D1297602

continued…

WARLORD

"A superb climax to an excellent saga...Romance and fantasy readers will appreciate this terrific trio as Elizabeth Vaughan provides a fabulous finish to a superior story."

—Midwest Book Review

"An outstanding conclusion to an inventive and riveting trilogy with a passionate, powerful love story at its core."

—The Romance Reader

"A top-notch series, well written and enjoyable."

—Curled Up With a Good Book

WARSWORN

"A moving continuation of the wonderful *Warprize*. Bravo."

—Jo Beverly

"Readers will be delighted...Unusual and thoroughly enjoyable."

—Booklist

DESTINY'S STAR

"Fans will relish this strong romantic quest fantasy."

—Genre Go Round Reviews

"Riveting...The plot moves at a nice clip, and the ending is a masterstroke... *Destiny's Star* is a terrific story."

—The Romance Reader

"Bethral and Ezren are marvelous characters to spend time with…[Vaughan] has a gift for bringing cultures and dialogue to life, and I very much look forward to more."

—*All About Romance*

"Vaughan's writing is rich and provocative. Her descriptions [are] gorgeous, watching Bethral and Ezren fall in love…was perfect…I didn't want the story to end."

—*Smexy Books*

WHITE STAR

"An engrossing story which will keep readers enthralled. The characters are interesting and appealing…Ms. Vaughan has crafted an interesting world where myths and reality blur. Filled with magic, gods and goddesses, and heroic deeds, the reader will never want to put this book down."

—*Fresh Fiction*

"There's tension, turmoil, and adventure on every page. The characters—main and side alike—are interesting and enjoyable. The sex is fun, and the romance is undeniably sweet."

—*Errant Dreams Reviews*

"Vaughan world-builds with a depth and clarity that allows you to immerse yourself in the world of the hero and heroine…If you are looking for a book with colorful world-building, solid characters, and sound storytelling, this one might be just what you're looking for."

—*All About Romance*

continued…

"A riveting and thoroughly enjoyable story."

—*Romance Reviews Today*

"Fans will appreciate the clever twist that Elizabeth Vaughan writes in *White Star*, as the latest return to her Warlands saga is a welcome entry in one of the best romantic fantasies of the last few years."

—*Alternative Worlds*

DAGGER-STAR

"*Dagger-Star* is the perfect blend of fantasy and romance...A really enjoyable read."

—*Fresh Fiction*

"An excellent romantic fantasy...Readers will enjoy Elizabeth Vaughan's superb, clever return to the desolate Warlands."

—*Midwest Book Review*

"Elizabeth Vaughan pens a story of love and adventure...You feel yourself being sucked into the adventure and don't want to put the book down."

—*Manic Readers*

"In a return to the world of the Warlands trilgoy, Elizabeth Vaughan successfully creates a new set of characters and a new story...A very satisfying read."

—*Romance Reviews Today*

WARDANCE

ELIZABETH VAUGHAN

Published by Birch Cove Press

ISBN-13: 978-0-9984501-1-7
Worldwide Rights
Created in the United States of America

Cover Art by Craig White
Cover Design by STK·Kreations

For
Dennis McKiernan
Author and Friend
whose wit, words and wisdom have guided me more
than he can ever know

and

Martha Lee McKiernan
Artist and Friend
who, in the fashion of a zen master, asked
'Why do you write?' and
opened my eyes to my own truths.

CHAPTER ONE

I t took everything Simus had not to plunge his sword into the chest of the arrogant warrior-priest who barred his way.

But that had been the exact mistake that Keir of the Cat had made when he had conquered Xy, hadn't it. Simus wasn't about to do the same.

Instead, he eased back in his saddle, took a long, deep breath of the sweet air of the Plains, and let his glare sweep down over the *bragnect* before him.

The warrior-priest stood, unimpressed. His hair hung in long, matted braids; his face, neck, and chest were covered with swirling red, green, black, and brown tattoos. Nothing marked him from his fellows except a long scar that ran along the side of his face, puckering the corner of his lip. He'd offered no name, no token, no courtesy.

Simus seethed, holding his temper in check. His warriors, gathered behind him, shifted in their saddles, muttering darkly, no doubt fingering the hilts of their swords. They'd no love for the warrior-priests, either.

"I say again," the warrior-priest said, his eyes as dark as Simus's own skin. His lip curled with disdain. "The Eldest Elder Hail Storm has decreed that all shall pull back, out of sight and sound of the Heart."

Simus focused behind the man, trying to let his anger go with the wind. Behind the warrior-priest, the Plains stretched out with the splendor of new, green grasses and the flowers that danced in their midst. They'd only to ride a few more miles, over a few more rises, and they would be at the Heart of the Plains.

Simus took another breath, letting the man wait. The spring air, the flowering grasses crushed under their horses' hooves, made every breath a pleasure. Especially after a long winter spent in the dark lodges, with naught to do but sharpen weapons, and talk and plan with Keir of the Cat as Xylara, his Warprize, grew heavy with their child.

Keir and Lara had left for Xy at the earliest hint of fair weather. For reasons Simus didn't fully understand the birth of the babe must occur in Xy, under the eyes of the nobles. Since that time, Simus had spent countless hours training and preparing for the Spring Trials, conducted each year at the Heart of the Plains.

Keir's plans required a weaving of new patters between Xy and the Plains, binding the lands together. No longer would Xy be subject to raids from the "dreaded Firelanders". No longer would those of the Plains be dependent on the raids for survival. But for those plans to come to pass; for Keir and him to hunt this prey successfully, Simus needed to enter the Spring Trials, face all challengers, and become Warlord.

Nothing would stop him from earning that status in his own right, with warriors sworn to his service.

Nothing stood between him and that goal except his survival of the Trials and this arrogant *bragnect* standing there with his curled lip and vivid tattoos.

Simus tightened his legs, and his horse shifted under him,

sensing battle. Simus's fingers twitched toward the hilt of his own weapon—

"Isn't Wild Winds the Eldest Elder of the Warrior-Priests of the Plains?" Joden spoke up from behind Simus, his voice calm and understanding. Far more understanding than Simus was prepared to be. "Who is this Hail Storm, to turn us from our traditional ways?"

Simus stilled his hand, glad for his friend at his shoulder, gladder still for his support. But he didn't ease up his scowl, since he'd missed what Joden had plucked from the warrior-priest's words. Who *was* this Hail Storm?

"Is it not the season?" Joden continued. Simus flicked a glance back to see Joden tilt his head to look at the sun. Joden's broad, brown face was deceptively pleasant as his dark eyes considered the sky. "Perhaps we now reckon time as a city-dweller and have missed the day?"

There was a ripple of laughter from the warriors gathered behind Simus, an easing of tension clear in their voices. Ah, Joden, soon-to-be-Singer, whose reasonable tongue had the sharpest of edges.

The tattooed man bristled, probably from Joden's insult, but maybe for his mistake in naming another warrior-priest. Certainly, this one had not so much as offered his name, appearing out of the tall grass to bar their path.

"It is the season," the warrior-priest acknowledged, his scar rucking up as he snarled. He tightened his grip on his staff. "But the Heart is needed for our purpose. Take yourselves off."

Simus's loathing boiled over. Skies, he hated the warrior-priests of the Plains, who had no truth, who claimed false powers, and worked not for the People, but to preserve their own status.

Mistake it might be, but the insult was not to be borne. Simus snarled and went for his sword.

But the snarl was still in his throat, and his blade not clear of its scabbard when other warrior-priests appeared.

The hair on the back of Simus's neck rose, and a feeling of dread washed over him.

They wisped up like fog from the grasses, their tattoos bright, some holding naked blades, others with staves adorned with bleached human skulls. They stood in silence, their disdain a pressure on his skin. They made no move, no sound, but the threat was clear.

Simus stilled his hand. He felt his warriors behind him, waiting for him to unleash their fury.

"It would be best," Joden said softly, in perfect Xyian, "to put this off for another time."

"Bastards," Simus cursed in Xyian, and thrust his sword back into its sheath. He turned his horse's head away with no further word. His warriors waited and watched, covering his back, and then turned to follow his lead. Silently, he led them directly away from the Heart.

Once his group was well away, Eloix came up beside Simus. Her skin still had that pale winter look, but she'd already a touch of redness on her cheeks. Her blue eyes reflected her fierce frown as she glanced back behind them. "Simus, they disappeared back into the grasses as the last of us rode away."

Simus grunted, letting his rage cool. He waited until they were a few rises beyond to turn to Joden. "What do you make of it?"

Joden urged his horse forward until he was even with Simus. Eloix slowed her horse, politely dropping back.

Joden shook his head, his face reflecting his confusion. "I know not. But that was a rare display of power for a warrior-priest. Every time I convince myself that their powers are false, they do something like this."

"Truth," Simus said. "Whatever they are doing, it must be important."

"And I do not know the name 'Hail Storm' either," Joden added.

Simus grunted. "Wild Winds was Eldest Elder when the Council sundered. That was but a season ago."

"It feels like a lifetime," Joden said.

Simus really looked at his friend then, seeing the lines of pain about the man's eyes. Joden bore the grief of having lived through sickness and death, strange to those of the Plains. 'Plague,' the Warprize had called it, and even her great powers had no cure.

"You keep your sorrow within," Simus said abruptly. "You need to sing of it."

"When I have the words," Joden said, and there really was no more to say to that.

Simus knew that the plague had caused Joden to doubt Keir, and he'd spoken his truths openly, making no secret of them. He'd come to see the truth of Xylara as Warprize, and had supported her before the Council. Simus trusted Joden's truth and honor. But that did not mean that Joden would support every change Keir and Simus were working toward.

"Riders!" Eloix called a warning to them.

Simus looked and saw two riders coming over a ridge, headed directly for them.

"That's Osa." Joden recognized her before Simus did. Odd to hear him use her name without the title of Warlord, but such was the tradition of the Spring. 'Warlord' had to be re-earned, each and every year. A warrior did not use it unless their oaths had already been sworn.

Joden continued with a tone of resignation. "And that's Ultie with her."

Simus kept his face bland but grimaced within. He lowered his voice, meeting Joden's gaze. "What was it Lara called him?"

"The arrogant, loud-mouth, over-bearing, obnoxious, bad-breathed Warlord Ultie," Joden said, his face bland, a smile dancing in his eyes.

"A woman of insight, our Warprize," Simus muttered, but then he couldn't stop from laughing out loud, letting his voice roll over the grasses. He and Joden shared a quick smile, but Simus sobered his face as the riders drew closer.

"Greetings, Osa. Greetings, Ultie," Simus called and urged his horse forward.

Osa and Ultie had both been Warlords in the previous seasons. Now they were his rivals, and if he survived the Trials, his equals. Simus felt no qualm in treating them as such.

What he wasn't sure of was their positions as to Keir's plans. Keir had made no secret of his plans for Xy. Nor had he concealed his hatred of the warrior-priests, and his desire to break their hold on the People.

But neither Osa or Ultie had expressed more than a passing interest in Keir's schemes, although both of them had courted the Warprize before her confirmation.

Before she'd formally chosen Keir as her Warlord.

Osa was the first to approach, looking ravishing as she always did, her hair like flame and her pale skin contrasting with the browns of her leather armor. Her whip was at her waist, her slight smile reflected her eyes. "Simus." She nodded. "You have come for the Trials then?"

"If these warrior-priests ever allow it." Ultie scowled, glancing off in the direction of the Heart.

"You were driven off as well?" Simus asked.

"They've prevented anyone from raising their standard," Osa said. "Of the few that intend to."

"What?" Simus asked sharply.

Osa raised an eyebrow in the direction of his warriors, and reached back into her saddlebags for a strip of bells. "We'd have private words, Simus. With Joden of the Hawk as well, if he is willing."

Simus gave a nod, and looked over at Eloix, summoning her closer. "Set camp," he instructed. "A temporary one, for the night. Let's not have those warrior-priests thinking we will wait patiently."

"Another rise or so to the north and you should be far enough off for the damned warrior-priests," Ultie said. The big man's weathered skin hadn't lost its tan over the winter months; his brown hair and beard were still long and shaggy.

"I'll see to it." Eloix nodded respectfully to all of them, and lead the warriors off.

Osa leaned forward and tied the bells in her horse's mane. All four of them drew their horses close, and cast a wary eye on the grasses around them.

"Who knows if the elements-forsaken warrior-priests would even honor the privacy of the bells," Ultie growled. "They shift like winds, and are not to be trusted."

Osa shrugged. "I mislike this, but they are the warrior-priests. It is within their rights."

"You said 'of the few'?" Simus asked.

Osa nodded, settling back in the saddle as her horse lowered its head to tear at the grass. "The warrior-priests drove us off yesterday at dawn. Ultie and I have ridden the wide circle around, to see who has appeared for the contests. We found fewer than I could wish."

"Four Warlords for each of the four elements are required," Ultie growled. "Less than half of that have appeared, and most of them new to the contests. Colts, all of them, and unsteady on their legs."

"Especially when you ride up and bellow at them like a rutting ehat," Osa said dryly, then focused on Simus. "But he states the truth. Few warriors have appeared to raise their banners for challenge, and fewer still of the elders of any tribe have gathered."

"Where are they?" Joden's frown was deep and worried.

"Made themselves scarce, and there's wisdom in that," Ultie said darkly. "With the Council sundered last season, and warrior attacking warrior, who is to know what to expect?"

"The Council was concluded," Joden said. "Eldest Elder Essa ended the Council after the out-casting, and before the Warprize chose her Warlord."

"Don't know what that city-dweller was thinking," Ultie groused. "I would have been a better choice. What does Keir have over me?"

"You dropped your trous to show her your 'weapon,'" Osa said. "Little wonder she stomped from your tent and declared the courting at an end."

Simus kept his face straight, and didn't dare look at Joden.

"City-dwellers," Ultie snorted in disgust. "I will never understand them. And Keir thinks we can—"

"Regardless," Osa cut him off. Her horse lowered its head to graze, the bells chiming in its mane. "Have either of you seen any of the Eldest Elders? Reness? Essa? Wild Winds?"

"Reness left with Keir and the Warprize," Simus said. "They have returned to Xy for the birth of her child, and Reness thought to attend her. She may have continued on with them to Xy. Of Essa, I have not heard or seen. And Wild Winds—" Simus looked at Joden.

"The warrior-priest who barred our way said that Hail Storm was the Eldest Elder of the Warrior-Priests," Joden said.

Osa and Ultie exchanged glances. "Not a name I know," Ultie said grimly. "Not that they share their names." He looked at all of them. "But I will speak this truth. I have held back the Elders among my warriors. They will not approach the Heart unless I send word."

Simus frowned. "Why would you—"

"To keep them safe," Ultie said. "To wait and watch and see what is. To not risk their knowledge and wisdom to the madness that seems to infect us now." He glowered at Simus. "Has Keir thought of that, eh? If there are not enough Warlords? How will the armies raid, to provide for our people and the thea camps? How will we survive, eh?"

"Liam will come, if needed, although he will wait at the border of Xy." Simus met Ultie's glare. "There is time yet, for others to appear and set up the challenge banners for Warlords and Token-bearers and to form the armies."

"And if they do not?" Ultie said, his horse as agitated as he.

"And if the sun does not rise?" Osa said impatiently. "I can say this much. Antas of the Boar was seen, cloaked and hooded, going into one of the camps of the warrior-priests."

Simus narrowed his eyes at that news. Antas had been the

Eldest Elder of the Warriors, until his betrayal of the Council. He'd tried to have the Warprize slain in the very Council tent. "I wonder what he sought there?" Simus mused.

Ultie just snorted. "Antas would be Keir, if he could."

"Perhaps he seeks to be WarKing as well," Osa said mildly.

Simus jerked his head up to stare at her.

"Oh, do not give me that look, Simus." Osa gave him a sly smile. "He may not have shouted it to the winds, but how else can Keir plan to repair the damage he has caused? He has cut the Council tent to ribbons and only a WarKing can mend the tears."

"He caused?" Simus asked.

Osa shrugged. "Many say so."

"The warrior-priests alone cannot make Antas WarKing," Joden pointed out. "That requires the full Council and the Eldest Elders."

"And round and round we go," Osa said. She tilted her head, and studied Joden. "And do you support Keir as WarKing?"

"I take no position," Joden said.

"And if you were Singer?" Osa pushed.

"You ask me to comment if I were Singer? If the Council reforms, if the Eldest Elders are found, if the Warlords are chosen and the armies formed?" Joden chuckled. "You might as well ask in what pattern the clouds will form tomorrow."

Osa's smile was wry. "A Singer's answer."

Joden shrugged.

Ultie started to turn his horse. "Well, this talk will not settle anything, and I've had my fill for this night. We can talk further as we sit and wait for the warrior-priests to finish whatever they would do at the Heart." He spat in the grass. "Elements grant that the prey they stalk turns on them."

"Night comes. Time enough tomorrow to beat theses grasses flat," Osa agreed. She took the bells from her horse's mane. "Seems we must wait on events." She wrinkled her nose, gave them both a nod and rode off.

Simus watched after them, then looked at Joden. "What do you think?"

Joden shrugged.

"A Singer's answer." Simus rolled his eyes, turned his horse, and headed for where his warriors were making camp. Joden followed silently.

As they rode up, warriors met them to take their horses. Eloix came up on foot as they dismounted. "We've strong kavage, and meat spitted over the fire." She looked them both over. "You've the look of too much thinking, Simus."

"Aye to that," Simus said, feeling anger simmering under his skin. "I'm in need of a sparring session to work out my frustrations."

Eloix sidled up next to him and nudged his hip with hers. "Perhaps I could offer a better distraction?"

Simus gave her a warm smile, and reached out to stroke her cheek lightly with his fingertips. "Afterward, lovely one. I would call a senel tonight. The warrior-priests may have kept us from the Heart, but I would keep us to the path I have chosen."

Joden straightened as did Eloix. They both lowered their eyes, and gave him the traditional bow of respect. "Yes, Simus."

Simus grinned. "We will begin the rituals tonight."

CHAPTER TWO

I call this senel to order," Simus announced, letting his joy and satisfaction ring in his voice.

From the faces around him, the warriors shared his pleasure.

They may have set a temporary camp with no large tents, but they'd done him proud with braziers heaped high, the flames burning merrily. The light surrounded the group with a golden glow, one that could probably be seen for miles since the sun had dipped beyond the horizon.

Simus stood among them and raised his hands. "The fire warms us," he recited.

The crowd responded, their voice rising together. "We thank the elements."

Simus raised his voice a bit louder and stronger. "The earth supports us."

"We thank the elements," they responded, raising their voices with his.

Simus let joy fill his voice. "The waters sustain us."

"We thank the elements," came the echoing response.

"The air fills us," Simus said, booming out the words.

"We thank the elements," his people shouted in adulation.

Simus grinned in shared pleasure, and his words echoed in

the air. "We thank the elements, for their gifts to the People of the Plains."

"*Heyla*," was shouted by all.

Simus waited for them to settle. "We have fought together for many a season under Keir of the Cat," he said. "We have faced dangers and enemies no other warriors of the Plains have confronted, and we have emerged alive, our weapons still sharp." He took a deep breath and let his smile grow wide. "It is fitting then, that I declare my intent to you, to enter the Trials and become Warlord in this season."

Shouts of "*Heyla*," erupted from all around. Simus couldn't resist a glance at Joden, seated at his side. His friend met him grin for grin.

"Joden of the Hawk intends to take the path to Singer this season as well. As such, as is our way, he takes no sword oaths to any warrior. His oaths will be to the Plains themselves if he succeeds in his Singer Trials." Simus bowed his head toward his friend. "Until such time, we will have his company and his truths—"

"Not to mention his songs!" Yers added, his white skin, dark brown hair, and crooked nose gleaming in the firelight. Simus joined the laughter.

"Truth!" Simus said. "Now, as is tradition, I would ask that Joden recite the rules of the Spring Trials for us." Simus settled back down on his gurtle pad.

Joden rose, his broad face flushed with pleasure. "I am honored," he said, and then raised his right hand, palm to the sky. "May the skies hear my voice. May the people remember."

The response rose from every throat, including Simus's. "We will remember."

Joden lowered his hand. "Now begins the Spring Trials, when

all may challenge for a place in the armies of the Warlords of the Plains."

His audience was still, and silent.

"Battle is for survival, for gain." Joden's voice was a melodic chant. "Battle is vicious, brutal, and no quarter given." He looked at the crowd. "Here, now, in the flowering of the Plains, in the new grass and the early rains, here is where we emerge from the winter lodges, sharpen our weapons, and show our skill." Joden paused, and took a breath. "For in the Trials, we appreciate the beauty of the blade in motion, the finesse behind the blow. The Trials display the best of us."

A soft murmur of appreciation came as the warriors nodded.

"So let it be that in our Trials we value more the grace and skill of the warrior. Each fight is to the first blood, but let that blood be no more than a trickle or a trace, the slightest whisper of metal parting skin. Let the contest within the circle of challenge be a dance, a display of all that is in the best of us," Joden continued. "Bring into the circle only your sharpest blades."

Blades, and not maces or warclubs. Blunt weapons meant to crush heads and break bones had no place within a challenge circle; pulling out a weapon of that kind signaled an intent to kill.

"The challenges take place within the circle, upon the bare earth, under the open sky, with water and fire as witnesses," Joden said. "In no other place are challenges permitted, except within the circle, under the challenge banners. And with a Singer as the judge, neutral and unquestioned in their truths."

Joden gave a small smile. "When we were children in the thea camps, our wooden weapons would be taken if we challenged and lost. Now, as adults, once the Singer has rendered judgment, the defeated warrior surrenders only their dagger," Joden said. "Gone are the days we spilled blood and lives in the challenge circles. Now we look for the skillful to lead us into battle. Now we form our armies for the Season of War. Long it has been so, and long will it continue." He raised his right hand, palm to the sky. "May the people remember."

Again, Simus joined in the response, "We will remember."

Joden sat.

Simus picked up the leather bundle by his side, and rose back to his feet, using his height to draw attention as he pulled back the folds to reveal his new token. "Here is my formal token that I will use during the Trials, for any to take up and share their truths with me." Simus lifted the gleaming, curved bone high. It was adorned with feathers, beads, and bells. "Keir gifted me with the tip of an ehat rib, from the four ehat hunt that occurred last season. I could not attend, but some of you were there—"

"I was honored to be on a musk team," Yers chortled.

"And I, on a kill team," Tsor laughed. "It was glorious!"

Simus lowered his token and gave them all a mock scowl. "I'll not hold that against you."

Laughter broke out then, for Simus had complained bitterly that he'd missed the hunt.

"Are you still crafting that song, Joden?" one of the warriors called out.

Joden nodded. "For use in my trials," he said.

"Which means we cannot hear it this night," another moaned as others expressed their disappointment.

Amidst the laughter and complaining, Simus knelt and placed the token on the gurtle pad that had been set before him. The white bone gleamed, and he could just make out the small hawk figure that he'd carved into the very tip.

The warriors grew silent as Simus rose back to his feet. "I seek to form an army," he said, "but not for the usual reasons." He turned serious, as did his listeners, focused on his words. "And this truth must be clear," he said. "It must be a truth spoken under the open sky before I take any warrior's sword oath this night." Simus settled his feet in the ground, swept his eyes around the campfire. "I support Keir of the Cat in his goal of breaking the warrior-priests' claims to power. I support him in the effort to join with Xy to bring new ways to our people."

Nods and mutters of agreement from the warriors—but these warriors had served with Keir and himself, and shared their views. Others would not be so easy to convince.

"Long have our people warred to survive," Simus continued. "But that way of life is not sustainable. Keir and those that support him would break that cycle and the false hold the warrior-priests have, and use the skills and ways of Xy to supply that which we raided for before."

"Damn the warrior-priests to the snows," Yers muttered, and there were nods of agreement all around.

"My intent is that the army that follows me will take up position at the border of Xy and the Plains, to protect Xy from any who might think to raid it while it is under the protection of Keir of the Cat and myself," Simus said. "When new warriors approach us with an interest in joining, let this truth be shared immediately. I'd have no one claim they were not told, or that my plans were not revealed. If I expect truth from a warrior in my service, I must offer truth to them."

Simus spread his hands. "I have shared my truths, and declared my intent. Who would offer me their swords under the open skies?"

Almost as one the warriors rose, pulling their weapons. They each stepped forward to kneel before him and swear the oaths that placed their truths and their weapons in his service.

Joy filled his heart as they proceeded one by one to swear. When the last had sworn and returned to his seat, Simus had to clear his throat before he could speak the ritual words. "I would be your Warlord. I take responsibility for your lives and hold them dear. Your blood is my blood, your flesh is my flesh."

"Heyla, Warlord," came the ritual response from all. Even Joden joined in the cry.

Simus released the tension in his own chest with a great laugh. "Now just let those 'bastards' allow us access to the Heart, and we'll raise my banners high."

His warriors joined in the mirth, and started to pass around the waterskins with fermented mare's milk. "To insult such a one in Xyian," Eloix chortled, "That would have them choke on their own wrath."

"Did the Warprize ever explain the meaning of that word?" Yers asked. "I never understood it."

"Cadr," Eloix called out. "You had training in healing with the Warprize. Did she ever explain the word?"

The younger warrior popped up out of the crowd, his long brown hair braided back. "No," he said brightly. "But she sure used it when she was riled up!"

That brought much laughter, for the temper of the Warprize was well known.

"Did she ever explain it to you, Warlord?" Yers asked.

"Something about the nature of one's birth." Simus shrugged. "I still don't understand how a birth could be unnatural." He settled down onto his gurtle pad, took up his drink, and decided to savor it. After this night, he wouldn't indulge. He'd need his wits the next few weeks. "I look forward to the Trials."

"To the dancing, more like," Joden said, laughing. "And will you be teaching others the Xyian dances that you learned?"

"Maybe I will," Simus crowed. "Wouldn't that raise hackles and ruffle feathers." He laughed.

"And the sharing after?" Eloix asked, her eyes dancing with mirth. "Or will you follow Keir's ways in that as well?"

Simus heaved a dramatic sigh. "Once my tent is raised, I will not share bodies during the Trials," he announced. "And while I know that all the women warriors will be deprived of my gifts—" He swept his hand down his body for emphasis. Laughter and protests arose from the group. Simus held up his hands. "Sharing during the Trials makes things…complicated."

"So you won't be adding foalsbane to your kavage in the mornings?" Yers taunted.

"Wouldn't taste right without it," Simus called back. "Besides, who knows? Like Keir, I might find my Warprize." He waggled his eyebrows. "And the need might arise, yes?"

Laughter again, and Simus settled back, well pleased with his warriors, with the night, and with what was to come. "So," he said to his warriors, "who intends to challenge for what positions?"

Yers jumped to his feet. "I, Yers of the Cat, will contest for Second!" With much laughter, the warriors pulled him back down.

Simus grinned his pleasure. Yers had served under Keir and Simus before, and he was a loyal and excellent warrior. So loyal, in fact, that it had been he who had given Lara's apprentice mercy when he had fallen ill of the plague. Yers had felt it best that he take her wrath, rather than Keir or Marcus. The Warprize had forgiven, in her own time.

If he met the challenges, he'd be a strong Second, not afraid to express his truths. Nothing was more valuable to a Warlord.

Many others called out to also contest for Second as well as Third. Eloix and Destal both declared for Token-bearer, and proceeded to glare at one another. Simus was pleased to see an interest in all positions. It spoke well for the Trials.

"No challenges for me," Oxna said loudly. One of his older warriors, she'd served with him under Keir. The flames made her amber skin glow, and gave her slanted eyes a wicked glint. "Not if you'll have me as Tenth, Warlord."

"That I will, Oxna," Simus said. "And pleased to have you. The Tenths are the strength of my army, being our warleaders. We need more in that same position."

Oxna lifted her mug in response.

"I'll take the scouts, if you will have me, Warlord," Cimor spoke up. The older man was grizzled, but his skill was in his cunning. "I've served as such under—"

Simus held up his hand with a laugh. "No need to list your campaigns, old friend. I accept."

They spent some time under the night sky as the braziers burned down, talking of the Trials to come and the positions that were normally appointed, not contested for.

"I'll ask for supply master," Sal said. "That is, if no other is interested."

"No one has spoken for it," Simus said. "And I'd be grateful if you'd take on the task."

"Consider it done," Sal said with clear satisfaction, but Simus was even more pleased. She'd served Keir in the same role, and understood the Xyian use of coin for trade.

"For those that would contest for Token-bearer, I have a

caution," Simus said. "We have all served under Keir, and have all known Marcus, his Token-bearer."

Some of the older warriors were nodding now, anticipating his words.

"But Marcus is not a traditional Token-bearer," said Simus, "due to his afflictions. Any who would contest for Token-bearer should be aware of this, for mine will fill all the traditional roles of one that speaks for the Warlord and is his voice and message-bearer."

He could see thoughtful looks and nodding heads.

"One last thought," he said. "Antas of the Boar shattered his oaths when he attacked the Council of Elders and called for the death of the Warprize in Council last season. There is no truth, no honor in him. I do not think he will appear for the challenges, but he is bold."

"I had not thought of that." Yers looked thoughtful. "Would he be considered a candidate?"

"That is for the Elders and Eldest Elders to decide," Simus said. "But I ask that you all keep careful watch over yourselves and any that pledge themselves to us. Attacks may not just come in the challenge circles."

Thoughtful looks all around, now. Simus was glad to see they were considering that warning seriously.

"For now," he said, turning the conversation to happier things, "I thank you for the gifts of your truths and declare this senel closed."

The warriors stood and stretched, and went to seek their tents, or to post the watches. Some started to gather gurtle pads and mugs, and stir the braziers to settle the coals.

"That was well done," Joden said.

"It was, wasn't it?" Simus said, well content with the day. He glanced off toward the Heart. "Now there's just the worry of what they are doing."

Joden shook his head. "Don't think on it," he said, then gave Simus a sly smile. "Didn't Eloix offer to distract you?"

"So she did," Simus said, catching Eloix's gaze across the camp.

Her answering smile matched his.

CHAPTER THREE

They walked away from the tents, but stayed within the circle of guards he'd set. Eloix was ahead of him, carrying a blanket, her sword bouncing gently against her swaying hip. Simus enjoyed the sight as he followed, feeling a warm curl of anticipation. They stopped just far enough from the camp to be out from underfoot as the warriors and horses settled for the night.

Eloix spread the blanket over the grasses and disrobed, placing her weapons close at hand, piling her armor neatly beside them.

"Your skin reflects the starlight," Simus murmured as he admired the silver shine on her skin. Even her golden hair seemed to mirror the stars. He moved closer to help her slide her trous off, down her long legs.

"Such words. Are you sure you are not a Singer in training?" she whispered back, then laughed, reaching to stroke his jaw, and run her fingers over his close-cropped hair.

"Just a humble warrior," Simus said into her ear as his dark hands wandered over her pale breasts. "With a desire to please."

"Oh, you please—" Eloix drew a long breath as he ran his thumbs over her taut nipples. She pushed him back slightly and reached for the clasps of his leathers. "But humble? I think not, warrior."

"Oh, yes," Simus said. "Humbled by your loveliness." He ran his hands up over her collarbones and felt her shiver under his touch even as she laughed again. He traced a path down her back, pulled her close and caught her lips with his.

Eloix leaned into him, moaning into his mouth, her hands moving faster to strip his armor and weapons and set them aside. They collapsed together to the blanket, lost in the pleasure of skin on skin. The air was filled with the scent of crushed grasses and the warm, musky scent of their bodies as they reached for one another, the heat growing between them.

Eloix pulled back, pushing him down, letting her hands stroke his stomach, ghosting over the long scar on his thigh. "Now the distraction I promised," she whispered, and straddled him, easing his length into her warm, hot wetness.

Simus moaned his appreciation, reaching for the breasts that swayed above him, and allowed himself to be completely and utterly distracted.

* * * * *

Afterward, Eloix curled beside him, her back to him, facing her weapons. Simus made sure the second blanket covered them both, then stretched out on his back, his hands behind his head. His body was sated and relaxed, the tension and tightness gone from his muscles. The warmth of the coarse blanket felt even better with the touch of the cool night air on his face and arms. He took in deep breaths, enjoying the scent of the night, the grasses, the blade oil on their weapons and the muskiness of their bodies. A warrior could not ask for more.

Better this than the stone walls of Xy surrounding him, shutting out the skies and stars.

He'd remained in Xy to secure the kingdom when Lara and Keir had left to confront the Council of Elders. Parts of that time he'd enjoyed, especially teaching the city-dwellers the ways of the Plains. He chuckled at the memory of strolling naked through the castle until Anna the Cook chased him through the halls armed with nothing more than a wooden spoon and the sharp edge of her tongue.

But there was much he would not miss. He hadn't cared for their thick walls, or their beds that wanted to swallow a man whole, thrashing in the softness, unable to rise. Nor their notions of pleasure, or their rules as to who slept with who, and the rituals of binding. They'd not seen a man of his color before, or any color other than their own, and their shock at the idea of women warriors had been something to behold.

And their senels, skies above. Simus winced at the memory of meetings held in stone rooms, talking endlessly about nothings, a waste of breath and sunlight.

It had been no hardship when the threat to Lara and Keir had called him back to the Plains.

Simus stretched again, relishing the slight tug of the scar on his thigh. There was no pain, no weakness in the limb, all thanks to the healing skills of the Warprize. He smiled in fondness of the little healer who'd followed her Warlord to the Plains. And now they'd left at the first break in the snows, returning to Xy for the birth of their child. Both besotted with each other, and Lara as big as an ehat.

Not that he'd ever say that to a life-bearer. He snorted at the very thought.

Eloix stirred at the sound, shifting so that her back touched Simus's hip before she melted back into sleep. Simus's own body stirred in response, anticipating a bit more 'distraction' when she woke. She was a joy to share pleasure with…and yet…

Simus frowned up at the stars.

He'd never seen the benefit of bonding as Lara and Keir had, never thought it was something he would have interest in. Limited to one partner? Bond together to the snows and beyond? No, sharing pleasure with multiple partners on equal terms suited him best.

And yet…there was something between Lara and Keir, something different. Simus narrowed his eyes as he considered it. It was a different kind of sharing, beyond their bodies, and it reflected between them.

He'd seen it in Anna and Othur too, those two fat city-dwellers who had earned his respect in the time he'd been in Water's Fall. Anna for her skill with that spoon, and Othur for his insights in the problems of bringing their two peoples together. They'd shared the same lives for many years, longer than any bonded couple he'd known. It seemed a fine thing, for them.

Simus took another deep breath, and laughed at himself. He wished his friends well, but for him, the Plains were where he truly wished to be.

For all its flaws.

The stars danced in the night, stretching as far as he could see. If he turned his head, a glow was visible in the direction of the Heart, as if every fire pit and torch were lit surrounding the great circular stone. He grinned and turned his head deliberately away. Another time, he'd have tried to sneak closer, and learn the warrior-priests' secrets. But he'd not risk it this night. There was too much at stake. Even if the skies favored the bold.

'The earth covers the stupid.' The dour, scarred face of Marcus,

Keir's token-bearer, floated in his mind.

Simus chuckled at the thought, but there was truth to Marcus's words. He and Keir and Simus had spent long hours during the winter in the deep lodges, sheltered in the earth, planning and talking. Keir had warned him that being Warlord was a far different matter than serving as Second. He felt it already, in the eyes of his warriors as they awaited, looking to him for decisions.

Simus drew a deep breath and let it out slowly. The stars twinkled above, seemingly cold and distant, as if waiting for him to prove himself.

'*I will,*' he vowed to them. '*I can handle whatever comes.*'

The stars were silent, and unimpressed.

Ah well. Enough of that. Simus stretched again, carefully brushing against Eloix with the lightest of touches.

She stirred, rolling over, smiling as she looked at him with sleepy eyes. "I see I have failed you," she said, her voice low and husky. "You have been thinking. Wasn't I distracting enough?"

Simus rolled over, covering her, settling between her thighs as she spread her legs to welcome him. "More than enough. So much so that I desire even more—"

A bell-like tone shivered in the air, stopping his words, his breath, his very thought. For long moments it held them, helpless and suspended, and then it rolled on and past, sweeping over them like a wind.

It came from the Heart.

Simus was up, his sword and dagger in hand, crouching low. Eloix had her weapons as well, her body close to the ground. The glow from the Heart had brightened.

Simus gestured, and Eloix reached for her armor as he watched the area around them. She dressed on the blanket, thrusting her legs into her leathers with quick, efficient movements. Her face did not reflect fear, but her eyes were wide, her breathing fast.

A match to his own heart beating in his chest.

Simus stayed in his crouch, turned a full circle, but saw nothing. Still he watched, paying special attention to the Heart, until Eloix hissed softly, fully armed and armored.

He placed his weapons on the blanket and reached for his leathers, keeping an eye on the surrounding grasses. He dressed swiftly, securing each buckle and strap quickly and quietly.

Eloix was kneeling now, her back to him as she tried to watch the entire Plains.

Simus was stuffing his feet in his boots when they heard a man's voice, accusing, sharp, insulting in tone, ringing over the distance.

"Can you make out what he's saying?" Eloix whispered.

"No." Simus fastened the last of his buckles and reached for his blades. "I don't—"

Another man's voice, not as powerful, but defiant could be heard. Growling, Simus stood and scanned the horizon.

"Simus, no." Eloix reached for him and he let her pull him back into the grasses. He knelt on one knee. "What did you see?"

"Nothing," Simus said. "We need to get closer—"

A woman's voice rang out, clear and strong, with the summoning cry used for horses. A mare belled at the same time, and Simus could have sworn the ground trembled beneath his feet.

Then he realized why. Every horse in their company was running for the Heart of the Plains.

He'd seen herds spooked before. He'd seen them run for the sheer joy in movement. He'd even seen horses dance with their warriors when returning to the Plains. But this…he'd never seen this. Every animal appeared focused and intent on a single goal.

The woman called again, commanding, demanding her call be answered.

Answer they did. Within a heartbeat, the herd was surging past them, neighing fiercely as they ran.

Simus jumped to his feet, pulling Eloix up for fear they'd be trampled. But the horses swerved aside, streaming past, ignoring them. Another heartbeat, and they were gone into the glow.

"Skies above," Eloix trembled next to him, her sword still firm in her hand.

"Well," Simus said, to cover his own racing heart. "If we are to get closer, we'll be walking."

"Are those voices coming from the Heart?" Eloix's voice was a rasp. "How can we hear them? What could they be doing that—"

The camp behind them was reacting. Warriors flooded out of tents, raised voices called out. Simus heard Joden call for him. He gave his own shout in response.

From the Heart, two voices, man and woman, thundered out, crying together with perfect clarity. "FOR THE PEOPLE OF THE PLAINS!"

There was a cracking sound, as if stone broke on stone.

Simus was on his feet, Eloix on hers. The very wind seemed to still. To pause.

Waiting.

A pillar of hot, bright power flared straight up from the Heart of the Plains, like a needle piercing the night sky.

CHAPTER FOUR

S imus stared up, blinking at the pillar that towered over them, swirling around and around like one of the deadly wind storms that came in the spring. Somehow he knew in the core of his being that it was so much more than light. It was power, vast and terrible and yet so beautiful.

Eloix threw up a hand to shield her eyes. Simus stood, enthralled, watching as the bright pillar swayed and twirled, linking the land and the stars.

A bell-tone sounded again. Simus had heard the big bells of the city-folk, but that had been nothing like this. This sound seemed to come from the land itself, from the very—

Something came rushing toward them across the grass, something deep in the grass.

Simus brought his weapons up, only to see a broad band of light flying toward them, expanding out. The thick band of pure sunlight looked like it was traveling under the earth, illuminating the grasses from below. It moved so fast, like fleeing deer.

Eloix took a few steps back, as if to run. Simus's knees shook, but he locked them and gripped his weapons. The bell-tone was still sounding in his ears, trembling in his chest.

The light passed under them so swiftly that there was no

chance of flight. For a moment, he and Eloix were covered in light. Then it was gone, climbing the rise behind them, passing beneath the other warriors. It left behind a sense of warmth… and joy? Yes, joy flooded through Simus, as if the earth and skies exalted together.

Simus turned to watch it go, and then turned back when another tone sounded, ringing through him as the light passed through him again. And again. But in the wake of the fourth wave of light, the horses returned from the Heart, prancing and tossing their heads.

The pillar of light was gone. Simus blinked, letting his eyes adjust as the stars came back.

As if nothing had happened, the Plains seemed to right itself once more. The stars returned in the night sky, the horses returned to their grazing. All that was left was the thumping of Simus's heart in his chest, and his fierce grip on his weapons.

"Did you feel that?" Joden ran up beside him, his sword in hand. "Did you feel—"

Other warriors ran up, all talking at the same time. Simus sheathed his blades and gestured for them to kneel, so as not to be outlined against the night sky. The grasses and the horses would shield them.

More warriors joined them, staying low, some taking up guard positions around the group, watching the land that surrounded them, all with strained faces and questions in their eyes. The joy was gone, leaving fear and uncertainty.

Simus waited until they'd all appeared, in various states of dress, but all with weapons at hand. He raised a hand, signaling for their attention. "I do not know what has happened, but we will discover the truth of this. We ride for the Heart, and we ride as if for war."

"Aye, Warlord," came the responses.

"We will go in tight formation. Have your lances at hand." Simus looked over his warriors, meeting their eyes. "I do not wish to shed the blood of those of the Plains. Let no warrior raise a weapon, except on my signal," he continued. "But if we are attacked, we will answer in kind."

His warriors all nodded their agreement. Their eyes held fear, but not doubt. Simus nodded, satisfied.

"Eloix." Simus looked at the woman at his side. "I have a hard thing to ask of you, warrior."

She waited, lifting an eyebrow.

"We will ride to the Heart, and I do not know what we will find there," Simus said. "But whatever we find or learn, Keir and Lara must know of it. Gear yourself with extra food, and extra horses, for if we are attacked, if swords are raised against us, don't wait for my command. Break off and ride for Xy."

Her eyes went wide, then narrowed. "Warlord—"

Simus cut her off. "You are known to Keir of the Cat. More so, you know Xy and speak their language. Your tentmate, Elois, she remained in Xy. What little we know, they must be told. No matter how wild the tale is, you will be heard and believed."

Eloix huffed. "I had hoped to contest to be your Token-bearer."

"If you wish to hear the winds laugh," Joden murmured, "tell them your plans."

"Keir must know." Simus glanced at the Heart. "He must hear the truth of this, and he knows you and will trust your truths. Stop at the border, where Liam of the Deer waits in protection of Xy. Tell him these truths as well, but do not linger."

Eloix sighed and nodded. "Warlord, I obey."

"Take this truth with you as well, when you go," Simus said. "Tell Keir that if the warrior-priests have destroyed the Heart of the Plains, they will die at my hands."

* * * * *

Three scouts, to the front, right and left," Simus directed as they started. "Stay within sight of us and each other," he continued softly. "Keep an eye on us, as we keep watch on you."

There was enough starlight to see by, and it was easy to follow the wide swath of flattened grasses left by the herds when they'd charged toward the Heart.

Three riders went forward, one at the fore, two off to the sides.

There was nothing about the night that set it apart from any other, silent but for the jingle of harnesses. Yet the tensions were there. Simus recognized the sharpened awareness of anticipated battle as the blood coursed through his veins. Even the breathing of the others seemed louder, harsher than normal. The colors were muted in the night, with only the occasional gleam of starlight off the armor and weapons of the warriors. Simus could feel his shoulders tighten as they grew closer to the Heart, the glow ever larger on the horizon.

The scout to the left signaled silently, and Simus led his warriors toward him.

The scout pointed. A man staggered through the grass, bare of chest, wearing nothing but trous, and leaning on a staff with a leather thong hanging loosely from its top, no skulls to be seen. Simus was willing to swear the man was a warrior-priest. But there was no arrogance now; the man's breathing was ragged, almost sobbing as he lurched forward, his trembling hand stretched out for the scout's horse.

But the horse, on its own, was backing away, ears flat to its head.

"What—" Simus started to ask but cut off his own words when the man lunged forward as if to catch the reins. The scout's horse lashed out with its teeth bared, snapping them shut on thin air as the man yanked his hand back.

"Warlord, I don't know why, but…" The scout struggled to regain control as the horse continued to back away. "But she'll have nothing to do with him."

Simus's own horse came to a stop, its ears flat. All the horses did, as if they'd caught the scent of something foul.

The man fell to his knees, his face lifted to the sky with a long cry of despair. Simus saw tracks of tears glistening on his face and chest. He looked closer, recognizing the scar that ran along the side of the man's face, catching the corner of his mouth. "You," he said, almost questioning his own thought. "You were the warrior-priest that blocked us from the Heart. What happened here?"

"We can't call them," the man wept, his voice cracked and wavering as he babbled out the words, spit gathering in the corners of his mouth. "They will not answer, will not come."

Simus urged his horse to step closer, but the animal stamped its foot and would not advance.

The man gasped, tried to catch his breath, then gave the warbling cry used to summon a mount from the herd. None responded, even the remounts that Eloix had brought with her. Not one animal advanced to his side.

Simus looked at the man in horror; all the warriors did.

"Our horses are one with us," Simus said, his voice thick. "Xyians might name their horses, and think to own them, but we live with them. What have you done, that they would refuse you?"

"What in the name of the elements did you do?" Joden's voice reflected Simus's own thought.

"The Sacrifice, the Sacrifice called them and then," the man collapsed to his hands and knees. "We have offended. We have—" The rest of his words were lost in his weeping.

Joden dismounted and went to the man's side, kneeling down beside him. He looked up at Simus. "His tattoos are gone," Joden said.

"Gone?" Simus asked.

"His skin is pale and new, as if the colors had been ripped away."

"We brought down the wrath of the elements." The man was choking and gasping out the words. "All of the elements, for it has returned and now I can see it. I can see it, but I cannot touch—cannot feel—cannot use." The man cried out in anguish, fisting handfuls of grass and earth.

Joden leaned over, whispering questions.

Simus gestured for the others to back the horses off, and they went willingly, keeping watch on the plains around them. But other than the man's cries, the night was quiet.

Joden finally stood, shaking his head. "His wits are gone," he said sadly. "Maybe after he calms, he could tell us more, but I have little hope of that."

"We will move on," Simus said sharply.

Joden nodded and turned, but the warrior-priest reached up, and grabbed his arm sobbing out a plea. "Mercy. I ask mercy."

Joden paused, and looked at Simus.

Simus returned the look, and shook his head. "Give him a dagger, Joden. With all that has happened in the past, with whatever has happened now, he does not deserve mercy at our hands."

But Joden didn't move. Didn't look away.

Simus frowned. It mattered little, since a warrior of the Plains who could not summon a mount was as good as dead. "Leave him," he commanded.

"I cannot," Joden said. "Any more than I could have left you."

Simus narrowed his eyes.

Joden returned the stare.

"Singers." Simus huffed out an exasperated breath and nodded to Joden. "Do it."

Two of his warriors dismounted, and approached as the trembling warrior-priest stretched himself out on the grasses at Joden's feet. Joden pulled his dagger and knelt, as the other two pressed down on the warrior-priest's shoulders and hands.

"The fire warmed you," Joden began.

"We thank the elements," came the traditional response from a few throats. The warrior-priest as well, his voice cracking as he bared his throat to the knife.

Simus did not join in the chant. He noted that others felt the same way. The warrior-priests had earned no friends among them. Besides, he knew Joden. He'd go for the heart thrust, a surer and far quicker death than the warrior-priest deserved.

Joden's voice was a murmur now, the responses softer as the elements of water, air, and earth were invoked and thanked. The man pressed to the earth seemed calmer now, although his breathing still rasped in the night air. His sobs had quieted, and seemed more of relief than anguish.

Simus frowned. The warrior-priest had been strong and arrogant when he'd confronted them earlier. What would drive such a proud warrior to such depths? And they'd offended the elements? The horses? A chill ran down Simus's spine.

"Go now, warrior," Joden's voice rang out, the ritual complete. "Beyond the snows and to the stars." With a swift move, he thrust the blade between the man's ribs and into his heart.

The silence was sudden and deep.

Joden cleaned his blade on the grasses as the others rose and returned to their mounts. He rose as well, and sheathed his blade.

Yers looked at Simus. "What did he mean, that all of the elements had returned?"

"I do not know." Simus shook his head. "But I know where we will find an answer." He looked toward the glow that still lit the horizon, and didn't let his own fears reflect in his voice as he issued his command. "Mount. We ride to the Heart."

CHAPTER FIVE

Dawn traced the horizon as they approached their goal. They encountered nothing and no one until they reached the area where the warrior-priests had established their camps.

His warriors were silent as they surveyed the chaos. Tents were clearly trampled, with gear strewn and tossed about. Cooking fires were scattered, the embers still burning, the pots and tripods askew, or knocked down altogether. The larger fire pits burned, true enough, but the fires were little more than coals.

And there were bodies everywhere.

All warrior-priests and priestesses.

All dead.

Simus gestured, and some of his people dismounted, checking for survivors. It didn't take long for them to look up and report.

"Dead," Yers said in hushed tones. "All dead, and by their own hands."

"All of them?" Simus asked. It wasn't possible. There had to have been a full camp here, and if it surrounded the Heart...could all the warrior-priests be dead?

"All," Joden said from off to the side. "There are no survivors."

"What in the name of the sacred flames happened here?" Simus wondered out loud.

"Our horses avoid tents unless provoked or stampeded," Joden said. "They do not bite or kick unless trust is lost. Why would they trample through the camp?"

"The Heart lies just a bit farther," Tsor said. The big man was subdued. They all were.

Simus urged his horse in that direction, and the others followed.

All around the great stone circle the fire pits were lit and smoldering, as if after a great ceremony. And there in the center the Heart lay, perfectly normal. Cool, grey stone, untouched and eternal. Perfectly circular, large enough to host the huge Council tent and all the Elders of the Plains.

Simus stared down at it, as if it could somehow give answers. There were none.

Simus swung down from his saddle. "Keep watch," he ordered as he walked up and onto the stone, striding to the center, looking for a mark, for a chip, for blood, for any sign of the source of that pillar of light.

There were none.

Simus frowned. The stone was perfectly clean. Usually whenever the tribes gathered around the Heart, it had to be swept almost hourly to keep it clear of debris. But the surface was untouched.

Joden knelt at his side, splaying his hand over the surface of the Heart. "I'd thought it would be hot, or…something," he murmured.

"Spread out," Simus called. "Look to see if all the camps that surround this place are like the ones we came through. Signal if you find anything, or anyone."

Joden rose to his feet, surveying the stone. Simus stood there, uneasy, as his warriors turned their horses and rode out. "That light, those sounds," he said to Joden. "There should be some mark, some sign."

Joden nodded his silent agreement, walking toward the edge of the stone, circling Simus as they both looked for some answers. The coming dawn made it easier to see that there was no trace of *anything* to be seen. Which made Simus even more nervous.

A short time later, the warriors returned, all of them reporting the same thing. Tents collapsed, the ground trampled, and the dead everywhere.

"I'd put it in the hundreds," Eloix said quietly. "I've never seen such a thing. Warlord, they were all stripped of their tattoos, and all showed signs of having died at their own hands. None of their staffs had skulls, either."

"I know where we might find some answers," Joden said slowly, pointing off into the distance.

"Where?" Simus asked and then turned his gaze to where Joden pointed. On a far rise a handful of tents stood against the horizon, lit with torches, with people and horses milling about.

* * * * *

Simus thanked all the elements that Joden obeyed when Simus ordered him to ride at his side. His friend would have plunged ahead at a gallop, regardless of the risks.

Not that Simus really blamed him. He wanted answers, too.

The scouts took up their positions. All of his warriors regrouped with him, and they rode at a slow pace, and constantly scanned the Plains. But here there were no trampled grasses; the herd had not come this way.

Simus felt his shoulders ease as they circled around to mount the ridge. This camp appeared normal from the looks of it, and as they drew closer he could see that here were mostly young ones.

"They've only partial tattoos," Joden noted.

"Which only adds to the questions," Simus said. Young warrior-priests were kept isolated and away from the warrior camps until they had earned their full tattoos. It was rare to see even one, and here was a camp filled with them. Simus did a quick count and frowned. Maybe twenty in all, their bare torsos decorated with tattoos in various places, but not covered in them as they would be when they reached full status.

He signaled the scouts back, and slowed their progress to a walk. He did not hail the camp, but made no secret of their approach. Yet they went unnoticed, the group's focus seemingly on a tall, fully tattooed warrior-priest in the center of the group.

"Wild Winds," Simus said softly. Joden nodded his agreement.

Wild Winds stood, staff in one hand, talking to four or five young warriors of the Plains. Still, there was no threat in any of their gestures or faces, no fear or anger. Instead, Simus could have sworn there was relief and even joy.

Yers caught Simus's eye, then pointed with his chin to where one of the young warrior-priestesses was seeing to a horse, removing its tack. The horse was nuzzling the young one's hair as she worked.

Something painful eased in Simus's chest. Still, it was no reason to relax. Even less to trust. Wild Winds was the Eldest Elder of the Warrior-Priests of the Plains. His cold disdain and opposition to Keir of the Cat was known. His refusal to consider any new ideas and his opposition to the confirmation of the Warprize had resulted in the sundering of the Council of Elders. Simus had no reason to expect a welcome. Even so, he had to try to learn the truth of all of this.

"Wild Winds," he called, louder than he intended, fully expecting a hostile greeting.

Which made the open expression on the tattooed face that turned his way even more of a shock.

"Simus of the Hawk." Wild Winds strode up and stood before him, planting his skull-less staff next to him. "How may I aid you?"

Simus studied the man. Wild Winds seemed stronger somehow, yet the three human skulls no longer dangled from the leather thongs on his staff. Wild Winds still bore his full tattoos, the only one in the crowd to do so. And his eyes...

Simus glanced at the others that surrounded him and saw the same things in the eyes of the others. Over-bright and wild, as if they'd drunk enough fermented gurtle milk to be seeing the dead. Or survived their first battle. Rattled, nervous, relieved, scared, anxious; it was all there in their eyes.

Except one. A woman standing just behind Wild Winds, at his shoulder. Lovely, with firm breasts and skin the color of kavage laced with milk. Her black hair was twisted into curls that crowned her head. Her bare shoulders were capped with green and black tattoos in a twisting vine pattern that trailed down her arms just far enough to cover the tattoos of her tribes and her birth offerings to the Plains.

But what really caught his attention were her cool, grey eyes, which regarded the crowd calmly. She, whoever she was, was keeping a calm face and a steady hand.

Their eyes met, and Simus was lost.

There was beauty there, but there were mysteries as well. Simus couldn't read her expression or her emotions. But there were secrets in the depths of those eyes that he wanted to explore.

Her gaze slid away from his. Simus realized that the chatter around them had died off.

It took Simus a breath to turn his attention back to Wild Winds and his greeting. A breath too long, since the old man seemed to sense his…distraction.

Simus narrowed his eyes, staring at Wild Winds. "An explanation would be a good start," Simus said carefully. If Wild Winds could act as if nothing had happened, so could he. "My evening pleasures were interrupted by a needle of light that pierced the sky, and a Singer with an itch of curiosity." Simus nodded his head toward Joden. "I had no choice but to leave my bed and seek you out."

Wild Winds greeted Joden, and continued talking, inviting them all into his tent, and offering to tell the tale. Simus listened, caught off guard by this change of tone from the Eldest Elder Warrior-Priest. Still…Simus opened his mouth to refuse.

Joden dismounted beside him, taking the decision out of his hands. Damn all Singers to the snows, he'd little choice now. Yet there would be no harm in listening, and any knowledge gained would aid them.

Besides, he was just as curious as Joden to hear what the man would say.

Simus signaled Eloix and Yers to join them. He'd listen.

Whether he'd trust was another tale entirely.

* * * * *

So this was Simus of the Hawk.

Snowfall wasn't impressed.

She'd been at Wind Winds's side all through the eventful night, ready to both serve and protect her mentor. She'd stay close, although he would claim she was hovering.

So she was slightly behind Wild Winds when the riders approached and hailed the camp.

Simus was tall and imposing, she'd grant him that. One of the largest, blackest warriors she'd ever seen, with skin that shone like obsidian rock. He sat his horse with confidence, dressed in fine chain, his sword on his back. His dark eyes flashed as they swept over them and the gold earrings in his ears caught the morning light.

Handsome, of that there was no doubt, but he knew that all too well, Snowfall thought. She'd heard tales of his wit and charm. But he was certainly rude, greeting Wild Winds without his honors. She wasn't fooled by his—

Their eyes met, and something sang through her, like the power of the Plains itself.

His eyes were dark in color but bright with suspicion, yet under that there was strength, and joy of life itself, as if every breath was a gift to be savored, enjoyed, relished.

The tattoos on her shoulders began to tingle. Snowfall didn't react, didn't gasp. She slowly slid her gaze from his and stood, trying to quiet her inner tremble as he and Wild Winds talked.

Her training kept her face a void, where no warrior could read her thoughts. 'A warrior-priest keeps their own counsel at all times,' was the command, and she'd learned her lessons well. But her tattoos—

They knew no restrictions, and she felt the twisting vines wanting to move, to writhe over her skin. They could not, of course. Her tattoos had been placed on her skin magically by her master, Wild Winds. As long as she was in training, they were under his control.

But they wanted to dance.

Snowfall watched as Wild Winds extended Simus and his people the hospitalities of his tent and offered to tell the tale of the night and the Sacrifice. Simus of the Hawk radiated distrust, but the one named Joden, the potential Singer, dismounted immediately to share in kavage and news.

Snowfall drew a deep, slow breath. So much had changed in a single night, a single moment, a single act by two city-dwellers strange to the Plains and hunted and abused by the warrior-priests. No one had known what would happen when Hail Storm had lured them to their deaths on the Heart.

But the pillar of light had sprung into the sky. Wild Winds had been healed, and those of the warrior-priests who had followed Hail Storm were dead or dying. And the magic, the power that the Sacrifice had returned to the Plains—that still made her skin tingle. She glanced at the coming dawn and wondered what else the elements had in store for them.

"You think that warrior-priests cannot change?" Wild Winds was asking Simus, drawing her attention back to their discussion. "Come and hear the tale, or not. As you choose."

"Keir is going to gut me," Simus grumbled, but he dismounted.

Well. Clearly, a warrior in servitude to a Warlord with dreams of ruling the Plains. Snowfall didn't let her disdain show. She moved off, back toward the main tent as Wild Winds gathered those that would talk and explain, including the young warriors who had served as Guardians to the Sacrifice.

What did her master see in this Simus? Why had her tattoos reacted?

Snowfall didn't heave a sigh, or even take a deep breath. She kept her outer face calm, even as her mind raced with questions.

She'd see to the brewing of kavage, see to the warmth of the tent, offer welcome to these warriors, as her mentor desired. But she'd also wait and watch.

And keep her blades sharp.

CHAPTER SIX

Simus may have accepted the invitation into Wild Winds's tent, but he took nothing at its face. Especially a face of an adversary, covered with the ritual tattoos.

And there was also that woman, but Simus would not allow that to divert him from his purpose. After all, as fascinating as she seemed, she too wore tattoos.

He gathered his warriors around him, and ordered them to make camp close by and wait for him. He lowered his voice when he arranged the watches. His warriors had all given him understanding nods. They'd watch both without and within, and keep their blades ready.

Only then did he lead Joden, Eloix, and Yers into Wild Winds's tent, already filled with warrior-priests in training and young warriors.

Wild Winds gestured Simus and his people to gurtle pads set to his right and offered mugs of kavage and bowls of gurt. Joden took the mug and drank. Simus took his and kept it in his hand.

Wild Winds settled cross-legged before the crowd, his staff on the ground, with no weapon in hand. Simus noted that the young woman with the cool, grey eyes knelt beside the warrior-priest to serve him kavage. "My thanks, Snowfall," Wild Winds said.

The equal of a Token-bearer, then, with no token to bear. She was truly lovely, and despite himself, he couldn't help but again compare her skin to the color of kavage with milk. Perhaps with a touch of honey for sweetness. How would her skin taste in the midst of pleasure?

As if she'd overheard his thought, she raised her eyes to meet his. Those eyes considered him, giving nothing away.

Simus widened his smile, and nodded at her.

Her gaze passed over him like a north wind and was lost to sight when she lowered her eyes, her dark lashes hiding her thoughts.

There was a slight snort off to his left; Joden had seen. Simus ignored him, and brought his mind back to the moment as Wild Winds raised his hand, his palm up in the traditional gesture.

"May the skies hear my voice," Wild Winds intoned. "May the people remember."

"We will remember," said everyone, echoing his words.

"This night, we share our truths together, with no exchange of tokens. Let no one take offense, let all listen with open hearts and minds," Wild Winds said. "I would ask that all speak of what they have seen and what they have done. The warrior that has suffered the most this night, one Gilla of the Snake, now rests within the safety of her tents. But we have her fellow guardians, Lander of the Snake and Ouse of the Fox. They will start our tale."

A warrior stood, young and as nervous as a colt. But he stood tall and steady and spoke his words clearly. "For us, this started when we were still in the thea camp of Haya of the Snake, days before our Rites of Ascension," he said. "For on that day the sky opened above our camp, and two people fell from the sky…."

At the mention of Haya, Simus exchanged a quick glance

with Joden. But the rest of the young warrior's words left Simus amazed. The youth described the arrival of the Sacrifice and his Token-bearer to the Plains, along with a horse fully encased in metal and a small four-legged creature they called a cat. Of the attack by the warrior-priests, and the Sacrifice's loss of control of the powers he carried. Of a desperate flight across the Plains, and then an even more frantic pursuit to try to rescue the warrior Gilla from Hail Storm and his followers. Until the final confrontation at the Heart of the Plains, and a pillar of light when the power, the magic was released.

"In the moment when the Token-bearer summoned the horses to the Heart, not just the living ones answered her call. The dead, too, both horse and warriors." Wild Winds went silent for a moment, his eyes distant. He heaved a sigh, and shrugged. "The Sacrifice cried out for justice, and the magic answered with a needle of power. Those that followed Hail Storm offended the elements, and they died for it. You have seen the results." Wild Winds raised his hand, his palm up in the traditional gesture. "May the people remember."

"We will remember."

"The sun is well above the horizon," Wild Winds said. "These truths will be repeated again and again as more warriors return to the Heart. For now, let us rest and sleep on the truths we have shared."

There was a rustle as the crowd roused and stood, yawning and blinking sleepily. They filed from the tent, their voices a soft murmur as they left.

Simus didn't stir. He sat and waited as the tent cleared, the mug of kavage in his hand long cold. Joden, Eloix, and Yers remained as well, until the only ones left were themselves, Wild

ELIZABETH VAUGHAN

Winds, and his Snowfall.

"You have heard my truths, Simus of the Hawk." Wild Winds shifted slightly so as to face him.

"I thank you for your truths," Simus replied, considering the man before him carefully, then made an abrupt decision. "Wild Winds, I would ask for your token."

Snowfall's eyes went wide. Around Simus, Eloix, Joden, and Yers all started, Yers actually reaching for the hilt of his sword.

Simus waited. Warrior-priests had never honored this ritual, never sought or gave tokens, always responded with silence or violence. If there was true change…

Wild Winds gave Simus a wry smile. He nodded to the full mug of kavage in Simus's hands. "You hold my token, Simus of the Hawk. What truths would you voice?"

"You've told me what has happened," Simus said. "For which I thank you. But you haven't told me what it means. For the warrior-priests. For the Plains."

"I will speak to your truths." Wild Winds sighed, his shoulders sagging. "I haven't told you what it means, because I do not know," he said.

Simus leaned back, struck by the plain honesty of the words. Even more, it was the worry in Wild Winds's eyes that made him think the older man was telling the truth. Simus glanced at Joden, who seemed to share his own confusion.

"In truth, I never expected to see this dawn. The Warprize had a name for my death, slow and painful. 'Cancer,' she called it," Wild Winds said.

"Yet you live," Simus said.

"I was healed." Wild Winds's eyes flickered to the side and Simus knew there was more to that tale than what Wild Winds was telling.

"You are not telling me everything you know," Simus said.

"Truth," Wild Winds said. "We all have our secrets. But these events have come at me like a violent storm across the Plains." Wild Winds shook his head, his long, matted braids moving around his face, "It happened so fast, I've had no time to consider the consequences."

Simus nodded slowly.

"I know this much," Wild Winds said. "There is work to be done." He gestured with his chin toward the Heart.

Simus grimaced, but nodded his agreement. "The bodies must be seen to, the camps cleared." He frowned, considering the full mug of kavage in his hand. "Osa and Ultie are not far, with their warriors," Simus pointed out. "Other candidates will be arriving. We will make short work of what must be done, and, if you are willing, share these truths with them as well."

"Yes," Wild Winds nodded. "This truth must be shared with all."

Simus stared at him, still not quite sure he believed what he was hearing.

Wild Winds chuckled then sobered quickly. "Do you know where Eldest Elder Reness is? Or Essa?"

"Eldest Elder Reness left with Lara and Keir to aid with the birth of their child," Simus shrugged. "I've heard nothing of Essa. Do you fear—"

"I do not know," Wild Winds sighed. "But always Essa has been the first to the Heart in the Spring. I feel the need for his truths now, and Reness as well. But I am too tired to think much past that thought." He frowned, opened his mouth as if to say more, only to be cut off by a yawn. He chuckled, and shrugged at

Simus ruefully. "It seems the night and day has caught up with me."

"With us all," Simus agreed, suddenly feeling his own weariness.

"Have I answered your truths?" Wild Winds gestured toward the mug, completing the ritual with a slight smile.

"You have." Simus drained the mug, and then offered it back with his own rueful grin. Snowfall advanced to claim it from his hand.

"Then let us sleep on these truths we have told each other," Wild Winds rose, and with him all in the tent rose as well, stretching stiff limbs.

Simus nodded. His own exhaustion was creeping up on him; he needed to sleep. "Until tonight, then."

* * * * *

Simus led the others to where his tent had been pitched, greeting his warriors on watch. "The camp is set?" Simus asked.

"Aye, Warlord," the First responded.

"Form a hunting party," Simus ordered. "With any willing to go. The others are to grab what sleep they can, when off watch."

"Aye, Warlord," came the responses as he ducked into his tent. He turned to face Joden, Eloix, and Yers as they entered behind him. He lowered his voice, not bothering with bells. "You heard it all. I've not the wits left to talk it out now. Eloix—"

"There's enough daylight for some hours in the saddle," she murmured. "A few mugs of strong kavage, and I can be off."

"Good." Simus smiled his approval. "Tuck yourself into the hunting party. Ride for Xy once you are clear of watching eyes."

"We should send two messengers," Yers suggested. "By separate ways."

"I cannot spare a warrior," Simus said. "There are few enough here with me that I trust, and the loss of another may mean failure on our part. Little good that will do our cause."

Yers crossed his arms over his chest, but nodded his agreement.

"Go carefully," Simus said to Eloix. "Stop at the border and tell all to Liam of the Deer if he is there. Then make haste to Xy. Keir must be told of this." He sighed. "I do not trust this sudden change, but for now we will take it as truth."

"I will tell him," Eloix said.

"Tell him this as well," Simus stared at the wall of the tent, organizing his thoughts. Eloix waited silently.

"We'd thought that this year would be spent in preparation," Simus said. "I would build my army; Joden would become Singer. Keir would build his strength in Xy, and then he would return next Spring to reclaim the title of Warlord, and then to WarKing. I will continue with that goal, but I think he should consider returning to the Plains now. This season. His presence could make a difference."

"Even if Eloix rides like the winds themselves, Keir could not get here before the Trials are concluded," Yers protested.

"Truth," Simus said. "But Keir's presence gives us more choices than his absence." He focused on Eloix. "He will have to decide."

"I will tell him," Eloix said.

"Say this as well to Lara," Simus said. "Little healer, I regret pulling him from your side."

"From your lips to her ear," Eloix promised.

"The elements ride with you," Simus said softly. Eloix bowed her head. Yers opened the tent flap and they both left together.

Joden stood there, blinking in the shadows of the tent. "Such a song I could write," he breathed.

"Not now," Simus said firmly. "Sleep, then we will see what the skies bring our way. Get to your tent, Joden. Or better yet—" Simus barked an order and one of the warriors threw back the flap and looked in. "Joden and I will snatch a few hours' sleep. See to it that Joden returns to his tent," Simus commanded, starting to remove his leathers. "And make sure he's bedded down before you leave, else he will make songs in his head the rest of the day."

"I'll see to it," the warrior chuckled. "Come, Singer."

"Not a Singer yet," Joden protested, as the warrior tugged on his arm.

Simus snorted his amusement as he stripped and crawled into his bedroll. He settled into the furs with a willing sigh of relief, and closed his eyes. His old thea had always said that a warrior sleeps when he can, the better to be prepared. But his thoughts raced, filled with his own questions.

With a huff, he rolled over and forced himself to think on something else. Something…distracting.

Like the mysteries in the depths of cool, grey eyes.

Those thoughts, that sense of curiosity. Simus smiled at himself. As if a warrior-priestess would share her secrets. That would be even stranger than the events of this day. He yawned and settled into sleep.

And dreamed of kavage laced with milk…and just a touch of honey.

CHAPTER SEVEN

Wild Winds tiredly stripped and curled up on his bedroll. Snowfall fussed as she carefully covered him completely with his furs, as if he were still ill. Still dying.

"So?" he asked sleepily, pulling the blankets to his shoulders. "What do you think of Simus?"

"I do not understand," she said softly, dodging his question and his eyes. "Why you would send me from your side."

Wild Winds rolled over onto his back, stretching under the bedding, then relaxing with a sigh as they warmed with his body heat. "Now it's more important than ever." He yawned. "And you are avoiding my question. Tell me your truths."

"He is a handsome, strong warrior, taller than most. But Simus does not trust you." Snowfall shrugged. "He does not trust us."

"No reason that he should," Wild Winds said. "One night will not change that. But I am still intent on my purpose. You must contest to be his Token-bearer."

"You have seen to my training," Snowfall countered, her voice crackling with pain. "You will need my help with the others."

"No." Wild Winds looked at her. "I need your help to win back the trust we lost with Hail Storm's actions, for he has destroyed what the warrior-priests were. Now we must rebuild what we are, and how better than to offer one of our own to serve Simus? To learn more of the man who would stand at the side of one who would bring change to the Plains?"

"He is an arrogant, over-confident wind blowing over the Plains," Snowfall blurted out. "Over-sure of himself, and rude as well."

Wild Winds fought a smile. "You know so much of the warrior, having watched him listen to our truths?" He tucked his chin under the blankets, hiding his mouth.

"He is all bluster and charm, with no substance behind." Snowfall glared at Wild Winds as she knelt beside his pallet. "You are my master and mentor and I have followed your ways in the dark times," Snowfall snapped. "Now the magic is returned, and you are healed, and you say to me, 'leave my side.' I feel like the rain is falling up from the ground."

Wild Winds pulled the blanket down from his mouth, and sat up. "Sit, Snowfall."

Snowfall sat beside his pallet.

"The dead spoke to me, when they healed me. Three old friends, who had been my skull spirits," he said.

"You freed them." Snowfall's eyes were wide.

"I did, but they returned to aid me." Wild Winds smiled at the memory of them supporting him, speaking to him once again after long years.

Snowfall waited.

"They told me three things," Wild Winds said. "And they bade me listen and learn well. That another battle looms."

Still she waited, silent and patient.

"'Magic is a blade that cuts both ways.'" Wild Winds could almost hear the echo of his friends' voices as he spoke. "'That which was taken is restored. That which was imprisoned is now freed.'" Wild Winds sighed. "'Embrace the old. Preserve the new.'"

"Master." Snowfall's tone was a gentle one. "You were ill and—"

"No." He shook his head. "They are my trusted friends, and while the words are cryptic, they are a warning. Since that moment, I have had this feeling of dread. The dead and the power that has returned are trying to warn me, but I do not have the gift to fully understand." He rubbed his face with his hand, his tiredness returning. "The Eldest Elder before me told me that in the ancient days there were Seers of the Plains. Ones who could foretell the future. Who knows? Perhaps those gifts will return to us as well, but how will we learn to use them?"

"You are tired." Snowfall reached for his blankets. "You should—"

"Who else can speak words of peace, Snowfall?"

She opened her mouth, then closed it.

"The warrior-priests who supported Hail Storm have paid for it with their lives," Wild Winds continued. "Keir of the Cat would think that a good start, and were he here I fear he might be tempted to kill us all. But Keir's Warprize seems more open to us." He thought back on his meeting with that young woman, and nodded. "And I believe that Simus and Joden, the would-be Singer, would also consider our truths."

Snowfall's face had fallen back into its usual, impenetrable mask. But he could see that she was considering his words.

Wild Winds sighed. "This has all been too much, too soon. We will speak of this—" Another yawn caught him off guard.

"Sleep," Snowfall commanded. "We will speak of this later, Master."

"We will," Wild Winds said firmly before he closed his eyes, and allowed himself to drift off.

* * * * *

Snowfall set herself the task of cleaning the outer tent, gathering dishes and piling up the gurtle pads. She was far too wound up for sleep.

But as even as her hands moved in familiar tasks, her thoughts raced like galloping horses, ranging over the Plains.

She'd been so proud to be selected as warrior-priestess at her Rite of Ascension, so many years ago. Proud to learn the power of her gifts, and how to use them with the limited resources the land offered. Wild Winds had explained, taught, encouraged her and Lightning Storm together.

But the powers of the warrior-priests had been in sharp decline for years and were continuing to fade as the small amount of power in the Plains was being consumed.

That aspect of being a warrior-priestess never sat well with her. The arrogance adopted by most, and the deceit of the true extent of their powers. Given that she was still in training, she'd had limited contact with warriors. Only those that had their full upper-body tattoos walked freely within the Tribes and were permitted to go to war. But still, her training was to conceal, to hide, and never show weakness or emotion.

She glanced at the colorful designs on the tops of her shoulders, and ran a hand over the green and black vine pattern. Would they ever be completed now?

The camp around her was settling for the afternoon, with many seeking sleep. Over by the tent of Simus of the Hawk, a hunting party was forming. The wind brought their words to her ears, talk of a herd of deer close at hand.

Snowfall bent over the washing tubs, using sand and hot water to clean the mugs and bowls they'd used. She could feel those warriors' eyes upon her, regarding her suspiciously. No special gift of power was needed to feel their confusion, and the weight of their mistrust.

Would one of them come forward, to talk to her? Why would they, when all they had known of warrior-priests was contempt and disdain?

Even before the Sacrifice, Wild Winds had asked her to seek out Simus of the Hawk and serve him as Token-bearer. The fact that he would be entering the Trials this Spring had long been known. Wild Winds felt that it was important that Simus come to understand warrior-priests, since he felt that the mind and heart of Keir of the Cat was filled with hatred of their ways.

Was her master right?

Snowfall reached for more mugs and bowls, and scrubbed each thoroughly before setting them out to dry in the grass.

She'd no desire to leave her master. Now that the Plains was awash in the power—

She paused for a moment, letting herself see the golden glow that lay within the land, pulsing softly, like a long, slow heartbeat. For a moment she considered how one could use it to wash dishes, and then chided herself at the idea. Foolish to waste power in such a way.

Besides, washing gave her time to think. To consider Wild Winds's position.

The hunting party mounted their horses, and set off at a trot. A weight lifted from her shoulders with their departure.

She glanced at the tent again, considering the man who slept within. Simus was handsome, certainly. Tall, muscular, dark, with a bright smile. But he knew it well, and she wrinkled her nose at his manner. Loud, boisterous, and with an arrogance of his own, much like elder warrior-priests. Snowfall allowed herself a slight quirk of her mouth. He'd expressed his interest in her body with his eyes, and she'd ignored him. She doubted Simus of the Hawk was used to being spurned.

Yet her tattoos had reacted to his presence. Snowfall winced inside. At some point she would have to share that with her master. She knew full well he'd use it to support his argument.

Snowfall sighed, and reached for another bowl. Wild Winds's insistence that she leave his side felt like he was rejecting her. Now that the power had returned, now that they could use their gifts freely, they could relearn all that had been lost. And yet, he would send her away.

A yawn caught her off guard. Enough thought. She turned back to her work, and finished quickly. Her own tiredness was stalking her now, and she would need to wake soon enough to prepare the evening meal.

The last of the bowls done, she cleaned the cooking area, and stood to stretch. She'd enough time to catch some sleep before—

Movement caught her eye. Lightning Strike was coming, running hard. He ran up to her, with an apologetic look. "Wake the Eldest Elder. There is something he needs to see."

"He's weary, as are we all," Snowfall said, frowning. "Won't it wait—"

"No." Lightning Strike shook his head. "It's Mist."

* * * * *

Wild Winds stood over Mist's body, sprawled in the center of her ruined tent. His old friend had made her choices, but it struck hard to see her cold and lifeless. She'd told him that she would seek the snows, but something was wrong—

"I couldn't sleep," Lightning Strike said. "I thought to seek her out, since she was special to you, Eldest Elder. I found—"

"Mist." Wild Winds knelt and reached out to take her left hand as he called her name in a ritual as old as the Plains themselves.

"She didn't die at her own hand," Lightning Strike pointed out in a low voice.

Wild Winds looked at the wounds that had been inflicted on her, by a sword nowhere to be seen. But as he touched her cold flesh, his skin crawled. There was a taint on her body, of a life drained with foul intent.

"Blood magic," he whispered.

Lightning Strike and Snowfall both stiffened, their hands on their weapons. Snowfall scanned the area, her eyes narrowing.

"Mist," Wild Winds called again, as the ritual required, taking her right ankle in his hand. "Mist, Elder of the Warrior-Priests, answer me."

Silence, her eyes lifeless and unseeing, stripped of her tattoos.

"Mist," he called twice again, grasping her left ankle and hand and when silence was his only answer, he leaned over her, and closed her eyes. He stood and looked out over the Plains that now contained a new danger.

"Hail Storm lives?" Snowfall asked softly.

"Hail Storm lives," Wild Winds confirmed.

* * * * *

Hail Storm crawled under the cover of some low aspens, by a

creek bed that ran fast and cold. He lowered his swollen forearm into the water, and hissed as it covered the angry red scratches. He looked about, fearing he'd been overheard, but the area was clear.

Curse them, curse them all: the Sacrifice, his Token-bearer, and that damned animal of theirs that had injured him so. His rage was greater than his pain, and his pain was fierce.

The four scratches ran the length of his forearm, deep and sore. He'd let them bleed, and the cool water helped leach out some of the heat, but it seemed to him that the red was moving up his arm. His fingers felt fat and swollen. It had been hard to grip the hilt of the sword when he'd killed Mist.

At least he'd been able to use her death. Drain her life force to add to his reserve of magic. And that was where the injury was the deepest. Far worse than the loss of his rank, pride, and tattoos. Far worse than his inability to summon a horse, for even that he could deal with.

Hail Storm clenched his jaw, taking up a handful of sand to scrub the pus from his wounds. The pain of his body was incredible, but not more so than what he suffered now. No. The very worst was the magic pulsing in the land, magic that he had once been able to reach out and touch. Drain. Use.

Now the power fled before him, even as he reached, faster even than the horses that avoided his presence. All he had now were the reserves he'd created from the blood magic he'd practiced.

He would have wept, but that his rage filled him with hate. For Wild Winds, for Keir of the Cat, and for any who supported them.

The water had cooled his arm, but it still pulsed with pain. He grunted, tempted once again to try to use magic to heal it. But every time he tried to focus his will to such a thing, the power would slip from his grasp, as if it opposed the healing. He'd waste no more on another attempt.

He pulled his arm out, and knelt down to drink deeply, feeling hot and dry. He'd managed to escape from the Heart without being seen, and he'd make sure to stay under cover. But he still had allies. Still had options. He'd wait for darkness, and find them.

The stars would show him the way to the camp of Antas of the Boar.

There he'd find welcome. Food, drink, rest, and aid for his vengeance.

CHAPTER EIGHT

"Warlord," Yers said from beyond the tent flap.

Simus came awake quickly, his eyes snapping open, reaching instinctively for his sword. Angry voices were just outside, but even as his fingers brushed the hilt, he recognized the normal sounds of the camp. Warriors moved about, meat sizzled over a fire, pots clattered, and the smell of kavage was in the air.

He eased back within his blankets, the gurtle furs soft against his skin. The recent happenings tumbled through his head. This change—the deaths of the warrior-priests, and Wild Winds's openness—could it be trusted?

The tent above his head held no answer, nor, he suspected, would the open skies. It was something he'd have to keep careful watch on, his eyes open, his weapons ready.

"Warlord," the voice repeated.

"Come," he said.

Yers pushed the flap aside. "Destal has taken Eloix's place for the time being. " He carried a mug of kavage in his free hand.

Simus threw back the bedding, and sat naked, cross-legged on his pallet. He reached for the mug as Yers offered it to him. "What news?"

Yers went to one knee beside his pallet and lowered his voice.

"The hunting party left soon after you slept and attracted no attention. They have already returned with two good-sized bucks. They tell me that Eloix left them as soon as they were out of sight of the camp."

The kavage was strong and hot in Simus's mouth. He welcomed the bitter taste, and the surge of energy it brought.

"There was some commotion in the camp of the warrior-priests shortly after you bedded down. Wild Winds went down to the dead, then returned to his tent." Yers looked over his shoulder at the tent flap. "And now the Warlord candidates have gathered outside, demanding to talk to you. Ultie, Osa, Nires, Reht, and Zioa are among them, along with others I do not know. I told them that if you did not have kavage first, you'd emerge from the tent with a bared blade." Yers flashed a grin. "They accepted it, but it is not in their nature to be patient."

"I take it they've talked to Wild Winds." Simus rubbed his hand over his face and yawned.

"They must have, as irritated as they all are," Yers agreed. "And did not like what they heard."

"Simus," Ultie bellowed from outside. "Drink your damn kavage out here."

Simus rolled his eyes, and handed the mug to Yers. He swept his armor and weapons into a great armful, and took the mug back. "Rouse Joden," he ordered and strode out the tent.

The Warlords were gathered just beyond his campfire. His warriors were clustered at the fire, cooking the evening meal. Their glances reflected their quiet amusement as he walked past them.

Simus marched right up to the center of the Warlords dropped his gear at Ultie's feet. Ultie scowled, but Simus just smiled.

Osa snorted, her green eyes bright as she admired his form,

standing in the middle of all of them, naked as a babe. He raised his mug to her, set it in the grass, and reached for his trous. "Ultie of the Needle-rat, how may I aid you?'

"You can explain what has happened," Ultie growled. "We return to find the Heart a battlefield, and—"

Simus made a great show of flapping out his leather trous and then put them on, hopping around on first one leg and then the other. While Ultie sputtered out his demands, Simus took the time to consider the others.

A few faces he didn't know; new candidates for Warlord, he assumed. Far too few of those, and that wasn't good. The Plains would suffer if the traditional number of armies didn't form.

Osa had her arms crossed over her ample breasts, clearly amused. Simus knew she'd talked to Keir about his goals and hadn't expressed more than a general interest. He already knew better then to offer her the warmth of his bed. Osa's preference was for women, and she held to her ways.

Simus already knew Ultie would offer no support. But no real opposition either, at least until anyone attempted to stop Ultie from doing whatever Ultie wanted to do.

Reht and Zioa were a different matter. Reht was a short woman: short of stature, short of hair, short of temper. The amber of her eyes matched the golden brown of her skin. Simus was not sure of her opinion as to Keir, but she was giving him an amused smile through her almond eyes.

Zioa was taller and easily excitable, always talking with her hands, always pushing her thick black hair back behind her ears. She reminded Simus of an old, ivory-handled dagger he'd had long ago, with weathered handle and a sharp blade. Zioa'd been friendly in the past to both Keir and him, and she was grinning at him now. Simus decided to count her as friend to their cause.

Nires of the Boar was off to one side, one of the most experienced Warlords. Blond of hair and beard with streaks of grey, his skin wrinkled and creased, but a warrior to be respected. The winds had it that Nires had lost track of the number of seasons he'd fought. He stood with one hand on his hip, the other on his sword hilt, but the stance was casual and interested. Simus caught his eye, and realized that the man was studying him even as he was being studied.

But at his side stood two whose faces were openly hostile.

Ietha, a tall, thin woman with a permanent scowl on her horse face. Her brown hair was pulled back in a horse-tail, which only emphasized her height. Her slanted eyes and sand-colored skin were lovely, but those dark eyes were unamused.

Loual stood beside her. The man looked like the weathered stone of the walls of Xy, but Simus wasn't about to tell him that. Loual wasn't looking at him, his eyes hooded, focused on the ground. Simus knew well that he had spoken against Keir. He stood now with arms crossed, as if to reject any new idea that came his way.

Last of all, Kiza, lovely Kiza was laughing at him, making no secret of her delight. Her of the pink skin like the morning sky, and reddish hair piled high on her head. The least likeliest of Warlords, but Simus knew her blade was dangerous, having sparred with her before. He flashed a grin at his old friend. She winked back.

"—dead warrior-priests, needles of light in the sky," Ultie said, not used to being ignored. "What say you?"

Simus didn't reply until he'd stomped his feet into his boots, belted his trous, and swept up his mug of kavage. "My thanks for your courtesy." He gave Ultie a mocking nod.

"Fool," Ultie growled. "Explain this." He swept his hand toward the Heart. "The dead strewn about, the camps torn asunder. This is no laughing matter."

Osa picked up Simus's leather tunic and shook it out, offering it so he could slip it on. He gave her a nod as he offered his mug to Kiza, accepted Osa's aid, then started on the buckles.

"What happened?" Ultie demanded again. "The night was filled with strange lights and noises. We return to the Heart only to find a battlefield with no enemy that any can see."

"Didn't Wild Winds and his people explain?" Simus asked, retrieving his kavage mug.

"We would talk to him," Osa said. "If he were here."

Simus stared at her, then turned.

Wild Winds's tent, and those of his followers, were gone.

Simus blinked, unable to believe. The tent was gone, the area clear, with only the grass swaying in the wind. "He was here," Simus said slowly, frowning. "He must have moved his camp."

"Nowhere that we can find," Ietha grumbled.

"What did he tell you?" Ultie demanded.

Simus caught a glimpse of Joden and Yers returning, both of them looking just as surprised as he was. They must have heard what Osa said, since both seemed as confused as Simus felt. The whole camp gone? Simus's frown deepened. Where had the old warrior-priest taken the young ones in training? And why? It made little sense.

Under his confusion, he felt a pang at the idea that he'd seen the last of those cool, grey eyes.

He let the regret go as he turned to Osa. "I'm happy to share what I was told," Simus said. "Joden heard everything as well, and can speak to the truths that—"

"I'll not listen to that city-lover's lies," snarled one of the group.

Joden roared, and charged to attack.

The other warriors faded back and away as the one who'd offered insult fumbled with his sword. A critical mistake, given Joden's speed and rage. Simus crossed his arms over his chest and settled in to watch.

Warriors tended to listen to Joden's calm voice and reasonable words, to hear his wisdom and songs, and think nothing of the sword at his side. But Joden, he of the broad smiling face and solid build, was a warrior first, even if his heart was full of song. Yes, warriors tended to forget that, until they saw him in battle.

Certainly, this one had.

The fumble with the hilt gave Joden enough time to close. Joden hadn't bothered to draw a weapon. He came in fast, leading with his shoulder and slammed into his foe. The man went down, hard, sword still in its sheath. He lay there stunned, his breath gone.

Joden backed off, pulling his sword, his eyes smoldering. "Draw your sword, *bragnect*, so that I might prove my truth on your ass."

Osa stood to one side, fairly close to Simus's shoulder. "Who is that?" Simus asked under his breath.

"One Wyrik," Osa muttered. "Of the Boar. He was Second under Reht of the Horse last season."

Simus grunted as he watched Wyrik stagger to his feet and pull his sword. A big man, hardened from long years of combat. "The same Tribe as Antas then," Simus said.

"With much the same attitudes as Antas," Osa observed. "But

the Tribe of the Boar are not all of one mind. Witness Nires there." Osa nodded toward the older fighter.

Nires was frowning, glaring at Wyrik with disapproval.

"Oh," Osa said and winced, which drew Simus's attention back to the fight. "Wyrik had better watch—"

Joden whipped in fast, fended Wyrik's blade with his own, and then punched him full in the face. With a satisfying 'crunch', blood began spurting from Wyrik's nose.

"Ever have I spoken my truths," Joden growled. "Even at the cost of friendship." He danced back from the blood spray.

Wyrik's only answer was to spit, raise his blade and charge forward. A charge that Joden met head on, catching Wyrik's sword with his own and forcing it up. For a breath they struggled, then broke apart.

"You lied to Antas," Wyrik snarled, his voice thick and wet. "You said the city-dweller was no Warprize, then turned and—"

"But I saw my mistake." Joden's anger distorted his face. "A Warprize must be discovered during the course of a battle, or on or near a battlefield. As Lara was. A Warprize must render aid to the Warlord or his men. As Lara did." Joden never took his eyes off his opponent, but he raised his voice for all to hear. "Finally, a Warprize must be attractive to a Warlord, must spark feelings of desire."

"As the heat of the sun that shines in the height of summer," Simus announced. "And that is certainly true of Lara and Keir. Lara is a true Warprize to her Warlord."

"Aye," Joden growled, circling Wyrik, looking for an opening. Wyrik watched him warily.

"I may not support Lara and Keir in all things," Joden said. "But I will ever speak my truth, even if it means I admit my mistakes. And I will prove it on your—"

"Enough," Nires's deep voice rumbled over them. "This gets us no answers. Withdraw your words, Wyrik. Or we'll leave the two of you to resolve your truths." Nires's voice went dry. "From what I have seen, I have a feeling that Joden will have the last say."

CHAPTER NINE

Wyrik stood, breathing hard as the blood ran down his chin to drip on his chest. His eyes never left Joden's.

"I'm willing to leave it here." Joden took a step back and sheathed his blade. "The day has been a long one, and I feel the need for kavage."

"Spoken as a Singer-to-be," Simus called out. "What say you, Wyrik?"

Wyrik swung his glare at Simus, then back to Joden. "I withdraw my words," he spat, then stomped off, pushing through the crowd.

Simus almost laughed out loud, but decided not to. The Warprize had forced a supply of bloodmoss on every warrior. He could offer Wyrik some bloodmoss to stop the bleeding.

But then again, maybe not.

"What say you, Simus of the Hawk?" Nires asked. Simus watched as everyone focused on him. "Where is Wild Winds?"

"I do not know," Simus said. "But he was here, and the warrior-priests were responsible for all that occurred. Joden and I can tell you the truths that were told to us; you can believe as you so choose." Simus eyed the clouds on the horizon. "There is a storm brewing. I can offer you the comfort of my tent, with hot kavage and food, or we can tell it here so that none are tainted by my courtesy."

Ultie snorted.

Nires frowned. "Take no insult, Simus of the Hawk. Sunset comes, and with it the winds bring a storm. I would hear the basics now; the rest can wait for another day."

"I would ask Joden to speak then," Simus said. "For he has witnessed all that was said."

"I will start with our approach to the Heart, after the needle of light pierced the sky," Joden said. His ire was still up; his tone was sharp, words clipped and terse. Joden recited the story as it had been told. Simus stood, listening, playing with his kavage mug as the wind began to rise. Clouds off in the distance promised rain soon to come.

"These are the truths I was told by Wild Winds," Joden finished, his voice once again slow and reasonable.

"I confirm the tale," Simus said firmly.

"I do not know what to make of this," Ultie rumbled. "Warrior-priests turning on each other now? Becoming more powerful, and telling the truth of such?" Ultie pointed a finger at Simus. "What has Keir wrought upon the Plains, with that Warprize of his?'

Joden jumped in before Simus could open his mouth. "You cannot lay all of this at Keir's feet. The warrior-priests seem to have brought this upon their own heads, no fault of the Warprize." Joden shrugged. "Other changes, yes. But this?"

"I would offer no offense, Joden of the Hawk, but I'd not believe a word of this tale," Ietha said. "Except my own eyes witnessed the fire in the night, and see the dead in the field."

"A field that needs clearing," Osa pointed out. "And with so many they must needs be given to the earth."

"There's truth to that, Joden," Nires said. "In all my seasons, we have always left the battlefield to the enemy. Now I find it here, on the Plains, at the very Heart." He shook his head, his face a mix of frustration and confusion and disgust.

"What of the Council?" Reht asked gruffly, picking at her gloves. "Will the Council form? Wild Winds is apparently here, but where is Essa? Reness?"

"And there is no Eldest Elder of the Warriors," Zioa said pointedly.

"Eager for the title, Zioa?" Reht asked.

"Antas holds that place," Loual growled.

"Antas of the Boar was stripped of the title when he called for violence against the Warprize in a Council meeting," Simus said firmly. "Nires was named in his place."

"But only for the Outcasting," Nires reminded them all. "A new Eldest Elder of the Warriors must be named by the Elders. I can lay no claim to the honor now."

"So what shall we do?" Reht asked as the wind began to rise, bringing the scent of rain.

Simus could see the uncertainty and fear rising, even as the storm did. He let loose with a laugh, as strong and confident as he could make it, and caught their attention. "We shall do as we have always done," he said. "Once the Heart is cleared, we shall set our tents, and raise our banners high. During the day, we shall offer and accept challenges and gather the armies of the Plains. And as the sun sets, we shall take down the banners, and dance as warriors dance, well into the night." Simus turned back toward camp. "That will bring the stragglers, if for nothing else than to join in the dancing and singing."

"Now is not the time for dancing," Loual snapped.

Simus looked back over his shoulder at the cluster of them, and gave the man his widest smile. "When better?" he laughed, throwing out a challenge to all of them.

* * * * *

As soon as he'd discovered that Hail Storm still lived, Wild Winds had ordered his camp broken and had his followers slip away quietly, under the protection of a veil. It had taken all their efforts, and a lot of power, but they'd managed to leave the Heart without raising any alarm. He required them all to hold themselves unseeable and silent once they were mounted and away, so that no eyes might track them.

"You will make them fear us," Snowfall protested.

Wild Winds had wondered how long it would take her to confront him, and he'd not been far off. They were mere hours away from the Heart and their camp, the storm clouds hanging heavy over their heads.

"They already fear us," Wild Winds replied as he rode at the back of the group, watching carefully for signs of pursuit.

"Is this wise?" Snowfall asked, riding beside him. "For us to flee?"

Wild Winds turned to look at her, the wind dancing the curling twists in her black hair. Snowfall studied him, with a thin worry line between her brows.

"Simus and Joden have heard our truths, and they will spread the tale. It will take time to clear the Heart of the dead, and one of us can return to confirm the telling once we've hidden away." Wild Winds urged his horse on. "Hail Storm is a threat to the young and untrained. He walks the blood paths. He didn't just kill Mist. He took her soul. Her life. In doing so, he has chosen a way that he can spread, if he wishes to." Wild Winds grimaced. "I suspect he will not want to. He will want all the power for himself."

Snowfall said nothing; a particular trait of hers. She could say more with silence than anyone he knew.

He sighed, meeting her gaze. "Snowfall, we are not who we were, but we can become who we truly are."

"If you are done being cryptic," she said, without a change of expression, "we'd best keep moving. The rains come."

He snorted, but gave a nod and urged his horse to a trot, Snowfall just behind. He pulled up when he realized that Lightning Strike wasn't paying attention; his horse was drifting off to the side. "Lightning Strike?"

The young man kept his seat, but he'd let the reins go slack, and was studying the sky, his head thrown back.

"Lightning Strike," Wild Winds called again, and the lad's head snapped back, a dazed look on his face. With a shamefaced look, he gathered up his reins and rode over to them.

"Where were your thoughts?" Snowfall asked as he drew close. "You seemed lost with them."

"The clouds dance with power," Lightning Strike explained.

Wild Winds glanced up, frowning. He could see no power in the skies above them. The land, though, *that* he could see, pools of sweet magic scattered all about them.

"And I see nothing," Snowfall said ruefully. There was envy in her voice.

"We all have different skills, different levels of talent," Wild Winds said. "Different ways we see and apply the power. We must learn and train those skills to the best of our ability, and learn control."

"I wonder," Lightning Strike looked up at the sky. "Would the magic control the storms? Call the lightning?"

"I wonder," Wild Winds said mildly, "what one would do with it if one did?"

That brought the lad's gaze down from the sky. "I hadn't thought of that," Lightning Strike confessed.

"Do so before anything else," Wild Winds said as they moved off. He urged his horse back to a trot. "You must think things through, Lightning Strike. That more than anything else, we must teach the others."

"I will," Lightning Strike said.

"And you," Wild Winds said to Snowfall. "You must challenge for Simus's Token-bearer."

"I do not see why I should leave your side," Snowfall said calmly as she retrieved her cloak from her saddlebags. The wind was coming up fiercely now; the rains would start soon.

"You must. If our people—not just what is left of us but the people of the Plains—are to survive, there must be change. And that is no easy thing." Wind Winds urged his horse forward. "I would have you return to the Heart. Watch Simus, Snowfall. Hide yourself, and watch him. You will see another side to him."

"I do not wish—" Snowfall started.

Wild Winds cut her off. "Keir, Simus, and Joden lead the herd in this. They must come to trust us."

"They would trust you," she argued.

Wild Winds barked out a laugh at that. "No, that deer has bolted. Simus must needs come to know us, and how better than to offer him your service? Besides, with Hail Storm alive, there is the issue of protection."

That brought a frown to her lovely face. "You think Simus needs our protection?"

"No." Wild Winds shook his head, his dreadlocks dancing over his back. "I think we may need his."

* * * * *

Pain filled Snowfall's heart. "Master." She slowed her horse, and met her master's eyes. "I have no wish to leave you."

Wild Winds stopped his horse. Snowfall did as well, letting her gaze fall to the reins in her hand. The others continued on. The wind was picking up, and the rain was starting to splatter Snowfall's hood.

"Snowfall." Her master's voice was a rumble. "I do not wish this either. You have been an excellent student, and we both know you are close to attaining mastery, closer than any other."

"Master." Snowfall didn't look up, letting the pleasure at his words mingle with her pain.

"This is a path you alone can walk to try to bring peace back to the Plains," Wild Winds said.

"Lightning Strike—" Snowfall started.

"Has a temper he still struggles with," Wild Winds said smoothly. "Can you see him trying to deal with Simus?"

Snowfall allowed herself a small snort. "No," she admitted.

"You have the patience and the cool head. Your skills, your use of the power lies more in protection and defense of others," Wild Winds said. "You are my truth that I send to Keir and Simus. My truth, my teachings—you have learned them well. Stand at his side, and let there be no more secrets. You can offer your blade, and your knowledge, and provide Simus with your truth."

Snowfall raised her eyes. "My oaths are sworn to you."

Wild Winds nodded, and gave her a bittersweet smile. "No longer can I hold you at my side, warrior-priestess in training. Dismount." He slid from his saddle to stand at her horse's side.

She obeyed from long habit, and they stood, facing each other, sheltered by their horses.

Wild Winds held out both his hands, palm up. "Give me your hands."

She placed her hands on his, and then with a long sigh, slid them up his arms to grasp his elbows. His warm fingers grasped hers as well.

"Snowfall, warrior-priestess of the Plains, let the elements witness that I release you from my service. Your training is complete, your powers under your control. Your tattoos are free from my control and—"

Golden light surged up from the ground, dancing along their bodies. Snowfall looked into Wild Winds's startled eyes, wide as her own as the light surrounded them.

Deep within, as if settling next to her heart, a feeling grew. Joy, and a feeling of wild freedom. But then an urgency, a sense of dread.

Their tattoos moved, powerfully. Wild Winds's writhed all over his body, the colors dancing as they watched. Snowfall's vines stayed on her shoulders and upper arms, but they danced as well, growing and adding new leaves.

Wild Winds licked his lips and continued to speak, his voice hoarse with emotion. "—and your gifts are your own to use in the Service of the Plains. Serve them well."

The golden light twirled about them once more, then sank within the earth.

"Does that happen?" Snowfall whispered.

"Never before," Wild Winds whispered back.

Snowfall tightened her grasp on his arms. "That feeling you spoke of, of uncertainty, of dread." She looked north again. "I feel it, Master."

"Master no longer." Wild Winds looked at her with a soft smile that set her heart aching. "Every ending is a beginning, and every beginning an end." He released his hold, and turned to mount his horse. Once in the saddle, he looked down at her. "Seek out Simus. Look deeper, Snowfall."

"And if he is not worthy?" Snowfall asked.

Wild Winds gathered up his reins, and urged his horse on. "Return to me," he said over his shoulder and left her there, following the others.

Snowfall sat, watching him disappear into the grey rain, lifting her face slightly so none would know if it was rain or tears on her cheeks.

So here was the sorrow of her heart, and yet pride as well, for she was a full warrior-priestess now, if that was what they still were. So many questions, so many changes to explore, and she wanted to do so at her...at Wild Winds's side.

But...an itch of curiosity turned her head toward the Heart. Toward Simus. Toward a new path. So many questions lay there as well, so many challenges, including the challenge to her fighting skills.

She could ignore Wild Winds's command. She was released, her choices were her own. She could mount and follow and take the path that walked at his side.

"Who else can speak words of peace, Snowfall?"

She stood for some time, in the sprinkling rain, fighting duty and her own desires, letting them war in her head, until her horse stamped in frustration.

She mounted, and turned her horse's head back toward the Heart.

* * * * *

For the first few hours of her ride, Eloix wallowed in her resentment and allowed it to fester. She'd had great plans to contest for Token-bearer, and yet here she was, returning to Xy with messages for Keir of the Cat, a task unlooked for and unwelcome. Destal was probably even now planning her challenges, and Eloix was certain she could've defeated her and claimed the place by the Warlord's side.

There were clouds on the horizon behind her, but she'd outride them easily.

When it grew too dark to see, she stopped for the night. She made a cold camp after she'd seen to the horses. After a few gulps of cold kavage, and a handful of gurt, she'd rolled herself into her blankets, and lay for a moment, letting herself relax.

She could hear the horses chomping at the grass, which rustled as they tore the shoots with their teeth. The scent of crushed greens surrounded her. She heaved a deep sigh, and let the hurt and disappointment go. There would be other times, other chances. The winds knew that there would be challenges again next season, and next, and the season after that.

Rolling over, she admired the field of bright stars overhead. She'd a task at hand, one that showed Simus's faith in her, so that bode well. While Xy was strange in its custom and ways, it was interesting. And the food was good. And she'd see Elois, and hear of her adventures.

Besides, she'd witness first hand Keir's reaction when she

brought word of the events on the Plains. Perhaps the Warprize had delivered her babe by now. Had the theas allowed her to keep the babe? Eloix rather suspected they had. She stretched under her blanket, glancing down at her own arm, wondering if the Warprize had gotten the traditional tattoo.

A smile drifted over her face as she settled down, fingers on the hilt of her sword next to her, and willed herself to sleep. She'd be up and riding at the first hint of sun.

CHAPTER TEN

Antas waited in one of the deeper gullies for his scouts to report.

The alders with their fresh green leaves hid him, and the stream that trickled past gave his horse a chance for a good drink. Antas dismounted, held the reins and patted the horse's neck as it slurped at the clear water.

Time was he'd have never hesitated to approach a thea camp openly, certain of a warm welcome and the courtesy of its tents.

But times had changed, now, hadn't they?

Keir and Simus had seen to that.

Antas stared at the leather reins in his hands, absently checking them for cracks or weak spots. He'd watched Keir and Simus and that foresworn Joden too. Watched as they advanced as warriors, through campaigns and the Trials.

He'd seen their loathing of the warrior-priests, listened to their first rumblings of change, but he'd thought nothing of it. Even when Keir had become Warlord, he'd shrugged. What could one fool young one do?

Keir had taken the northern most city of Xy as his target, and then announced to all his intent. Made no secret of it. Bad luck to him and good riddance had been Antas's first thought, and who could blame him that? Who was Keir to speak of conquest? Of holding, occupying? Of dancing new patterns?

Foolishness.

Yet Keir had done just that, with Simus at his side. Against all odds. And then, to add insult to injury, he'd claimed a Warprize.

A Warprize. Antas growled under his breath as a sudden rage swept through him. Here he was, Antas of the Boar, a warrior, a Warlord, and Eldest Elder of the Warriors, and he'd no Warprize. How many seasons had he seen in battle, with no sign of such a prize.

Then for Keir to claim that his Warprize had healing powers that challenged the might of the warrior-priests? It was outrageous and an offense to the elements.

Antas rolled his shoulders, and twisted his head, trying to ease the knots of tension in his shoulders.

His horse sensed his anger, and stamped its foot. He reached out, stroking its neck until it relaxed and started to tear at the browse it could reach.

When Joden, that false Singer-to-be, had shifted like the winds to support the Warprize, that had been the last blow. The Council had forced his choice, forced him to take sword in hand to protect the Plains. Pity his blades hadn't brought Keir down, and Simus and Joden for that matter.

But the elements had not been with him, and he'd withdrawn with his warriors and those that agreed with him. Withdrawn to spend the winter in their lodges, discussing, planning, talking.

A simple enough plan. First to solicit more warriors to his cause, theas included, to join their voices to his. Then to enter the Trials at the Heart, contest for Warlord, and confront the Council when it gathered. Reason with them about the paths they were seeking. They could not ignore his voice, especially with the other Elders behind him.

And when Hail Storm had approached him, and talked of replacing Wild Winds as Eldest Elder, well, that had been a blessing from the skies themselves.

Except something had gone wrong.

Hail Storm became cagey, saying only that there was a ceremony that the warrior-priests needed to conduct at the Heart, and that the warriors would all be driven back, the Trials delayed.

Antas had shrugged at that, for it seemed no matter. A day, a night, how could that make a difference? He'd continued his rounds of other camps, leaving his main force farther away from the Heart. He'd avoid conflict with others until he chose to start it.

Until this last night, with strange voices echoing over the Plains, horses running off as if summoned by the elements themselves—

A pillar of light that appeared, piercing the night sky, so bright he'd had to shield his eyes. And then the rings of light that had followed, racing through the grass and disappearing.

No word had come, from Hail Storm, from the Heart. Antas had ordered his warriors not to approach the Heart. Whatever ceremony the warrior-priests had conducted, he'd wait to hear from them before approaching. But it was unsettling, and he wondered—

A rustling in the alders alerted him, and Antas raised his head. It was Veritt, his Second, who threaded his horse through the alders and drew close.

"The camp that lies over two rises," Veritt pointed with his chin, "it's a thea camp. Haya of the Snake is the Elder Thea." He gave Antas a quick grin. "Not the friendliest of warriors."

Antas frowned. "With a tongue as sharp as her blades and not afraid to speak her mind."

"Do we approach her?" asked Veritt. "We could return to our camp, wait for word from the warrior-priests."

Antas considered. "Her voice cuts like a dagger, but it carries weight. If she moves the camp again, we may not find her until after the Trials. Let us talk to her, then return to our camp." He mounted, ducking alders as he settled in his saddle. "Nothing ventured, nothing gained."

Veritt lowered his eyes, and bowed his head. "Yes, Warlord." Then he snapped his head up, and flashed another grin. "Just as glad you're the Warlord. You have to do the talking."

* * * * *

Antas made no secret of their approach, leading his men in a slow walk over the rises toward the tents of the thea camp.

Haya was waiting for them, the canny old gurtle, standing there, tall and straight and silent. Her white hair shone against her tan skin. Her dark eyes were like flint, cold as the Snake of her Tribe.

Antas slowed his horse, glancing around, looking for likely young warrior-children, but the camp was unusually silent. Antas wondered at that as he signaled a stop to his warriors, and dismounted.

"Greetings, Elder Thea Haya of the Snake," he said lightly. "I'd speak with you, if you would."

Haya studied him, then her gaze swept over the warriors of his party. Her eyes returned to Antas and she gave him the slightest of nods. "Antas of the Boar."

Leaving off the honors he was entitled to. Antas kept a scowl from his face.

"The bodies of two of our young warriors have returned to the camp." Haya's voice was flat and hard. "We are preparing to mourn our dead," she continued, giving a pointed look to the clouds on the horizon. "Now is not the time."

"Death comes in an instant," Antas said. "Even to the young." He heaved a great sigh of sympathy. "But the dangers that threaten come in an instant as well. Best to be prepared."

There was movement in the tent behind Haya. A man emerged, his head bald, his face brown and wrinkled in a frown.

Antas gave him a nod. "Greetings, Weaponsmaster, Seo of the Fox."

Seo nodded in greeting, but said nothing.

"Do you bring news of the Heart?" Haya asked, not relaxing her stance. "Of the lance of light that pierced the sky?"

"No," Antas answered truthfully. "That is a concern for the warrior-priests and I have had no word as to its meaning." That was honest enough, although he was certain that Hail Storm would have a tale to tell when next they met. "No, Haya, I would speak of the Trials, and the dangers to our young ones."

There was a long pause then, with nothing to be heard but the wind in the grass.

"It would be good to hear whatever news you bear," Seo said.

Haya's face was unreadable, but she lowered her arms. "I offer you and your warriors the shelter of my tent. Come within. Speak your truths."

Antas entered Haya's tent to find that her courtesy was a warm one, with a brazier glowing, hot kavage offered, and bowls of gurt placed within easy reach. But there was no warmth in Haya's eyes as she gestured him and his Second to take their seats.

"This is Quartis," Haya said shortly, indicating the younger man already seated to her left. He had the tattoo of a bird's wing around his eye, and feathers braided into his long hair.

"Greetings, Singer." Antas eyed the man warily, but Quartis's face and nod were neutral and proper in all respects.

Antas gestured to the warrior who had followed him within the tent. "My Second is Veritt of the Bear."

Haya sat, her back still and straight. "My people will offer kavage for your men, and see to their horses. As I said, I can offer you little time. I've two young warriors to mourn for this night, and a sorrowing camp."

"Death comes in an instant," Antas repeated, taking the kavage. The young warrior who served him limped slightly as she moved about with mugs and a pitcher. "A hard lesson for the young of the Plains to learn."

"So it is," Haya said. "Your truths?"

Blunt and to the point. Antas cleared his throat. "As Elders, you were at the Council of Elders when—"

"No," Haya cut him off. "I was not in the Council that day." She caught Antas's glance at Seo. "Nor was Seo," she continued. "Reness was there, but I have not heard her truths." Haya paused, studying Antas intently. "I have heard many tales of what happened, but we did not see."

"Ah." Antas leaned forward, feeling a bit more confident. "But you know that the Council of Elders have failed us. Failed to protect the Plains from Keir of the Cat and those of his ilk."

"I hear that blood was spilt," Haya said, staring into her mug of kavage. "I hear that a Warprize was claimed, and that Keir of the Cat was stripped of his position, Warlord no longer. What dangers do you speak of, Antas?"

"The threat to our ways, our traditions," Antas said. "The loss of respect for our warrior-priests—"

"If it's lost, it's their own fault," snapped the young warrior who had served them, the pitcher of kavage clutched tight in her white-knuckled hands. "They—"

"Tenna," Haya cut her off. "See to the warriors without."

Tenna pressed her lips together, bowed her head, and limped from the tent.

"Forgive her lapse," Haya said tightly. "The dead we mourn this day were of her tent."

Antas gave her an understanding nod. "Haya, you are known as a thea of strength and ability. For years you have raised strong young warriors to serve the Plains—"

"I have already released my young ones to the Plains," Haya said. "If you seek warriors, you must go the Heart and raise your banner."

"I seek your entire camp, Haya, to place it under my protection," Antas said.

That shocked the old gurtle into silence.

"I protect this camp," Seo growled.

"I honor that." Antas gave the Elder a nod. "You are weaponsmaster to the young, and keep them safe from the normal perils of the Plains. But these are not normal times, Seo. And the dangers can come in many forms. We must keep to the old paths and restore the old ways. The young ones must be kept safe and free of taint."

The three before him were still and silent, waiting.

"There are those of us that feel that the Council itself is a danger, when it allows strange ideas and brings changes to our ways," Antas continued. "I would gather those that would resist those changes, so that we may protect the Plains by any means necessary."

He met their unblinking stares with his own.

The sound of wailing came through the tent walls.

Haya rose. "I thank you for your truths," she said. "We will consider them."

There wasn't much more he could do but rise from his seat, and allow her to escort them from the tent.

Veritt waited until they were mounted and moving away from the camp before speaking. "She mentioned Reness," he said under his breath. "Do you think she knows?"

Antas settled himself into his saddle. "She knows nothing of what has happened," he huffed. "Else we'd have not been met with welcome." He set his horse to a trot, and the others moved with him.

"And now?" Veritt asked.

"We've convinced three theas to join us," Antas said, thinking aloud. "We'll return to our camp. I hope to find Hail Storm there with word of what has happened at the Heart."

Antas glanced over his shoulder at the tents behind them. Haya stood there, her arms crossed over her chest, watching them depart. He smiled grimly to himself as he faced forward. "From there, we will see. Decisions must wait until I know more."

"Simus of the Hawk will be raising his banner," Veritt warned.

"Let him," Antas growled. "It will do him no good. If those that challenge him fail to take him down, I will face him myself, mace in hand."

* * * * *

Haya watched as Antas and his warriors rode off. She felt Seo move up behind her, his warmth at her shoulder. "Of all the Councils I did not attend," she muttered, irritated with herself. "It had to be this last one."

"You had three life-bearers giving birth," Seo reminded her.

"Truth," Haya said.

"And if you had been there?" Seo asked. "Would you have supported Keir?"

"I don't know," Haya admitted with a shrug.

"But you weren't there," Seo said. "Besides, what are Councils but hot breath, wasted words, and stale kavage in a tent?"

"Useful, to have my words returned to me," Haya said dryly. "My thanks for your truths."

Seo chuckled.

"Antas drew first," Quartis said as he emerged from the tent. "He called for the death of the city-dweller before she could be named as Warprize. Or so Essa said last season."

"I would have preferred to have seen this truth for myself, or heard it from Reness." Haya frowned as she watched Antas and his warriors disappear over a rise.

"You did not tell him of your role with the Sacrifice, the Token-bearer, and the Guardians you provided," Quartis observed with a neutral tone.

"A Singer's question," Haya gave him an amused look. "Singers, ever asking without actually asking."

Quartis returned her look with a half-smile.

Haya turned back to watch the departing warriors. "It seems to me the less said of that the better. Especially after last night."

Tenna limped up, a basket of dirty mugs in her hands. Her hands were shaking, but she stood tall before them. She'd been one of the Guardians. Haya's heart filled with pride, but it wouldn't do to show it.

"Did you recognize any of them?" Haya demanded.

"No, dea-mine—" Tenna stopped, and gulped, her eyes going wide.

Haya let herself smile and reached out to brush back a lock of Tenna's hair. "You're an adult now, warrior. Such childish names are not for you anymore."

Tenna blushed. "Yes, Elder."

"A hard habit to break," Seo chimed in.

"Yes, Weaponsmaster," Tenna responded.

Haya watched with pride as Tenna took a breath to continue. "No, Elder Thea, I did not recognize any of his warriors." Tenna met her gaze. "We were attacked by warrior-priests, and there were none in with his warriors. Even if there had been," she added, her truth in her eyes, "I am not sure I would have been able to recognize them."

"Fair enough." Haya sighed, and gestured to the basket. "See to those later. Join Arbon and the others, and tell them we will be there shortly. We will mourn El and Cosanna this night."

Tenna's eyes glistened, but she gave a silent nod in response and left them.

Haya sighed, and lowered her voice so that only Seo and Quartis could hear her. "I'd thought I'd moved our camp far enough that we couldn't be found easily. Yet Antas found us, and I fear the next time his request will be a demand."

"Where can we go?" Seo asked. "To keep the young ones safe?"

"Where else? The Heart."

Both Quartis and Seo stared at her as if her wits were gone with the winds.

"The young do not go to the Heart in the Spring, during the

Trials. That is not done." Seo glared at her. "The camps do not mingle except in the Fall, to gather for the final Council of Elders. Young ones underfoot of warriors preparing for war? That is not done," he repeated.

"We know things that the Council will need to know," Haya said. She turned to look at the horizon, her knowledge of the Heart's location unerring.

"So, too, I need to find Essa," Quartis said. "The Eldest Elder Singer must know as well."

"But this is not done," Seo protested again. "Thea camps do not mingle with—"

"Seasons change," Haya said grimly. "So must we."

* * * * *

Simus paused to wipe his brow with his forearm. His skin was gritty with sweat and dirt.

"I'll thank the skies if this is the last," he muttered to Joden as he reached for a large roll of sod and packed it back into the earth to cover the mass grave.

"It is." Joden paused himself, raising his head to look around at the others.

Simus grunted, pressing the grass roots down harder than really needed. It had taken far longer to clear the Heart of the dead then he'd expected. Hours of digging so that the bodies could be returned to the earth; there was no way so many could be given to the air, water, or fire. Then too, there was the sorting out of supplies and gear, distributed equally among those who worked. No item would be allowed to go to waste. It wasn't so much the time it took, but the work itself that dragged down the hearts and minds of the warriors around him.

Simus rose to his feet, dusting off his hands, then paused.

Someone was watching him.

"Something?" Joden asked softly, still pushing the sod into place.

Simus stretched, turning about, scanning the grasses, but all he could see were his own people, busy at their tasks. No one was staring, or trying to get his attention.

"Felt eyes on the back of my neck," Simus admitted.

"A threat?" Joden stretched as well. "I don't see—"

"Eh," Simus said, brushing it off. "I'm weary. So are they." He looked around, taking in his warriors. "You'd think they'd been defeated in battle," Simus said.

Joden rose to his feet as well, cracking his back. "We of the Plains raid, Simus. We gallop in, wage the battle, and ride away. We are not used to dealing with the aftermath. The only other time we've had to deal with this…" Joden's words trailed off, his eyes distant.

Simus knew well enough that Joden was in the past, burying the dead from the plague.

"Enough," Simus put his hand on Joden's shoulder, calling him back. "Enough, my friend. We'll eat and rest and in the morning we'll start fresh, and raise our tents for the Trials."

CHAPTER ELEVEN

Snowfall had ridden as close to the Heart as she dared, using her powers to mask her presence and protect her from prying eyes.

She'd released her horse back to the herds and cached her bedroll, gear, and saddle before she'd gone to watch Simus of the Hawk. She'd crept in close, an easy task given that there were few warriors and fewer camps established.

She'd watched, and as the sun had set, she'd returned and made a small, cold camp. Wrapped in her blankets, she looked up into the endless sky full of stars and thought on what she had seen, trying to ignore her nervousness.

Fireflies appeared, dancing in the air around her. Snowfall smiled to see them, remembering chasing them as a child in the thea camps.

On impulse, she worked a hand free of her blankets and called the power to her. She concentrated, trying to re-create the tiny bits of light in the air.

She wasn't completely successful. Golden glitters just fell from her fingers and didn't float like the living bugs. But as she waved her hand, it left a trail of bright light, like a ribbon that hung in the air before settling to the ground.

Guilt seized her then. It wasn't proper to waste power on such things, even if the land now glowed with it. She stopped, pulled her hand back into the warmth of her blankets and forced herself to consider what she had seen.

She'd watched as Simus had helped his people clear the dead. Watched him do the actual work, not hover about giving orders to his warriors.

And he'd offered the dead respect, which had caught her by surprise. Simus of the Hawk was known to despise warrior-priests, yet the bodies of the fallen, punished for their offenses to the elements, were picked up and laid in rows, not tossed about like so much dried dung.

Her surprise had been enough that she'd made a mistake. She'd gone too close, stared too long.

Simus had sensed her watching.

A thrill went through her even now, as she lay under warm blankets. The memory sent shivers that went to her toes and made her skin prickle.

Her tattoos had tingled as his eyes had seemed to meet hers. She'd dropped her gaze in that instant, and pressed herself down in the grasses, holding her breath, afraid that he'd seen her. Somehow he'd known he was being watched.

She'd kept her eyes down, concentrating on her veil, on the grass, on her breathing, until he had shrugged and turned back to his duties.

That had never happened before. She vowed silently that it would not happen again. For she intended to keep watching, and listening, if she could get that close. There was something about Simus, something different.

More and more warriors would be pouring into the area

around the Heart, and she'd need to have her wits about her if she wished to remain undiscovered. She'd have more care next time.

And there would be a next time.

* * * * *

Simus made it a point to rise early at first light, strike the tents, and with his warriors head to the Heart to choose his camp's location for the trials. He got there first, much to his satisfaction, and claimed an area both close to the Heart and directly north, placing his tent between the Heart of the Plains and Xy. It put him in a place of prominence, and made clear his intentions. Both were important for the Trials.

He planted the first pole himself, and then his warriors gathered to aid in raising the large structure. Keir had loaned him his tent, looted long ago from one of the fat cities of the East. It was a clever thing, large enough to hold senels, and yet portions could be closed off for sleeping, eating, and private discussions. But they'd had to haul the support poles from Xy, and it was difficult to piece together. He and his people had a grand time, swearing and laughing loudly as it collapsed on top of them more than once.

He was glad of it, for at least among his people spirits were rising. As they should be, for the Spring Trials were a relief from the long, cold days of winter. Now was a time to prepare one's gear, try one's skill, and find one's place within the armies of the Plains, and to dance one's heart out in the evening revels. Simus grinned to himself as he tightened one of the last ties for the tent and stepped back to admire their handiwork. His warriors stood with him in the sun, smiles bright as they congratulated themselves.

"Let it be said that we were first," he called out. "Let the Plains remember when we dance this night." His warriors cheered his words. "But there's still work to be done," he reminded them all.

"We'll start cutting the sod for a challenge circle next," Yers said. "I'll pace it out from your tent. About ten paces, I should think."

Simus laughed his agreement. "Make it wide, so I can run them in circles." He strode over to where Destal was directing the warriors unloading the packs from the horses, moving the gear into his tent. "We'll need a hunt," he said as he bent to pick up two packs.

Destal nodded. "I figured after the camp is established. There's plenty of daylight left. We'll put the individual tents behind yours, leaving spaces for cooking fires and the like. The privies are already dug, and the wells uncovered. It's a good site, no question there."

"We'll call for a dance tonight, first at the Heart with our drums and patterns," Simus said, well satisfied. "I'll raise my banners at dawn."

"There's something to be said for waiting a day or two," Destal pointed out as they carried the packs into the tent. "Saving your energies, assessing the challengers and watching their weak points…" Her voice trailed off as she studied his face, and then chuckled and lowered her gaze in respect. "And then, of course, there is your way, Warlord."

Simus laughed and clapped her on the shoulder. "Truth. Do you intend to challenge for Token-bearer?"

She nodded. "I do."

"Then let's see this finished, so we can spar a bit before the dancing."

Destal shook her head. "No, Warlord. I'll set up your weapons rack. You see to your armor and weapons. We'll deal with the camp." She flicked him a sly look. "You'll burn off that energy in the dancing tonight. And after."

"Fair enough." Simus grinned as he ducked into the tent, and entered his private chamber.

He'd spent his time in Xy wisely. No more cobbled-together armor pieces plundered during raids. Othur, Seneschal of Water's Fall and Warder of Xy had taken the time to assist him in 'commissioning' new leathers and chain from the craftsmen of Xy. Simus shook his head, contrasting the welcoming faces of the craftsmen to the dead he'd looted in the past.

He'd taken full advantage, and had even indulged in gold trim to the chain, with leathers underneath dyed black. He racked the set piece by piece, making it ready for the morning. He shook out the black cloak, with the brooch Keir had given him pinned in place. He'd cut a fine figure tomorrow, that was certain. A pity that lovely warrior-priestess in training wouldn't see him. Her dismissive gaze would have warmed, of that he was certain.

He'd just settled with his sword and whetstone when a voice came from the outer chamber. "The glitter of the armor matters little if the sword's not wielded well."

Simus pretended to shiver. "You sound like our old Weapons-master," he snorted. "And where have you been, having managed to avoid all the work establishing camp?"

Joden pushed through the flap, looking hot and sweaty. "Doing what a would-be Singer does. Listening. Talking. Observing."

"And what have you observed?" Simus gestured his friend to a seat beside him.

Joden sat, settling his sword on the ground next to him. "As to that, my throat is far too dry to talk."

Simus laughed, even as Destal entered with a tray of kavage and gurt. She knelt to place it on the ground before them. "I thought this might be welcome, Singer."

Joden smiled at her. "No more Singer than you are Token-bearer, but we are striving, eh?"

Destal tilted her head in acknowledgment. "Do you wish to speak under the bells?"

"No bells," Joden said, reaching for a mug as he glanced at Simus. "Unless you—"

Simus shook his head.

"Then I will leave you to your words," Destal said. "The set-up is almost complete. Only the senel chamber remains." She chuckled as she raised the flap. "Already there are those that hover nearby."

"A good sign," Joden said as she left.

Simus nodded, set aside his blade, and took a handful of gurt from the bowl, popping one of the pieces in his mouth. "So?" he asked. "What did you learn?"

"I went looking for Essa, Eldest Elder of the Singers," Joden said. "I did not find him."

Simus frowned, and reached for kavage. "Odd. Essa is never far from the Heart of the Plains. Even if he was driven off as we were, he'd be close."

"He's not been seen," Joden said. "The Singers I did find have not seen him either. Nor have they heard word of his whereabouts."

Simus shrugged. "He will come, eventually." He flashed a grin. "Nothing pulls Essa out like an audience or a dance."

"Truth," Joden said. "When the people are ready to listen, a Singer appears."

"Now, who did you see?" Simus asked. "And in what numbers?"

Joden shrugged. "The Warlords that you know of, so far. Ultie's people have appeared, with Elders among them."

"Good," Simus observed.

Joden drank deeply. "The candidates for Warlord are trickling in. Osa and Ultie were hard on your heels and have set their tents." He lowered his mug. "Those that oppose you have spread their tents all around the Heart, the better to talk against you, I suspect. Loulal, Ietha, Nires—"

"Not a surprise," Simus said.

"Rhet was talking to Zioa and Kiza as I walked past," Joden said. "Their greetings were warm enough."

"Rhet has not supported, but not opposed," Simus mused. "Perhaps she can be convinced to join us."

"Or perhaps she waits to support those who appear to be winning." Joden gave Simus a warning look over his mug. "She has ever been quick to take advantage."

Simus shrugged. "What else did you learn?"

"There is confusion and fear about the warrior-priests," Joden said. "And much talk after Wild Winds's disappearance." He paused, a smile flickering over his face. "I caught a brief glimpse of Wyrik. Enough to see a bruised face and blackened eyes."

Simus laughed. "Where have you set your tent?" he asked.

Joden hesitated. "I hadn't decided. If I wish to be impartial, I must—"

Simus snorted. "As if all do not know that we are friends. That you support Keir."

"I supported Keir in the claiming of his Warprize," Joden said mildly. "That doesn't mean that I will support him in all things. A Singer must be loyal to the truth, impartial, fair—"

"Warm," Simus said dryly. "Fed. Comfortable. This tent is cavernous, and all know you support me in my challenge for Warlord. Put your bedroll down here, at least until you start your own Trials."

Joden smiled his long, slow smile, and shrugged. "I will, and thank you."

"And you'll sing tonight? Lead the drumming at the very least?" Simus mock-scowled.

"Of course," Joden said.

Simus smiled and took another swig of kavage. The truth was that Joden's singing would say more for his support of Simus than which tent he slept in. As well his friend knew. Both of them had taken Keir's lessons to heart. 'You win more warriors with dance and drum and talk around the fires than with a naked blade,' he'd said, and Simus knew it well, having watched Keir recruit these many seasons.

Now, it was his turn.

The flap stirred; Destal stood just behind. "Forgive the interruption," she said, her tone a pleased one. "Two young warriors are without and would speak with the Warlord. They say they are here to offer their swords."

"So it begins, the gathering of my army," Simus intoned in a solemn voice.

His gaze caught Joden's and they both started smiling, their grins growing wider and wider until Simus almost laughed out loud. The first to offer their swords! But he settled his face and tone to conceal his excitement, and rose to his feet. "I will see them."

* * * * *

Lander stilled himself as they waited outside the Warlord's tent, in the manner of a warrior. Ouse stood beside him, attempting the same stillness.

It was not to be.

"It's huge," Ouse said in a whisper. "There's no tent so large in the thea camp." He craned his neck and went to his toes, trying to look over the thing. "You could fit four thea tents in that one, for certain."

"I know," Lander said and pressed his shoulder against Ouse.

Ouse dropped back on to his feet and huffed out a breath, giving Lander a worried look. Lander smiled back fondly. Ouse's red curls tossed in the breeze, and his pale skin was even paler under his golden freckles.

"It will be fine," Lander reassured him.

"I don't know," Ouse said softly. "We don't really have permission to do this and—"

The main tent flap pulled aside and Destal, the current Token-bearer to Simus of the Hawk, appeared.

"You may enter," she said with a nod, gesturing them into the tent.

Lander pushed through the flaps, with Ouse so close behind he could feel his breath on his neck. Blinking to adjust to the dimness within, Lander took in the large area filled with gurtle pad seats spread out in front of a wooden platform.

Simus of the Hawk was seated in the center of the platform, studying both of them with a serious look. But what made Lander's breath catch was that Joden of the Hawk was seated beside him. He knew of the warrior, rumored to be about to start his Singer Trials.

"Welcome, warriors." The Warlord's voice was deep and warm, befitting a man so big. "What truths would you share?"

Lander couldn't seem to make his feet move, but Ouse jostled him from behind. Somehow he found himself kneeling before the platform, Ouse at his side. Lander opened his mouth, but to his horror, no words came.

Joden of the Hawk gave him a puzzled look, then lifted his eyebrows in recognition. "I know you both," he said. "You are the warriors that told us of the Sacrifice. You were the guardians and guides, were you not?"

"We were some of them," Lander blurted out. He swallowed hard and continued. "I am Lander of the Snake, and I would pledge my sword to your service for the coming season."

"I am Ouse," Ouse's voice cracked. "Ouse of the Fox. I too would pledge my sword to your service for the coming season."

The Warlord considered them carefully. "From which thea camp did you emerge?" he asked.

Landers winced, exchanging a quick glance with Ouse. How did he know? "Our thea was Elder Thea Haya of the Tribe of the Snake."

He watched as Simus and Joden both glanced at each other. "Well, then you are well-trained," Simus said dryly and Joden snorted as if over a private joke.

"She permitted us to escort the Sacrifice." Ouse's words spilled out from him in a rush. "But we were to aid him to reach the border of the Plains and find his way home. We were given no further instructions beyond."

The Warlord didn't smile, but the corners of his eyes crinkled a bit, and Lander's heart lifted.

"So it is in battle," Simus said, "that sometimes a warrior must think for himself. Still, tradition would have it that your thea would send you to Loual of the Snake, Warlord for many years." He gave them a stern look. "Why me?"

"Because we have heard of the Warprize," Ouse blurted out again. "We know you support her and Keir of the Cat. This is where the action will be, and who would not wish to be a part of that? Besides, Lander wishes to be a Singer."

Lander blushed, wishing the earth would open and swallow his lover. "Ouse," he hissed, even as Joden gave him a wide smile.

"What?" The Warlord was openly grinning now, his teeth white against his dark skin. "Not for my prowess? Not for my skill or strength or cunning?"

Ouse blinked at him, and Lander closed his eyes in resignation. "That too, Warlord," he offered, but it sounded weak even to his own ears. "But I do wish to be a Singer, once I have met my obligations as a warrior of the Plains."

"He's already started an epic song of the Sacrifice," Ouse said firmly.

"I'd be happy to hear it, if you wish assistance," Joden said.

Lander felt a rush of gratitude, and heat to his cheeks. "My thanks," he managed, without his voice breaking.

"Sit," Simus commanded, gesturing them to gurtle pads close by. "Tell me this: What do you think of the warrior-priests?"

Lander exchanged a glance with Ouse as they sat. "Truth be told, Warlord, we are uncertain."

"They pursued the Sacrifice," Ouse said. "Killed two of our friends, and then took another friend hostage. Ezren, that's the Sacrifice's name." He paused a moment to order his thoughts. "Ezren and his Token-bearer could have kept on, toward their home. Instead they chose to give chase to rescue Gilla of the Snake."

"But we were met by a warrior-priestess who offered herself as hostage and took us to Wild Winds," Lander added. "It would seem that the warrior-priests were not all of one mind. Then the Sacrifice occurred, and—" He swallowed, remembering the column of light and the swirling herds of horses around the Heart. "I do not know what to think," Lander repeated. "But I try to remember that those responsible for what happened are not the warrior-priests that are now with Wild Winds."

"Well said." Joden nodded. "You think like a Singer would, and should."

Lander dared to hope. "You'd take our oaths?" he asked, his eyes locked on the Warlord's.

"Yes," came the reply.

Lander's heart rose in his throat.

"Pull out your swords," the Warlord commanded. "I will take your oath here and now, conditioned only on my surviving the Trials. Destal and Joden will act as witness to your words."

"Willingly," Lander said, with mounting joy, and pulled his sword, taking care not to injure himself in his nervousness. It wouldn't do to bleed on his Warlord.

The oath passed in a blur, and he found himself stumbling out of the tent, Ouse at his side, as Destal escorted them. He tried to focus on her advice as to the location of their tent, but all he really felt was the heady relief of success. They'd done it; they'd serve Simus, Warlord of the Plains, and who knew where that might lead.

Ouse nudged his arm and they exchanged grins, stumbling after the Token-bearer like two warriors giddy on too much drink.

CHAPTER TWELVE

Simus stepped out of his tent at dawn the next day, dressed in his new armor and ready for battle.

A wide circle of bare earth awaited him, and clustered around were his warriors. Almost all faced him, their faces filled with joy and anticipation. But there were also those with their backs turned, looking out over the Plains, keeping watch.

Simus's heart swelled and he returned their grins with his own, his face feeling like it might split at any moment.

He strode forward to the edge of the circle, and bellowed to the skies. "HEYLA!"

His people roared their response.

"We have bared the earth," Simus chanted, making sure his voice could reach the entire crowd. "We ask the earth to witness these Trials."

"We thank the earth for witnessing our truths," came the traditional response.

Two braziers sat off to each side, one filled with water, the other with a fire that leapt brightly from precious wood.

Simus moved to the one filled with water. "We have lit the fire," he chanted. "We ask the fire to witness these Trials."

The crowd responded. "We thank the fire for witnessing

our truths."

Simus moved to the opposite side. "We have poured the water," he said, his words a steady beat. "We ask the water to witness these Trials."

"We thank the water for witnessing our truths."

Simus returned to the center, and laughed as he lifted both hands, palms up, and tilted his head back. "Skies, we invite you into our midst. We ask the skies to witness these Trials."

"We thank the skies for witnessing our truths."

And without prompting, all joined in the last shout of "HEY-LA!" followed by laughter, clapping of hands, and pounding of feet.

"I declare myself a candidate for Warlord," Simus proclaimed, and walked back to his tent entrance where the challenge pole stood. He raised his banner swiftly, a long streamer of red against the sky, cracking against the wind. "Red for the flame that is a Warlord," Simus recited.

Destal stepped forward. "I request permission to contest for Token-bearer," she said, and at Simus's nod hung her banner below his. "Brown," she said. "For the earth that is a Token-bearer."

"I request permission to contest for Second," Yers said, and when Simus gave him the nod, he attached his banner below Destal's. "White for the air that is a Second."

"And I for Third." Tsor stepped forward, and at Simus's nod, attached his blue banner to stream out with the rest. "Blue for the water that is a Third."

His warriors, still clustered about, were laughing and smiling. Simus stood in their midst and shared their joy, admiring the banners for just a moment. But he was also very aware of the risks they were taking, tying their success to his. If he failed, they'd have to seek service with another Warlord, losing rank and status. Or worse, return to a thea camp to wait out the season.

But they gathered and stood, smiling and confident, and his heart swelled at the sight.

"Now the hard part," Destal said after a moment. "The waiting."

Sighs and groans, and the other warriors started to wander off to see to their duties.

Destal sighed as well. "I've a belt to re-stitch." She settled on a gurtle pad beneath the challenge pole.

Yers shrugged. "I'm off to make the rounds of the Tenths, and see if I can talk to some that have not yet sworn their oaths. Summon me if a challenger appears."

Tsor placed his pad by Simus's weapons rack and pulled out a whet stone, clearly intent on sharpening his sword.

Other camps were starting to form around them, but for now few warriors wandered freely. It would be some time before challengers appeared. Simus resigned himself, retreated back into his tent, seated himself on the platform in all his finery, and decided to brood. Majestically. Powerfully. As a Warlord should.

He did not fear the Trials. But waiting was not something he did well.

The dancing the night before had been sparsely attended, but that had not been unexpected. Most of the others had barely picked their sites, much less erected their tents. Simus and his people had danced and chanted until they were tired enough to sleep. Tonight he hoped for more warriors to attend.

Destal had set watches, and Simus couldn't fault her there. It was not the traditional way, but he'd rather break tradition than not keep his warriors safe.

And then again, tradition didn't plan for change, did it? Warrior-priests all dead, yet their powers increased?

So much could go wrong. Othur and he had planned for a supply caravan to arrive in Xy during the Trials. He'd hoped they'd arrive soon, but only the winds knew when or if they would come safely. Then there was Antas and his plots, and that was concern enough for any warrior.

Voices rose from outside the tent, and Galid stepped within. Simus gave him a nod.

"I wish to challenge for Token-bearer, Warlord," Galid said, his white teeth flashing against skin the color of dried grass long under the sun. "And would ask your permission."

"Given," Simus said, and Galid wasted no time stepping back outside. He could hear Destal's voice as they moved off toward the fighting ring, and soon he heard the clash of swords.

"Fretting, I see." Joden emerged from one of the side chambers, kavage in hand. They had agreed that he wouldn't take part in the opening of the challenge circle. Even Simus saw that it would violate any sense of neutrality on Joden's part.

"Warlords do not fret," Simus pointed out, straightening and lifting his chin. "We brood."

"Ah," Joden went to the main entrance and lifted the flap to look out. He shook his head. "I see Destal is in fine form this morning. Her challenger is already offering his dagger in surrender." He dropped the flap and took a seat next to Simus. "And just what are you brooding about?"

"The other Warlord candidates," Simus sighed. "Who supports, who might oppose. If I can persuade them to aid us. What tactics or even treachery they might use against us."

"And?" Joden asked.

"Whether Eloix has reached Keir," Simus admitted. "Whether she encountered the supplies caravan. Whether the supplies will arrive intact, timely—"

"There's no way to know," Joden interrupted. "Unless the warrior-priests have ways of divining such answers that we know nothing of."

"Then there is that, too." Simus frowned. "The whole issue of warrior-priests, with almost all dead, and those that remain wielding powers beyond imagining who appear to have a change of heart and then disappear with no word." If he also thought on that woman, Snowfall, he'd not mention it to Joden.

Joden shrugged. "As to Eloix, it's unlikely she's reached Keir. I doubt she's even at the border."

"She's fast," Simus argued. "She might be—" He stopped his own words. "Perhaps I do fret," he admitted.

"Chess." Joden settled on the seat beside him. "I'll take city-dwellers."

"I rise to your challenge." Simus settled back. "Let us prepare for battle."

* * * * *

Every morning Eloix rose with the dawn, saddled a fresh horse, and moved off at a run. She'd done long rides like this in the past, and fell into the familiar trance of the pounding of the horse's hooves and the movement of its muscles under her. Day and night passed swiftly; it was times like these that Eloix felt as one with the elements, for all that existed was the horse, the land, her heartbeat, and the distant mountains of Xy on the horizon.

She was lucky enough to encounter herds where she could release the horses she'd ridden, and summon fresh ones to her side. She'd always check those that had run with her, but they were hale and hearty, and while ready to return to grazing with a herd, unharmed for their travels.

She saw a few groups of warriors in the distance, headed for the Heart. But they didn't attempt to greet her, and she rode on and past without incident. But one nooning, as the sun rode high in the sky, she saw a lone rider headed toward the Heart, and something in the warrior's posture gave her pause. She blinked against the sun, shaded her eyes and stared, uncertain if she recognized the rider. But if it were true...

She warbled one greeting, and then another from her days in the thea camp, and held her breath.

The rider swerved toward her, coming on at a gallop, returning the warble with a high, joyous call of her own.

"Heyla," Eloix called and laughed when she saw it was indeed Elois who'd answered her greeting. Their horses slowed to a trot, and they drew close enough to hug from horseback, pounding each other's backs.

"Eloix." Elois was flushed and weary but clearly glad to see her tentmate. "Do you come from Simus? Do you bear truths for Keir?"

"I do." Eloix grinned as their horses danced around each other. "I'm charged with messages from Simus for Liam and Keir, and the Warprize. You came on that errand?" she asked hopefully. "Return with me to Xy, and I will share my news."

Elois shook her head, her face falling. "No, there is a truth I must carry to Simus. Othur, the Warder of Xy, is dead. Slain on the night of the fire-needle, at the hand of Lord Durst."

Eloix shook her head in sorrow, then focused on Elois's last words. "You saw it from Xy? The lance of fire?"

Elois nodded. "And heard it. You?"

"Oh yes," Eloix said. "And carry word of its cause from Wild Winds himself."

Elois whistled low. "When did you leave?"

"The day after," Eloix said.

"You made better time than I," Elois huffed.

"Better horses," Eloix said, with a smirk.

"Truth," Elois agreed. "Are the Trials over?"

"No," Eloix said, and didn't hide her regret.

Elois lit up. "Then maybe there is time for me to challenge as Token-bearer. In your stead," she added slyly.

"Don't gloat," Eloix chided. "But defeat Destal for me."

"I will," Elois said, humor in her voice. "And we've no time to waste, if we are to carry our truths. The skies go with you."

"And with you as well," Eloix called out as she turned her horse toward Xy and urged him on.

And so it went, night following day, following night again, until at last she spotted the outpost at the border of Xy.

She slowed then, not eager to give an impression of frantic importance that might attract the wrong attentions. Various scouting groups saw her and hailed her, but she did little more than return their greetings. One group she did stop, since she recognized a few of the warriors. They assured her that Warlord Liam was at the outpost. One laughed, and warned her to 'mind the crush within' as they waved her on.

Puzzled, Eloix pushed on through the foothills, and the winding path that led to the building on the top of a sheer rise. As she emerged from the final stand of trees, she gasped out loud.

The last she'd seen the place, it had been a ruin, long abandoned by the Xyians. But now the stones were restored, and she could see within the walls a large yard filled with warriors, horses, oxen and wagons loaded with packs, all milling about in chaos. She pulled her horse to a stop just at the gates and gawked at the sight. So *many* laden animals, wagons, and warriors.

"Something to see, eh?" A Xyian guard stood there, pike in hand.

Eloix nodded, then dismounted. "I bear messages from the Plains for the Warlord Liam."

The guard glanced at the sun above and gave a nod. "He'll be in the Great Hall, most like. You been here before?"

Eloix shook her head. "Last I saw the place, it was scattered stone and vines."

"Aye, the trades have been hard at it," the guard said with a grin. "By order of the Warder of Xy." He whistled and a young lad came running up. "Take this warrior to the Warlord," the guard ordered him, then turned back to Eloix. "We'll see to your horse and gear."

Eloix followed the lad, although walking felt odd for the first few strides, as if her body had forgotten exactly how to do it. Still, she pushed on as the lad skirted along the wall to avoid confusion, and led her through two large doors into a shadowed hall, cool and dark.

Warlord Liam, tall and regal, sat at the end of the hall, facing a small crowd of Xyians and Plains warriors, all of whom seemed agitated. One in particular, a small balding man with a paunch, argued loudly with a taller warrior, who looked ready to pull a blade.

Eloix thought it best to hold herself back, but Liam spotted her over their heads. With a look of relief, he gestured her forward. "Are you from Keir or Simus?" he demanded, silencing the group before him with a gesture. "I've been expecting a messenger."

"Simus, Warlord." Eloix advanced and would have gone to one knee, but Liam shook his head and rose to his feet.

"Warrior, I know the look of one who has had nothing but kavage and gurt for days on end." Liam walked through the crowd.

"You and I will talk in the kitchens. As to the rest of you, settle these issues among yourselves before you depart for the Plains on the morrow. If I make the decision, no one will be pleased." Liam stepped away, and gestured to Eloix. "Come."

He strode off, and she followed with some trepidation. Eloix had served under her share of Warlords. Some good, some bad, but they almost all could be unpredictable at times, until one knew their ways. She'd not served under Liam, but had heard good things for the most part. She followed as he walked, and flicked her glance to his ear, which was woven with wires and gems that caught the light. She hurriedly dropped her gaze, not wanting to be caught staring. Most of the talk about Liam was of his broken bonding with Marcus, Keir's Token-bearer, and that was in hushed tones under bells.

They entered through a large arched doorway, and Eloix walked into a room filled with people, warmth, and the smell of bread and roasting meats. Her mouth started watering, and her stomach gave a mighty rumble.

Liam strode past the large spits covered in roasting birds, and the grand ovens where the servants were working. Xyian cooks from the look of things, and her stomach grumbled again at the scents of spices and meat.

Liam called for food as Eloix trotted to keep up with his long legs. She found herself seated at a table in a kitchen that reminded her of the one at the Castle of Water's Fall. As she sat on the bench, adjusting her sword and dagger, a large platter with a loaf of warm, fresh bread was placed in front of her by a serving maid, with a crock of butter and a knife for spreading.

"Eat," Liam commanded, seating himself opposite her.

Eloix tore off a piece off the loaf, made good use of the butter, and crammed it in her mouth.

"I've barely arrived from Water's Fall, but it seems they've stored up all their disputes for me to resolve. That chaos in the outer yard—" Liam tore off a hunk of bread for himself. "That chaos is the supplies that Othur has sent to Simus."

Eloix's mouth was full, but she raised a questioning eyebrow, then leaned back to let the girl place a plate of roasted fowl before her.

"The Seneschal thought to send a healer with the supplies," Liam said. "I am not sure that was wise decision. You have met the Warprize?"

Eloix nodded, tearing the leg from the bird, and bit into the succulent meat.

"Well, let us just say, he is not Lara." Liam grimaced. "Be that as it may, I will hear your news, have you sleep this night within my walls, and then send you on your way with two warriors as escorts as soon as the sun rises."

"But, there's no need," Eloix protested then choked, and reached for kavage. The meat was sweet and tangy, with spices she didn't know. Good, though.

"Eat," Liam commanded again. "I know there remains hours of daylight yet, but you will be all the better rested for the journey ahead. You met no opposition on the way here?" At her nod, he shrugged. "That may not be so for the rest of your journey. There has been no word from the Plains since the night of the fire needle that reached into the sky, and sounded the tones that shook us all to our very marrow." He narrowed his eyes at her. "You will tell me what occurred, yes?"

Eloix swallowed and nodded.

"Finish your meal first. Keir has asked that I secure this place for a time, then continue on to the Heart to aid Simus," Liam continued. "No word has followed me from Water's Fall. That worries me, but it may be too soon to expect a rider, or it may be that nothing of consequence has occurred." Liam scowled. "I dislike silence."

Eloix kept eating, since she was fairly certain he wasn't talking to her. Not really.

"If nothing else, he promised to let me know if aught threatened anyone within the walls of the City." Liam shook his head. "Marcus, you foolish old badger…"

His voice trailed off, and Eloix did the smart thing and kept her eyes down and continued eating. Nothing good could come of that topic, and she'd no mind to speak with no token in sight.

Skies, even if he'd had his token there, she'd a mind to stay silent. Her thea didn't raise a fool.

"At any rate, I have messages that I would have you take to Keir and Lara," Liam said, then held up a hand before she could stop eating. "Written messages, for there is a Xyian here who takes down my words. When you leave you will take them with you."

Liam drummed his fingers on the table. At first Eloix thought he was impatient with her, but his eyes were far away and lost in thought. She ate steadily then, finishing the meal with a sigh and a long drink of kavage. She set down the mug, a burp catching her by surprise.

But it served to bring the Warlord back from his wanderings. "Done?"

She nodded.

"Then give me your truths," he commanded.

"On the morning of the night of the pillar of fire," she began, settling in for a long tale. "The warrior-priests drove us from the Heart…."

CHAPTER THIRTEEN

S imus dodged his challenger's blade with an elaborate spin, bringing his dagger within a hair's breadth of his opponent's cheek. But she dodged, shifting just enough to avoid his blade. Simus laughed in pure pleasure as she danced back away from him.

Clearly this Misa of the Cat was wary of his next attack.

The Trials may have gotten off to a slow start, but like a waking sleeper, they were rousing. The Heart of the Plains was beating, growing stronger and faster as warriors gathered around the great circular stone. More warriors arrived every day, adding to the chaos, confusion and growing strength of the Heart.

Simus feigned a charge, holding his sword low, and his dagger high, pulling up short as she darted just at the edge of the circle, trying to get behind him. He laughed out loud as he spun again, daring her to close with him.

She didn't rise to the lure. She stood, breathing hard, swords at the ready. Her pale brown hair stuck to the sweat on her face.

Simus stilled, watched, and waited.

Fighting with two swords was all well and good, but Simus preferred the sword and dagger. The shorter blade offered strikes one couldn't achieve with two longer weapons. Not that two swords were a bad choice; Keir preferred that style. His opponent was good with them, there was no doubt of that.

Simus was better with his.

He drew a deeper breath, enjoying the warm looseness of his arms and legs, the sheen of sweat on his face. The past days had been filled with questions and problems as others sought his leadership and guidance. Simus dealt with them all, taking charge of his growing army, worrying about tent placements, organizing rosters and hunts, knowing that this too was the work of a Warlord.

But he relished the challenges. Blade against blade under the open sky, with his blood singing through his body. And, of course, the admiring glances of those that gathered to watch.

And they did gather. Simus grinned, but he wasn't fool enough to glance around to see who watched.

His opponent seemed to take his grin as a dare. Her eyes narrowed, and her nostrils flared as she darted toward him. She brought both swords up, aiming to slash through his guard.

Simus waited, then slipped to her right at the last moment, parrying the first blade and dodging out of the reach of the other. He slashed with his dagger at her wrist as she went past him. She continued on, turning to face him, but cursed as blood dripped from her hand.

"Done," called the Singer from the side. A murmur of approval from those gathered, as talk rose around them.

Simus lowered his weapons then. "Well fought," he said.

"Well stuck," she replied. She pulled her dagger from her belt, and held it up, the blade at her heart, blood dripping down her fingers.

"Misa," Simus took the offered dagger, token of her surrender and nodded toward her hand. "I'd offer bloodmoss for that, if you would."

She cocked her head with a curious look. "I've heard of the Warprize's blood-eating plant. I'll try it, and thank you for the offer."

Cadr, young warrior with long brown hair, and large brown eyes, stepped forward with a leather sack, and applied bloodmoss to her hand. Speaking softly he explained how it worked.

Simus watched them as he accepted a scrap of cloth from Destal, and started wiping down his blades. It was all well and good for Simus to talk about the changes a Warprize would bring, but better yet to show hard-headed warriors the benefits of new ways. And if there were those in the crowd that listened, and leaned in to see, well, all the better.

"Use it only when the wound is clean, like this," Cadr was explaining. "Never if there is dirt or debris within. And once it's used, throw it to the ground." The dried yellow leaves on Misa's hand turned pale green. "It will seed itself to the earth and grow more for the next season."

"Hmmm." Misa nodded, her eyes wide as she stared at her hand where the cut had been. She lifted her hand so that others could see. "Maybe even drop some where you field-dress a kill."

"Not a bad thought," Simus said, giving her an approving smile. "That's an idea to spread."

Someone in the crowd snorted, and moved off. Simus caught a glimpse of Loual walking away, Wyrik at his side.

Misa tilted her head and caught his eye once again. "I would come to your next nooning," she said.

"You would be welcome," Simus replied. "I will see you to-morrow, then?"

"Tomorrow." Misa accepted a small bundle of dried blood-moss from Cadr before she walked off.

"She'd be a good one," Oxna said softly. As his first Tenth, she'd be watching for likely recruits.

Simus nodded absently as he sheathed his weapons and cast an eye at the sky. The sun had reached the horizon; that would be the last challenge for this day.

Yers was already reaching to pull down the challenge banners for the night. "It goes well so far," he said glumly. "But I worry for the lack of Tenths."

"They will come," Oxna said. "I suspect they are taking our Warlord's measure."

Simus shrugged. "It is a concern, but it is also early days yet." He clapped Yers on the shoulder. "Give it time."

"And if they don't join us?" Yers said.

"I've given it some thought," Simus admitted. "We've a fair number of warriors that could be trained—"

"You wish to speak with the Warlord?" Destal's voice cut through his, drawing Simus's attention to a tough-looking older woman warrior standing near them. She was grey and wrinkled, but there was strength in her stance.

"I do," the woman said, and bowed her head to Simus. "I am Faela of the Deer, Token-bearer to the Warlord Ultie. He asks you to his tent for this night's meal."

Simus raised an eyebrow, and shared a glance with Yers. "When?" Simus asked.

"Now, if it would so please you," she answered. "I would take you to him." She glanced around. "He asks that you come alone."

Simus raised both eyebrows.

"Warlord," Yers cautioned.

Simus just shook his head at Yers and gestured toward Faela. "Lead the way."

* * * * *

The grass tickled Snowfall's nose as she pressed herself down and watched Simus of the Hawk walk off toward Ultie's camp.

She considered following, but only for a moment. She didn't know Ultie by sight, but by reputation, and that was formidable. His camp was bigger, with many seasoned warriors moving around. She wasn't sure she should try to overhear what was said; it bore the risk of discovery.

To her chagrin, it wasn't the easiest thing to conceal herself, even with the bright power that lay at her hand. She had to concentrate on her veil at every moment. Sitting in one spot wasn't bad, but she did press the grass down under her. Moving was harder, and if she forgot herself she could lose her concealment altogether.

She didn't want to find out how the warriors would react to her sudden appearance in their midst.

No, it was enough for now. She pulled in her powers, settled the veil over her body, and started to slither through the grass between the tents to return to where she'd camped. She'd hunt tonight; eat something more than dried meat and gurt. A hot meal, hot kavage, a warm bed…then she would think on what the last few days had shown her.

She paused to let a group of warriors leading horses move off before she continued. Their talk was teasing, and light. Scouts, it seemed, about to make their rounds.

Such a difference between this and a warrior-priest camp. The old camps full of warrior-priests had been quiet, stifled, aware of their loss of powers and the secrets they kept. But here? Laughter, work, shared tasks. So very odd, and yet, very welcome.

She waited, patient, until they moved off.

Once she was far enough, she stood, stretched and walked the rest of the distance. She'd moved her camp to a small pond where the alders grew thick. There was nothing but game trails around it, and she deemed it safe enough. She used her power to keep her veil up, though. Just in case.

The sun was high enough that she could set a few snares for rabbits that were as thick as the alders. Once that was done, she walked to the other side of the pond, knelt, dropped the veil, and focused.

The power was there, all around her, golden and bright, moving like water around her. She took a moment to bask in its glow, feeling its presence, slowing her breathing to match its rhythms.

She turned her attention to that sense of dread that lingered under her breasts. It was still there, and yet not there, and as much as she tried to commune with it, there was only apprehension. An underlying fear…no, that was too strong. Worry was a better way to describe it.

But no amount of focus, or probing, provided more information. Snowfall opened her eyes, blew out a breath in frustration, and once again wrapped her veil around herself.

She would keep trying. For now, she needed to move.

She put herself through the paces of fighting an imaginary foe with her knives. The moves were old and familiar, but Snowfall pushed herself to make each form perfect. It wouldn't do to lose her skills now. Besides, the leather corselet she wore was still uncomfortable, chaffing in places. She was so used to nudity that any cloth on her breasts felt odd. But naked skin offered no protection against a blade. Maybe if she reworked the lacings, the fit might be better.

Once she was done with her forms, sweat dripping into her eyes, she decided that lacings could wait. She stripped down, easing herself into the cold water of the pond, and scrubbing herself with sand. It felt good to be clean. It felt even better when she heard a squeal from one of the snares. She'd caught a fine, fat rabbit for her supper.

She cleaned the meat, wrapped it in wet leaves with some ogden roots, and set it roasting in a small fire pit that she dug. Kavage brewed close by, and her stomach rumbled as she settled in to wait for it to cook.

She pulled the corselet over, and started to work on the laces. But while her fingers picked at the strings, she glanced over her shoulder and considered all that she had seen.

Her mouth had dropped open when Simus had planted the first pole to raise his tent. With his own hands. She shook her head at the wonder of it.

He'd laughed, wrestling with the sides, cursing mistakes that he made, and bellowing with joy even when the pole and tent had collapsed on his head.

Simus strutted, true enough, certainly putting on a display. But there was an openness about him, a joy in living, in breathing, as if he was inviting the elements to admire his prowess in a way that didn't offer insult to others. Snowfall frowned at the fire as the wet leaves sizzled. It was hard to explain, but certainly his warriors had taken no offense, sharing in his mirth.

Snowfall shook her head, puzzled. She'd not taken offense either, even catching herself laughing with him at one point.

Simus was like no warrior-priest she'd ever met before, and she was fairly certain that he was unlike other Warlords as well, although she'd not dealt with any directly. But Simus had looked every inch a Warlord when he had stepped from his tent to open the challenge circle.

Gleaming armor, his gold rings in his ears glittering in the sun. The smile, so bright, so hopeful.

It would be hard to see that smile dimmed.

Snowfall frowned at herself, and poked at her dinner with a stick. That was not a consideration. Wild Winds had charged her to see for herself, and she needed to stay on task.

She'd never seen the ceremony for the opening of a challenge circle before, although she knew the ritual from her days in the thea camps. She'd known the words, but not the excitement, the pride of the warriors involved. It seemed to her that they'd all felt the power of the man they called Warlord. Simus was charming, handsome, and there was an allure about him that she'd felt brush her own skin.

He was skilled with his weapons as well. She'd watched him meet every challenge, and his fights were a pleasure to watch. For such a big man, he moved with grace and speed. Moreso than she had expected.

Yet, again, he didn't crow of his victories, or shame his opponents on their loss. He was polite and gracious, and quick to offer aid, as he had offered the bloodmoss.

Snowfall frowned again. It had to be false. Simus was, of course, trying to win hearts and swords, and as such would seek to hide his flaws.

The meat was sizzling, and Snowfall pulled the bundle from the fire, hissing in pain as she pulled back the leaves. A good meal, hot kavage, and she'd sleep well. Tomorrow she'd return and get as close to Simus's tent as she could.

There were flaws, she thought as she took a bite of the juicy meat. And she would find them.

* * * * *

Ultie's tent wasn't quite as large as his own, but Simus frowned when he saw that it had been placed at the center of his warriors' tents. Not the usual set-up for the Trials. Still, there was a wide pathway, and the usual challenge circles. But as Faela lead the way Simus noted a tension more at place in a camp at war than at the Trials. Instead of preparing to enjoy the evening meal, warriors seemed guarded and alert.

They watched him pass with less than friendly eyes.

Faela strode right up to the tent and entered without so much as a greeting. Simus followed, to find himself confronted by Ultie, a few Singers, and a thin, bruised man in battered armor.

"Essa?" Simus blinked, uncertain. This was not the proud Eldest Elder Singer that he'd last seen at the Warprize's confirmation, with his splendid colored robes. The Singer's tattoo was around his eye, but—

"Simus of the Hawk," Essa said and there was no mistaking that voice, even if it was filled with anger. "I would ask for your token."

Simus's hand was on his brooch before he could gather his thoughts.

"I hold your token, Simus of the Hawk. Are you the one trying to kill me?"

CHAPTER FOURTEEN

Essa's face was a mask of calm, but Simus could see a wildness in his eyes. Essa held the brooch in one hand, the other resting on the hilt of his sword.

The other Singers, clearly Essa's guards, also had their hands on the hilts of their swords.

"No," Simus said quickly and firmly, keeping his face still, hiding his shock. Now was not the time to mock this man.

"Hunting us like ehats, attacking both night and day, destroying my tents and supplies, killing my people?" Essa's voice cracked, but he brought it back under control.

"No," Simus said. "And if you wish, I will repeat my words for the open skies to see and hear."

"Told you," Ultie said to Essa.

Essa stared at Simus hard, but Simus met his glare and didn't drop his gaze until Essa looked away.

"Well, someone is," he said. "Someone has." He ran his free hand over his face. "What was Reness thinking to wander off to Xy? And where is Wild Winds? And what in the name of all the elements was that shaft of light? Ultie says that you witnessed that night and spoke with Wild Winds. Where is he?"

"I don't know," Simus said.

"What did he say?" Essa demanded.

"I will tell you all I know," Simus said. "Although Joden would tell it better."

"Why in the name of the elements would I trust Joden?" Essa spat.

"What?" Simus demanded, startled.

"I am not sure I trust any of the Plains at the moment, except those of my tents," Essa continued. "I came to Ultie because—"

"Because if I wanted you dead, you would be," Ultie rumbled. "And since you aren't, I don't."

Essa choked out a laugh. "The only certainty left in an uncertain world."

"Sit," Ultie commanded, gesturing to the gurtle pads. "We need kavage and food for this talk, and bells on the flaps. Faela, see to the bells, then see to our meal. Essa, return Simus's token. You will eat, yes? And then we will listen as you speak of what has happened to you."

Simus settled on the gurtle pad Ultie indicated, arranging his sword and dagger beside him. The other warriors sat as well, except Essa. The man was clearly agitated and started to pace back and forth as Faela wove a strip of bells into the tent flaps.

Ultie himself passed the water and cloths for hand-washing. "Faela has enough to see to, and I want no more warriors within."

Simus nodded his understanding, and whispered a prayer to the elements as he washed. They all did, except Essa, who continued to move around the tent, muttering under his breath until they all had completed the ritual. Then he spun on his heel and glared at Simus.

"Never, in all my years as Eldest Elder have I been assaulted," Essa growled, his anger clear in every gesture. "I usually winter in the lodge closest to the Heart," he continued. "But there was a—" Essa hesitated. "A Singer that I wished to speak to, about the events of the last Council. So I went south, and when the snows grew deep, we took to a lodge and wintered there."

He continued to pace as he talked, his scabbard swinging on his hip, threatening everyone's heads. Faela dodged around him as she served spiced gurtle meat, flat bread and roasted ogdan roots. Simus's stomach rumbled.

Ultie gestured for the others to start eating. Simus reached for bread and meat.

"When we emerged, I conducted the Rites of Ascension for a few of the thea camps, as was normal. But the warrior-priests conducting those rites with me acted strangely." Essa still held Simus's cat brooch in the hand he was waving about. Faela ducked under his arms with the kavage pitcher and mugs. "I should have listened to my instincts, for they were telling me something was wrong. Perhaps Adaya would still live if I'd—"

Essa's warriors were shaking their heads, and one spoke. "There is no way to know that, Eldest Elder. And no one blames you but yourself."

Ultie rolled his eyes and gave Faela a nod. She stepped into Essa's path with a mug of kavage and waited.

Essa stopped, sighed, and took the mug.

Simus helped himself to more of the spicy gurtle and roots.

"We were attacked." Essa stood there, staring at the kavage. "It was clear they wanted me captured and my warriors dead. We managed to break free, but more warriors appeared and harried us. I lost warriors and gear to them as they would appear out of nowhere—" He took a swig of kavage, and cleared his throat. "Then one night a warrior-priest appeared with warriors and attacked me with foul power, freezing me in place so that I could not so much as move. My warriors fought, and fought well, but the only thing that saved us was a bolt of light piercing the night sky. The warrior-priest fell to his knees, screaming, and suddenly I could move and breathe and I killed him."

"Well done," Simus said.

Essa stopped there, looking at him as if seeing him for the first time. "After, I noticed his tattoos were gone, as if ripped from his body. What do you know of that?"

"Sit," Simus said. "Even if you did not hold my token, I would share what I know."

"Hard to listen, much less think when you are stomping around like that," Ultie muttered around a mouthful of bread.

Essa huffed, but settled on a gurtle pad. He balanced Simus's brooch on his knee, and held his kavage mug in both hands.

Simus cleared his throat. "For me it started when a warrior-priest popped up from the grass and forbade us to approach." He continued, going through the events of that day and into the night.

One of the warriors closest to Essa nudged his arm, and offered bread and meat. Essa's eyes never left Simus's face, but he took a piece of the flat bread and nibbled at it. Yet as Simus's story progressed, the bread was abandoned as Essa listened in grim silence.

"And Wild Winds disappeared?" Essa demanded at the conclusion of Simus's tale.

"I awoke to find him and his people gone, and angry Warlord candidates gathered outside my tent demanding explanations." Simus glanced at Ultie.

Essa closed his eyes and rubbed the corner of his eye. "What in the name of the elements does this mean?"

"Nothing," Ultie said. "We are gathering for the Trials as we always have and always will."

"Nothing?" Essa gave the man a hard look. "Ultie, the Council was sundered and now the warrior-priests are—"

"You have trusted Wild Winds in the past," Ultie said. "Trust him now."

Essa sighed, shaking his head, but remained silent, giving Simus his chance. He leaned forward, intent to know the answer to the question that had nagged at him since this strange meal began. "Why do you not trust Joden?"

Essa shrugged at Simus's question. "Joden supported Antas against the Warprize until he changed his mind. If he were to become Singer, what is to prevent them from killing me and making Joden Eldest Elder, with Antas's backing?"

"No," Simus shook his head. "Joden opposed the Warprize when he faced the devastation that was the 'plague'. Antas used Joden's doubts to support his own claims."

Essa raised an eyebrow. "Perhaps. But Joden's acknowledgment of the Warprize came at a convenient time, didn't it? When Antas seemed to have gone too far?"

"You twist his actions—" Simus replied hotly.

"All I know," Essa overrode him, "is that Joden was all you say before he followed Keir of the Cat to Xy. But since that time, he has broken with our ways, and his truth seems—"

"You hold my token, Eldest Elder Singer." Simus glared at the man. "But I will not sit and listen to you insult Joden of the Hawk."

"I will share these same truths with him, face to face," Essa said calmly. "For he will approach me to become Singer, will he not?"

"Of course he will," Simus said. "All who know him know

his intent."

"Even I know it," Ultie muttered.

"Joden of the Hawk is an honorable warrior," Simus continued. "He is not treacherous. He would not—"

"If you had told me that Antas would attack the Council, I would have laughed and called you fool," Essa said. "This wind of change you would bring blows the seeds of our destruction as a people."

Simus would have protested, but Ultie raised a hand and stopped his words. "Essa, who do you think sent warriors and warrior-priests after you?" Ultie asked.

"I have no proof," Essa said, shrugging. "But Antas seems likely."

"I doubt that Antas will appear here," Ultie said. "Too many hold his actions against him. You are here now. You can call the Council of Elders together. Reness will arrive at the last moment; she always does. Nires is here, who was named Eldest Elder Warrior to replace Antas."

"That was a temporary measure for the Outcasting." Essa frowned. "And that needs doing as well. It's the warriors gathered that will name the next Eldest Elder Warrior." He sighed. "It's complicated."

"No," Ultie said. "It's simple. You will shelter here with me for a time, regain your strength. You will sing at the dances, and replenish your gear. You will gather the Singers and would-be Singers to you, and then you will sort things out."

Essa gave him an exasperated look. "Ultie, it's not that easy."

"Yes, it is." Ultie reached over and plucked the brooch off Essa's knee and tossed it to Simus. "We thank you for your truths."

A clear and simple dismissal.

The spicy gurtle meat didn't sit easy as Simus made his way back toward his camp.

The sun was lower now, the camps finishing their challenges and meals, and preparing the night's dancing. The scents of fry bread and kavage floated on the air, along with various bits of talk. Simus ignored it all as he strode along, thinking on Essa's words. Dreading having to tell Joden of this talk.

And as if he'd heard Simus's thought, Joden appeared beside him as he walked, matching him step-for-step, his broad face smiling. "You look as if you are planning a battle. Why so grim?"

"Later," Simus muttered. "And under the bells."

Joden glanced at him, but thankfully didn't press. "You missed a good match," he said. "Osa was challenged by a warrior barely out of the thea camp." He laughed. "He challenged with sword and shield. Osa chose her whip."

"And the arrogant pup cowered behind that shield most of the fight?" Simus asked.

"For all of a few breaths," Joden snickered. "First time he lifted his head to see where she was, she lashed out and caught his forehead. He stood there, blinking through the blood, like a dazed ehat. An easy enough challenge to judge, that is certain."

Simus tried to laugh at the image, but it sounded forced even to his ears.

* * * * *

It was much later that night and far too soon for Simus when he found himself alone with Joden again. They sat together in his tent, after the dancing had ended and the camp had gone quiet.

Joden sat across from him, with a pitcher of hot kavage between them and bells woven into the tent flap ties.

"What troubles you so?" Joden asked, pouring kavage for both of them.

Simus played with the cat brooch between them, the light from the glowing braziers glinting off its shiny black surface.

Joden waited, as patient as always.

Simus heaved a sigh, and told him.

Joden listened, truly listened, until Simus ran out of words and reassurances. The silence seemed to echo around him as he took in Joden's face. "You're not surprised," Simus said, rubbing his thigh, feeling the scar even through the leather.

"Are you?" Joden asked mildly. "I made my decisions in the moment," he continued. "And they were my honest choices. I would not call them back." He gestured toward Simus's thigh. "Any of them. I spoke my truth as I saw them at the time, and admitted my mistakes when I saw the flaw in my truth. But that doesn't mean there won't be consequences for me."

Simus stirred, frowning. "But you were punished for it, back in Xy."

Joden rolled his eyes. "Being asked to sing of my decision not to grant you mercy is not a true punishment, Simus."

"But you will sing of it," Simus pressed.

"I will," Joden nodded.

"I do not like to think my life has come at a cost to you," Simus growled feeling the press of guilt. "That you might not become a Singer because—"

"Simus, did Essa refuse to consider me as a candidate for Singer?" Joden asked.

"No," Simus said slowly.

"Essa is the Eldest Elder Singer," Joden said. "A candidate for Singer must pass through Trials as the Warlords do. They must let me try," he continued. "And if I pass through the Trials, then I will face their judgement." Joden shrugged his shoulders. "It is a challenge, and I will confront it in my time."

Simus sighed. "Challenges are so much easier when you can swing a sword at them."

"True enough," Joden agreed with a heart-felt sigh. "True enough."

CHAPTER FIFTEEN

S ome nights later Simus woke when the night-watch whispered his name through the tent flaps. "Warlord, a messenger from Xy."

Simus rolled out, pulled on trous and boots, and grabbed his sword and dagger. He went out into the main tent to find the watch standing there, a woman warrior in their midst.

"Elois, it is good to see you," he said as one of them stoked up the coals of a brazier. "Come from Xy?"

"Aye, Warlord," Elois went to one knee before him then rose when he gestured her up. "I bring word from Warlord Keir of the Cat and the Warprize."

Elois had the look of one too long alone with only the herds. She stood tall and straight, but her eyes held a bright, dazed sheen. Simus knew that look all too well, as did the watch. It took time to adjust back to normal after days and days in the saddle. They softened their voices and gave her respectful space.

"When did you leave Xy?" Simus asked, trying to determine how much he could ask of her.

"The morning after the night of the pillar of light," Elois responded.

"You made good time." Simus was impressed.

"Once I had decent horses," she said ruefully, swaying slightly. "But I bear truths you must hear, Warlord."

"Should I waken Joden?" one of the watch asked.

"No, let him sleep," Simus said. "Give me the meat of it, Elois. I'll hear the whole tale once you've rested and slept." He could not stop his own eagerness. "How does the Warprize?"

"Well," Elois's face lit up. "She has borne twins, and all were well and healthy when I left."

Simus crowed a soft laugh as the other warriors slapped each other on the back. "Two," he laughed. "Well, done, Little Healer! Keir and Reness must have burst with pride."

Elois smiled and nodded, but then the joy drained from her face. "But there is grief as well, Warlord."

His joy fled in a breath. "Tell me," Simus demanded.

"Lord Othur, Seneschal and Warder of Xy was slain by one of the Xyian nobles." Elois drew a shaky breath. "He died speaking peace, with no weapon in his hand, and they killed him for it."

Simus felt the words like a blow to the chest. He stood for a moment, not fully understanding. "Dead?'

"Dead," Elois said. "He died with his bonded, the Warprize, and Heath of Xy by his side."

Simus rubbed his face with one hand.

"There is more, but that is the meat of it, Warlord." Elois drew a deep breath but Simus cut her off with his hand.

"In the morning," Simus repeated. "Bed down here, in one of the chambers. Do not stray from me, for I would hear all the truths you have."

Elois nodded, her exhaustion starting to show. "I was sent to ask for word of the needle of light, but I saw Eloix on the way here, and I know you have sent word. The Warlord bid me obey you in all things, but he also freed me to take oath with you if I remained."

Simus nodded. "My thanks, Elois."

"Just one more thing, Warlord." Elois yawned, then caught herself. "Forgive me, but you mentioned the Eldest Elder Thea."

"Reness?" Simus asked. "What of her?"

"She was not present at the Warprize's birthing." Elois blinked at him, her tiredness clear. "She is not in Xy."

"Where is she?" Simus demanded.

"Best I know, she got word at the border that had her turning back," Elois yawned again, and blinked at him as she rocked on her feet. "So far as I know, she never left the Plains."

"Let's see to you," Simus took her elbow. "We'll sleep on this news."

* * * * *

Except Simus couldn't sleep.

He lay on his pallet, looking at the roof of his tent until all went back to stillness. The watch was in place, it was quiet and dark, and yet sleep eluded him like the swiftest prey.

Othur dead? It seemed so wrong to even think those words. Othur was a city-dweller, in a home of stone, surrounded by guards who were skilled enough…how could this be?

And yet, death comes in an instant. Even to city-dwellers, it seemed.

The words of that truth stuck in his throat, and he rose from his bed, dressed and armed himself quietly, and stepping out into the cooler night air.

The night was clear and dark, with the stars ablaze in the skies.

The watch stirred, and rose to their feet, but he shook his

head. "I need to walk about," Simus murmured as they settled back. "Alone."

"As you will, Warlord," they replied, although one sharp-eyed woman gave him a look of understanding.

"At least give us a direction, and a time," she said crisply. "So we are not wandering about as if looking for a lost gurtle from the herd."

Simus snorted softly, but she had a point. "To the Heart," he said. "No more than an hour's time."

He strode off, walking through the grass that had yet to be trampled down by warriors and horses. As was traditional, none made their camps close to the Heart of the Plains, and no tent touched its border. Not at least until the Council was summoned and its massive tent raised.

Simus tried to think of nothing but the scent of crushed grasses below his boots and the brilliant skies above him. But the pain flooded in as memories of Othur appeared before his eyes. Laughing that great laugh of his, sitting in the warm kitchen eating the fine cooking of his Lady Wife, his pride in his Castle and his Kingdom. Of the morning he'd—

Simus stopped dead, the memory was so strong. *Of standing in the middle of the hot baths, with water to his waist. He'd smiled at Othur. "We've yet another Council today."*

"Yes." Othur had nodded with a bemused look on his face. "I fear that in many ways the Warlord and Xylara have left us with a heavy task, trying to bring our people together. To work in harmony. In peace."

Simus felt his grief well up. He resumed his steps.

The Heart was the same cool, grey stone it had always been, and his boots rang on the surface as he strode to the middle. The only sound here was the rustle of grasses, and the far noises of the various camps that ringed the Heart. The water in the lake next to it lapped at the shore, but only softly.

"He died speaking peace, with no weapon in his hand."

Simus shook his head in regret. A city-dweller, perhaps, but in his own way a warrior for his people.

The stars hung above him, seeming to sparkle with the beat of his own heart.

Simus drew a deep breath, and faced north toward Xy. He spread his hands, and lifted his face to the stars. "Othur." His voice cracked as it echoed against the stone.

The whisper in the grass was the only answer.

Simus faced to the west, and cried out to the night. "Othur of Xy."

And again, he turned south, and let his tears flow. "Othur of Xy, hear me."

And then, turning east, a final plea. "Othur, Seneschal of the Castle at Water's Fall, Warder of Xy, my friend, please."

The skies and stars were silent.

Simus dropped his head and his arms, letting his grief flow through him. "One day, my friend, I'll hope to see you beyond the snows."

He stood there for a moment, letting the wind take his tears, letting his breathing settle. Then he turned back, to head for camp.

Joden stood waiting, just beyond the stone. "They told me," he said as Simus drew near. He fell in step with him. "You knew him longer than I did."

"A good man," Simus said shortly. "Poor Lara, for such joy and such sorrow all in the same day. And Keir has lost an advisor of great worth." Simus looked north. "I wish I knew what was happening there."

"They wish the same," Joden said. "And we'll know more when Elois wakes. If I know her, that won't be long after sunrise." He sighed. "But I had another reason to seek you out. Late last night I learned that the last of the candidates has established a camp, and the bulk of the warriors have arrived. The mood is changing, and the challenges will be more serious from here on."

"That was to be expected," Simus said calmly, but his heart sped up as he headed back to his tent. "The next few days will tell the tale."

* * * * *

Eloix saw clear field beyond the trees and sighed with relief. She'd caught glimpses of the towers of Water's Fall as they rode, but she'd be glad just to be out from under the forest. Once in the open, she'd be able to breathe. She didn't like the way the trees hung over her and blotted out the skies and sunlight. It felt unnatural.

The horse's ears perked up, and she felt it quicken its pace. No doubt the animal saw the walls, and was ready for its stall in a barn. Strange Xyian customs, that went against the elements in every way. But it was what the horse was used to, and that she could understand.

She'd be just as glad to be off its back, that was certain.

Her two escorts, both Xyian warriors, had been friendly enough. The road had been good, and they'd made decent time for Xyian horses. But she'd be glad to see the Warprize and Warlord and finish her task. And Lady Anna's bread, so different from the Plains. Fluffy and white and good. Eloix's stomach rumbled at the thought.

They were half way up the road when horns sounded from the walls. "They're hailing us," one of the escort said.

Eloix looked at the walls, to see the warriors there, waving their arms, and calling out. "That looks more like a warn—"

A huge shadow moved over them, blotting out the sun. There was a sudden gust of wind, bringing the smell of rotting meat.

Eloix's horse laid its ears flat, and jumped into a gallop. Eloix kept her seat and looked back, over her shoulder.

A monster flew in the sky behind her, a huge beast with wings outspread, clawed feet reaching for her horse's rump. It was dark and leathery, with cruel eyes in a head topped by two wicked, spiraled horns. It had missed its target, hissing with frustration. It beat its wings to climb higher into the sky, raising a cloud of dust and debris.

Her escort was shouting now, one galloping off the road. Horrified, Eloix watched as a second beast tore that warrior from his saddle, and pulled him into the air. Its tail was long, arching over its body. It stung the man, who screamed again and again.

Arrows and bolts arched over her head, from the walls. Eloix went flat against her horse's neck, and urged it on, thinking only of shelter.

The shadow drew closer, coming at her across the grass. Eloix snarled and reached for one of her lances, determined to strike a—

Pain ripped through her shoulders as the sun was blotted out; the sound of hissing filled her ears. She flung herself to the side, hoping to tumble off. There was the road, and then grass, and then…blackness.

CHAPTER SIXTEEN

Simus acknowledged that Joden was right. The tone of the challenges had changed. It was in the winds that blew warmer, in the rising sun that shone hotter, in flowering grasses where the petals were falling away. In the sounds of the camps, and the talk of the warriors…

And in the blade of his opponent.

Simus held his sword and dagger before him defensively, drew a breath and considered the man. One Pero of the Badger, who had served as a Tenth with Keir in the past and knew Simus well. An older, seasoned warrior of many campaigns. Grey of hair and dark of skin, Pero was a short and wiry warrior, with strength behind his blows.

Pero had started the fight with cautious intent, probing Simus for weaknesses. No reckless moves from this one. Nor was he quick about it. They'd been at this for some time. Careful, steady, relentless: that was the challenge this Tenth gave Simus. Testing him, that was certain.

The change of tone was also in the faces of the other Tenths who stood around them, silently watching their combat. Simus felt the weight of their judgment as a knot between his shoulder blades.

Simus rolled his shoulders to release that knot as he waited for

Pero to make his next move. He'd need to conserve his energies. As tempting as it was to attack, better to—

Pero's teeth flashed in a grin, as if he'd read Simus's mind, and rushed in low and fast.

Simus's sword rang as he blocked Pero's weapon, and then shifted to try to bring his dagger to bear. Pero was ready for that, and blocked with his shorter blade. Pero stepped back, and to Simus's surprise, darted a glance off to the side. As if looking for a signal? Approval?

It didn't matter. Simus took his opportunity and struck hard with his sword. Pero blocked that, but seemingly stumbled and almost seemed to turn into Simus's dagger, letting the blade cut his cheek.

They broke apart, breathing hard, as the Singer called out Simus's victory.

Simus stood silent as Pero sheathed his sword with a shrug, and then offered his dagger, hilt toward Simus, the point at his heart. "I offer my surrender, Warlord."

Simus gave him a long look as he sheathed his own weapons, then grasped the hilt. "I accept your surrender," he said as he took the dagger. "Well fought, Pero of the Badger."

"I'd offer my sword as well," Pero added. "And to serve you as Tenth, if you'll have me."

"Willingly," Simus said. He could see Yers, his Second, off to the side, grinning like a crazed ehat.

"A mistake, Pero," a voice called from the crowd. "Where's the gain to be made in an army that does not raid?'

The crowd shifted, and Wyrik stepped forward, a sneer on his face.

"I've made my decision, Wyrik," Pero said mildly. "My Warlord will see to his people's needs, and the needs of the Plains."

"Pero's word is good enough for me." Another warrior stepped forward. More warriors nodded around him. "I'd offer my blade as well."

"Fools." Wyrik was contemptuous, bordering on offending. "How will he provide for you, and for the Tribes? How will he supply the thea camps and see to his warrior's needs? What of weapons? Armor? Supplies?"

"I will provide," Simus rumbled, facing the warrior. "There will be no lack for those who serve me."

"So you say," Wyrik scowled. "But—"

"So I say," a new voice called, high and joyful. They all raised their heads to an incoming rider. Simus almost laughed out loud when he recognized her.

"So I say," the rider repeated as she pulled her horse to a halt. "And I should know, for I have escorted the supplies these last few months and came on ahead to find you. Hail, Warlord Simus."

"Hail, Methla of the Deer," Simus laughed, even as he noticed Wyrik fading back into the crowd. "How stood Xy when you left it?"

"Your news would be newer then mine, since we left Xy months ago." Methla dismounted. "Elois came just as we were planning to leave the border. I did not speak with her, but the Warlord Liam gave me her words." She dropped her voice, aware of the watchers around them. "Hard to learn of Lord Othur's death when he was the one that sent his greetings and well wishes with us, and all weapons and supplies you'd asked for, including some of those Xyian crossbows."

Since Elois had shared her news in senel the day before, all of Simus's people knew of Othur's death. Simus clapped a hand on Methla's shoulder. "Let me take the oaths of these warriors," Simus said. "Send word back to the caravan of our location. Then we will talk."

* * * * *

Methla stood on no ceremony once they were in Simus's tent, but threw her thin, lanky body down on a gurtle pad with a grateful sigh. "Oh it's good to be back on the Plains." She glanced at Simus. "I feared that I would have to be the one to tell you of Lord Othur's death."

Simus grimaced as he settled down beside her. "A loss to us all, but especially to Lara."

Methla's face brightened. "Good to know she had her babes, and twins at that. The elements blessed her." Methla flashed a grin. "I wonder if she'll get the traditional birthing tattoos?" she chuckled, gesturing towards her own left arm.

Simus shared her chuckle as Destal served them kavage.

"How goes the formation of your army?" Methla asked.

Yers folded up his long legs to sit on a gurtle pad next to her. "It goes well. With the Tenths that swore oaths this afternoon, I am certain the numbers will increase."

"It's late in the season for Tenths to be making their choices," Methla lifted an eyebrow. "But I am glad to hear things go well." She paused. "Othur gathered everything he thought might aid you and piled it into wagons. Weapons, leather work, supplies, blankets, pots and pans, and such food stuffs as he thought made sense. I fear it slowed us, but there weren't enough horses in Xy to carry it all in packs."

Methla scowled. "Once we reached the border I tried to shift it all to horses, but that damn fool insisted on bringing his wagon." She ran her fingers through her hair in frustration.

Simus questioned Yers with a glance, but his Second shrugged. Who was she talking about?

"I tried to explain that the Plains lack roads and something called a 'wheelwright'," Methla continued. "That our horses are not trained to pull wagons, and that oxen are damned slow. Now the damn thing's only fit for firewood as far as I can tell, but he slept in it every night." She drew in a breath. "Simus, I honor you as Warlord, and I offer honor to Warlord Keir and the Warprize, but if ever I was tempted to kill a Xyian it would be this one. He—"

"Wait." Simus frowned. "Othur sent a Xyian with you?"

Methla looked at him in surprise. "I thought you knew," she said. "Othur said you would need someone with his skills. He's a healer."

"Like Lara?" Simus asked.

"Oh, no." Methla rolled her eyes. "He's a skilled healer, but he's no Warprize."

The tent flap rustled, and Destal stuck her head in. "Warlord, the caravan arrives."

"Send them into the camp," Simus ordered as he rose to his feet. "We'll meet them there."

* * * * *

The main camp was soon awash in milling horses and warriors as the supplies were unloaded, the packs carried into tents set aside for storage. Sal, as supply master, took charge of the chaos, standing back to watch with a growing sense of satisfaction as they unloaded new swords, blankets, pots and pans. Simus was especially pleased to see the weapons, and Othur had included the obsidian and shafts for the making of new lances.

And under every pack, each horse had a new saddle, ready to be given to his warriors. More bounty than from a minor raid, and all in good condition.

Sal came to stand next to him as the laden horses continued to stream into camp. "Othur did well by us," she said.

"He did," Simus confirmed. He grinned as he watched Pero and Misa admiring the supplies and the new saddles. His new Tenths, sworn to his service. And word would spread to other warriors that Simus of the Hawk provided for his warriors. His grin threatened to split his face.

Sal coughed, bringing him back.

"See to the distribution in the morning, once you have an idea of what we have here," Simus said, trying to look serious. "Meet the greatest needs first."

Sal wasn't fooled, and her smile was just as blinding. "I will, Warlord. But I'll also set some aside for the others that will swear soon."

The creak of a wagon wheel warned Simus, and he looked to see one lurching toward him, pulled by two Xyian oxen that looked weary and worn. The man in the wagon looked just as tired, although nothing could disguise that he was a city-dweller. Fat, balding, dressed in Xyian trous and robes in a muted blue, with no weapon in sight. Simus judged him to be at middle-age for a city-dweller. As he walked over, he changed his mind. Not fat, really, just soft around the middle. Pale of skin, like all city-dwellers, and sweating in the afternoon sun. Simus gave the man a smile as he approached. "Greetings," he said.

Only to receive a blank look in response.

Methla appeared on the other side of the wagon, and gave

Simus a look and a shrug. "Warlord Simus," she said in Xyian. "This is Healer Hanstau of Water's Fall."

"Finally," Hanstau said with a sigh.

"Greetings—" Simus began again, but blinked when Hanstau cut him off.

"I've healing supplies that need to be unloaded." The wagon creaked and groaned as the man struggled to climb down from the wagon seat. "If you will direct me to where I can set up camp and stake my oxen, I'd be much obliged. Some place with an adequate water supply, if you please."

"You do not speak our tongue?" Simus asked. "Why did Othur send you?"

"Lord Othur." Hanstau made the correction clear. "Lord Othur called for healers; none answered," he said grimly. "To run off to the wilds of the Firelands? Anyone would be mad to do so."

"So, why are you here?" Simus asked.

"Because I was the only one willing to come," Hanstau pulled out a large white square of cloth and mopped his brow. "Lord Othur and Master Healer Eln made offers such as I could not refuse." He tucked the cloth away again, and straightened up, staring Simus in the eye. "In exchange for my service for one year, they promised to aid my eldest in setting up his own smithy, as well as a fine apprenticeship for my youngest son as a scribe. My daughters were given positions in the Castle, to serve the Queen and Lady Anna. My late wife would have been pleased and honored to see our children so placed. I considered it my duty."

Simus glanced at Methla, who refused to meet his gaze. "Well, you have my thanks for your adherence to duty," Simus said dryly. "I shall have someone escort you, and aid in setting up your camp. Be welcome to the Plains, Hanstau of Xy."

Simus walked off, and Methla fell into step beside him. "He's not really that bad, once you get past the pompous stubbornness," Methla said quite cheerfully. "He knows a few words, like 'yes' and 'no' and 'where is the privy?'"

"My joy knows no bounds," Simus said and caught Yers's eye. "Our healer has arrived, and speaks nothing but the Xyian tongue. Have Cadr assigned to him. He'll need aid setting up his camp, and have someone see to his oxen."

Yers nodded. "Cadr is a good choice. The lad speaks Xyian and has an interest in healing. He can learn from him."

"Well, also put guards on the man. I fear he'll not adapt to our ways as quickly as the Warprize, and I want someone watching over him at all times. The elements alone know how much trouble he'll get into."

"I'll see it done," Yers promised. He smiled. "Best you return to your tent. When word of these supplies spreads, I think more will ask to serve. You'd best be ready to take their oaths."

"I will," Simus said, and grinned.

* * * * *

There were few challenges that afternoon, but many warriors with questions, and no few offering their swords. Simus took pleasure in the moment as his ranks filled. Tenths appeared as well, which would ease Yers's concerns. Destal kept up a steady stream of kavage for all comers.

When the time came to lower his banner, Simus emerged from his tent with a feeling of quiet contentment, only to find a challenger waiting. Destal had followed him out, and made a soft sound of surprise.

This one had waited until late in the day and hadn't made

her presence known. No doubt she'd thought Simus worn and tired. A younger woman, holding her shield in front of her body as if to ward off complaints.

Simus sighed as if with regret and glanced at the sun not yet touching the horizon. He sighed again, looking up at the challenge banner, still flapping in the breeze over his head.

"I am Sesson of the Hare," the warrior announced, her voice only quavering a little, and not with amusement. "I offer challenge, Simus of the Hawk."

"I accept." Simus heaved another long sigh of resignation and stepped within the circle. He was careful not to glance at his Token-bearer or Second, for fear they'd dissolve into the laughter they were struggling with.

A Singer was there as well, rather conveniently.

And the hairs on the back of Simus's neck rose in warning.

The woman warrior stepped into the circle…and pulled a mace from behind her shield.

CHAPTER SEVENTEEN

Destal sucked in a breath, but Simus knew it was already too late. He was within the circle and a Singer was at hand. And if the eyes of the fearful warrior now glittered with hate, well, Simus had no one to blame but himself.

She'd made her intent clear enough. Simus gave her no quarter. He crossed the circle at a run, ramming into her shield with the shoulder of his sword arm.

She stumbled back, not expecting his rush. It put her off balance, but she managed to keep her shield up, and swing with her mace. Simus grunted but took the hit in order to strike upward with his dagger.

She failed to block him. He thrust the blade deep into her throat, hitting gristle and bone.

The glitter in her eyes vanished. She collapsed to the ground.

Simus stood over her body, breathing hard. For a moment, no one moved.

The Singer cleared his throat. "Done," he said, "with Simus the Hawk the winner."

'The survivor,' Simus thought grimly as he sheathed his sword. He leaned down, feeling the burning of rising bruises along his ribs and grabbed the dead woman's mace. Blood still dripped from

his dagger onto the ground.

Two warriors approached and both went to one knee before him. "Warlord," one said. "We were of her camp, and would see to her."

Simus gave them a nod, and they stepped forward to pick up the body. The onlookers moved away, talking quietly among themselves.

Simus added the mace to his weapons rack, making sure it was easily seen. He grabbed up a cloth and started to clean his dagger. Joden appeared from around the tent and stood silent at his aide.

"A change in tone, indeed," Simus growled under his breath, angry at himself for not taking the challenge seriously, and for letting her past his guard. His ribs would ache for some time to come. He turned away from the rack to watch the departing warriors with the body between them.

"What was behind that, I wonder?" Joden murmured, as he watched as well. "Did she decide on her own to make a death challenge, or was she sent?"

"Can you find out?" Simus asked.

Destal stood close. "Let me send someone else instead. Joden is a bit too…obvious. But this is hardly a surprise. Warlord, you are going to be a target for—"

"I, PIVE OF THE SNAKE, CHALLENGE FOR WAR-LORD," a voice boomed from behind them, and something hard smacked into Simus's calf.

Simus reacted swiftly and instinctively, jumping forward to gain space from his attacker, then spinning to face him as he drew his sword and dagger. Joden and Destal each jumped to the side, their own weapons out and facing the threat.

Simus's heart leapt in his throat as his blades came to bear on his attacker—

—a small girl-child, who barely came up to his waist, wielding a wooden sword and dagger, holding them in the position for another assault.

Simus stared.

The child was frozen, her wide eyes taking in his blade hovering inches from her head. "I—" her voice cracked high in fear.

"Pive," came an older, calm voice. "Hold."

Simus knew that voice. He rolled his eyes in its direction, as did the girl-child.

Haya of the Snake stood there, her arms crossed over her chest.

"Dea-mine," Simus blurted out in astonishment.

Haya raised an eyebrow at him. Simus flushed with embarrassment, but Haya paid him no mind. She focused instead on the girl. "Pive, you have erred. You have attacked an adult warrior, one fresh from a challenge. You struck with no warning and no ritual, and he would be within his rights to kill you."

Pive swallowed hard, her face screwed up with anger and fear. Simus could see tears starting to well up in her eyes.

"What say you, Pive?" Haya demanded.

The child lowered her weapons, her shoulders sagging in defeat. Her mouth was trembling as she offered her wooden dagger to Simus, placing the blunted point at her heart. "I offer my sur-surrender, Warlord."

Simus sheathed his weapons, and took her dagger, careful not to smile at this smallest of warriors. "I accept your surrender."

"Pive…" Haya chided her.

Pive sighed, and gave over her sword to Simus as well.

"Go back and join the others," Haya said and the girl was

off in a flash.

There was an awkward moment as the adults recovered themselves under Haya's gaze.

"Greetings, Elder Thea Haya," Simus recovered first. He offered the wooden weapons to Haya, but she shook her head, and gestured toward the rack.

"Impetuous, that one," Haya said. "She needs to learn consequences."

Simus snorted softly, but racked the weapons accordingly.

"So, you are not yet a Warlord, I see," Haya observed. She cast her eye over Joden. "And you, not yet Singer?"

"I—" Joden stumbled. "It is good to see you, Thea. You look well," he finished lamely.

Haya snorted. "Seo will join us shortly. He is checking locations for our camp."

"Our weaponsmaster is here, too?" Joden blurted out, his dread clear.

"You brought your thea camp to the Heart?" Simus asked with a strong sense of impending doom. "In the Spring?"

"Yes." Haya walked over to the tent flap. "We have much to discuss. Perhaps you will offer me the courtesy of your tent? Offer kavage?"

Destal scrambled forward. "Allow me to see to your comfort, Elder Thea."

They both disappeared within Simus's tent.

Joden puffed out his cheeks and let his breath out slowly.

Simus rolled his eyes. "Theas," he whispered in resignation.

Joden nodded.

"Perhaps you'll join me?" Haya's raised voice came through the flap.

They both hastened to obey.

* * * * *

Snowfall glowered at Simus's tent from her hiding place in the deep grass. Rare anger coursed through her; her tattoos tight and tense on her skin. She'd found the flaw, sure enough.

Simus of the Hawk was an arrogant idiot.

He'd walked into the challenge circle, acting all put-upon, like an arrogant fool. No warning, none of his people had checked, the man was blessed by the elements to be alive, much less the victor.

He'd reacted quickly, and took his opponent down fast and hard, but still. He never should have entered the circle unprepared. Snowfall faulted him for that, but she also faulted his people. His Token-bearer especially.

Snowfall had watched Simus fight, but she'd also watched her potential opponent in the ring. Destal was good, true, but not good enough. Snowfall looked forward to challenging her.

Simus of the Hawk had no caution. He needed protection; needed someone to watch his back. Destal was not the one to do this. What would happen if he failed in this? How could the Plains unify under the Council of Elders if the fool got himself—

The pounding of feet came at her and children ran past her, heedless of the tall grasses and established paths.

Snowfall hunched down.

The Heart was becoming too crowded, too difficult to travel even hidden. And now, with a thea camp added, well…

She needed to retreat to her camp, but it would be best if she waited until the camp had settled and the sun was a bit further behind the horizon. She'd plenty to think on in the meantime.

"Look deeper," Wild Winds had said, and as was almost

always the case, her master…her former master was right. There was more there than pomp and arrogance.

He'd impressed her when he'd treated those young warriors with dignity, taking their oaths seriously, and welcoming them into his service.

He'd impressed her more when the horses had arrived loaded with supplies—and those saddles. Skies above, Snowfall had never seen a new saddle before, only those looted or stolen at war. Certainly, she'd never had one. The warrior-priests took the best for themselves and the leavings were for those in training. But Simus hadn't even blinked at new weapons, new saddles, and ordered them distributed to his people based on their needs.

She had not expected such fairness from him.

Voices were raised, calling the children to order, and back to their tents. Snowfall didn't move; patience was a form of protection in and of itself.

There was one more thing about Simus, and this one made Snowfall chew her lip and wish she could contact Wild Winds to talk of it with him.

Simus of the Hawk had mourned a city-dweller.

She would not have believed it if she hadn't followed him, and seen with her own eyes. His words, his prayer, his tears all spoke of a great truth, that he had lost a friend.

A city-dweller.

Snowfall shivered, and then forced herself to concentrate on her power, flowing into the veil that kept her hidden.

If Simus could mourn someone so different than a warrior of the Plains, then maybe…maybe he would listen to a warrior-priestess. Or whatever she was now.

Snowfall swallowed hard and shoved the thought away. She

didn't even know herself, and that was terrifying and exciting at the same time and in the same breath.

The area around her was clear enough. She started to crawl off, taking care to keep herself concealed.

Time to prepare. She'd sharpen her knives, see to her meal and her rest, and then when dawn came—

Let it be as the elements willed.

* * * * *

So you brought your thea camp to the Heart?" Simus asked again after they had settled within his tent, kavage and gurt all around. Haya had told them of her hostile encounter with Antas of the Boar. Weaponsmaster Seo had joined them, as had a Singer, one Quartis by name. Yers settled on a gurtle pad, eyeing Haya warily. Joden sat next to Simus, as silent as Simus had ever seen him.

"I have," Haya said.

"The entire camp?"

"All," Haya confirmed calmly. "Down to the last newborn and gurtle in our herds."

"This is not wise, Haya," Simus said, feeling like he was pointing out the obvious. "Live children around live steel? It is asking for trouble."

"Wise enough, young one, to take the action I must to protect what I have sworn to shelter."

"But I can't offer—"

"You can and you will." Haya held up her mug for more kavage. Destal moved hastily to fill it. "For isn't that the truth of your message? That you and Keir will protect the children? Provide a better future for them?"

"I—" Simus had no answer for that. "The thea camps have always protected themselves well enough."

"Do not challenge your thea's decision," Seo growled.

Simus rubbed his hands over his face. "Elder Thea—" he started, but she didn't let him finish.

"It is clear to me that Antas is a threat," Haya said. "The added strength of your warriors combined with mine will see to it that he makes no moves. That, and the nearness of the Council."

"The Council of Elders in the Spring is not attended by the theas," Joden said carefully.

Haya shrugged, as if that was a matter of no importance.

Yers chimed in. "We could widen the perimeter of the camp and bring the children within its circle. The herds could remain outside, under guard."

"I do not think Antas seeks the animals," Seo said firmly. "He seeks control of the thea camp itself."

"Spread the word among my warriors that children roam the camp," Simus said to Yers. "Warn them, or else that Pive might not be so lucky the second time." He offered Haya a smile. "That one will be a Warlord someday."

"If she survives bearing five children," Haya said starkly. "Survives the pain that is a life-bearer's to bear."

Simus went silent for a moment. "I hadn't thought of it that way."

"I do," Haya said. "Every day. For they are my charges. Why do you think that Reness supports these ideas of yours and Keir's? Because theas know the true price in death that the Plains pay."

"There is a healer here," Simus said. "Sent from Xy. With supposedly the same skills as the Warprize."

"Ah." Haya nodded. "I have heard much of the healing skills

of the Warprize. I will have words with this healer. In the meantime, I've a camp to see to." She rose to her feet, Seo and Quartis following her example. "And you've a title to win, Simus of the Hawk. See to it that you rest well this night. And have the healer see to that injury you are trying to hide."

With that she was gone, Seo and Quartis after her.

* * * * *

In the morning, Simus felt worse than he had the night before, but that was to be expected with such bruising.

Yers and Destal raised their challenge banners at dawn, but Simus sent for the healer, drank the bitter tea he made, rubbed on an ointment that smelt of mint, and squirmed back into his pallet for another hour or so. Warlord's privilege, he thought drowsily to himself as he faded back off to sleep.

Only to awaken to a commotion of angry and bitter words from a gathering crowd outside his tent. He grumbled as he pulled on trous and his armor, stomped into boots and burst from his tent into their midst.

"What now?" Simus roared, silencing the crowd with his outburst. "Are horses demanding to speak truths at a senel? Are the skies falling? Or rain falling up?"

"She offers challenge!" Destal was in Simus's face, enraged. "To me! For Token-bearer!"

"Who?" Simus demanded.

"I do," a cool voice answered him.

Simus looked over—

—to find Snowfall standing in the center of the challenge circle, her grey eyes cool and collected, her arms crossed over her chest.

CHAPTER EIGHTEEN

The uproar was getting louder and intense and drawing even more attention. Everyone around them had an opinion, and wished to be heard.

Snowfall stood in the center of the challenge circle, ignoring it all, her calm gaze focused on Simus. The morning sun made her sweet brown skin glow bronze. She stood with her hip cocked to one side, two oddly crooked long-knives belted at her waist. She had abandoned the traditional dress of a warrior-priestess. She still wore leather trous, but her chest was covered by a sleeveless leather corselet that laced up the front. Her shoulders were bare, but for the tattoos that capped them. There was a tightness in those muscular shoulders, but Simus couldn't fault her for that.

Destal was screaming at the woman, standing at the edge of the circle. "You dare? You, who have never done service under a Warlord? Never seen battle? Never taken oaths of service?" She put her hand on the hilt of her sword. "I am going to thrash you to within an inch of your life."

"You may try." Snowfall shrugged, as if it was of no matter.

Destal bared her teeth and started to pull her blade.

"SILENCE," Simus bellowed.

Everyone froze, jaws snapping shut mid-word.

"Sit, all of you," Simus ordered.

He was obeyed, everyone sitting, cross-legged, sorting themselves out as the crowd settled. Snowfall still stood, facing him. But Simus noted that she glanced around as those closest to her eased down to the ground, and some of the tautness left her.

Some, not all. She was right to be wary. None of his people had any love for warrior-priests.

Yers and Joden both appeared, threaded their way through the crowd and sat closest to Simus. Simus gave them each a nod, but stood silent until he was sure he had everyone's attention.

"Warrior-priestess Snowfall, what in the name of skies do you do here?" Simus asked mildly.

She didn't change her stance, just lifted that heart-shaped chin a little and met his eye.

"I offer challenge to Destal for the right to serve as your Token-bearer."

Those grey eyes still had hidden depths, but this was far more at stake here than a sharing of bodies. Whether she knew it or not, Snowfall had presented him with a decision that would test his leadership as Warlord.

"You cannot." Simus kept his voice at a moderate tone. "Before you can offer challenge for Token-bearer, you must first offer me your sword. You have not."

"I would do so," Snowfall responded.

Simus narrowed his gaze at her. "You cannot. You are under oath to Wild Winds."

"I am not." Snowfall glanced to the north and Simus saw a flash of pain deep in her grey eyes before she turned her attention back to him. "Wild Winds has released me from his service."

A murmur of surprise rose around them, and Simus found

himself almost without words. "Why would he do that?"

Snowfall drew in a deep breath. "Wild Winds says we, the warrior-priests, are no longer what we were, and in what we were, we erred. That we, the warrior-priests, must become other than what we were and are, and yes, while I know that his words are cryptic, more I cannot say. I am—" She paused. "I was his student in-training. His thoughts are beyond my full understanding."

Joden stood and looked to Simus for permission. At Simus's nod, he addressed Snowfall. "You understand if you give Warlord Simus your oath and lose the challenge to be his Token-bearer, you are still bound to serve him? The oath binds you, even in defeat," Joden pointed out. "You understand this?"

"I do," Snowfall said. "If it cannot be that I serve as Token-bearer, still I have a place within this camp and duties of service owed to the Warlord."

"You'll be given scut work," Destal snarled from where she sat. "The newest of the new will rank above you and—"

"Destal," Simus warned.

Destal stood and appealed to Simus. "Warlord, she has no skills."

"I served Wild Winds in the same office," Snowfall said. "There is no difference with a Warlord, surely. Pots must still be cleaned and linens washed."

A faint murmur of amusement washed through the crowd. At Simus's gesture, Destal sat down with a huff.

"With respect, Warlord," Yers rose to his feet. "She knows nothing of our ways, never having served within an army. And she and her kind are not to be trusted."

"You do not hold my token." Snowfall's voice was cold. "And your words are offensive."

"Warrior-priests offer no tokens." Yers didn't look at her, just kept his eyes on Simus.

"I do and I will," Snowfall said, pulling out a square of red silk. "Wild Winds gave it to me, saying that I would have a need."

Simus stood, shaking his head. "I do not understand this." He gestured toward her and the challenge circle. "Why would you do this?"

"Do you doubt my oaths, once given?" Snowfall asked, twisting the silk in her hands, the first sign of worry he'd seen in her.

"No," he said slowly. "I would have no doubt of oaths given to me, for they will be taken before the elements for all the skies to see." He smiled slightly. "But you must admit, Snowfall, that this is not a path taken by a warrior-priestess before."

"I am not a warrior-priestess." Snowfall's face didn't change, but there was a sadness in her tone. "Wild Winds says that we are not what we were, so we must become what we are. I will swear an oath to you for this season, and then I will contest for Token-bearer. What happens after that is only for the skies to know.

"But this I do know. A leather belt does not re-stitch itself together. If I am silent, who will speak to mend the mistakes of the past?" Snowfall spread her hands out. "If I do not speak of peace and understanding, if I do not reach out to bridge the gap between what we were and what we will become, who will?"

Simus's stomach clenched, thinking of another who'd spoken of peace and died for it. At least Snowfall had the good sense to have a weapon at hand.

A cough drew his attention to the back of the crowd, where Lander and Ouse, the first warriors to pledge to him, were rising to their feet. They each looked at the other, then Ouse nudged Lander's shoulder. "Warlord," Lander's voice cracked nervously.

"Speak," Simus said.

"We told you of our part in the journey of the Sacrifice," Lander said. "This warrior-priestess, she was the one who came to the Sacrifice and his Token-bearer and offered herself as hostage to them." He stood a little straighter and his voice grew stronger. "She came unarmed, and was true to her oaths with us, Warlord. We would speak for her."

Simus gestured, and everyone resumed their seats. The challenge banners flapped in the morning breeze, and Simus raised his eyes to the skies and considered. Was she to be trusted?

The skies held no answers. It was up to him to decide.

He chose to trust.

He lowered his gaze back to the waiting crowd. "I will accept your oath, Snowfall."

There were gasps, then silence as she pulled her blades, knelt before him and swore her oath.

"My first command is that you are to use none of your powers without my knowledge and permission."

That got him a startled glance of grey eyes that fell away, hidden under dark lashes. Clearly, she hadn't expected that. There was a long pause before she spoke.

"I obey, Warlord." Snowfall rose to her feet in one swift, graceful move.

"Further," Simus said, "you may challenge for Token-bearer."

Destal leapt to her feet, snarling. "I will kill you, *bragnect.*"

"It is not my wish that you kill her, Destal," Simus said calmly.

"Is that an order, Warlord?" Destal snapped.

"It is if it needs to be," Simus replied coolly.

Destal glanced at his face and looked away. "That will not be necessary, Warlord."

"Quartis, will you judge?" Simus asked the Singer.

"It would be my honor," Quartis responded quickly.

"Whoever wins should serve me my kavage," Simus announced, turned, and went into his tent. The roar behind him indicated that the crowd was on its feet and had already chosen sides.

The clamor almost drowned out the voices of Yers, Joden, and Seo as they followed him within.

"What are you thinking?" Yers demanded.

"Haya will not be pleased," Seo announced as they moved further into the depths of the tent, the better to hear one another. "She bears no love for warrior-priests."

"Where is the Elder Thea?" Simus asked.

Seo beamed, his tanned face turning into a mass of wrinkles. "She's trying to pry knowledge from that healer. She knows no Xyian, so he keeps speaking louder and slower as Cadr tries to translate. It's going like a grassfire. I suspect that Haya may burst from sheer frustration."

"Are you out of your mind?" Yers demanded again. "She is one of them."

Simus sat on his gurtle pad at the head of the room. "I doubt she will survive the challenges. But if she does, as a warrior under my command she is a valuable source of knowledge about the warrior-priests, and she is sworn to my service." Simus raised his eyes to Yers. "And you forget yourself."

Yers drew a deep breath, clearly calming himself. "Warlord, I would be doing less than my duty to you if I did not point out that you are making a mistake. You yourself reminded us that the position held by Marcus is not the traditional role of a Token-bearer. You would have her speak for you? A warrior-priestess?"

Joden looked troubled. "Simus, he is not wrong. The choice—"

"The ultimate choice is mine," Simus said. "At the end of the Trials, I pick my Token-bearer from those that have won the right to contest for it. It is a process, not an elimination. Allowing her to challenge is no risk to me."

A roar came from outside the flap.

"But it allows her within your camp, and confidences," Yers said. "If she doesn't poison your kavage, or attempt to bewitch you with her powers. What would Warlord Keir think of this if he were here? He'd never trust—"

"Keir is not here," Simus hardened his voice. "I will be Warlord within my own right. And have you not given me your oath?"

Yers dropped his gaze and lowered himself to one knee. "Yes, Warlord."

"Do you wish to rescind your oath?" Simus pressed.

"No, Warlord," Yers said, his eyes still down.

"No battle plan survives first contact with the enemy," Simus stated firmly. "I will see this done as best I know how, knowing our goals. But the choices and decisions are mine to make." Simus paused. "If you feel differently, give me your token, tell me your truths, and I will release you from my service."

There was silence, then Yers bowed his head. "No, Warlord, I obey."

"Like Keir, I wish to hear your truths," Simus said. "But in the end, I will make my decisions and expect to be obeyed. Is that clear?"

"Yes, Warlord," Yers said. With that, he seated himself at Simus's side.

Simus glanced at Joden, who said nothing, then turned to look at Seo. The older man gave him a nod. Was that approval from his old weapons-master? He had to be mistaken.

Seo's wrinkled face folded into a smile. "Can't wait to tell this to Haya. She'll have a few things to say, that is certain."

The tent flap flew open, and Destal stomped through, a look of rage on her face and a cut on her cheek. Snowfall followed behind her, her face calm, her knives sheathed. They disappeared into the serving area, and Simus found himself holding his breath, listening. But there was only silence and the clatter of pottery.

Finally, Snowfall emerged carrying a pitcher of kavage and mugs. She walked up to them, still cool and calm. "Kavage, Warlord?"

"Yes, Token-bearer." Simus took the mug from her hand.

Snowfall turned and offered kavage to Yers, who declined, and then to Joden and Seo, who both took a mug. She then turned back to Simus. "Should I raise your challenge banner, Warlord?"

"Yes," Simus took a sip of the kavage.

"More warriors would ask permission to challenge for Token-bearer, Warlord," Snowfall said calmly. "They are lining up outside."

"Send them in," Simus instructed.

Snowfall nodded, set the kavage pitcher down at his side, and walked out of the tent.

"That woman is in for one hard day," Simus mused. "Meanwhile, we have work to attend to."

* * * * *

Simus approved some handful of challengers, and then left the tent through the back way to oversee the placement of the thea camp with a very cranky Second. Simus was willing to give Yers time to adjust to his decision, but he wasn't going to tolerate much else. They both concentrated on the duties before them, and when a warrior informed them that Destal had left on a long-range hunt, neither made comment to the other.

All during what was left of the morning, Simus was approached by warriors wishing to challenge for Token-bearer. Except for a few clearly unsuitable candidates, who had no skills to be a Token-bearer, and a few hotheads spoiling for a fight, he granted the requests.

But by the time the sun was almost at its height he was tired, and hungry and curious, so he returned to his tent with two of his Tenths.

Snowfall was facing another opponent, her wicked knives out and flashing, and had him cut before Simus drew close.

"Done," Quartis the Singer declared. "With Snowfall the winner."

The loser offered his surrender, and Snowfall took the dagger with a nod. She had quite a nice pile of them at the base of the pole.

"Quartis, have you been judging all morning?" Simus asked. "I thank you for your service."

"As do I," Snowfall added softly.

"It was an honor," Quartis grinned. "And I will return after the nooning to continue, for I wish to see how this song will end."

"I would offer food—"

"My thanks, Simus, but Haya will gut me if I do not find her and tell her the tale so far," Quartis said as he headed off toward the thea camp.

"Take down the challenge banners," Simus ordered, even as another challenger came up to the circle. The warrior looked about to protest, but Simus fixed him with a glare. "She will raise her banner again shortly," he said. "But first I want my nooning.

"Which I will take privately," he continued, turning to the

Tenths. "Deny me to any who seek me out for this nooning. Let them know I'll speak with them later. I will send messages when I am ready."

The Tenths gave him a nod, and settled down on watch.

Snowfall was standing in front of the tent entrance, the banners in her hands.

Simus held open the tent flap. "In," he ordered.

Snowfall obeyed.

CHAPTER NINETEEN

Simus wove a strip of bells into the tent flap as Snowfall vanished within to prepare their meal. He was confident the bells, and the Tenths outside, would ensure that even Ultie wouldn't barge in during this nooning.

The tent was cool with the flaps down, the light dim. He wanted to see Snowfall's face for this discussion, so he went to the platform and stirred the coals of the brazier.

Snowfall came out balancing various bowls, and a platter of flat bread.

Simus eyed the food. "Bring your meal out here too. We'll talk as we eat together."

Snowfall hesitated, then nodded, set down the dishes and disappeared again.

Simus settled down on his gurtle pad, feeding the brazier enough fuel so that a flame flickered to life, then settled down to a steady burn.

From outside, he heard voices. The Tenths, talking to someone, and then the faint chime of the bells as someone tested the flap. He smiled to himself as the voices faded away. Essa, by the sound of it.

Snowfall returned, balancing more dishes in her hands and

arms and set her additional burdens down before making another trip. Simus arranged the bowls of gurt and dried meat and a platter of flat bread between them as she returned with kavage and mugs. She settled on the gurtle pad opposite. They both removed their weapons, and placed them by their sides, within easy reach.

She held out the water pitcher and bowl for hand-washing and they both went through the ritual silently, murmuring their own private thanks to the elements under their breaths.

Simus dried his hands and reached for the bread.

"I would offer an apology," Snowfall said, her hands folded in her lap. "I was not able to prepare a warm meal."

"Eat," Simus said, pushing the strips of dried meat toward her. "You would not know this," he continued, "but every challenge need not be met immediately. You may take them at your own pace. Challengers know they may have to wait if the one challenged is seeing to their duties."

"That makes more sense," Snowfall said slowly. She broke off a piece of meat and started to chew.

Simus took a moment to watch her as he poured his kavage. Her grey eyes sparkled, but their brilliance was softened in this light. There was a soft scent of sweet honey in the air as well, which Simus was certain came from her warm skin.

Snowfall offered him a bowl of gurt. Simus gave her a half-smile. "I wasn't sure you would survive the mornings' challenges," he said.

"They underestimated my knives and my speed," she said.

"Unusual blades, those," Simus nodded toward them.

"I believe they were raided in the far south," Snowfall said. "Wild Winds received them as tribute, and gifted them to me."

Simus took a few pebbles of gurt. "They won't underestimate

you this afternoon," he pointed out. "They have seen you fight."

Snowfall shrugged. "We shall see," was her only reply.

"It surprised them," Simus said. "Surprised me as well. We tend to forget warrior-priests are capable of fighting, since they do not spar with warriors or enter the Trials."

"We spar with each other," Snowfall said. "Fellow warrior-priests, none of whom were forgiving or kind. Brutal in their own fashion, or—" She hesitated. "At least, they were."

There wasn't much Simus could say to that. For a time, they both just concentrated on the food, lost in their private thoughts. There were voices outside the tent now and again. Simus reminded himself to ask the Tenths who had visited during the nooning.

The silence was comfortable as they ate, until Simus reached for the last bit of bread, and winced.

"That mace hit bruised you badly, didn't it?" Snowfall asked.

Simus nodded. "Hit harder than I care to admit," he said. "I have something for it," he stood and headed toward his sleeping area.

"I'll get more kavage," Snowfall said behind him.

Simus returned first, with his ointment, and remained standing as he stripped off his armor and padded tunic. Snowfall walked silently across the room, sat, and poured for him as he removed the wax plug from the jar. "What is that?" she asked.

"A healing ointment," Simus said as he lifted his arm and looked at the discolored and swollen area. He took some of the cream and rubbed it in carefully, hissing as the cool lotion touched heated skin.

"It looks better than I would expect," Snowfall looked up from where she sat, studying his body.

Simus couldn't help but suck in his stomach a bit as he applied more salve. "It does seem to help," he admitted. "Our new healer seems to know his craft."

"So it is true that you have a city-dweller in the camp?" Her eyes widened. "I have only ever seen the Sacrifice and his Token-bearer, and they seemed like people. I'd heard that all city-dwellers are so fat they waddle like water-birds. Is that true of yours?"

"You must judge for yourself," Simus chuckled, then stopped to think. "You saw the fight? The one with the mace?" he asked casually as he stoppered the jar again.

* * * * *

He surprised her, and caught off guard she blurted the truth. "Yes."

"You used your powers?" Simus's eyes were dark and hooded.

"Yes," Snowfall admitted. "I was hidden in the tall grasses by the Heart." She looked away. "I wanted to learn all I could before I challenged."

Simus wiped the remaining lotion off on his chest with his hands. "You can hide yourself?" And at her nod, he frowned. "Show me."

She obeyed, wrapping a veil around herself.

"Skies," Simus breathed, his eyes wide and startled. "Are you—" He reached out to touch her, and brushed against her hair.

Snowfall caught her breath as a tingle ran down her neck.

Simus frowned. "I can feel you."

"I do not vanish into thin air," she said. "I hide myself from your sight, that is all. I still make noise, breathe, and move as you do."

"How hard is it to do this?" Simus asked, his eyes narrowing. Snowfall could see him thinking, assessing the benefits and the dangers.

"Before?" Snowfall shrugged. "Even if one could locate enough power, there was a danger in using it, that it would leave you at a most vulnerable time. But now? After the Sacrifice? Power abounds," she said simply. "But there is still the risk that I would lose my concentration, or have someone touch me as you have. The veil only conceals, it doesn't protect."

Simus nodded. He seemed so much bigger, here in the tent, towering over her. Yet he moved with a warrior's grace as he settled on the gurtle cushion.

He looked up at her. "There is an ehat in the tent with us, and I would take it by the horns." Simus leaned back and watched her in the firelight. "I have questions, Snowfall, and I would ask for your token. So that there are no misunderstandings between us."

Snowfall nodded, and handed him her piece of silk. Simus took it carefully, running the cloth between his fingers. "And I would offer my own in return," Simus nodded toward the stump of wood where his formal token rested.

Snowfall reached over and took it in both hands. The bells chimed as she held the curved bone, smooth under her fingertips.

"So," Simus asked. "Now we exchange truths with one another. Whose idea was this? To become my Token-bearer?"

"Wild Winds," Snowfall admitted, and something of her pain must have reflected in her voice. Simus's face softened as she continued. "And I came to agree with him."

"Where is Wild Winds?" Simus asked.

"North," she said. "I do not know where for certain. He indicated that he would keep his people on the Plains unless the danger grew, and then he would retreat into Xy."

That caught Simus off guard. "For Wild Winds to think he'd

be safer with Keir…the threat posed must be greater then I know."

Snowfall nodded. "The warrior-priests are no longer of one mind. Wild Winds fears for the young. Hail Storm would take them and train them to his advantage, maybe even teach them the blood ways. Those ways distort the soul, and pervert the lives it touches. The elements reject it, and those that practice it. Although—" She hesitated. "There are times when it is practiced for good. When the blood sacrificed is your own." She hurried on. "It is hard to explain, when you do not have gifts."

"How do you know I don't?" Simus asked.

"You were tested," Snowfall said. "At your Rite of Ascension. All of the Plains are tested, and those with the gifts were taken as warrior-priests. No matter how strong or weak the gift within the person." She drew a deep breath. "In the past, the young were given no choice. Recently, Wild Winds was giving those with weaker gifts a choice. Your Ouse of the Fox is one such." Simus raised an eyebrow as she continued on. "Night Clouds follows Wild Winds's ways. He gave him a choice, and he chose to be a warrior."

"What powers do you have?" Simus leaned forward. "Healing, as the warrior-priests have always claimed?"

Snowfall shook her head. "Maybe in the past," she said. "But our ability to heal is limited. Certain plants that help with fever. Dried mushrooms that deaden pain."

"Purple smoke," Simus snorted.

"A special mixture of dried grasses and mushrooms," Snowfall nodded seriously. "It confuses the senses. But the chants, the rites that were used? They seemed to have little effect." Snowfall hesitated. "That may no longer be the case. Wild Winds was cured of a wasting disease on the night of the Sacrifice. And I was told that the Sacrifice healed his Token-bearer of a broken leg with his power. But how? I cannot say."

"Cannot say?" Simus's question was hard and sharp.

"I mean, I do not know," Snowfall lowered her eyes. "It is harder than I thought to tell these truths to an outsider,"

Simus huffed out a breath. "Joden will want to pry your head open and learn all your secrets."

"Wild Winds says we no longer have any." Snowfall lifted her head. "I am to tell all, as you command. Some will believe, he says. Some will not. Either way, truths told will serve us better then secrets have in the past."

Simus waited, silently. It took her a moment to realize she had not answered his question.

"I am not so powerful as Wild Winds," she admitted. "I can conceal myself from sight, as I did in the grasses," Snowfall kept her gaze on his, that he might know she spoke the truth. "I have a gift for using the element of fire, and can use it as a weapon. I can send messages."

"Messages?" Simus perked up. "And get a response?"

"As if we are talking in the same place," Snowfall said proudly. "But only if I have a kind of token from that person. Something that links us." She nodded toward the piece of silk. "That was a gift from Wild Winds."

"So if Keir had a token—" Simus started.

"And one of us at his side," Snowfall finished for him. "You could talk to him as if he was in the same room. But there is a risk," she confessed. "I am exposed when I do that, and the message can be overheard."

"A warrior-priest at Keir's side." Simus snorted. "Maybe when ehats fly."

"It may be possible, with the power that now resides in the

Plains, to send a message without a warrior-priest to receive it," Snowfall suggested. "But I have not tried, and will not, not without your permission." She hesitated, not quite sure how to explain the next part.

Simus waited silently.

"There is a new gift," she said slowly. "One that only appeared to Wild Winds and myself recently. He thinks it is a kind of foreseeing, but…" She let her voice fade away as she thought on her next words.

Simus was still, those dark eyes watching her.

"It is no more than a feeling, of apprehension, that something is coming," she said. "A looming threat of danger over the horizon."

"Is it specific?" Simus asked. "To a person? Or an event?"

"No," Snowfall said, and some of her frustration must have carried through her voice, because Simus's eyes crinkled in sympathy. "I have tried," she said. "To probe for more, but there is only this lingering feeling. Wild Winds says that there was a time when those with the gift could see the future. But that knowledge is lost to us." She shook her head. "The vagueness is not helpful."

"A warrior heeds every warning," Simus said. "Even if it's just a gut feeling." He took a sip of his kavage. "My warriors are already on alert. But if that feeling becomes more, tell me." He tilted his head to the side. "How hard will it be, to not use your powers except with my consent?"

Snowfall shook her head. "Not hard. Remember that the power has been scarce, and we were trained to conserve. I have never used it with abandon. I would ask, however—" She hesitated, then plunged on. "I would ask that you lift the restriction upon me if needed for your protection." Snowfall dropped her eyes. "We—I—have staked much on your success. If you should fall—"

Simus considered her suggestion, as he considered her.

How far could he trust her? Trust a warrior-priestess? No matter that she had sworn her oaths; oaths had been shattered before, with no formal recession and no warning.

Yet, there was something there. For all that Snowfall held her emotions inside, there was an honesty to her truth.

He'd trust, until his trust was betrayed.

Simus gave her a half-smile and shook his head. "In battle, I would never instruct a warrior not to use any weapon at hand. But this is not a normal battle. You mean well, Snowfall, but the risk is too great. We tread a new path here, and there are those that would use any excuse against you—against me—to deny the change we bring. My restrictions stand." Simus hesitated. "Do you need to use your powers to receive a message from anyone?"

"No," Snowfall shook her head. "Only to respond. And I will report to you any message I receive and I will not respond without your permission."

Simus nodded. "I thank you for these truths, Snowfall." He returned the piece of silk.

"And I thank you for yours, Warlord." She rose and returned his token to its place on the tree-stump. She strapped on her knives as he reached for his own weapons.

"You're in for more challenges," Simus warned. "I will not reject good candidates."

"I do not expect you to," Snowfall said, her hands filled with piled dishes. "This will mean nothing if I do not earn my place. I will clear this, and raise my banner again."

"And mine as well," Simus said as he strode toward the tent

flap, and began to untie the bells. "But Snowfall, prepare for a large meal tonight, and get extra servers."

"Warlord?"

Simus grinned at her. "I am calling a senel this night, and I am certain there will be a crowd, for I intend to invite all who wish to hear. I am sure the debate will be hot and thirsty work."

She nodded and turned away, taking the dishes with her. Simus paused, watching the sway of her hips.

He was glad he hadn't stopped taking his foalsbane.

CHAPTER TWENTY

Simus announced the senel for sunset and had Yers send messengers through the camp, so that all of his people knew of the meeting. From his Second through to all his Tenths, he made it known that they were invited. And he sent messengers running to Essa and every Warlord candidate that he knew, and even some who were only names to him. If Wild Winds thought that 'truths told were better than secrets kept,' he could only agree.

The afternoon hours passed slowly, for he isolated himself within his tent, re-wrapping the hilts of all of his weapons, listening to the sounds of battle outside the tent as Snowfall and Yers met their challengers and saw to their duties.

At one point, Elois entered his tent, looking rested and ready for combat. She knelt before him, offered her sword, and then surprised him with a question. "Warlord, I ask permission to contest for Token-bearer."

"Granted," Simus said, then grinned. "Snowfall seems to be in fine fettle today, though. So far she has taken down all comers."

Elois didn't return his smile. "She's good," she agreed. "But I am better. However, I will challenge in my own time."

Simus shrugged as she slipped out of the tent. The timing was her choice, so long as it was before the Trials ended.

He'd half hoped for a challenge to himself, for nothing would break the boredom like a good fight, but none were forthcoming. Given that his last challenge had been to the death, it might have discouraged the faint of heart. So Simus sighed and sat within his tent, and brooded.

Majestically, of course.

At one point, he'd run out of weapons to re-wrap, and emerged to take a few swords off his weapons rack. Yers was nowhere to be seen, but Snowfall was seated under the challenge pole, twisting her silk between her fingers.

"It's quiet," he said to her.

There was an odd glint in her eye as she tilted her head toward the Heart.

Simus frowned, but didn't react otherwise. He stepped to the weapons rack, picked up a sword, and pretended to test the blade as he looked out over the grasses.

A shiver of movement gave them away, the grass moving with no wind. Another shiver and he caught a glimpse of a rump held a bit too high and the sound of a frantic whisper. Children, it had to be, crawling and hiding to sneak a peek. Maybe to even get to see a challenge.

Simus dropped his gaze, and stifled a laugh. It wouldn't do to mock them. Still, they were not supposed to be anywhere near the challenge circle.

Snowfall stood and stretched, yawning as she turned and faced the area where the watchers were hidden. She pulled her knives, glared at the area and said a sharp, "Hey."

Shrieks erupted as six children leaped high and ran off with their wooden weapons, screeching in their excitement. Pive was one of them; Simus was glad to see that she had acquired a new wooden sword and dagger.

The children disappeared behind his tent, leaving silence in their wake. Snowfall turned back, her eyes sparkling, and the corner of her mouth slightly curved up.

"Is that a smile?" Simus asked.

The curve disappeared in an instant. "Warrior-priestesses do not smile." Snowfall resumed her seat. "Everyone knows that."

Simus disappeared back to his own tent, and focused on his work. But he couldn't help but wonder what she'd look like if she smiled.

* * * * *

As the sun set Simus stepped outside to lower his banner. There stood a straight-faced, victorious Snowfall and a sullen Yers. Both had survived the challenges of that day. Simus made no comment as the banners were lowered.

Yers strode off toward his tent as soon as the banners were down for the night. Snowfall darted into the tent the instant her banner was down, to start issuing instructions and commands to her servers just like a Warlord. The sides of the tent were rolled up, and lamps and braziers lit and stoked, for company was sure to arrive.

Haya was the first. "She will murder you in your sleep," she announced, her hands on her hips.

"If she does, I don't deserve to be Warlord," Simus said calmly.

Haya turned her glare on Snowfall, who waited with water for washing. "I know of you," she growled.

"I stood at Wild Winds's side. I stood hostage to the Guardians of the Sacrifice."

"So they said," Haya sniffed, refusing to give an inch. Simus gestured her and Seo to pads he had set off to the side. They were his guests, but not part of the senel, and Simus hoped Haya could keep her opinions to herself this night.

He spent some time welcoming his leaders and seeing them seated, as well as his guests. Yers returned and Simus gestured him to a place of honor on his right with his current Third, Tsor, on his left. He'd offered to seat Joden on the platform as well, but Joden had declined.

His people mixed in with the Warlord candidates, since by tradition they had no better rank than any other until they were confirmed by the Council. Essa, on the other hand, was Eldest Elder, and he was given pride of place in front. Simus was interested to note that Quartis sat with him as opposed to Haya, but thought no more of it.

Once the crowd was seated, fairly spilling out of the tent, those that would serve went through the ranks, offering water and cloths for hand-washing. The tent quieted as all gave thanks. Essa seemed to be scanning the crowd, as if searching for someone. Simus frowned, wondering, but he'd no time to consider further.

When the last had been seen to, Simus rose. "I welcome you all to my tent. My current Token-bearer, Snowfall, has prepared kavage and food for all this night. Let us eat before we talk. Then I will open the senel to speak of events, hear your views, and announce my decisions."

Snowfall emerged from the back, leading servers bearing wooden platters filled with roasted venison, flatbread, and ogdan roots. The smell of the meat set Simus's mouth to watering as he waited for his share.

"I do not hold your token, Simus." Reht, one of the Warlord candidates, rose from the back. "But as this meeting involves your

Token-bearer's presence in this camp, she should not be here."

"I take no offense to your truths," Simus said with a smile. "She has earned her place and I will hold her to her duties." He took his platter from Snowfall's hands. "If you fear the food, do not eat. More for us."

Ultie scooped up his meat with a piece of bread and started eating.

Simus smiled widely and followed his lead. The meat was hot, and its juices ran into the bread as he ate, and drizzled on the roots.

Some paused for a moment, but most started eating. Hard to ignore roast venison; harder still to waste food. It was too difficult to get, and one never knew what the next day's hunt would bring. Simus finished his platter and took more. Might as well have a full stomach before he took on the storm to follow.

The meal went quickly, and there was fresh kavage all around while Snowfall and those serving collected platters and bowls.

And as the last mug of kavage was re-filled, Zioa marched forward, grabbed Simus's token, and shook it in his face. "So all your talk of hating the warrior-priests was a lie?"

* * * * *

Well, I think that went well," Simus announced, surveying the empty tent, littered with gurtle pads and mugs.

Snowfall and Joden stood and stared at him.

"As well as could be expected," Simus amended.

"Except for the shouting," Joden said.

"Well, there is that," Simus agreed.

"Except for the fact that everyone seems to think that you have brought a viper into your tent," Snowfall said. "Or that I have betrayed all that the Plains stands for by giving you my oaths."

"Well, that is true," Simus said cheerfully. "Did you see Wyrik of the Boar's face? I thought he'd have a brain storm. Too bad he didn't." Simus frowned. "I wonder if that healer can treat those?"

"Simus." Joden rubbed his face with one hand. "I don't think you are taking this seriously."

"You thought this would be easy?" Simus grew serious. "You thought everyone would smile and nod and welcome this?" He shook his head. "No. As Keir has said, we are weaving new patterns." Simus flashed them a grin. "Patterns he doesn't even know of yet. This will not be easy. My token will most likely wear out before I am even recognized as Warlord." He looked at the poor, bedraggled thing, its feathers slightly worse for wear.

"I need more kavage," Joden said, taking up his mug.

Snowfall nodded, and slipped from the area.

"What other choice is there?" Simus lowered his voice. "Keir's plan was to break their hold on our people, and then unite the Plains under a WarKing to find a better way." He gestured toward where they could hear the clatter of kavage pots. "They have broken themselves. So now it seems to me, my choice is to ignore the outstreched hand, or reach out and take it."

"I think that Keir would reject that hand," Joden said carefully.

Simus slowly nodded his head in agreement. "You are probably right." He looked at his friend. "Do you think I am wrong?" he asked, almost dreading the answer.

Joden drew in a heavy sigh. "Maybe," he said, then countered with, "What do you think Keir will do when Eloix arrives with your message?"

"I do not know," Simus said.

"Have you thought of sending another in light of all this?" Joden asked.

Snowfall slipped back into the room, fresh kavage in her hands.

"Yes," Simus snorted. "But I need people I trust near me, even when they tell me I am wrong. And yes, I thought of sending you back, but the need for you is here, not there." He narrowed his eyes at Joden. "Were you avoiding Essa?"

"No," Joden said shortly.

"Have you talked to Essa?"

"No," Joden said, his voice still clipped.

"Ah," Simus said. At the look on Joden's face, he decided not to press the issue.

Snowfall started to straighten the gurtle pads, moving around the area with a gentle grace.

"Enough serious thoughts," Simus said, and laughed. "Come," he said, addressing them both with one expansive gesture. "There is dancing tonight. We will chant and dance patterns and exhaust the opposition. The morning will bring what the morning will bring. For tonight, we dance."

Snowfall looked at him as if surprised he would include her. She shook her head. "Warrior-priestesses do not dance."

There was a hidden sadness in her words that made Simus stop and think. Warrior-priests were isolated from warriors, maintaining their own camps. But not to dance? Another mystery in the depths of her eyes, and he wanted answers.

"You must," Simus insisted, putting a hand to his chest with a flourish. "You are my Token-bearer; you must come. If only to watch me."

"To watch," she agreed. "Just let me check on the servers in the back, that all is done properly."

"And then perhaps tonight, we could share our bodies," Simus suggested as she walked away. "If only to celebrate."

Snowfall paused, and looked at him with her calm, grey eyes. "No," she said.

Joden choked on his kavage.

"What?" Simus said.

"No," she repeated calmly. "It would complicate things."

And with that, she disappeared into the back.

Simus stood there, staring after her in astonishment.

Joden was coughing, talking and clearing his throat at the same time. "Thought you didn't share during the Trials?" he choked and laughed. "Thought it made things complicated?"

"Show more respect for your Warlord," Simus growled.

Joden just kept laughing.

CHAPTER TWENTY-ONE

"You understand, I do not wish to trouble the Warprize?" Amyu asked anxiously, embarrassed to be seeking reassurance.

The stone walls of Master Healer Eln's chamber were covered in shelves, filled with bottles and jars, more than she'd ever seen in a Xyian building. She stood by the large wooden table, glancing around. It made her feel even more nervous, all these things surrounding her. She felt hemmed in. Trapped.

Master Healer Eln sat on his stool by the table, his long grey hair braided down his back. He had a calm presence, a very quiet man. The braid was unusual in a city-dweller; for Amyu, it made him seem safer somehow. Like one of the Plains.

"It's just that she, the Warprize," Amyu hurried on, "she has other worries right now, with her kingdom, and her new babes."

Master Healer Eln nodded, studying her. "You want to talk, as if under the bells, correct?" he asked gently. "That's why you came here to see me?"

"You'd think they were the first babes ever born." Amyu reached up and pushed her brown hair behind her ear. "They are good babies, mind you, but—"

Eln snorted with amusement. "But all new mothers are like

that, even Master Healers." He paused. "But that is not why you are here."

Amyu dropped her gaze, glad that she'd made the journey from the Castle to his shop in the City. Far more private then any tent, with stone walls and closed doors. "The Warprize has said that Xyian Healers hold words told them to their hearts, yes? Like the Singers?"

"I will tell no one what you confide in me," Eln said softly. "And that is the second time you have asked me that, Amyu. What troubles you so?" The concern in his voice was clear, and reassuring. She looked up when he continued. "Does it have to do..." His glance fell on her left arm.

So he knew about her lack of tattoos, of her barrenness. Knew that to her own people she was still a child and a failure. Yet still he treated her as an adult, as a person of worth. Xyians were odd that way. It felt so strange, and yet, so wonderful at the same time.

"No, it's not about that," she said softly, and cursed the tears that welled up in her eyes when he just nodded, and didn't press the matter. "It is—" Amyu tried to find the words. "Since the night of the pillar of light, I have—"

Raised voices cut through the quiet and the door to Eln's chamber burst open. Amyu spun, her weapons in her hand.

"Wounded, Master," an apprentice explained, holding the door open. Into the chamber rushed a group of four in the uniform of the City Guard, all talking at once, carrying an unconscious warrior face down between them. "Master Healer," one of them grunted under his load. "Wyvern sting."

"Here, quickly." Eln was up, moving his stool to the side, gesturing toward the table. "Where's the wound?"

"Lower back," one said.

Amyu pressed herself against the shelves to make way. Jars and bottles rattled behind her. Eln called for his apprentices and the other healers.

The unconscious warrior's lower back was a mess of torn leather armor, blood, dirt, grass, and sizzling flesh. Amyu wrinkled her nose as the stink of the poison rose from the wound. It smelled as rank as ehat musk.

"Two of the wyverns came swooping down as they rode out of the woods," a guard explained. "Poor bastards didn't know to watch for them. The others with her didn't make it."

The guards settled the warrior onto the table facedown, as gently as they could. "She's breathing still," one said. "We think maybe she's from the Plains."

Amyu sucked in a breath at that, and craned her neck to see the warrior's face. "Eloix," she said, recognizing the lax face. "She was with Simus of the Hawk."

"Send word to the Warlord immediately," Eln commanded, and one of the guards leaped to obey. "I need a few of you here," Eln said. "In case—"

"Aye," the oldest Guard said, nodding in understanding. "Best to be careful." He reached over, and removed Eloix's weapons from their sheaths.

Amyu slid toward the door, feeling in the way, but Eln stopped her with a look. "Stay." He jerked his head into the corner near Eloix's head. "You speak Firelander, and we don't."

Amyu obeyed, darting into the corner, and trying to make herself small as Eln called for supplies. "Wine," he ordered his apprentices. "Water hasn't worked before this. I need this armor cut away. Be careful not to let any of that venom get on you."

There was another rattling of jars and bottles as they all moved about the room, getting into position. An older apprentice with leather gloves stepped forward, and started to peel back the shreds as another cut with a large knife. The sight of the wound got no better as the leathers and padding were removed.

The city guards were stoic, but they averted their eyes. One was having a hard time, and started to retch.

"Go," Eln commanded and the guard released his hold on Eloix's arm and darted for the door. "Amyu, take his place," Eln instructed, and she did so. But even as she gripped Eloix's wrist and shoulder Amyu couldn't help but stare in revulsion and fascination. The bloody flesh bubbled and frothed before her eyes. She'd heard that wyvern poison ate away the flesh it touched, but she'd never seen it. She glanced at Eloix's lax face, glad that the warrior wasn't feeling the pain of the wound.

But that ended at the first touch of wine on her back. Eloix heaved up, half off the table, her hands clutching the edge with a white-knuckled grip. Her pained howl filled the room as hands pressed her back down.

"Skies above," she panted, her eyes wild and unseeing as she was pressed back down on the table. "What has happened?"

"You were attacked," Amyu spoke in the language of the Plains. "Injured by a flying beast."

Eloix was gasping, taking in air, her eyes wild and dazed. Amyu kept talking, repeating the words as Eln worked furiously.

"Wine isn't working, Master," one of the apprentices said.

"We will try milk next, but only to a small area," Eln instructed. "Keep trying the wine."

Amyu looked down to see sanity return to Eloix's eyes. "You," she struggled to speak. "Child."

"Yes." Amyu set aside the all too familiar pain of rejection.

"We have sent for the Warlord," she said.

"We will give her something for the pain," Eln said. "Tell her to drink it."

Eloix blinked up at her. Her sweat-soaked hair was plastered to her skull. "What kind of wound is this?" she gasped out.

Amyu took the small bottle from the apprentice. "A sting, from a creature they call a wyvern."

Eloix's breathing came in harsh pants. "How bad?"

"Bad," Amyu said. "This potion he offers you will take away the pain."

"And my wits?" Eloix asked, taking the bottle.

"Probably," Amyu said honestly.

"No, then." Eloix took a breath, her face contorted, her voice shaking with strain. "These city-dwellers are soft. We are of the Plains. Give me the truth, child."

"As you request," Amyu said in their language as Eln and his people worked around her and Eloix. "It is said that the poison of the beast eats the flesh. The Warprize has told me that they have not found a way to heal it."

"He can't cure it?" Eloix drew in air between clenched teeth.

"The cure has been to cut off the struck limb." Amyu felt her own voice quake. "But you were struck in the back."

Eloix panted and rested her forehead on the rough wood of the table. "Is there an adult of the Plains near that I can give my message?"

She was so used to being dismissed as a child, Amyu wasn't even surprised. "Eln sent word to the Castle, but there may not be enough time." She tightened her grip on Eloix's sweaty arm. "I swear that I will deliver the words you speak, and I will see that your rites are done properly, by a warrior of the Plains."

Eln swore under his breath, and Amyu glanced over in time to see the despair on his face. He caught her looking, and scowled. "Have her drink," he ordered.

"She will not," Amyu said in Xyian. "She has messages to deliver."

"She will when it gets bad enough." Eln turned back to his work.

Eloix took the bottle, and gripped it tightly. "He forgets," she snorted. "I speak Xyian."

"If I try to grant you mercy, they will try to stop me," Amyu said. "It is their way." She loosened her hold on Eloix's wrists for a moment. "There is a dagger on my belt."

"When I have given you Simus's words," Eloix said through clenched teeth. She coughed wetly, and spit. There were flecks of blood on her lips as she started to speak. "I hold you to your oath, child. Listen well. On the morning of the night of the pillar of fire," she began, panting between words. "The warrior-priests drove us from the Heart…"

Amyu listened carefully, as Eloix recited Simus's message to Keir. She focused on those painful words, ignoring the sounds around her. Of sizzling flesh, and frustrated healers.

Toward the end of her message, Eloix let out a surprised gasp. "The pain. I can't feel—"

Eln lifted his head, his eyes so stark and so old. The healers around him all paused in their efforts, moving back. The guards paused, confused.

"I can't feel my legs," Eloix finished in Xyian.

"Yes." Eln's voice was little more than a croak. "It's eaten through—" He swallowed hard. "Are you in pain?"

"It's harder to breathe," Eloix said, more cough than voice.

"It's working toward the lungs." Eln sounded harder now. "If you understand me, know that I am not stupid. I would ask, before you—" He stopped, his jaw working.

"Snows," Amyu said. "We say she is going to the snows."

"I know," Eln snapped and Amyu almost stepped back at the rage in his voice. The apprentices flinched, glancing at one another.

"Clear the room," Eln commanded, and the guards and apprentices bowed their heads and left, some murmuring soft prayers.

"Amyu stays," Eloix demanded, grabbing her wrist.

"I know what she will do," Eln repeated, his voice filled with sorrow. "I would ask that she let me try one more thing on the wound, before—"

"Yes," Eloix said, coughing. "Try what you will."

Eln didn't hesitate. He reached for a large basket on a top shelf and pulled out a handful of bloodmoss. Amyu watched as he took the plant and placed it on the edge of the wound, where the poison still glistened.

The pale yellow leaves curled, turned brown, and crumbled into dust. Eln stared at it, and then closed his eyes.

"He is finished," Amyu whispered.

"The fire warmed me," Eloix choked out the beginning of the ritual. "I thank the elements."

Amyu released her hold, pulled her dagger, and placed it in Eloix's hand. Eloix gripped it tightly, her fingers bone-white. Eln had stepped back from the table, his face buried in his hands.

"The earth supported me. I thank the elements," Eloix said, but started coughing, bringing up blood. She struggled to continue.

Amyu knelt by the table, shaking inside, but striving to be the warrior Eloix needed her to be. "The waters sustained you," Amyu picked up where Eloix had left off. "We thank the elements."

Eloix's eyes were wide, focused on Amyu, but unseeing. She nodded as she choked, and placed the tip of the dagger at her throat.

"The air filled you. We thank the elements." Amyu's voice shook despite her best efforts. "Go now, warrior. Beyond the snows and to the stars."

Eloix thrust the dagger home.

And for long moments both Amyu and Eln stood silent as the last breath of life left her body.

Eln finally moved, striding over to jerk open the door. The guards outside came to attention.

"Amyu carries a message for the Queen and Warlord," Eln's voice rasped. "See her to the Castle."

CHAPTER TWENTY-TWO

The city guards hustled Amyu to the Castle, hugging the sides of the buildings, keeping a wary eye for the flying beasts as they trotted along deserted streets.

The Castle was a brooding presence, guards with bows and crossbows at every window. The Palace guards rushed her through the gardens and the kitchens, avoiding the courtyard. The monster that had attacked the day before was still laying there, its carcass being rendered for removal.

"Nobody's tried to eat it yet," one of the guards muttered. "But there's interest in the leather and other bits."

Amyu nodded silently.

"The Queen's in the Council Chamber, with the Overlord. The Seneschal's there, with the others."

Amyu nodded again. Up the stairs then and through the corridors. She knew the way, but the guards didn't leave her side. Amyu didn't complain; everyone was jittery and on edge.

So was she, if she were honest.

As they climbed the stairs, Amyu realized that Eloix's blood was still on her hands and leathers. Amyu shuddered, trying to conceal her fear. She'd never been in battle, never killed another, never watched a warrior bleed out before her eyes.

Maybe being a child was not such a bad thing.

But before she could scold herself for such a cowardly thought, they reached the double doors of the Council room, and heard voices raised inside. Amyu paused, drawing a steadying breath, and then opened the doors, hoping to slip in quietly.

The large stone room was darker than normal, with wooden shutters drawn closed over the windows. Candles flickered as her entrance stirred the air, causing the tapestry behind them to rustle against the wall. The airion on the tapestry almost seemed alive as the cloth moved. A blend of horse and eagle, its wings flaring in the candlelight.

All of the chairs that normally surrounded the large Council table had been pushed back. The table was covered with large swaths of paper. 'Maps,' as Xyians called them. Many people were crowded about the table, but Amyu focused on the Warprize and her Warlord.

The Warprize was the first to speak, her fey blue eyes wide. "Amyu, is that blood?"

The talk in the room went silent, and every eye focused on her.

Amyu flushed, and looked down at the blood smeared on her leathers. "It is not mine," she assured her. "I was at Master Healer Eln's when a messenger from the Plains was brought in with a wyvern-sting." Hopefully, none would question as to why she had been there. Amyu lifted her gaze, only to be caught by the Warlord's piercing blue eyes as he stared at her.

"Report," he commanded.

Faces grew grimmer all around as she explained Eloix's injury. They'd known the warrior and they knew what happened to those wyvern-stung. But the Warprize held out hope. "Was Eln able to counter the poison?" Lara asked. Her face fell when

Amyu shook her head.

"Were Eloix's rites seen to?" Wilsa asked, her face a mask of pain. She stood next to Lord Marshall Warren.

"I aided her to thank the elements before she went to the snows. I did not presume to do more." Amyu kept her voice steady, trying to hide her trembling. "Eln said he would keep her body there, until a warrior could perform the rites."

"And her words?" Keir demanded.

"I have them," Amyu said. She took a deep steadying breath and began, repeating Eloix word for word, translating it into Xyian as she went.

It was only when the Warprize went pale that Amyu realized she was reciting it as Eloix had spoken it, with every gasp and moan as she'd fought past her pain to deliver her charge. Amyu looked away, closed her eyes, and continued, concentrating on the recitation. But she made sure to stop before the death ritual began.

"That was all," Amyu finished. "Other than her death."

"Skies above," Keir said, his voice a bare whisper. "You did well, Amyu."

"You did," Wilsa said. "I will see to Eloix's rites myself."

Lord Marshal Warren was standing next to the Warlord, and he frowned at her. "Are you sure that was all?" he asked. "That you got it right?"

Amyu stiffened at his words, but surprisingly Wilsa came to her defense. "Warren, you city-dweller. Remember our memories."

"Ah, lass, I meant no insult," Warren said ruefully. "I ask pardon."

"What does it mean?" the Warprize asked.

Keir stood, his arms crossed, staring at the top of the table, brooding. "I don't know," he said slowly. "Simus is facing those *bragnects* alone."

"Not alone," Atira of the Bear spoke up from where she stood next to Heath of Xy, Seneschal of the Castle. "Simus has his people, including Yers. And more will flock to his side."

"Should you go to him? Go to the Plains?" Lara asked quietly, and the pain and the strength in her voice was clear.

Keir shook his head, and wrapped an arm around her, pulling her to his side. "We are under attack by these monsters," he said. "I must see to the safety of Xy before we discuss leaving. Let us deal with the troubles before us."

"Here is what we know," Lord Marshal Warren said, spreading out a large map of the City and the fields beyond.

The others drew closer to the table, but Amyu faded back to stand against the wall. She debated leaving, her message delivered, but she didn't want to disturb their work. She'd wait, and slip out at the first chance. The solid stone felt good on her back, and its coolness seemed to leech out her tremors.

"The first attack was just yesterday, on the day of Heath and Atira's wedding," Warren continued.

"Bonding," said Atira, giving Heath a fond glance.

"That was the first we saw of the beasts. Heath managed to kill it with one of the Plains lances," Warren said. "We lost one man to the sting that day. As far as we could tell, it came down from the mountains, and its target was the horses in the courtyard."

"The stinger," Lara said. "That was given to the healers, correct?"

"Yes," Warren said. "They're still clearing the carcass. Hard to believe the size of its claws, and its horns."

"It's a fearsome creature," Wilsa agreed. "But we know they can die. Since the first attack, dozens of the creatures have been sighted, all hunting in the fields beyond the walls. Since that first attack, we've kept the people and the animals in the City under cover."

Warren spread out a new map, a larger representation of Xy. "It seems that the creatures roost in the mountains. Once we moved the herds down into the trees, there were fewer attacks. But they still go after horses and cattle."

"And any riders on the roads," Keir said grimly.

"Lances work best to kill them," Heath said. "Crossbows as well."

Detros, head of the Palace Guard, nodded his head. "I've men trained with both on the walls and on watch. They'll not take us by surprise again."

"How far have they spread through the land?" Keir asked.

"I don't know," Warren said. "But the gods help anyone caught out in the open with no warning."

"We've taken down all the flags and pennants from the Castle walls," Detros said. "They're attracted to movement."

"The Trials have started," Keir said. "The challenge banners will have been raised."

"The Plains…" Xylara whispered.

Amyu's stomach clenched at the idea of the monsters attacking her home.

"Before his death, Father sent crossbows and bolts in the supply caravan," Heath said firmly. "And obsidian for making lances."

"And we don't yet know if the wyverns have attacked the Plains," Atira said. "It may be they are only here in the mountains."

Truth, to be sure, but Lara didn't seem any more reassured then Amyu was. The warriors would have no warning, and the poison in their stings—

"The Plains will fight." Keir's voice was a rumble. "And they will kill the beasts. Remember, on the Plains, one can see open sky for miles around." He shared a look with the Warprize who smiled, but did not look any more confident.

The door behind Amyu opened and Archbishop Iian stumbled through, his arms filled with scrolls and books, followed by two acolytes, their arms just as burdened.

"I may have found something," Iian said as he tried to thrust part of his load into Amyu's arms. She took a step back, and he stopped and blinked at her, noticing the blood.

"Are you hurt?" he asked urgently.

"I'm fine." Amyu suppressed a smile. The archbishop had come into his office suddenly, and was not much older than she was. But he handled his duties with skill and dignity. He'd been the one to recognize the wyverns and give them a name.

"What have you found?" Keir leaned forward eagerly.

The archbishop recalled himself, and deposited his books on the table. Iian pulled out one that looked the oldest to Amyu's eyes and opened it to a place marked with a ribbon.

"An ancient reference, with illustrations, if you can believe." Iian let the book fall open.

Amyu gasped at the vibrant colors. Both pages were covered in a picture of what had to be the Castle and the city of Water's Fall. In the air, wyverns flew, and were being attacked from the air by airions, and from below by some sort of contraptions.

Everyone leaned in to look.

"I know it seems fantastical," Iian said. "With the airions in the skies. But look at—"

"Are those riders on their backs?" Amyu breathed, caught by the image of people riding the airions. A wave of longing swept through her. "Is that even possible?"

"There are stories," Lara said. She chuckled. "But they are old tales of fey times. Kalisa, in the marketplace, claims her ancestors rode them."

"I care not for fantasies," Keir said as he drew the book closer. "But those crossbows on the towers—"

"They are called ballistas," Iian said, pulling out another scroll. "And here is a reference to their manufacture."

"Something like that, even if we could learn the way of it, would take time," Heath protested.

"And here—" Iian drew out yet another scroll, "—is a reference to where the parts were stored when they were disassembled after the creatures were banished."

"Stored?" Heath asked. "Where?"

"Banished?" Lara asked. "How?"

"In the old passages into the mountain. As to the banishment, I don't know," Iian admitted. "Perhaps with more time to research—"

"Those old passages are a maze," Heath said. "But there are storage places here and there. Whether the parts remain is another story. In the meantime—"

The door opened, letting in a fresh breeze that set the candles dancing and the tapestry moving against the wall. "Warlord," a guard said tersely, clearly struggling with his composure. "Five more of the fell creatures are overhead."

The warriors all headed for the door, orderly, but wasting no time.

"Keep looking," Keir said to Iian. "The past may yet aid us in this fight."

"I will," Iian promised.

"We could still send a messenger to the Plains," Lara said hurriedly. "Get word to Simus."

"I can spare no warriors," Keir said firmly.

"Amyu could go," Lara insisted.

Amyu flushed, and looked down.

"No, Lara," Keir said, but his eyes were not unkind. "Aside from Amyu's status, I will risk no one until we have contained this threat."

With that, he was gone with the others.

"Amyu," Lara sighed. "I—"

"I will clean up," Amyu said. "Before I return to my duties."

"That would be best," Lara said with a smile, and followed the others out of the room.

The door closed behind her, and with the drafts gone, the tapestry settled against the wall. Although the airion's eyes caught Amyu's eye, for they still seemed to gleam in the light.

What would it be like, to ride such a thing?

Iian was gathering up his scrolls and books. "I've more reading to do," he said, sounding pleased.

"I would help you with those," Amyu offered.

"I thank you, but—" Iian gestured at her leathers and wrinkled his nose.

"Ah." Amyu grimaced and nodded.

Iian returned her nod amiably, as he rolled and stacked his scrolls carefully. "Amyu, why didn't the Warlord send you as a messenger?"

Amyu's throat closed, but his question was an honest one. He was Xyian, he'd have no way of knowing. "It would not serve," she replied. "To my people, I am a child who will never go through the Rite of Ascension. I should have gone to the snows long ago for my failure to produce warriors for the Tribe. In their eyes, I am a failure."

"Oh. I see." Iian studied her, no judgment in his gaze, just a natural curiosity. Then, like a wise Singer of the Plains, his gaze sharpened, and his eyes bored into hers. "And in your eyes, Amyu? In your own eyes, what are you?"

She found she had no answer.

CHAPTER TWENTY-THREE

Antas of the Boar felt no need for the usual courtesy. He just threw back the tent flap and stepped in to Hail Storm's tent without so much as a greeting.

"Ugh." Antas curled his lip at the stench. He stared at the mound of bedding before him. "You stink like a rotting carcass."

The tent reeked of stale, sick sweat and piss. Hail Storm lay on his pallet of gurtle pads, covered in blankets and furs. At least Antas thought it was Hail Storm. As he'd been told, the man's ritual tattoos were gone.

Hail Storm turned his face toward Antas, eyes dull and glazed. There was a sheen of sweat on his forehead that glistened as he blinked against the light.

"So." As much as it disgusted him, Antas stepped farther in and let the tent flap close behind him. "I return to my camp, expecting to find a powerful Eldest Elder of the Warrior- priests, his followers with him, rejoicing in the Sacrifice and ready to join with my warriors."

Hail Storm closed his eyes and turned his face away.

Antas crouched by his pallet. "Instead, I am told strange tales about that pillar of light and the deaths of all of the warrior-priests. Except you, who crawled into my camp more dead than alive and demanded succor."

"Not all." Hail Storm's voice was a rasp. "Wild Winds and his followers live."

"Even better," Antas snorted. "You could not even kill that sickly old man? What of your plans, Hail Storm? What of your magic?"

"I still have power," Hail Storm turned his head back and snarled.

"And what of this?" Antas waved his hand over the mound of blankets.

"It is nothing," Hail Storm said. "A minor wound."

Antas reached out and yanked back the blankets.

Hail Storm's arm was swollen to twice its normal size, the skin purple and bloated. White puss oozed from the wounds, and red streaks traced vivid paths up toward his shoulder.

"Nothing?" Antas said grimly. "I don't wonder at the smell, now. You look like a bloated, dead gurtle." He paused, considering the man. "Why do you not heal yourself?"

"My powers are strong, but they do not lend themselves to healing," Hail Storm admitted stiffly.

"Anyone else, and I'd grant mercy without asking," Antas said.

Hail Storm fixed him with a glare, and Antas saw strength flood into those dark eyes. A quick move, and Hail Storm flourished a dagger in his good hand. "Do not think it," he growled.

"As you wish, Eldest Elder." Antas rose to his feet. "I will leave you to your suffering."

The dagger disappeared under the blanket. "We had a plan, you and I," Hail Storm said. "You should follow through with it."

"Aye, true enough," Antas said. "I planned to go to the Heart, set up camp and join the Trials." He curled his lip at the thought.

"But that was with the support of the warrior-priests with you as Eldest Elder. Now—"

"I am Eldest Elder," Hail Storm rasped.

Antas looked down at the sickly man before him. "You just said that Wild Winds lives."

"I am Eldest Elder," Hail Storm repeated, his eyes glazed, the sweat pouring off him. "Attack the Heart."

Antas gave the man an astonished look. "Attack the Heart? Do you think me a fool?"

"You ignore my advice at your peril."

"I will listen to your advice if you live." Antas spun on his heel, and strode out of the tent, grateful for the fresh air.

He swept the stench away from his nose with a deep breath of clean air.

Veritt, his Second, and Leda, his Third, were waiting for him, a polite distance away. Antas walked toward them shaking his head. "Come," he said. "I've a need for kavage after that."

They fell in beside him. "You saw?" Leda said.

"I did," Antas growled. "And I think it's likely he will die of that wound. Any other warrior, and I'd grant him mercy. But we need him."

Leda nodded. "I'll assign some warriors from punishment detail to care for him. At the very least they can see him cleaned and fed."

"See if any of the theas who have joined us have any ideas how to help him," Antas said.

"They have no more healing skill than we do," Veritt pointed out.

"No, but they deal with the cuts, scrapes, and bruises of children all through the day," Antas said. "It's worth trying." He paused. "But do not let them know of Reness. I am not sure their support would last if they knew we held her."

"I will see to it," Leda said.

"How bad is her leg?" Antas kept his voice low as they walked through the camp.

"Bad." Leda shook her head. "She fought like she was enraged. We tried to tend it, based on the tales told of the Warprize. But those are twice-told tales and we have no skill."

"How did this happen?" Antas said, feeling his anger rise. All of his careful plans seemed to be unraveling. "She was to be guarded at all times, controlled by the warrior-priests."

"She was," Leda said calmly. "But the warrior-priests collapsed when the pillar of light rose in the night. In the confusion, she took her opportunity." Leda shrugged. "But for the warriors that spotted her fleeing, she'd have succeeded."

"A fine thing." Antas rubbed his hand over his face. "I go to seek out theas and return to find my prisoner wounded in an escape attempt, my all-so-powerful warrior-priest sweating in his bed, and all of his warrior-priests dead. And Hail Storm says 'attack the Heart.' Cursed fool—"

"Not all dead," Leda said. "According to Hail Storm."

"That's what he said. But can I trust it?" Antas asked.

"When he first crawled into camp, he babbled out a lot of information," Veritt said. "It felt like the truth, and his skin supports his tale. His tattoos are gone."

Antas grunted, continued on to his command tent, and gave the nod to one of the guards to open the flap. "Kavage," he called to Catha, his Token-bearer, and settled himself on his seat on the wooden platform.

Veritt and Leda settled beside him, and after the handwashing ritual, they ate in silence. Antas thought as he chewed, considering all the events as he washed down the meal with kavage.

He waited until the food was cleared, and bid Catha weave the bells in the flap and join the talk.

Catha settled beside him, the heat of her body a familiar comfort.

Antas broke the silence. "We must consider our options. Hail Storm still urges an attack."

"Hail Storm is a fool," Veritt said softly. "But his suggestion has some merit to it. The Heart is concentrating on challenges, not defense. We could strike hard and fast. Those candidates that support the old ways would come to our aid if we got word to them."

"You might even secure Essa for your purposes," Catha added quietly.

"Are we so certain of the support of the candidates?" Leda asked.

"Ietha for certain." Veritt held up a finger, ticking off the name. "Loula, Nires, they are all—"

"No." Antas took more kavage. "I cannot be sure of Nires of the Boar's position."

Catha nodded. "He outcast Iften, did he not?"

"He did," Leda confirmed. "And there are many other candidates who have not expressed support. Ultie being one of them. An attack may cause them to turn against us." She glanced at Antas. "Our truths are more effective than our swords."

"We need a Singer." Veritt looked into his kavage glumly.

"True." Antas frowned into his mug as well. "I had hoped that Joden of the Hawk would claim that place, but he betrayed us. Still, there are others who may be persuaded."

"So we wait?" Veritt asked.

Antas scowled. "I hate waiting," he said. "I am not good at it."

"We know," Catha said and gave him her soft smile. "Yet in its way, patience is as powerful a weapon as your sword."

"Fine. Yes, we wait." Antas took up his mug. "It is enough for now to build our strength. Although, I want far-ranging scouts sent out, to locate Wild Winds if possible. Especially if he has those with him who still wield power. They might yet be brought within our camp to serve our purpose."

Leda nodded.

"We've voices and eyes at the Heart," Veritt said. "They'll let us know the ways the winds are blowing. They will tell us when the Council tent is raised."

"When do we strike at Simus?" Leda asked.

"Perhaps we don't," Catha said.

Antas opened his mouth to protest, but Catha raised her gentle hand. "Our allies can strike at Simus and his allies. Shoot the horses out from under them while we wait to see how the Trials go."

"Then, when the Council tent is raised, we act." Antas nodded reluctantly. "The Elders must see reason." He raised an eyebrow at his warriors. "And if they do not, my patience will come to an end."

CHAPTER TWENTY-FOUR

Simus awoke to the first chirps of the grass birds. A slight breeze was playing with the sides of the tent, bringing with it the scent of promised rain. His camp was just starting to stir as the night watch prepared for dawn.

He stretched under the blankets, and grinned in delight. His camp. His army. Considering how this season has started, it was coming to a satisfactory close.

Provided of course, everything went according to plan.

His grin faded as he gave a groan at that thought. After all, he knew well the truth of, 'If you wish to hear the winds laugh, tell them your plans.'

There was a scratching at the flap to his sleeping area.

"Come," he said.

Snowfall entered, gracefully carrying a tray with kavage. "Good morning, Warlord."

She stood, holding the tray, in her leather trous and corselet. A sheen of rain covered the tattoos that capped her strong shoulders, and the droplets also gleamed in her hair. Her face was neutral.

"Morning." Simus sat up, feeling the bruising in his ribs all the more this morning. He groaned, throwing back the blankets and sitting cross-legged on his bed. He reached up and stretched.

Snowfall was giving him a critical look. "The bruising seems less," she said. "You should use more of that ointment."

Simus lowered his arms and gave her a bright, hopeful look. She'd declined to share before but this was a new day. "Perhaps you could rub it on for me?"

To Simus's disappointment, Snowfall didn't even blink. Didn't even raise one of those delicate eyebrows. "No. Here's kavage for now," she said calmly.

Simus admired the movement of her lovely hips as she knelt to place the tray next to him. She rose just as smoothly, displaying the long length of her legs. "I will have your meal ready shortly."

"Send word to Yers that I would hold a senel as soon as I have eaten," Simus said with a sigh. "Ask Joden to join us as well." He reached for the kavage. "Do not raise the challenge banners this morning."

Snowfall bowed her head. "As you wish, Warlord."

With that, she was gone.

Simus deflated slightly with another sigh, then reached for the pitcher. She hadn't seemed interested.

On the other hand, she hadn't seemed un-interested. Simus's grin returned. He'd take his victories where he may.

He stood, twisting and stretching, warming stiff muscles. It was odd, how comfortable her presence was within his tent. Snowfall was…restful. A quiet strength beside him.

She'd maintained his tent, showed in visitors, and met every challenge offered to her blades. Even Yers, as wary as he was, offered her respect. But those grey eyes revealed nothing in a face that was forever calm and serene.

Yet she also didn't let him get away with anything. She never laughed at Simus's asides or wild statements. Never rolled her eyes. Her face was always serene and cool.

It was annoying. Fascinating. Enticing.

He thought on that as he finished his kavage, and reached for his armor and weapons.

"Don't forget the ointment," Snowfall called from the main tent.

See? She cared. Simus grinned to himself, put down his padded tunic, and rummaged for the jar.

As he attended to his side, he thought on Snowfall. The mystery behind her eyes. It must take a great deal of work to control herself like that. To keep her face smooth and unresponsive, not cracking the slightest smile. A lot of control.

What would it take, he thought, to cause her to lose her mask? To see her smile, or laugh, or watch those eyes spark in rage. Or melt into pleasure at the touch of his hands?

A goal, Simus resolved as he strapped on his sword and dagger. Something to think on as he went through his day. Something to work on.

It was good to have goals.

* * * * *

It occurred to Snowfall that in one thing, Warlords and warrior-priests did not differ. At least, in the males.

She'd declined his offer of sharing with regret. He was a fine-looking man, well formed in all ways, and she had to suppress a certain curiosity as to his other…skills.

But there would be complications, with the other warriors if no one else. But also the magic. What if it flared as they shared their bodies? Her tattoos were already expressing some of her emotions. What if they responded in ways she couldn't control?

No, that was not worth the risk of satisfying her…curiosity. Even if his offer had heated her body. This was not the time or the place.

Still, her refusal had taken him back. That pleased her. Not that she would display that pleasure, one way or another.

What pleased her more was his acceptance after his initial shock. He accepted it. Oh, he pouted a bit, not that he would think of it as such. But still, she doubted few declined his offer of bedding as she had.

But while her Warlord's mood was a good one, it seemed the Plains were of a different opinion. The wind was cold and biting, setting the leather tent sides to moving back and forth. The damp crept into the corner of every tent and every bone in a warrior's body. No need to keep the challenge banners down; every warrior in camp not on duty was within a tent, seeing to tasks done well out of the rain and cold.

Snowfall sent out the messages as commanded while Simus ate.

She set the braziers burning in the command tent, and made the kavage strong and hot. She greeted his Second and Third with steaming mugs as they entered and shed their dripping cloaks. All of them accepted the mugs gratefully, even Yers. As others entered behind them, she greeted them as well.

And when all was in readiness, she ignored the stares and the side-ways glances, took up her Warlord's token, and waited for him to call the senel to order.

* * * * *

Simus was amused to see that Ouse and Lander were aiding Snowfall with the serving at the senel. Trust the young ones to try to be present when decisions were to be made.

Simus seated himself and then leaned over to Yers, seated to his left. "There's a few missing yet, I see."

Yers nodded, interrupting his sip of kavage. "It might take them a few minutes," he explained. "Sal wanted to make sure that the Xyian supplies were well covered against the damp. And that Xyian healer was having some trouble with a leak in what he calls a 'still tent'. Made quite the fuss."

"How is Healer Hanstau?" Simus asked. "I have not seen much of him the last few days."

"Because Haya claimed him," Joden spoke up, approaching to take a seat off to the side, mug in hand. "She's been having him help with the children, and demanding he explain his healing secrets to her." Joden sat down. "Which is fairly amusing, since his command of our language is not strong, and Haya speaks no Xyian. Cadr has been kept busy, trying to explain one to the other."

Simus chuckled, but looked at his friend with a careful eye. Something was off, something he'd not noticed before. He wasn't sure what was wrong, but something troubled Joden. Perhaps he'd approached Essa to become Singer? Simus caught Joden's eye, and raised an eyebrow.

Joden shrugged, and dropped his gaze to his kavage.

Well, whatever it was, it would have to wait until after the senel. The last of his staff had entered, and were doffing their cloaks. Simus caught Snowfall's eye and gave her the nod.

Snowfall waited until all were seated, then moved to stand before the wooden platform where Simus sat, and lifted his token high. "Rise and hail Simus of the Hawk, Warlord of the Tribes."

All the warriors rose, and heads were bowed.

Simus smiled at them all as Snowfall placed his token before him on the platform. "My thanks, warriors. Please be seated. I have called this senel to discuss our status and preparations and avoid having to stomp through the rain to ask the things I must know."

Laughter filled the tent, with nods of agreement all around.

"So let us start with our status. Yers, what say you?" Simus asked.

"The Tenths have organized well, and I am satisfied with their numbers and placement of warriors under their command," Yers began. "While recruitment has slowed, the numbers are more than we had planned."

Simus listened well as Yers spoke. He'd noted the slowing of new warriors pledging their swords over the last few days, but that was normal. Warriors were making their final choices. The Trials were fast approaching their end.

"Our supplies are good," Sal said. "The Xyian caravan filled any gaps. We'll use this day for making arrows and lances. We'll fill all the quivers we have, and stockpile more. We also found strips of bells and cymbals buried deep in one of the last packs. Whose idea was that?"

"Mine," Simus laughed. "For the dancing. If the rain clears, we'll make such a noise tonight as to set the other camps as jealous as the winds."

"In truth, Warlord, the army is ready," Yers said. "All waits on your confirmation."

"To the news then," Simus said with a nod. "How go the other challenges?"

"Osa and Ultie are firmly in place," Tsor told him.

"No surprise there," Simus said.

"Zioa was knocked out of the running by Wyrik," Tsor added.

"We might be able to recruit her," Yers said. "If we offered her a Tenth position."

"Once her temper cools," Sal said wryly.

A stir at the back of the tent, and Haya and Seo walked in. Snowfall greeted them, gesturing toward the front of the tent.

"What of Nires of the Boar?" Simus asked.

"Still a candidate for Warlord," Yers said firmly. "As are Ietha and Loual. I have been talking to Rhet, but she will not commit one way or the other." Yers shrugged. "I think she thinks that the issue need not be dealt with here, but in the Council held after the Season of War."

Haya and Seo wove their way through the group to seat themselves beside Joden.

"So Eldest Elder Essa may be close to the calling of the Council," Simus said.

"If one can be formed," Haya spoke up. She took a mug of kavage from Snowfall with a nod of thanks. Seo settled in beside her on a gurtle pad, and accepted his own mug.

"Elder Haya, Weaponsmaster Seo, welcome to the senel," Simus said. "I hear you are learning from Healer Hanstau."

"That man spoils children rotten. All soft and kind words over every scrape and cut," Haya grumbled. "Still, he has skills we do not have, and I would learn them." She rolled her eyes. "Would that he learned our language as quickly as the Warprize."

"I'd ask a question about that," Yers said. "Should we consider sending another messenger to Keir? Perhaps—"

Another commotion at the tent flap. Simus looked to see that Snowfall was talking to someone outside in low tones.

"Snowfall?" he called out.

Snowfall turned, and it seemed her eyes were just a bit wider than normal. "Warlord,

Eldest Elder Essa demands to speak to you."

CHAPTER TWENTY-FIVE

S imus gave a nod. He and his warriors rose to their feet as one. Snowfall pulled back the tent flap, and Essa swept in with his warrior escort. He threw back his black cloak to display silken trous and a tunic in vibrant hues of red and black. This was the Eldest Elder Singer Simus remembered of old; Essa appeared to have regained his confidence and balance. But Simus also noted the sword and dagger at his side, and that his escort was double the usual number. Quartis the Singer was in their midst.

Simus knelt and his warriors followed his lead. "We welcome you to my tent, Eldest Elder Singer," Simus said.

"You honor me," Essa said, his voice rich and strong. He walked forward, and four warriors followed him within. "Rise, please, all of you."

Simus rose, and vacated his seat, gesturing for Essa to sit in his place. He stepped down off the platform to join the others, and they all seated themselves before the Eldest Elder.

Essa settled himself on the seat, his escort arranged around him, and waved off kavage. "Simus of the Hawk, as candidate for Warlord, I bring you word that I have called for the Gathering of the Council at the Heart of the Plains. The Council tent will be raised over the Heart. On that day, present yourself and ten of your strongest to aid the Council in this matter."

Simus's heart swelled, and started beating faster. It was here, finally, finally here. "My thanks, Eldest Elder. My warriors and I will present ourselves as you require."

"Excellent," Essa said.

Simus bowed his head.

There was a rustling, and then Elder Haya rose to her feet. "Eldest Elder Essa, I would ask for your token," she said, her face wrinkled in a frown.

"Elder Thea Haya." Essa gave her a nod of his head. One of his warriors produced a leather strip adorned with copper wires and small bells that gleamed in the light. The warrior handed it to Haya with a bow.

"You hold my token," Essa said. "What truths would you interrupt me with?"

Simus exchanged a glance with Joden. That was not the tone one used to address an Elder.

Haya was not put off. She gave Essa a frown. "I do not understand how you can summon a Council—"

"As I do not understand the presence of your camp here during the Trials," Essa said smoothly.

Haya continued. "The Spring Council is for Warriors, Singers, and Warrior-Priests. Wild Winds is not here—"

"He will be," Essa said firmly.

"There is no Eldest Elder Warrior," Haya pointed out. "After the Sundering last Fall."

"There will be," Essa responded. "One will be selected."

"And last of my truths," Haya said, her tone defiant. "The Eldest Elder Thea always attends the Spring Council, the sole voice of the theas. Reness is the Eldest Elder Thea. And Reness is not here nor has she sent word of her intent."

"Then I would expect that you, as the only thea within the camp, to step into her place," Essa said, raising an eyebrow. "As is traditional and appropriate and necessary."

Haya's mouth closed with a snap.

Simus would have laughed at her expression, but he had better sense. Weaponsmaster Seo had no such restraint, chuckling out loud.

"I thank you for your truths, Elder Haya," Essa said. "If there is nothing further?"

Haya returned the token to the warrior, and sat down. Simus saw Seo poke her in the ribs and whisper something in her ear. Simus looked away, careful to control his own face.

Essa was not finished. "Tonight, if the rains clear, the drums will call all warriors to the Heart for the dancing. We shall gather as one before we divide into the armies of the Plains. Organize your watches accordingly."

"Heyla," Simus said, and clapped his hand on Yers's shoulder. Yers grinned, and all the warriors around them exchanged smiles and laughter. Soon, the Trials would be at an end. Essa held up a hand, and the warriors went silent. "This ends my words for now," he said. "But I would have further words with you, Simus of the Hawk. Under the bells."

"Of course," Simus said, and rose to his feet as he turned to face the group. "This senel is at an end," he said, and the warriors arose, talking amongst themselves. "Yers," Simus said, turning to his Second. "Stay and—"

"No," Essa said from behind him.

Yers's eyes widened. Simus went silent and looked back at the Eldest Elder.

"Clear the tent," Essa said calmly. "Of all except for your Token-bearer and yourself." Essa turned to look off to the side where Joden hovered, looking almost wary. "And you, Joden of the Hawk." Essa pointed to one of the gurtle pads directly in front of him. "Sit."

Joden obeyed and sat.

Yers gave Simus a worried look, but herded the other warriors out. Snowfall moved to close the flap, but Essa stopped her.

"My warriors will see to the bells. Sit." Essa looked up at Simus. "You too," he said.

Simus sat next to Joden, and Snowfall sat next to him. "This is my tent," Simus said mildly, keeping his anger in check.

"Truth," Essa said. He watched as his escort secured the tent flap, and wove bells into the ties. "But there are some truths that I wish to tell that are best not shared with all." He raised an eyebrow, and fixed Joden with an imperious look. "You have been avoiding me," he said.

Joden blinked and shook his head. "No, Eldest Elder. I was just waiting for the best time to—"

"A Singer must be impartial in all things," Essa said, overriding Joden's explanation. "A Singer's word is above suspicion of any influence or taint. You understand this?"

"Yes, Eldest Elder."

"Have you offered Simus your sword?" Essa demanded.

"No," Joden exclaimed, startled.

"At least you have that much sense," Essa said. "You would be a Singer?"

"Yes." Joden sat up straighter.

"And yet you are housed in Simus's tent, and fed by his people," Essa scoffed. "If you are to enter the Singer Trials, you must do better, Joden of the Hawk. Gather your gear. You will leave this tent with me, and you will not return."

Simus exchanged a startled glance with his friend, and then opened his mouth to protest. "Eldest Elder—"

Essa held up a hand to forestall him. "No. Joden, go."

Joden rose and headed to his sleeping area.

Simus made to speak again, but Essa shook his head and they sat in awkward silence until Joden emerged with his gear and left with one of Essa's warriors.

"Quartis, escort Joden to my tent. The rest of my warriors will wait outside," Essa commanded.

Simus watched as they departed, thinking to catch Joden's eye, wish him well if only with a nod. But his friend kept his head down as he and Quartis left, leaving only himself, Essa, and Snowfall in the tent. The tent flap was closed from the outside, and Simus heard the chiming of bells as it was secured.

Essa spoke. "It's for the best, Simus. He must walk his own path. Worry more about yours."

Simus kept still, feeling the loss of his friend. It felt wrong, to have him taken so quickly. But Joden had dreamed of being a Singer for as long as Simus had known him, and he would not stand in his way. Still…

He glanced over his shoulder. "What harm in a simple farewell?"

Essa ignored him. "Snowfall," he said. "Has there been any message from Wild Winds?"

Snowfall looked at Simus.

Simus scowled at Essa. "None. And if there had been, I'd have sent you word."

Essa gave an exaggerated sigh. "Not that kind of message."

"Oh," Simus said, and looked at Snowfall.

Snowfall dropped her eyes. "I am no longer in Wild Winds service, Eldest Elder."

"What does that matter?" Essa said.

"I have given my word to my Warlord to not use any gifts without permission."

"You know about this?" Simus blurted out to Essa. "That she can speak to those far off?"

"Yes, of course," Essa said. "And the price they pay for it."

Simus glanced at Snowfall. "The risk you mentioned."

"As I explained, Warlord," Snowfall said with an apology in her voice. "There are limits. And risks. Wild Winds warned me not to—"

"But you must," Essa interrupted. "It is urgent that I speak with him." Essa took a deep breath, and for the first time Simus saw worry in his eyes. "He must be here in time for the summoning of the Council, or the Council may splinter again. There must be an Eldest Elder of the Warrior-Priests present."

Snowfall sat silent, her hands in her lap.

Simus considered. "There is sense to your argument, but I am concerned about the risk to Snowfall."

Essa raised an eyebrow, but said nothing.

Simus frowned, thinking it through.

"Well?" Essa demanded impatiently.

Essa was right; Wild Winds needed to attend. "Do it," Simus commanded. "But if you sense that another hears, then end it. Understood?"

Snowfall's gaze lifted to his, her grey eyes wide. She nodded. "I need a few things for the casting," she warned.

"Get them," Simus said.

"We will wait," Essa agreed.

Snowfall got to her feet and disappeared within the depths of the command tent.

Essa settled back on his seat with a satisfied sigh.

Simus could not bear to sit still. He rose and started to pace before the platform. "Such a thing," he said. "Such a thing would have made such a difference. If they had shared this knowledge. If you had shared this knowledge."

"Remember that power did not flow so freely to them before," Essa said. "And when have any of us ever shared all of our secrets with the other? Each Tribe, each role, has its secrets."

"That needs to end," Simus growled, thinking as he walked. More importantly, Keir needed to know. If others had this power—

"I doubt Antas has any knowledge," Essa said, as if following his thought. "Who would share this with him? All of the warrior-priests are dead. And the few that survived are apprentices and they travel with Wild Winds."

"They shared this with you," Simus pointed out.

Essa shifted on his seat. "Eldest Elder Wild Winds shared this with me, when I became Eldest Elder Singer. And he and I were tentmates before he became as he is. As he was." The older man rubbed his hand over his face, and Simus saw the weariness there. "Accuse us all you wish, Simus. That was then. This is now."

A soft step and Snowfall appeared from the cooking area with a large flat copper bowl and a pitcher.

"Is that all you need?" Simus asked as she set the bowl on the platform, placing it before Essa. "I was expecting, I don't know, flames or smoke, or maybe a sacrificed gurtle."

The corner of Snowfall's eyes crinkled in amusement for just a moment. "If you wish, Warlord," she said, all seriousness, "I could go and get an animal."

Essa all but rolled his eyes at both of them. "If you don't mind," he said impatiently.

Snowfall knelt by the platform, and poured clear water into the bowl. "It will only be his face that appears, Eldest Elder. A larger image usually takes more warrior-priests, and much more effort." She looked at both of them. "Do not disturb the bowl or the water," she warned.

"How quickly can you find him?" Simus knelt as well, settling well back on his heels.

"That depends," Snowfall said, "on where his attention is, what he is doing."

"Best be about it," Essa growled.

Snowfall nodded in obedience and closed her eyes. She took a long deep breath, as if steadying herself, and then started to chant.

The words were odd, and not of the Plains. Simus frowned as he watched her. For just sitting and chanting there was a strain in Snowfall's face. He was disappointed. He'd been expecting fire and smoke and that purple cloud the warrior-priests usually invoked when working their so-called magics. Yet here was Snowfall doing real magic, and it seemed dull. Almost boring.

Essa was ignoring both of them, staring down into the bowl.

It took a moment for Simus to realize that something had changed. The bowl—no the water—was glowing, golden and soft. Snowfall's voice had a smooth cadence, and now she too appeared to glow, the golden light highlighting the beauty of her brown skin. This close he could see her dark lashes, admire the beauty of her heart-shaped face. She was so very—

"Wild Winds," Snowfall called softly. "I seek Wild Winds."

The air around them seemed to shift, blowing the rain hard

against the tent sides. The tent grew darker, and Simus swore the fires in the braziers crackled with malice, as if jealous of the power that stirred within.

"Wild Winds," she repeated, and the hair rose on the back of Simus's neck.

The light in the bowl flickered, and Wild Winds's face appeared, looking startled and wary. Until his gaze fell on Snowfall. Then his face, covered in the traditional tattoos of a full warrior-priest, broke into a wide smile. Simus blinked to see it.

"Snowfall." His voice was a rumble and the bowl seemed to tremble at the sound. Wild Winds's smile faded. "What has happened, that you risk this?"

"At my request," Essa said.

"Essa? And Simus?" To Simus's shock, the man's face turned toward his. Within the bowl. "Are you Token-bearer, then, Snowfall?"

"For so long as my knives are fast and sharp," Snowfall's voice was full of wonder, even as she nodded to the image. "But wait, Master. There is so much power…." Her voice trailed off as she closed her eyes and drew a deep breath in.

"Snowfall," Wild Wilds's voice was sharp.

Simus blinked as the image changed, and he scrambled back and to his feet as the colorless image of the man grew, as if made from the water itself. Wild Winds stood before them, hovering over the bowl.

Snowfall was blinking at it, as if surprised at her own success.

"There is a danger in that too, Snowfall." Wild Winds glanced at Essa. "This can only be your doing," he said.

"Are you well, my friend?" Essa rose from his seat to face the image. "I have heard such tales—"

"I am well," Wild Winds said gently, even as he cut him off. "We have much to discuss, you and I, but not here. Not now."

"What other risk?" Simus demanded, stepping closer to Snowfall's side. Snowfall still knelt by the bowl, her eyes on Wild Winds.

"The power is fresh and strong and can overwhelm an inexperienced warrior-priest. Also, the use of power is detectable by any watchers," Wild Winds answered. "And we could be overheard—"

"The other warrior-priests are dead, yes?" Essa demanded.

"Hail Storm lived." There came the sound of voices in the distance. Wild Winds looked over his shoulder. "I am not alone here, Essa. We are not under the bells." He glanced down at Snowfall. "And this is not without limits."

"Then I will keep this short. I would announce the ending of the Trials tonight."

"So soon." Wild Winds glanced at Simus, as if assessing him. "I had hoped for more time."

Essa shook his head. "To wait is to court disaster. When will you arrive?"

"I had not planned to come." Wild Winds frowned. "My students are still—"

"Who else to represent the warrior-priests?" Essa's frustration was clear. "And before you start a long-winded and vague speech about how you are not what you were, I would ask this. If not you, who?"

Wild Winds eyes flicked down to Snowfall.

"No," Essa said. "Snowfall has pledged her sword. That will not happen. Never mind all the other arguments against that."

"I had not thought it through," Wild Winds said, folding his arms over his chest. "I will come. Alone. Look for me at sunset tomorrow."

"Not alone," Essa said quickly. "I was hunted. You will be, too."

"But old friend, my power is more than my voice and my sword." Wild Winds laughed. "Besides, I have learned—"

From behind him came shouts. Wild Winds jerked his head around. "I must go."

With that, the image dissolved. Tiny droplets rained down in to the bowl.

Snowfall gasped. "He severed our link."

"Are you alright?" Simus offered her his hand, and she took it with a firm grasp, rising gracefully to her feet.

"I am," she said, and there was surprise in her voice. "I'm usually exhausted after such a casting. But not now."

Thunder rumbled, but at a distance. From the sound of it, the storm was moving off.

"Excellent," Essa pulled his cloak around himself. "Wild Winds's presence will aid those that dither to make a decision one way or another. The Council will form. And with any luck," he continued, "the skies will clear for the dancing tonight." He stepped off the platform and walked toward the tent flap. "Open," he called to his warriors outside. "We are done here."

His warriors unlaced the bells to open the way. Essa turned with a dramatic flair. "Use this day well, Simus of the Hawk, for the Trials end at sunset tomorrow."

With that, he was gone.

CHAPTER TWENTY-SIX

Simus spread the word to his people quickly, warning them of the coming announcement. As he walked his camp with Yers, he was pleased to see that preparations were moving along well.

They stopped for a brief time at the thea camp.

"We will see to it that the children are kept close, and our Xyian healer as well," Haya said, her usual scowl even deeper than normal. "Or scattered farther out beyond the camp to watch the gurtle herds." Weaponsmaster Seo nodded his agreement.

"Best to keep them out with the herds," Simus said. "Away from the tents and the excitement." He grinned at her. "I doubt they could resist the temptation of watching the final challenges."

"One can only hope that they obey better than you did as a child," Seo said pointedly.

"They will," Haya snapped irritably.

"Of course, Eldest Elder Thea," Seo said, a twinkle in his eye.

Haya rounded on him with a glare. Simus knew when to leave, and he took himself off with a nod of farewell.

"The Elder is unhappy," Yers muttered as he and Simus strode off.

"She is," Simus said under his breath. "Best to leave a raging ehat to itself, eh?"

Yers snorted his agreement.

Various warriors hailed them as they continued to walk through the camp. Simus was satisfied. It was orderly and organized, and his people looked ready. Tomorrow would be a long one for him, but at the end, after the challenges, success would be theirs.

"Join me for the nooning?" Simus asked Yers as they returned to his command tent.

Snowfall stood beside the entrance, arms crossed over her chest, watching the activity around her.

Yers glanced at her, frowning. "No," he said shortly. "I've a few things to see to yet this day."

"Well enough," Simus said cheerfully, but then paused. "Something?"

Yers nodded, his face grave. "There is talk…"

"What talk?" Simus asked.

"It is said that Joden left because of her." Yers jerked his head in Snowfall's direction. "That you argued about the warrior-priestess and he left in anger."

"Joden left with Essa to pursue his own path," Simus said patiently. It had only been this morning, but word travels with the winds. He drew in a slow breath. "And those that say this, what else do they say?"

"Some doubt you." Yers looked away. "Some fear her," he added. "But so far all say better to stay to serve you and Keir then to sever their oaths."

"Joden will be at the dancing tonight," Simus said, hoping he was right. "He'll tell his truths."

Yers looked him in the eye. "I hope so, Simus."

* * * * *

That night, as the sun set and the torches and fire pits were lit, Simus settled into the grass with his warriors fanned out behind him, seating themselves before the Heart of the Plains. The other candidates did the same, so that each claimed a section around the Heart.

As the warriors gathered and sat, Singers stood scattered in their midst. They would serve as Essa's voices, repeating his words for all to hear.

The storm had passed over and the skies had cleared, but a slight mist hung in the air. Simus was certain he'd never seen such a night sky before, black and deep with all the stars glittering above as if in approval. The air was cool and sweet; the ground around the Heart just dry enough to dance. Perfect, to his mind. He grinned, and looked over to his left.

Snowfall sat at his side, her face its usual mask of serenity. Yers sat to his right. The army—his army—sat with them, spread out behind. At least, those that were not on duty. He and Yers had left a strong guard behind. The warriors would rotate through, so that all could dance this night.

Simus craned his neck, trying to look without being too obvious. The other Warlord candidates were seated around the Heart. Some were beyond his vision; the Heart was wide enough that he couldn't make out faces. But close by him he could see Nires and Loual, and Ultie. They and their warriors settled down, all laughing and talking. Anticipation was high, for this night.

At some secret signal, the Singers all lifted their horns and blew out a blast calling for silence. Simus focused on the man standing at the center of the Heart.

"I am Essa, Eldest Elder Singer of the Plains," Essa called

out into the night. "Draw close and heed my words."

The Singers about them repeated his greeting, and the horns sounded again. Simus was amused at the 'draw close'. With all of the armies gathered there was little space left to 'draw close'. But Singers obediently repeated his words, echoing them so that all could hear.

"May the elements be with us this night," Essa called out again He turned to face in all directions as he spoke. "Warriors of the Plains," Essa said. "The raiding season comes, when we take what we need for our People. Are your swords ready?"

"HEYLA," was the cry that rose from the mass of warriors. A thrill went down Simus's spine as the voices rolled over the grasses, seeming to go on and on to the very edges of the sky.

"I hereby summon the Elders of each Tribe to the Spring Council," Essa commanded. "To confirm the Warlords for this season, and release them to battle."

The crowd stirred with excitement.

Simus shared a glance with Yers. Every warrior had known this was coming, but now it was set. Simus felt his own heart speed up at the thought.

"The Trials will end at sunset tomorrow," Essa continued. "The Council tent will then be raised, and the contenders will present themselves before us for confirmation."

Simus kept a smile on his face, but frowned within. The Trials alone were not the only part of this; Joden had warned him that he would face opposition before the Council even if he defeated all of his challengers. Thinking on Joden…

Simus narrowed his gaze, focused on the Singers all around him, but he did not see his friend.

"Tomorrow at dawn raise your challenge banners to the winds, for at sunset the banners will be lowered for the final time," Essa said. "But for now, we rejoice and thank the elements for their gifts. May the skies take pleasure in our dancing!" Essa moved off to the side of the large stone where a stool awaited him. As he sat he called a command. "Drummers!"

With a large BOOM, the drummers started a wild, fast rhythm. Cheers rose from all the warriors, and dancers flooded onto the Heart, swirling into a complicated pattern dance.

Simus craned his neck to look around.

Yers leaned over. "What do you seek?" he asked.

"Joden," Simus said. "I do not see him."

Snowfall craned her neck around, looking behind him. "It's possible that he is on the other side of the crowd."

"Do you think he was forbidden to attend?" Yers asked.

"I don't know," Simus said. He thought for a moment, watching the dancers as he considered his options. "It's possible as a Singer-to-be he is on the outer edges." He looked around again. "Send the question back. Does anyone see Joden?"

"Is that wise?" Yers asked quietly. "It might raise more doubts."

"I'll risk it. Better to know," Simus said.

Yers turned to Tsor and sent the question out through Simus's warriors. A gentle murmur rose and fell behind them, fading off as the question passed through the warriors.

The dancers swirled together, hands lifted to the skies, as the drums continued to beat.

The murmur returned through the crowd behind him and Yers reported. "No."

"Perhaps he is not here at all," Snowfall said, earning a scowl from Yers.

"I intend to find out," Simus rose to his feet. "Stay here," he commanded, and started to walk forward, skirting the edge of the crowd, toward where Essa was seated.

The warriors watching the dancing were laughing and talking. A few called out a greeting to Simus. He gave each a smile and a wave but continued on his way, intent on his target.

Essa was seated on a stool at the edge of the Heart, four warriors guarding him. He looked like he was watching the dancing, but a flicker told Simus that he had been seen. Simus strode up onto the stone, determined to get answers. But before he could get close, Essa raised a hand.

The drums stopped.

The dancers froze, and then ran back off into the crowds.

"Simus of the Hawk," Essa called out. To Simus's shock Essa's greeting echoed through the crowds around them, repeated by his Singers.

Simus froze, wary now. To confront a Singer privately was one thing, but to do so publicly risked being made a fool. Simus drew a deep breath as he faced Essa. "Eldest Elder Singer," Simus bowed his head, giving proper deference, stiffening when his own words were echoed by the Singers. The warriors of the Plains were to be privy to this conversation, then.

"You have spent time among the city-dwellers in the north," Essa said.

"I have." Simus gave him a wide smile. "I was very popular with the ladies of Xy." He assumed a modest look, covering his heart with his hand. "They fancied me."

Laughter arose from the crowd as his own words were echoed.

"More like you fancied them," Ultie bellowed out, but his words were not repeated so Simus ignored him. He kept his gaze on Essa.

"What else have you learned from those fat city-dwellers?" Essa asked, looking nothing more than curious.

What was that cagey old buzzard after, Simus wondered. This seemed dangerous ground to traverse at a...

Simus spread his arms and gave Essa his widest grin. "Why, to dance, of course!" Simus laughed even as his words echoed out.

"They dance?" Essa asked.

"Filthy city-dwellers do not dance." Ietha of the Badger stood, and folded her arms. Big-chested, blonde, and glowering at Simus, her words rang out over the crowd.

Simus couldn't figure out how Essa arranged that, but the challenge must be answered. "Yes, of course they dance," he said. "They even have special places within their stone tents for dancing."

"City-dwellers are nothing but prey to our hunt," Ietha spat. "What need we to know of them?"

Her words were not echoed, and in the silence after Essa gave her a cool look.

Ietha sat down among her warriors.

Essa turned back to Simus. "And what patterns do they dance?" he asked, and his words were repeated.

"Patterns," Simus scoffed. "Xyians use no patterns." He waited as his words echoed around. "Better to show you," Simus said. His heart skipped a beat in excitement, and on impulse he threw out his hand. "Snowfall," he called. "Come and dance with me."

CHAPTER TWENTY-SEVEN

Snowfall looked at Simus's outstretched hand, and then into his eyes.

With anyone else she'd suspect that they were trying to make her out to be a fool. She hadn't danced since her days in the thea camps. He could make her stumble, show her lack of grace…

But Simus's eye were filled with hope, anticipation, and that joy that seemed to underline his every breath.

When did she become so certain that she could trust him?

It was confusing and yet it stirred something within her in return. An answering joy. A hope.

She stood, walked to him, and took his hand.

A murmur rose from the crowd as word passed back among the warriors.

Simus's hand was warm in hers, his hardened calluses rough against her fingers. She gripped his hand tightly as she drew closer. "Warrior-priestesses do not dance," she said to him softly.

But soft or not, her words were echoed through the crowd. Snowfall glanced at Essa, suddenly wary.

Simus squeezed her hand, as if in reassurance, and gave her a smile. "You are not what you were," Simus said ignoring the echoes of his own words to focus on her face. "Or so Wild Winds has told us. I will teach you."

Snowfall raised an eyebrow.

"It's simple," Simus faced her. "Nothing so complicated as our patterns." He seemed very conscious of the echo, taking the time to explain his movements for those that could not see. "So we face each other, but our bodies do not touch. To be respectable in Xy, one must keep one's distance."

Snowfall watched as he took a position before her.

"I take your right hand in my left hand," Simus said, holding their joined hands together and out to the side. "And my right hand goes here," and he reached for the middle of Snowfall's back. His fingers brushed the warm flesh between her corselet and her trous.

Snowfall gasped, allowing the slightest intake of breath between her parted lips. His fingers seemed to burn her. Her tattoos rippled over her arms and shoulders as seeking more of his touch.

Simus's gaze dropped, and his lips curved in a sly, satisfied, irritating smile.

"And my left hand?" Snowfall prompted.

"Goes on my upper arm," Simus said. "Now we shift a bit so that we are off-center, so our knees and feet don't knock together."

Snowfall adjusted her position slightly, glancing down to see the positioning of their knees and feet. Simus glanced around, and she realized that some of the warriors around them were standing and mimicking their actions.

"Our arms act as a frame for our movements. Now count with me, and watch my feet," Simus said. "You must step backward in an opposite motion."

"Why must I step backward?" Snowfall demanded.

"Because you are the woman," Simus said. "The males 'lead'."

"You lead by pushing me backward?" Snowfall asked, and

laughter rose as her words echoed around them.

"Watch now," Simus admonished. "Step forward, side-step, feet together, step forward, side-step, feet together."

Snowfall put her head down, watching their feet.

"One, two, three," Simus chanted. "One, two, three," he said and then brought them to a stop. "Do you have it?" he asked, glancing over at Essa.

Snowfall looked up. "I think so—" she started.

Essa raised his hand, drums sounded—

Simus swept Snowfall off into the dance, swirling them both around the Heart.

* * * * *

Simus felt her gasp through his fingers rather than heard it, but other than a slight stumble at first, Snowfall flawlessly matched his movements. Simus waited until she was a bit more confident, then he started to move them about the Heart in a slow circle in time with the music.

For a moment it was as if they floated there on the Heart, the dark sky above reflected in the glitter of Snowfall's eyes as she looked into his. Simus sighed with pleasure at the sight, and drew her closer. She felt good in his arms as they moved as one, the sweet scent of her skin filling his senses. He drew her closer—

Snowfall stopped the dance, and pushed him away. "You said that bodies do not touch," she pointed out and he had to laugh as those words echoed around them. Laughter rose from the crowd.

"Truth," he said, standing there, feeling the loss of her in his arms.

"Again," Essa demanded.

"This time," Snowfall said, grabbing his right hand, "I lead."

Laughter rose at her words, but Simus willingly conceded control to her, only to discover how hard it was to move backward with any grace. But he only stumbled a bit before he caught on. Snowfall lead him in a graceful swirl around the Heart.

"The male always leads?" Snowfall asked. She had a look of concentration as she led him through the dance.

"Yes," Simus smiled at her. "It is the way of Xy."

"Foolishness," Snowfall said sharply.

Simus shrugged. "It is their way." He grinned at her. "Besides, there is a practical reason." He stopped dancing and the music stopped. "Xyians do not dance alone," Simus called out. "They would fill the entire Heart. Who will join us?"

Yers jumped up, holding his hand out to pull a protesting Elois to her feet. Other couples ran forward as well, not all from his people, Simus was glad to see.

"What is the pattern?" Essa called, for he had joined the dancers with a partner.

"There is none," Simus said.

"How do they avoid running into one another?" a warrior called.

"I don't know," Simus laughed. "They usually just got out of my way."

The drums sounded again, and the couples started to dance.

Snowfall lead again, and it was a struggle. "Ah, I see," she said. "The male leads because it's easier for the taller partner to watch for obstacles. That makes more sense."

Simus nodded. "It requires an awareness of the enemy, for the one who leads watches. If I may?" he asked, and they reversed their hands, and swirled with the music.

Soon it seemed that all the warriors were dancing, except a

few old fools Simus saw glowering at him. But he paid no attention. He had the lovely Snowfall in his arms, and the very skies seemed to sparkle in approval.

He glanced out over the crowd, at the warriors dancing on the Heart and around it. "What would it be like, if we could get them all dancing?"

He heard a soft, short, snort of a laugh, and looked down quickly. But Snowfall's face was calm and serene. "Did you just laugh?" he asked.

"Of course not," she replied. "Warrior-priestesses do not laugh."

Simus rolled his eyes at her, and swirled them around again.

Essa raised his hand and the music speeded up, the drums pounding faster. Around and around they danced, Simus watching carefully to keep them from a collision. But it was inevitable, and three couples spilled off the Heart on to the grass, laughing as they struggled up from an untidy heap.

"Enough," cried Essa. "Let us see a pattern."

The Heart cleared to allow the more traditional dancers to perform.

Simus walked back to his people, joined by Yers and Elois, both laughing as they settled back down. Snowfall took her place beside him. Someone passed forward skins of fermented mare's milk, but Simus waved them away. He was content, with his people around him, the stars above, and pattern dances that would go late into the night.

And if Snowfall was looking at him with a new light in the depths of her eyes, well, he would count that a win as well.

* * * * *

Snowfall felt breathless as she took her place beside Simus. She could still feel the tingle on her palm and her waist from his touch. She drew deep breaths, trying to calm her racing heart. But it didn't help that she could still smell him, a mixture of metal, leather, sword oil, and sweat. She bit her inner lip, and set about to calm her mind and body.

It was interesting, to watch him interact with his people, with Yers and Elois. He was still scanning the crowd as well; looking for Joden no doubt. The man had a deep sense of loyalty to his own.

Was that what made her trust him?

She fully expected the invitations he received, from warriors that asked him to join in their patterns. But he declined all of them with a friendly laugh and a smile. He even refused to join Yers in a battle dance.

She said nothing, but after a while, he caught her gaze and chuckled. "You wonder that I do not dance?"

She gave him the slightest of nods.

He faced forward. "The other Warlord candidates are not dancing either."

She casually looked around, and searched her memory of the night. "They have not," she confirmed.

"Not stupid enough to get themselves hurt dancing. We of the Plains do everything with abandon, and to risk injury so close to the end of the Trials is foolhardy," Simus pointed out. "A pulled muscle, a sprain, could make all the difference tomorrow."

"Ah," Snowfall said.

"Besides, you can learn a great deal about a warrior by how they dance a pattern." Simus gave her another smile, his eyes warm. "And I would deprive them of that knowledge."

Snowfall glanced over to where Ietha was talking to Nires.

Wyrik stood with them, glaring at Simus. "A good point," she said softly.

"Praise?" Simus straightened, and placed his hand over his heart. "My dear Token-bearer, I—"

"Enough." Essa was standing in the middle of the Heart, and once again his words were being echoed. "Let the drums go silent and the dancing end. Seek your beds. The morrow brings the final challenges."

CHAPTER TWENTY-EIGHT

No words were spoken between him and Snowfall the next morning as they prepared for the day. There was nothing to say. Simus ate, put on his armor, and took up his weapons with but one thought: This was the day that would see it done.

Snowfall waited for him by the tent flap, his token in hand, challenge banners in the other. His token would be needed if any warrior wished to rescind their oaths.

Snowfall looked him up and down, probably checking to make sure all his buckles were closed. Simus couldn't resist, and did a spin for her benefit, ending with a graceful Xyian bow.

She didn't even blink.

Simus sighed. A loss, then. Hopefully the only one of the day. He gestured for her to precede him and stepped out into a dawn just rising from the edge of the Plains. The sky filling with all the colors it had, from the palest blue to a blue so dark as to almost rival his own skin. Simus took it all in with a deep breath…

…and then dropped his gaze to find a young male warrior standing across the challenge circle from him, sword and dagger already in hand.

"I haven't even raised the banners yet." Snowfall's disdain was clear.

Yers came to stand close to Simus. "He's seen one, maybe two seasons of war, at the most," he sniffed, his crooked nose twitching. "More insulting than challenging."

A crowd had already gathered and more were coming. Mostly Simus's warriors, but a few that had clearly come to see their friend fight.

Simus stood, contemplating the young warrior as Snowfall raised his banners. "Truth, but there is muscle there."

"More ego then brains," Yers muttered. "Needs to be taken down hard for that arrogance."

Simus flashed him a smile. "And where would Keir and I be without arrogance?" he asked.

Yers rolled his eyes.

The young warrior walked into the circle. "I give challenge, Simus of the Hawk."

Simus yawned, and stretched as obnoxiously as he could. "So I see," he said as he scratched his chin.

Anger flashed through the youngster's eyes. "I am Beom of the Fox," he said, almost dancing in his impatience. "Answer my challenge."

"Of course, of course," Simus said. "But this sword won't do. A moment," he said, and turned toward his weapons rack.

"Come on, come on," Beom snarled. "Delay will not assist you."

"Let me just find the perfect…" Simus's eye fell on the wooden sword and dagger he'd won from Pive.

Snowfall was watching him. He gave her a sly wink. "Oh, here's just the thing."

With that, he snatched up the child's weapons, turned and brandished the wooden sword and dagger.

A startled gasp rose from the watching warriors, followed by snorts of laughter. Yers gave out an angry oath.

Beom's mouth dropped, and then his face filled with rage. "You mock me," he growled.

"Why, yes." Simus strode into the circle. "Yes, I do." He took up a dramatic defensive pose, as youngsters often did with their first weapons, and gave Beom his best vicious smile. "What are you going to do about it?"

Beom charged.

Simus waited, dodged, and swung at the lad's wrist, dealing a stinging blow, calculated to enrage his opponent.

It worked. The lad slid to a stop at the edge of the circle, turned and charged again.

His choice of weapons had been impulsive, but Simus wouldn't take another risk. He went on the defensive, warding off the blows as quickly as they fell. The lad was young and strong and fast, but angry, and it showed in his strikes.

Simus waited, using the wood of his blades to counter the steel of his opponent. Waiting for—

Boem's sword bit deep into the wood.

It was what Simus had been waiting for. He jerked his blade, forcing Boem's sword down, and then twisting it, hoping that the wood would hold long enough to—

Boem's sword went flying from his hand just as Simus's blade cracked in half.

Simus skipped back, his wooden blade broken off with a jagged end. Boem just stood there, stunned.

"Enough?" Simus asked.

Boem blinked at him, and for a moment Simus was sure he'd attack. But the anger in Boem's eyes cleared, and his mouth twisted in resignation. "Yes," he said, twirling his dagger and placing the point at his heart. "I would offer my surrender, Warlord."

Simus gave him a grave nod. "Accepted," he said as he took the dagger.

A buzz of talk rose from the watching warriors. This story would be all over the camps before the nooning.

Boem turned on his heel, and walked off, surrounded by what Simus hoped were friends. The lad would need them this night. Simus chuckled, and turned to rack his weapons.

Yers was standing there, scowling. He jerked his head toward the command tent.

Simus followed him in.

* * * * *

Simus settled on his gurtle pad, accepting kavage from Snowfall. Looking into those eyes, nothing showed.

Didn't mean he couldn't feel her disapproval.

Yers's reaction was clear. The warrior paced in the area before the platform. "I would ask for your token, Warlord."

"There is no need for tokens between us, Yers." Simus gestured with his mug. "Speak your truths."

"Have the winds taken your wits?" Yers demanded, coming to a halt before him. "That you would risk all on a child's weapons?"

Simus paused with his mug before his mouth. "The skies favor the bold," he said, raising his cup in a salute.

"And the earth covers the stupid," Yers snapped. "Marcus would gut you were he here, for risking everything Keir of the Cat has worked toward on a stupid—"

"You already said that," Simus said mildly.

"—rash, foolish, gesture." Yers started pacing again.

"I agree with the 'rash'," Snowfall said softly. "But he accomplished this much: No other young warrior will offer challenge and risk humiliation."

Ah, a win. Simus smiled into his mug. "See," he said smugly. "Snowfall thinks I am right."

Yers gave Snowfall a glance, opened his mouth to reply, but a call came from outside.

Tsor stuck his head in. "Snowfall, a challenger for you."

Snowfall gave a nod of her head and left the tent. Yers watched as she left.

"You wish her defeated," Simus said, his pleasure in the moment fading.

"Yes," Yers said shortly. "It would be for the best. Bad enough to have one in your ranks. In a position of trust…" Yers shook his head, then gave Simus a sharp look. "And do not think to distract me from my point."

"Yers." Simus set down his kavage. "I thank you for your truth. It was a calculated risk. I knew he'd lose his temper at the insult—"

"Don't try to convince me that you had thought it through," Yers said. "And how much of that was an effort to impress her?" Yers jerked his head in Snowfall's direction.

Simus stopped smiling. "None," he said shortly.

"This was not Keir's plan." Yers shook his head. "You haven't changed. I thought you would step up, embrace the trust Keir placed in you and take your duties seriously. Instead, you hazard all to impress a warrior-priestess," Yers continued. "For your own pride, you—"

"Enough," Simus growled.

Yers drew up short, staring at Simus.

"What battle plan survives the first sight of an enemy?" Simus said. "Keir seized upon the opportunities the skies gave him; I will seize mine. That is my choice, and my decision to make."

"If you survive the challenges," Yers said.

"If I survive," Simus agreed with a nod.

"I ask leave to go," Yers said, his anger clear in his eyes.

Simus nodded his permission and watched him go with regret. If Yers was having doubts, what of the rest of his warriors? He picked up his kavage as he thought about it, then shook his head. Enough. For this day, there was only one thing to focus on.

"Warlord." Snowfall appeared in the tent entrance. "Another challenger."

* * * * *

At the nooning, Simus entered the tent, grateful for the break.

Snowfall had prepared a full meal, but Simus shook his head as he took up a cloth to wipe the sweat from his brow. "I won't eat that heavily," he said, gesturing toward the food. "And don't bother with more kavage. Water only."

"But—" She looked at the dishes. "You've fought more challengers this morning than the last three days combined. You need to keep up your energy."

Simus gave her a grin as he sat on his gurtle pad. "I forget that you haven't done this before," he said, taking a handful of gurt. "Yers should have said something to you."

"I didn't know to ask," Snowfall said quietly, fetching him water. "Those of us in training as…warrior-priests…were not permitted to mingle with warriors. Only those that had earned their full tattoos had that privilege."

"And strutted around like arrogant cocks." Simus nodded. "Still, this is normal, the number of opponents, the speed of the combats. But I won't eat heavily tomorrow, and will drink only water. Which I will sweat out; I'll have no need to make water."

"So water, gurt, and drying cloths," Snowfall said.

Simus nodded again. "Dried meat, and berries. And salt the gurt," he said. He took up another handful of the white pebbled cheese and stood. "And don't worry if I pace. I don't want to risk getting stiff."

"They will keep coming at you like that?" she asked.

"Yes," Simus said. "But the more serious challengers will wait, watch, and approach when they think I am weary. Later this day." He glanced over at her somber grey eyes. "But remember I control the pace. I can rest and renew between, as long as I don't keep them standing overlong. The same is true for you."

"Some don't seem serious contenders," Snowfall said.

"No," Simus said. "Their goal is to wear me down for what is to come."

"You can outlast them," Snowfall said and it pleased him that there was no doubt in her voice.

"I can," Simus confirmed. "I have been training and preparing for this day for seasons. I will win."

Snowfall tilted her head. "Unless they get lucky."

"Ah, but luck has always been on my side," Simus grinned.

"That would be the arrogance," Snowfall pointed out.

Simus laughed. "Sunset will prove me right. The serious contenders will challenge close to sunset. Then we shall see." He paused, and frowned at the gurt in his hand. "Snowfall, make no move out there that would cause any to think you were using your magic. That would make things worse for both of us. Do you understand?"

"Yes," she said.

He gave her a nod of approval, and started on some of the dried meat. He ate quietly, lost in his thoughts as he chewed. Snowfall wasn't one for idle talk; she was quiet as well. The silence was comfortable and welcome.

Simus finished his food, and refilled his mug with water. "Snowfall," he said. "If I die this afternoon—"

She jerked her head around to stare at him.

Simus held up a hand. "We must consider every possibility. If I die, all warriors will be released from their oaths. Yers will take what warriors he can gather and head to Xy. Yers may try to re-form the army, or Liam of the Deer will. Either way, I command you to use your powers and return to Wild Winds."

"You will not die," Snowfall said firmly.

"But if—" Simus started, but Snowfall held up her hand.

"And where is your arrogance now?" she asked, but then she bowed her head to him. "I will obey, Warlord."

Satisfied, Simus finished his water, and stepped out into the sun.

* * * * *

Snowfall watched him leave the tent, and heard him greet his challenger. She stood there for a moment, listening to the sounds of combat, and tried to make sense of the man.

A warrior who declined to dance, but took the risk of using wooden weapons to a younger, stronger challenger.

A warrior who displayed such arrogance, and yet planned in the event of failure.

A warrior who expressed concern for her well-being even in the face of the hatred of his own people.

He was such a contradiction. Such a fascinating—

A shout from those gathered outside brought her back to her duties. She fetched more gurt, dried meat, and water. The rest of the food she told her helpers to eat. It would not go to waste.

And while she worked she considered her own truths.

There was something about his smile, the joy underneath it. It wasn't wide-eyed foolishness. It was the strength of his convictions. Hope with the practical truth of reality woven in.

Yet she believed Simus could walk this path. Weaving the new with the old to aid all their peoples. But that made her pause, and frown.

When had that happened? When had their desires, their goals, woven into one pattern?

A cry went up from outside. He'd defeated another challenger. Snowfall allowed herself the smallest of smiles.

"Snowfall." Tsor stuck his head within the tent. "You've another challenger."

Snowfall nodded, and headed outside to meet her opponent. She wished to stand beside Simus, aiding him, working with him. He'd not be defeated.

Neither would she.

* * * * *

By mid-afternoon Simus had met all of the challengers. They'd come like a steady rain. He took care to rest, to eat and drink between bouts, but he met and defeated them all. The fights were fast, some ending in mere heartbeats. But Simus took nothing for granted.

A few were latecomers, more testing his skill than offering a real challenge. One even offered his blade after their fight. Simus accepted him, then turned to face the next.

Snowfall faced quite a few of her own, and so far remained the victor in her bouts.

Yers and Tsor had fewer challenges, which pleased Simus. They were almost assured of their positions in his service.

The crowd of watchers grew larger, warriors sitting in the first few rows, others standing behind. His own people, and other warriors, come to see. Elois was hovering on the fringes of the crowd, watching as well. Simus paid them no conscious mind, focused solely on his opponent.

The hours became a blur of blades, strikes, counterstrikes, and victories. Simus kept pace, not concerned that his strength would hold, but always with an awareness of the sun on its path through the sky.

Offered yet another dagger, Simus stepped from the circle and added it to the growing pile. He glanced over his shoulder, but no other challenger stood opposite. A break then, in the shade of the tent. "Snowfall," Simus said. "I would have—"

"Nothing for you, *bragnect*." Wyrik of the Boar stepped through the crowd, shield and axe in hand. He positioned himself at the edge of the circle opposite Simus. "I challenge you, Simus of the Hawk. Come and die."

CHAPTER TWENTY-NINE

'Finally,' was Simus's first thought.

"I will kill you," Wyrik snarled, waving his axe around. "I will kill you and scatter your army." Wyrik looked around at Simus's people, curling his lip. "Then I will take my warriors and raid Xy for what we need."

Yers and the warriors around him were scowling, fingering the hilts of their swords.

As if she'd read his mind, Snowfall came up beside Simus, water and platter in hand, a few clean cloths over her arm. "Warlord," she said.

Simus took up a cloth, and ran it over his face, head, and the back of his neck. It felt good to wipe off the sweat.

"Come, Simus of the Hawk," Wyrik bellowed. "Pick up your children's weapons now, I dare you."

Simus continued to wipe his face.

Snowfall stood patiently.

Wyrik continued to rant.

Simus tossed the cloth off to the side, and accepted a mug of water. It was cool and sweet and he drank carefully. Deliberately.

"Your death will be at my hands, and mine alone," Wyrik shouted.

Snowfall continued to patiently wait. Simus thought he could see a glimmer of approval in her eyes. He looked over the selection on her platter, and picked out a hunk of the dried meat. Not too big, but not too small either.

He tore off a bite, and started to chew.

"Death to you!" It seemed Wyrik was starting to repeat himself. Some of the warriors exchanged quick glances with each other, and smirks. Simus tore off another bite and made sure to keep his face bland as Wyrik screamed at him. It wouldn't take long for—

Someone in the crowd snickered.

Which was all it took. Tension shattered, smiles broke out all around, and warriors eased their stances. Wyrik's flair for the dramatic had stumbled.

Wyrik realized it as well, glaring at the warriors. He then focused on Simus. "You stall," he snarled. "Coward."

Simus swallowed the meat, and then finished off the water. He took another cloth to wipe his hands. "My thanks," he said to Snowfall.

She gave him a nod and stepped back.

Simus considered his weapon's rack, and took up an axe and a shield. He turned, brought his shield up, with his weapon ready and fixed his gaze on Wyrik with an intent stare.

"Finally," Wyrik roared, bringing up his own shield and banging his axe upon it. "Face me, Simus of the Hawk. Face my—"

Simus leapt into the circle and charged, not wasting breath on words.

Wyrik warded him off, and it began. There was no art in this fight beyond survival. This was brute force, with axes clashing against shields, looking for any opening. This was battle, life or death, and no quarter taken or claimed.

Simus reached deep within for the strength he needed. Wyrik was fresh, but Simus was warm and ready. They were equal in strength, as far as he could tell. Equal in skill, perhaps. Yet Simus knew there was more to fighting than strength and skill, for he was determined to win.

Strangely, Wyrik grew oddly cagey, wary even, as sweat ran down his pale, white face. Simus frowned at the change of tactics. He pressed his advantage, but Wyrik was cautious, backing away. Simus followed up, taking a swing at Wyrik's legs.

Wyrik went down on his back, for no reason that Simus could think of, but he wasn't about to lose his chance. He raised his axe high, swinging for—

* * * * *

The power rose, took Snowfall in its grip, and tightened around her.

She was frozen, suspended, with all movement stopped. Her breath in her throat, the dread exploded in her chest. *Here. Now. Simus.*

The crowd shifted then, as if allowed. She saw one warrior pull a light, handheld crossbow out from under concealment, loading a bolt with slow movements.

Here. Now. Simus, rang through her soul.

The warrior took aim.

"DOWN," Snowfall screamed.

* * * * *

Simus heard Snowfall's warning, dove for the dirt, and rolled, bringing his shield up to defend himself.

A bolt hit his shield, biting deep.

A warrior stood frozen behind him, a crossbow in his hand, aimed at Simus. For a long, timeless moment there was silence. Then with a roar, Simus's warriors reached for the assassin and plunged their daggers into his body.

Simus rose in fury, and spun to face Wyrik. "This is your honor?" he shouted. "This is your truth?"

Wyrik scrambled to his feet. "Yes," he screamed back. "Yes, yes, a thousand times over, for the sake of the Plains and the elements themselves. You—"

Simus threw away his shield and took his axe into both hands. "This for your treachery," Simus spat, and swung.

Wyrik raised his shield, but Simus's rage gave him a new strength. His axe fell again and again as he beat Wyrik back, until the wooden shield finally cracked into shreds and fell off Wyrik's arm.

Simus raised his axe again. Wyrik attempted to ward off the blow. But Simus bore down and his axe broke the haft of Wyrik's weapon, slicing down into his collar bone. It continued on, parting flesh and cracking ribs.

Wyrik stood for a moment, life fading from his eyes. Simus yanked his axe up, and Wyrik's body fell to the dirt.

Simus stood, breathing heavily into the silence, as blood stained the challenge circle. He made a sharp gesture, and hands reached out to drag Wyrik's body away. "So much for his truths," Simus said, and then stepped out of the circle to clean his weapon.

"Anyone else?" he asked, keeping his tone casual, glancing at the setting sun.

"Warlord," Yers spoke from behind him. "I would ask for your token."

Stunned, Simus looked up. Yers stood opposite him, over the

bloodied challenge circle, his face taut with anguish.

Simus opened his mouth to protest, but thought better of it. He gestured for Snowfall to take his token to Yers. "You hold my token, Yers of the Cat," Simus said. "What truths would you tell me?"

"I would rescind my sword-oath," Yers said simply.

Simus dropped his gaze to his token. The decorative feathers moved; Yers's hands were shaking.

"I would ask the reason," Simus said, wishing desperately that this wasn't so public, for warriors to witness. The tale of this would be all over the camps. Even now, more warriors came running to see. The very air was filled with silent expectation.

"We started this venture, you and I, at Keir's side." Yers voice was low and intense, but his words carried. "Keir of the Cat has made it clear that he would see the destruction of the warrior-priests and changes to our way of life."

"Truth," Simus said. "Nothing has changed."

"Yet you cavort with warrior-priests," Yers pressed. "You allow one to contest for Token-bearer. Joden is nowhere to be found. His truths have been silenced for all I know." Yers took a deep breath. "You are bewitched. You are under the sway of our enemy."

"Bewitched by one that just saved me from treachery?" Simus glanced over to where Snowfall stood. Outwardly, she seemed cool and calm, but he sensed that she was shaken. He wished he had time to reassure her, but he turned back to Yers. "She could have just as easily let that warrior shoot me in the back." Simus drew a deep breath. "And as I told you before: Joden has gone with the Singers to face his own Trials."

"Yet he has not been seen," Yers said. "And no word as to his going? No farewells? No. He does not support you and I fear you have silenced him." Yers glanced at Snowfall.

"Yers, plans never last beyond the first exchange of blows," Simus argued. "We are warriors, we know that." He spread his hands for emphasis. Heads began to nod in the crowd. "From the moment that pillar of light pierced the sky above us, we have had to adapt. As the grass bends to the wind, so must we bend in the winds of change."

For a moment, Simus thought he'd reached him, then Yers's eyes went hard. "No. I cannot bend that far."

Simus rubbed his forehead and sighed with regret. "So be it. I release you from your oath." He watched as Snowfall retrieved his token. "I cannot thank you for these truths, Yers, for I am sorry to lose you at my side. Will you return to Xy? If so, I ask that you take word to—"

"No." Yers reached out and took a shield and mace from another warrior. Simus watched in disbelief as he stepped into the challenge circle and took a defensive position. "I offer challenge."

The crowd's reaction was no less stunned then Simus's. His jaw dropped. "Yers—" Simus was almost without words. "Yers, what are you doing?" Simus didn't bother to hide his pain.

"What I must." Yers's face screwed up in determination.

"Yers." Simus's anger rose. "You offered your truths to me, and I heard them and released you from your oaths. This—this is different."

"I cannot let you become the Warlord that aids Keir," Yers spat. "I do not trust you." He jerked his head in Snowfall's direction. "I do not trust this."

Simus's gut lurched. "Does it come to this?"

"I would be the better choice," Yers said. "Most of these warriors gathered here will support me once you have been defeated."

Simus bared his teeth. "I will not offer you my dagger," he warned.

"Nor will I," Yers said.

Simus glanced at the sun as he armed himself. The glowing disk still hung over the horizon. Not that it mattered. Even were it full dark, this challenge from within must be answered.

Simus took up his shield, and paused for a moment, as if considering weapons. He was tired; Yers had not faced nearly the number of challenges Simus had this day. He was determined; so was Yers. No, what gave Simus pause was that Yers knew him. They'd sparred for years, fought beside one another. Simus drew a breath. Should he offer his dagger? Preserve both their lives?

But even as he had the thought, he knew he would not yield. Yers had fallen in the same trap the warrior-priests had—that doing the same things in response to change was to court defeat.

Simus took up his own mace, and entered the circle.

If Yers knew him—well, the same was true for Simus. He knew Yers, now didn't he?

In moments, they clashed in the center of the circle, the first exchange of blows a violent one. Yers drove Simus back, and then retreated, circling him, looking for weakness.

Simus kept his guard up, turning to face his enemy. Whatever else Yers had been, he was the enemy now.

Yers moved in, and pressed Simus hard, to the very edge of the circle. The watching warriors faded away, giving them room.

Simus kept his shield high and defensive, striking only when he had advantage, getting in blows more often than Yers, but not enough to stop the man. Sweat rolled down both their faces, but Simus never dropped his gaze.

Yers backed away, as if catching his breath. Simus didn't follow up on that, too experienced to take such an obvious opening.

Yers grinned, and for just a moment Simus saw his sparring friend of old. But then the moment passed, and Yers's eyes narrowed and he rushed in, trying to bash shields and get close enough for a killing blow.

Simus took his rush head-on, and fended off Yers with a flurry of strikes that forced the other man back. Rage filled him then, pure anger that coursed through him, giving strength to the blows he hammered down on Yers's shield.

In the end, it wasn't strength or skill, but pure luck that caused Yers to leave an opening. Simus surged forward, striking for Yers's head.

In the split-second before he hit, Simus pulled his blow. Not all the way, but just enough, just enough to render...

His mace struck Yers's head.

Yers slid down in a boneless pile.

In the silence that followed, Simus stood, heaving in gulps of air. Yers didn't move, but he was still breathing.

Simus took a step forward, and stood over Yers's body, mace and shield in hand. He gave the crowd around him a hard look. "I am the Warlord of this army," he roared out in his anger and frustration. "Who would offer challenge? Who would rescind their oaths?"

He waited in the last light of the sun, the air thick with silence. Simus drew a breath, feeling the sting of sweat in his eye. He blinked to clear his vision and watched with satisfaction as the warriors around him knelt and bowed their heads until none were left standing except Elder Haya and Weaponsmaster Seo.

Haya stepped to his side. "Warlord," she said, acknowledging his rank with a nod of her head. "No one will offer challenge. No one will rescind."

Simus waited, looking over the bowed heads, waiting for a protest. "So be it," he said. "Tsor, you are Second. See to Yers. Get him to the healer."

Tsor rose to his feet. "I will see it done."

Seo was at his other side. "Let me see to your weapons, Warlord."

Simus glanced over, but Snowfall was talking to Elois, so he let Seo take his mace and shield from his hands. With Haya at his side, he stepped inside the tent, grateful for the dim coolness within. Simus stopped. It seemed like a fog surrounded his mind and body.

"Dea-mine," Simus spoke, his voice sounding odd to his own ears. He blinked, trying to focus on Haya, but she was right by his side.

"Battle-fatigue." Haya was brisk as she started unbuckling his armor. "Not a surprise, given your efforts this day. Let me see to you."

Her words echoed, as if from a distance, just as it had when he'd been in her tents. That familiar sound meant 'safe' and 'secure', and Simus let himself relax into that reassurance.

And just as she had in the past, she stripped him down, bid him drink water as she wiped him down with cool cloths, and then chivied him into his pallet and under a blanket. "Sleep, Warlord," she commanded, as only a thea could.

Simus gave in at that point, closing his eyes. For just a moment, he relished the pleasure of victory, but sleep was swift to claim its own.

* * * * *

Snowfall reached for Simus's banner, her hands shaking. Tsor was stripping down Yers's banner, and his own, his face a snarl of anger. She'd lower Simus's, then hers, then follow them into the tent. Her heart was pounding in her throat even as she moved. It had been so close, the warrior with the cross-bow, then Yers. It was a wonder that—

Someone came up from behind her.

Snowfall spun, dagger in hand without thought, Simus's banner in the other.

Elois stood there, grim in the dying sunlight. She glanced at Snowfall's banner, still streaming from the pole, then fixed her gaze on Snowfall.

"I offer challenge, Snowfall of the warrior-priests, for Token-bearer."

* * * * *

Simus woke, warm and relaxed, and then drew a breath as the memories hit him. He'd won.

At a price.

He lay there, letting it all sink in. Wyrik's treachery. Yers's betrayal.

Wyrik, he dismissed. That warrior had found his own death. But Yers…that struck deeper. Simus wondered if there had been anything he could have done to convince Yers otherwise.

Perhaps, and for that he regretted events deeply. But Yers had chosen a public display to rescind, and had then chosen to challenge, making his truths known. And that, Simus had to answer.

Relief swept through him. He'd survived the Trials. Now to face the Council and deal with the weapons they would wield.

With a laugh, he swept back the blankets, relishing the cool air on warm skin and—

—drew a sharp breath as his body reminded him of another truth.

He groaned and grit his teeth against the pain. Stiff and sore, the price of fighting so many over the course of a day.

Still, the worst was in the waking, and the sooner he forced himself up and moved, the quicker the pain would leave him. But the first movements were the worst.

He got to his feet with another groan, and started stretching, trying to work every muscle to ease the ache deep within. He could hear Snowfall moving about in the main tent, so there'd be kavage, and breakfast soon enough. His stomach rumbled at the thought. He reached for his clothing as the flap was pulled back.

"Morning," he said as he pulled on his tunic.

"Good morning, Warlord."

Simus jerked his head around.

Elois stood there, tray of gurt and kavage in hand.

CHAPTER THIRTY

If Elois were to be honest, she rather enjoyed the stunned look on her Warlord's face.

"Where is my Token-bearer?" Simus's dark skin furrowed into a deep frown.

"I am the current candidate for your Token-bearer," Elois said. She couldn't keep her satisfaction from her voice, and didn't bother trying. "I challenged and defeated Snowfall in the dying light of the evening sun." She held up the pitcher. "Kavage, Warlord?"

Simus ignored her offering. "Why wasn't I told?" He was still frowning as he reached for his trous.

"Elder Haya forbade it," Elois said. "She said you were not to be woken."

Simus finished pulling on his trous and stomped into his boots. "Where is she?"

"Elder Haya?" Elois couldn't resist asking.

"Snowfall," came the growl as Simus finished dressing.

Elois dropped her eyes and her teasing tone. "I do not know, Warlord," she said. "She showed me how your tent was set up, told me you like your kavage strong, and left with her gear." Elois raised her eyes then and gave him a narrow look. "As is the way of challenges, yes?"

"Yes." Simus belted on his weapons.

Good, he wasn't going to be difficult. One never knew with Warlords. "Tsor says to tell you that Yers is with the healer," Elois said. "Yers is well enough, although he has not yet woken. The Council tent will be raised today, and Eldest Elder Essa has sent word that warriors should—"

She kept talking, even though she knew he wasn't really listening. He was distracted, clearly.

"You need to eat something," Elois finally gave up. "Since you aren't hearing anything I say."

"Uh," Simus said. He took the mug she thrust in his face. He looked down at it like he'd never seen it before. "I need…I have to find…" Simus drew in a deep breath. "Do you think I am bewitched?" he demanded.

Elois looked at him seriously. "No, Warlord," she replied. "But it is better for you and the army you lead that she is not Token-bearer. I am the better choice."

The stunned look vanished from the Warlord's eyes, replaced by a flash of heat. "That choice is mine to make," he growled, raising the mug and draining it in a gulp.

Elois lowered her eyes and bowed her head. "Yes, Warlord."

"Have Tsor gather the necessary warriors for the tent raising," Simus commanded, taking a handful of gurt from the bowl. "I will return shortly."

"Yes, Warlord." Elois watched as the tent flap fell closed behind him. Only then did she let herself grin.

Tsor stuck his head in the tent. "The Warlord is headed for Essa's tent."

"Eldest Elder Essa's tent," Elois scolded. "If you would be Second, best you use his title at all times."

"I will." Tsor stepped in, eyeing the tray in her hands. "Is that kavage?"

Elois nodded. "We may as well eat. I doubt he will be back soon. He seeks Snowfall."

"Not a surprise." Tsor helped himself to the gurt, and let her pour him a mug of kavage. "Yers was wrong," he said, his mouth full. "I agree with Simus that he needs to take the chances the winds send his way. Better to have her with us than not. Warlord Keir would be the first to understand that."

"I hope so," Elois sighed. "But I agree with you. Warlord Simus is one I can support."

"That warrior-priestess challenges him," Tsor smirked. "The first I've seen to resist his charms. He is not bewitched."

"Oh, he is bewitched," Elois laughed. "He just doesn't know it yet."

* * * * *

I don't think you appreciate how difficult this will be." Eldest Elder Essa made a fine sight in his silk robes as he paced back and forth in the confines of his tent. Wild Winds took a moment to appreciate the sight as he scooped a bit more of the spiced gurtle into his flatbread and started eating.

"I am Eldest Elder Singer, but not all will heed my words." Essa was glaring at the floor, talking with his hands. "They will also listen to the likes of Ietha, or take a neutral path until forced to decide otherwise. Yet the Warlords must be chosen, the armies must raid as they always have. Our truths may be enough to carry the day, but what of Nires? And where is Reness?"

To Wild Winds's mind, silence seemed the best response.

"You took a risk, coming without escort. If you had gotten here earlier…" Essa turned, and his robes flared around him dramatically.

The spiced meat burned Wild Winds's tongue and he grunted in appreciation. He hid his smile from Essa with a quick sip of kavage. Essa continued to scold. He waited for a break in the flow of abuse to venture a word. "I got here as soon as I could."

"You and I are the only Eldest Elders—"

"I am no longer Eldest Elder," Wild Winds pointed out.

"Stop that," Essa scowled. "The Elders are gathering, true enough, but I am uncertain that Nires of the Boar will agree to remain as the Eldest Elder Warrior. And Reness is nowhere to be found. For all I know, she is still in Xy, seeing to the Warprize."

Wild Winds raised an eyebrow. It was not like Essa to repeat himself.

Essa stopped pacing and scowled at Wilds Winds. "Hurry up with that. The warriors will be waiting, and the tent must be raised."

As grateful as he was for Essa's hospitality, Wild Winds wasn't about to rush. His friend needed to work off some of that worry before he dealt with the day.

"Have you eaten?" he asked Essa.

The man shook his head as he paced. "Not hungry."

"It would be well if you ate something," Wild Winds suggested.

"I don't see how we can—" Essa broke off at the sound of a commotion outside the tent. "What now?"

Essa's guards were arguing with someone. "Eldest Elder," one of the guards called. "Simus of the Hawk would speak with—"

"WILD WINDS," came a roar from outside the tent.

"Let him in," Essa called and with that the tent flap blew

open as if the winds themselves demanded entrance.

Simus of the Hawk stood there, chest heaving, eyes flashing. "Where is she?"

Wild Winds raised an eyebrow and took another bite.

"Where is who?" Essa asked, clearly irritated. "Having survived your Trials, shouldn't you be gathering your warriors for the raising of the tent?"

Simus only had eyes for Wild Winds, and his glare was dagger-sharp. He took a step closer, to tower over him. "Where is she?"

Wild Winds took a drink of kavage, and raised an eyebrow at the warrior. "Who?"

"Snowfall," Simus grated out. "She lost a challenge as Token-bearer. Where is she?"

Wild Winds studied the tall, dark man before him, breathing fast and clearly agitated.

Interesting.

"I do not know," he said calmly. "Why would you expect to find her here?"

"You were her mentor," Simus said. "She would—"

"Did she not swear her sword-oath to you?" Wild Winds asked.

"Yes, but—"

"And when a warrior swears a sword-oath, and loses a challenge, that warrior is still oath bound to your service, yes?" Wild Winds asked.

"Yes, but—"

"You have not released her from her oath, yes?" Wild Winds said.

"Yes. No." Simus stumbled through his words. "I mean that

I have not released—"

"Then her proper place is in your army, serving the duties of a warrior," Wild Winds said. "Yes?"

Simus looked stunned. "Yes."

"Then why would you think to find her here?"

Simus stared at him, blinked, spun on his heel and left the tent.

"Were we ever that young and stupid?" Essa mused.

"You are not so old that you have forgotten those feelings," Wild Winds chuckled, and reached for the bowl of gurt.

"Aren't you done eating yet?" Essa huffed out a sigh and sat on the gurtle pad next to Wild Winds. He reached for the flatbread and spiced meat. "Still, I expected him to ask after Joden."

"Ah." Wild Winds smiled as he poured them both more kavage. "I think his mind is on other things."

* * * * *

What kind of sloppy sword-work is that," Destal bellowed at the two warriors sparring before her. "Ouse, keep your blade up. Lander, don't just wave your dagger around like a stick. It has a point. Use it."

Both young warriors were circling each other, swords and daggers at the ready. Destal snorted at that idea of 'ready'. Both of them fresh from the thea camps and it showed. She'd have to give them other partners. They might be free to share bodies and tents, but not bad habits. They'd improve if they had to fight others.

She caught a glimpse of the Warlord coming, stomping through the tents, looking riled up and irritated. Elements, but he looked to be in a mood, a rare thing for her Warlord.

"Where is Snowfall?" the Warlord demanded.

Ouse and Lander had stopped their sparring, staring at the Warlord.

"Here now," Destal commanded. "Who told you to stop?" When the young ones resumed their clash she continued. "She's been assigned duties, as any young warrior would be."

"What duties?" The Warlord was looking about, clearly seeking the warrior out.

"Collecting fuel for the fires," Destal said, and didn't blink when the Warlord flashed her a glare. "As all young warriors do," she reminded him. "I'll give her this much, there was no complaint out of her."

"Where?" came the growl.

"At the farthest edge of the gurtle and horse herds, behind the thea tents," Destal said. "You'll need a horse." She looked over to where a group of older warriors were preparing for their scouting run. One had a horse ready, saddled and equipped with lances. "Here, Amer," she called. "Give the Warlord your horse."

Amer came and handed over the reins. The Warlord mounted. "I'll be back soon," he said, and started off at a trot.

Destal waited until he was out of earshot. "Might want to get another saddle out of supplies, Amer."

"You think he might be a while?" Amer asked, shading his eyes to watch the Warlord gallop off.

"Aye," Destal said. "I'm thinking he might."

* * * * *

The horse was fast; Simus urged it to go faster.

She'd be at the edge of the herds, more than like, well beyond the thea tents. If he circled the thea camp, he was sure to see her. The idea that he might not had his heart beating faster in his chest.

The morning sun inched up, the air cool and still. The herds were quiet, the horses concentrating on grazing, occasionally lifting their heads to watch him ride past. Another rise and he spotted the first of the gurtle herds, grazing steadily toward him.

He pulled his horse to a stop, patting its neck as it huffed at him, restive and ready to go. He scanned the area looking for any signs of humans.

"Muwapp."

Simus turned his head to see a gurtle coming closer. Mounted on its back was a young girl, her hair pulled back and high on her head. He recognized her at once.

"Greetings, Warlord." The young one pulled the gurtle to a halt a respectful distance away, and bowed her head to him. She was wearing leathers, and had a new wooden dagger and sword at her belt. She also had a small horn on a cord, which meant she was in charge of her herding group.

"Pive." Simus gave her a nod. "I see you have won back your weapons."

Pive straightened, clearly pleased. But her face remained serious. "Yes, Warlord. May I be of service to you?"

Her gurtle started to graze, looking for the best grass.

"Have you seen a warrior collecting fuel?" Simus asked. "She has tattoos on her shoulders—"

"Yes," Pive said, nodding. "We are keeping close watch on her. She is a warrior-priestess and not to be trusted."

Simus drew a breath, looking into the child's eyes. A child only repeating what she had been told.

"This one can be trusted," Simus said. "Take me to her."

"As you wish, Warlord," Pive said, tugging on the reins of her gurtle, and turning it back toward the herd. "Hup, hup" she told her mount.

"MUWAAAAP," the gurtle protested, but did as it was bid.

Pive plunged into the herd, and the other gurtles moved aside, protesting as they shifted to one side or another. Simus nudged his horse to follow.

Pive angled off, toward another rise. There were other children scattered about, watching over the herds. Not that gurtles took much tending, but it was a common task given to younger children who had not earned their first metal weapons. Simus could remember his days of gurtle tending, not to mention the gathering of fuel for the fires.

They topped the rise, and Simus spotted her, surrounded by a 'guard' of children. Her horse grazed nearby, with just a plain saddle, and straps for carrying baskets.

The tightness in Simus's chest eased. "My thanks," he said to Pive and urged his horse forward at a faster pace, causing the gurtles to raise a storm of protest.

Simus saw Snowfall raise her head at the sound. She watched as he approached, her face blank and expressionless.

* * * * *

She watched as Simus urged his horse down the rise and headed toward her.

Her heart sped up, and she lowered her gaze to the basket in her hands.

She'd doubted he'd come. After all, she'd lost the challenge. Her duties were now no more than an ordinary warrior's. His was the role of the Warlord. He should be gathering his warriors and aiding to raise the Council tent this morning, as Essa had commanded.

But her heart had dared hope.

And now that he was here, she found herself torn between joy and a terrible trembling in her bones. It felt as if she had always known that Simus of the Hawk's loyalty, once given, was absolute. But she didn't understand where that knowledge came from. That trust. It thrilled and frightened at the same time.

But her heart ached for the one truth she knew well. She'd failed him. She could still serve, but not at his side, as she'd come to wish.

How to face him? How to admit—

But there was no delay, no escape. His horse pounded up, and she lifted her eyes to meet his.

* * * * *

Simus galloped close, and then slid from his saddle. "Snowfall," he said, and didn't try to hide his relief.

"Warlord," Snowfall said, nodding her head.

"I needed to find you." Simus stepped closer. "To see—"

"I lost," Snowfall said abruptly.

"I know," Simus said. "Where did she score on you?"

Snowfall touched her left cheek.

Simus stepped closer again to look.

"She's good," Snowfall said, but there was a hint of grudge in her respect.

"There's no scar." Simus made it a question.

"I used bloodmoss," Snowfall said. She looked at him closely. "You are well?"

"Well enough," Simus said. He took a deep breath. "I had to come find you," he heard himself babble. "To see if…" Simus stopped himself.

"Well, you have found me." Snowfall gestured to the baskets of dried dung that surrounded her. "At my duties."

"We are watching her," Pive piped up. She trotted closer to the two of them. "We told her she has to find the driest bits for a good fire."

Snowfall's mouth quirked ever so slightly. "Yes, they did," she said.

Simus just stared at Snowfall.

The sun was higher now, and for some reason Simus could see clearly. Clearer. Snowfall was all the more beautiful, standing before him, surrounded by baskets of dried dung.

Her eyes were clear and quiet, but he could read her shame. Her curls danced in the light, framing her face.

The pounding in his heart, the need within his soul...by all the elements above and below, he finally saw the truth.

It wasn't just her beauty, it was her, all of her, that he wanted. Needed. Her strength, her courage, her—

Snowfall tilted her head. "Shouldn't you be at the raising of the Council tent?"

Joy filled his mind and heart. Simus started to laugh, at himself, at the skies, at his own stupidity, laughing until the horses, the children, the gurtles were all staring at him with concern.

"Warlord?" Snowfall asked slowly, as they all, the horses, the children, the gurtles, all stared at him like his wits had been taken by the winds.

And still he laughed at his own blindness, and the realization that filled his heart.

"Warlord, are you well?" Snowfall asked. She glanced toward the thea tents. "I could fetch Hanstau. I think he is with Haya—"

"I love you," Simus said.

CHAPTER THIRTY-ONE

Once again Amyu found herself pressed against a wall within the Council Chamber of Water's Fall. This time she stood behind Archpriest Iian's chair, her arms filled with his books and scrolls. She'd offered to aid him, and the Warprize had smiled and nodded. But Amyu had another purpose for this morning meeting and she quivered to tell it. But not now. Not yet.

The room was stifling with clusters of candles burning on the table and mantle. The large tapestry of the winged horse-eagle hung heavy against the wall, still and silent. As if waiting.

Amyu forced herself to look away, and still herself to patience.

Warlord Keir stood at the head of the table, never content to just sit. The Warprize sat beside him, her face tight and anxious. The Lords of the realm, and those that served, were crammed in tight, some seated, others standing along the walls.

"What do you mean, gone?" Keir asked.

Lord Marshal Warren answered. "The reports are coming in, the last from scouts well outside the walls. Over the last few days the wyverns had been gathering on the mountainsides, clinging to the rocks and hissing. Then they launched, all of them, and flew south."

"All of them?"

"Like a cloud," Warren confirmed. "I've had watchers on the Castle walls, and have sent scouts as far and wide as I dared. There are no sightings of the monsters, and no attacks."

"Then perhaps we could open the shutters," Lord Korvis said, mopping at his sweaty face with a cloth.

No one moved to do so.

"Let's not take the risk just yet," Keir said dryly. "How certain can we be?"

Warren shrugged. "It's possible that they've hidden themselves in the wooded areas or caves. Only time will tell. But those that saw the flight said it was dark clouds of the beasts rolling down the valley."

The Warprize caught her lip with her teeth, and made a soft noise of distress. When Keir glanced at her she looked at him with her fey blue eyes. "The Plains," she said.

Keir jerked his head in a nod, but turned back to the table to scan those gathered. "We cannot be certain that they are gone, nor can we assume that they are gone forever."

"I am fairly certain they are not," Archpriest Iian spoke up, which caused a stir.

Amyu smiled slightly as he spoke. She could barely see his head over the back of the chair. But his words carried weight.

Iian stood and started to unroll a thick scroll of soft leather such as Amyu had never seen.

"Have a care with this," he demanded. "It's already split in places."

"What's this?" The Warprize craned her neck for a better look.

"The Sun's Book of Days," Iian said absently, gesturing for the Lord next to him to hold one end as he unrolled the other. "An ancient copy. The part I want you to see is—"

Everyone shifted slightly in order to see. Amyu pressed back against the wall. She had already seen. She'd already been convinced.

The Warlord was asking something of the Warprize and she was smiling at him as she answered. "A very old book of the Church of the God of the Sun, that sets out all the days of the year. It tells when to plant, when to harvest, sets out the holy days and festivals."

"You track your days with words?" The Warlord shook his head in disbelief.

Amyu agreed, it was odd.

"Here," Iian said finally. "Look. Each month begins with a picture." His finger jabbed down but never touched the scroll. "Here, you see wyverns. In all other months, you see wyverns. But for the spring months, the months of late spring, early summer? No wyverns."

"You think they will return, then?" Warren asked.

"Yes." Iian was confident. "What's worse," he said as he rolled the scroll open further, "I think they return with their young." Now he pointed down again, and necks craned, but Amyu had already seen the pictures of wyverns, large and small.

The Warprize frowned. "Iian, for such an event, wouldn't the litany have been more specific? There is no mention of the wyverns in the words, is there? Certainly none in the versions I have read."

"There's no mention of the dawn or dusk either," Iian said. "Why repeat what all know? That the sun will come up and set again. That the wyverns will leave and return. The lack of words does not trouble me. The fact that they pictured the event? That does."

"So you think they are gone?" Warren leaned forward. "And

will return?"

Iian shrugged. "There may be stragglers. But yes, I think the wyverns have left, and will return." He touched the symbol of his office. "With the Grace of the Sun Lord, after the harvest."

"Amen," was the whisper from many of the Xyians.

"We will not lower our guard," Keir commanded. "Heath, what of the search for ballistas?"

"We found parts hidden in various tunnels," Heath said. "But the leather and gut that held them together has dried and cracked. I have craftsmen working to reconstruct, but they need time."

"Maybe we have that time now," Keir said. "Still, have the warriors remain alert." He glanced around. "Unless there are other matters, this Council is at an end."

The members rose from their chairs as they started to file from the room. Iian took his time rolling his precious scroll, delaying until the room emptied and the door closed.

Warlord Keir seated himself next to the Warprize. "You wished to speak to us, Amyu."

"Aye, Warlord." Amyu stepped away from the comforting wall, and placed her burdens on the table, hoping that no one could see the trembling in her hands. "Warlord, Warprize." She drew a breath to slow her words. She felt the urge to kneel, but forced her knees to stiffen. Children knelt when asking; warriors stood. "I ask to be released from the service of your tent to pursue another path."

Warlord Keir studied her, his bright blue eyes piercing her intently. The Warprize leaned forward. "What do you mean, Amyu?"

"They are traditional words," Keir rumbled. "For a warrior who wishes to take on other responsibilities under a Warlord's service."

The Warprize tilted her head, and gave Amyu a puzzled look.

"I do not understand."

"I wish to seek out these creatures." Amyu glanced at the tapestry. The horse-eagle's eyes glittered back.

"Airions?" the Warprize asked. "But, Amyu, they are little more than legends. The stuff of story and myths."

"So were wyverns," Iian noted quietly, placing his scroll in its case. "But mere days ago."

"How can we know?" Amyu asked. "Unless someone goes looking for them?" It burst from her now, her ideas. "I would learn with Iian, seek out the eldest Xyians, listen to their tales and glean their truths. And then I would climb, for the mountains hold the answers, I am sure of it." She forced herself to stop, and breathe. "And show myself worthy to my Tribe and my Warlord."

"Amyu," the Warprize said, frowning. "You have nothing to prove."

"To us," the Warlord murmured. "But to herself?" He looked at her again, and once again his blue eyes regarded her closely.

And here it was, the moment of all her truths. Child or not in the eyes of the Plains, Amyu had to take this chance. "Yes, Warlord."

Keir looked at the Warprize. "You are her thea—"

"She is not a child," the Warprize said, frowning.

Iian spoke up. "It's worth trying, to seek out the older parishioners and ask for the old tales."

"The oldest person in Xy that I know of is Kalisa the cheese-maker," the Warprize said. "It's not a bad idea to seek out the old stories, but to go into the mountains? They are dangerous enough to Xyians. Especially to one who has only ever lived on the Plains."

"Find out what you can," Keir said. "Any knowledge aids us."

"But no more than that," the Warprize said, gentling her

words with a smile. "And no more talk of release from my service." She glanced at the tapestry. "There are others with far better skills for searching the mountains. You are of the Plains, Amyu, you do not know the risks."

Amyu stood, crushed. Denied. Her glance went to the tapestry, but the airion no longer met her eyes.

"But she can help me," Iian said. "Seek out knowledge?" He glanced at Amyu, clearly trying to soften the blow.

"Yes, of course," the Warprize said. She put a hand on Amyu's arm. "Even if we found creatures like that, I don't like the idea that you may be killed trying to find and ride those things," she said.

"Oh, I can ride," Amyu said, trying to hide the defiance in her truth. "I want to fly."

* * * * *

Simus laughed at himself, as Snowfall's mouth dropped open; as the horses, gurtles, and children all continued to stare. He laughed until he couldn't breathe, and then tried desperately to suck in air even as he wanted to shout out his stupidity and his joy.

Snowfall's mouth snapped shut, her lips a thin line, and those blank eyes, those lovely blank eyes he'd longed to see sparkle with joy, with laughter, were filled with anger. "You mock me," she snarled. But it wasn't enough to cover the pain in her voice.

"No," Simus denied. "I do not." Sudden deep fear coursed through him, like a cold wind. That sobered him, looking into her grey and hostile eyes. He dropped to his knees before her.

"I would speak my truth to you, here, under the open skies for all the elements to witness," Simus said, trying to slow his breath, trying to put his heart in his words. "I do not understand how it happened, but I do understand this. I love you."

"We have not even shared—" Snowfall protested, but Simus shook his head and held up his hands to stop her.

"This goes beyond sharing our bodies." Simus drew a deep breath. "The day is not right without your presence," he said. "Without drinking your kavage, without hearing your voice. There is no joy in the day if I cannot try to lure out your smile. There is no rest at night if I cannot hear your breathing in my tent." Simus paused, staring up at her. "I would not lose this. I would not lose you."

Snowfall's eyes glistened. Her anger had faded. "Simus," she breathed, and it seemed to Simus that she breathed out his soul in a single word.

Simus rose to his feet. "Snowfall," he said as simply as he could. "Without you, my life and breath are empty."

Snowfall's anger may have faded from her eyes, but he saw her doubt and uncertainty.

Simus took a slow step forward. "I know we haven't shared, I know we haven't so much as really touched—"

"We danced," she whispered, and hope flared in his heart. Simus moved closer, watching her eyes for any sign of rejection. When she didn't move, didn't retreat, he reached out and brushed his thumb along her cheek. Her skin was soft and warm and he leaned in ever so slowly, and she leaned forward, and—

"Ewwwww," a chorus shrilled.

Simus jerked his head around.

Pive stood there with five other children, all staring at them with their faces screwed up in various expressions of disgust. "Are you gonna kiss?" asked one of the smaller ones.

"Don't you have duties?" Simus asked.

They all recognized his tone, and scattered, mounting up on

their gurtles and charging off into the gurtle herd. Simus watched them flee, afraid that he'd been too harsh, until he heard some of them giggling.

Relieved, he turned back to Snowfall, and his heart sank to see the blankness back in her eyes. "Snowfall—"

* * * * *

It was too much too fast. She wasn't sure that she could trust, and yet she wanted to so very much.

Too much.

Simus turned back to her, his face so eager.

And what would that mean, for him, for his people. How would they react, how would Keir react?

She made her face a blank. "Warlord." She took a step back, away from him into the midst of her baskets, seeking their protection. "You have duties to attend to."

"Don't be afraid." Simus didn't move closer, his voice a gentle whisper.

Snowfall bristled. "I fear nothing."

"I do," Simus said with a wry smile. "I have left myself open to your attack, Snowfall. For a fatal blow from your hand."

"Warriors do not die from rejection," Snowfall said sharply. She edged farther back.

"Maybe not die," Simus said. "But I would break. I would be lost."

Snowfall looked away, at the grass, at the dung baskets, anywhere but at him.

She heard him sigh, and reach for his belt.

"Here is my dagger." He pulled it from its sheath. "I offer my surrender to you, Snowfall of the Plains."

That drew her eyes. Simus took a step closer, keeping his dagger point aimed at his heart.

Horns sounded in the distance, the deep echoing horns of the Singers.

"The Council tent," Snowfall said. "The raising has begun. You should be there."

"You are more important," Simus said.

Snowfall's eyes went wide. "You don't mean that."

"I do."

Snowfall glanced away. "It seems more complicated now," she whispered.

"No," Simus said, taking a step toward her, shaking his head in denial. "No, it isn't."

"I never thought…" Her voice trailed off. "I did not think…"

Simus shifted the dagger hilt toward her. "Accept my surrender, Snowfall. Accept my heart."

"I think we should be cautious." Snowfall didn't move any closer, but she didn't back away.

"I think we should be bold," Simus countered, stepping around the baskets.

"We may end up killing each other," Snowfall said.

"Or not," Simus said, and took another step.

"We will hurt each other," Snowfall murmured, eyeing the dagger hilt.

"Or not," Simus said. He started to smile.

"We will regret of this haste," Snowfall said.

"Or not," Simus said.

Snowfall tilted her head at him. He was so close, she could feel the heat of his body, see the spark in his eyes. "And that would be the arrogance?" she asked dryly.

Simus laughed and then leaned closer. "Kiss me, or kill me, Snowfall."

Snowfall hesitated, then reached for the dagger hilt.

A child's horn called out, a rude bleating noise jarring both of them.

"Pive." Simus swung his head around, growling at the interruption.

The children, scattered through the herd, were all pointing north.

Both she and Simus turned, squinting into the morning sun to see a cloud of black high above, stretching over the horizon to the north.

CHAPTER THIRTY-TWO

A storm?" Snowfall asked.

"Odd sort of storm," Simus said slowly, watching as the line seemed to grow larger. It pulsed with movement. He sheathed his dagger.

"Birds?" Snowfall asked, shading her eyes.

"They're coming too fast," Simus said. He watched for a moment, uneasy. "Those are no birds."

"They—" Snowfall bit her lip. "They glow."

"What?" Simus asked, watching the line with growing unease.

"As if they use magic." Snowfall seemed confused by her own words.

The herd around him stirred, gurtle heads coming up and looking north. The horses, too, his and Snowfall's, stopped grazing and lifted their heads, ears flicking nervously.

"Secure your mount," Simus ordered. Snowfall moved to obey.

The line was larger now, something large and winged, and coming fast. The numbers were massive, uncountable to his eye.

"That dread." Snowfall pressed her hand to her chest. "It's—"

Something old stirred deep in Simus's mind, like a muscle rarely used. He needed no more warning. "Pive," he shouted as he sheathed his dagger.

All the small herders turned toward him, their bows and arrows out, waiting to defend their charges. The gurtles stood, their heads up and alert.

"Back to the tents," Simus commanded.

Pive screwed up her face, but obeyed, calling a command to her fellow herders to move off as fast as their gurtles could go. Pive's ponytail bounced behind her as they ran.

Snowfall mounted, her horse stamping as it sensed the danger. Simus ran to his, and pulled himself up in the saddle. His horse snorted, dancing. "Snowfall," Simus yelled, as he pulled free the bow secured to his saddle. "Your magic? Permission granted."

Her glance was puzzled, but then her eyes went wide with understanding just as she turned to face the foe.

It was as if all the Plains had gone completely silent. There was only the wind, and the sound of leathery wings down-stroking against the wind.

The creatures were huge.

The first ones passed over head, paying no attention to them. Simus's horse trembled, but didn't move, obedient to his commands.

Simus saw dark, leathery wings, and lizard-like heads topped with long, black, curling horns as they sailed past. Their tails were long and spiked at the end. The downdraft of their flight carried the stench of rotting meat to his nostrils.

They were headed for the Heart. Perhaps they would—

The gurtles milled nervously, then broke as the first monsters flew over. They bolted at a run, away from the threat.

Simus's stomach sank. The gurtles were following the children.

Two of the creatures hissed and dropped down into the herd, landing on their clawed back legs. One snaked out its long neck, caught a gurtle in its jaws, and tossed it into the air.

Simus watched in horror as the monsters hopped through the herd, lashed out, killing anything that moved. In heartbeats they had killed so many.

One of the monsters launched up, and he heard Snowfall gasp as it soared high, carrying a dead gurtle in each claw as it flew away toward the Heart.

The remaining creature hissed and pinned its prey with long claws, and bent its snake-like neck for the killing blow. The gurtle screamed as it died.

The rest of the running herd collapsed to the ground, disappearing into the tall grass.

Simus couldn't believe the suddenness of it.

Neither could the creature. It flapped its wings, peering about for more prey, and then focused on the only movement in its line of vision.

Pive and the others.

The children were fleeing, their gurtles continuing to run. Pive glanced back, and even at this distance Simus could see her fear.

Simus cursed himself for a fool. He'd sent those children to their deaths. "Pive, down, down," Simus bellowed, knowing it was too late, knowing he'd—

He brought his bow up without thought, and launched two arrows, aiming at the creature's chest.

The arrows didn't pierce its hide. Didn't even draw its attention.

The creature hissed, spread its wings, and then gave a hop before it jumped into the air, beating down with powerful wings, lunging after its prey.

* * * * *

Here,' the power whispered. *'Now.'*

Snowfall didn't have time to curse at its idea of a warning. She'd only time for one thought. *'Not the children,'* rang through her head, making her own decision. *'Not Simus.'*

Snowfall clamped her knees around her trembling horse. "Stand," she commanded as she raised her hands over her head and called the power to herself, seeking a weapon.

The power answered.

Fire danced around her hands, hot, destructive, and eager. She screamed at the monster, and flung a hot bolt of fire at its head. Over and over, one after the other, as fast as she could conjure them.

The first hit the creature's snout. It shook its head and hissed.

Her horse stood beneath her, terrified but obedient. Snowfall narrowed her eyes, and threw again and again, watching as the creature turned toward her. The bolts of fire hit, and seemed to trail down the creature's side.

With no harm done.

Snowfall's heart caught in her throat. From the corner of her eye she saw Simus using his bow, but his arrows bounced from the leathery hide.

The magic…Snowfall could see the glow within it now. The creatures were not using the power, but they used the power naturally.

The monster turned in their direction, lowering its head with a glare, its beady eyes fixed on both her and Simus.

Now the danger was to them, but better her than Simus. It wasn't even a thought, more instinct that sent one last blast of power right into that hideous face.

"HEYLA," Snowfall screamed, turning her horse in circles

with her knees, waving her arms. "Come here, come here." She sent out ribbons of light, golden sparkles twirling in the sun as she tried to catch the beast's eye.

The creature hissed, launched itself into the air, headed toward her.

Snowfall dropped into the saddle, and her horse bolted away. Snowfall kept her seat, both hands high in the air, the ribbons of light streaming out behind.

She had its attention. The creature flapped its dark, leathery wings, gaining height and following.

Even in her panic, Snowfall watched over her shoulder, eyes wide, as the creature used the power to launch itself in flight. What manner of beast?—but she cut that thought off, concentrating, weaving the ribbons from her hands, fleeing away, drawing the threat from the children, away from Simus.

The monster followed, taking flight and gaining.

* * * * *

He was going to kill her.

Simus almost howled when Snowfall created the distraction, successfully luring the creature away.

He urged his horse after them, and the animal responded with a leap, galloping along. He gripped his mount with his legs, and continued to launch arrow after arrow.

But the arrowheads didn't pierce, didn't even make it turn its head to look.

Its prey was Snowfall, and in another few feet—

"Circle," Simus bellowed. His lance; it was the only hope of a kill.

Snowfall never looked back, but her horse began to turn as

it ran. The creature shifted its flight.

Simus guided his horse to run alongside it.

The creature ignored him, intent on its prey. Simus reached for the lance in its quiver. One shot—he'd have one throw.

A tremor of fear for Snowfall passed through him, but Simus pushed it down and away, focusing on the beast, on the wings, waiting for them to rise, to give him that one precious target, one throw at the lungs—

The creature flapped its wings to gain height, and then plunged down with its wings spread high and wide, extending its claws at Snowfall's back, shrieking its rage—

—exposing its chest.

Simus threw. And he threw true.

The creature screamed, even as its claws plunged down. Snowfall's horse stumbled, and both she and the horse fell into the grasses.

The creature screamed again, biting at the lance, then it hit the earth, tumbling and writhing, its tail lashing about as it struggled. Clods of earth and grass flew as flailed about, its wings beating desperately against the ground.

"Snowfall," Simus whispered in a wordless prayer to all the elements. He dismounted and ran forward as her horse struggled to its feet.

He found her in the grass, face-down and limp. His hands trembled as he turned her over, her face bruised and scraped.

"Snowfall," he called, checking for wounds on her arms and legs, checking—

Her eyes flew open, and she gasped in air, clutching at his shoulders. He pulled her into a hug, relief flowing through him. But Snowfall was pushing him back, and he released her for fear—

She took his face in her hands, pulled him close, and kissed him.

The taste of Snowfall exploded in Simus's mouth.

Her lips were warm and sweet. Simus closed his eyes, wrapped his arms around her tight and reveled in the pure pleasure of the kiss. But in a breath Snowfall jerked back, her eyes wide as the same thought struck both of them.

"The children," they both breathed.

Simus pulled her to her feet and they both scanned the grass around them. The creature lay dead, their horses close, but all that was to be seen was grass. The thea tents were gone. Simus took a few steps, his heart in his throat. They'd run in an arc… the bodies…

"Oh skies, no," Snowfall started to run with him, speaking under her breath. "Skies and stars and sacred fires, please—" Her voice was half sob, her prayer his.

A gurtle head popped up from the grasses, looking about. "Muwaaaap," it called as it staggered up.

Simus sucked in a breath, running full out. "Elements, please—"

Horns sounded from where the thea tents had been, and warbling cries rose, calling to the children. The pit in Simus's stomach grew as the wind shifted, bringing with it the scent of blood and death.

"Muwaap, muwaap." More gurtle heads popped out of the grasses as the herd rose and complained.

Pive's head popped up as well.

Simus's knees went weak, stumbling in his relief, but he kept running as four more little heads appeared. Alive. They were alive.

"Praise the elements," Snowfall choked out.

Simus kept running.

Pive was blowing her horn in response to the theas's call. She squealed in surprise when Simus scooped her up and hugged her. For just an instant, she hugged him fiercely, and then pushed back at his chest. "Warlord," she protested, and struggled to be let down.

Snowfall knelt, gathered the others, checking them for injury. Simus closed his eyes in relief. None were harmed.

The gurtles had not been so lucky.

"What were those things?" Simus demanded of Snowfall.

"I have no idea." She rose to her feet, looking back at the huge, dead monster.

Warriors ran from the thea camp toward them, Seo at the lead. Behind them, huffing and puffing, was Hanstau.

The warriors formed a circle around the children, bows and swords at the ready. Seo strode toward Simus as Hanstau checked the children. Other warriors watched the skies.

"Those things attacked and wrecked our tents." Seo faced Simus. "I've deaths among my warriors, and dead horses." He nodded toward the huge carcass. "What is that thing?" he asked.

"We don't know," Simus said.

"I do," said Hanstau.

CHAPTER THIRTY-THREE

Hanstau stood as he spoke, adjusting the strap of his satchel, sweat gleaming on his pale pink head. He spoke in rushed Xyian, breathing hard. "My grandfather would tell us scary stories by the fire late at night. He'd talk of tales told by his grandfather, of monsters that once lived in the mountains, huge flying lizards. 'Vicious and cruel, with sharp claws and a poison that pierced men's hearts.' Wyverns, he named them." Hanstau drew in a deep breath to calm his panting.

Simus translated what he had said.

"I caught some of that. But 'grandfather'?" Seo asked. "I do not know that word."

"Father's father," Simus replied and turned back to the healer. "I saw none of these when I was in Xy."

"They'd not been seen in my grandfather's lifetime either." Hanstau's eyes were a bit wide. "Only in my grandfather's grandfather's time. Honestly, I thought them only stories. Myths."

"Not so," Simus growled.

"They came from the north," Snowfall said quietly.

Simus looked toward Xy, and spared a moment of fear for his friends. But then he remembered stone tents. Relief and envy flooded through him. "Seo, spare two warriors, and have them examine the body. We need to know all that we can."

"Tell them to beware the tail," Hanstau said. "If memory serves, that is where the sting is."

Seo nodded, an odd look on his face. Simus knew he had not yet adjusted to the Xyian way of forgetting things told them.

"Take the children and life-bearers into one of the winter lodges," Simus started, but Seo interrupted.

"There will be no stores, no food—" Seo argued, but Simus cut him off

"Regardless," Simus said. "Look."

In the distance, another black mass approached.

"Skies," Seo breathed.

"Everyone down," Simus bellowed, and they all flattened into the grass.

"Hold the horses, if we can," Simus commanded, and Snowfall nodded.

The wyverns passed overhead as Simus stood close and tried to soothe his trembling horse. Once again, a few creatures swooped in to take gurtles, but most flew past.

When the sky was clear, Simus rose to his feet.

"We will shelter," Seo said. "And you, Warlord?"

"I will take Snowfall and return to the Heart," Simus said.

"Take Hanstau," Seo said grimly. "You will have a need."

Simus considered, then nodded. "He can ride double with Snowfall."

"But," Hanstau started, but Simus cut him off.

"I don't trust your riding skills if we are attacked," Simus growled as he mounted his horse.

"Warlord." Hanstau's tone was dry as Snowfall went to aid him mount. "I have all the skill necessary to fall off a horse and hide in the grass."

Snowfall's eyes crinkled in the corner, but her face remained blank, unreadable to most. Simus's heart swelled, but there was no time for such things now. He turned his horse's head to go.

Seo reached out, his hand on Simus's boot. "Warlord, find Haya. She was to attend the tent raising. She was at the Heart." Seo's worry was clear.

Simus gave him a sharp nod, and turned his horse toward the Heart.

* * * * *

Awareness flooded into Hail Storm, through his fevered dreams. He'd heard—

"Here, Warlord," came a voice. "We've found him."

Hail Storm was hot, suffocating, the leather of the collapsed tent covering his face, sticking to his sweat, his own stink all around him. He opened his dry mouth to gasp as the debris was ripped away. Sunlight flooded his eyes, blinding him.

"Alive?" came a distant bellow, one he recognized. Antas of the Boar.

"If you want to call it that," said another above him.

Hail Storm blinked at the muck in his eyes, trying to understand what was happening. He lifted a hand to rub the crust away, bringing his swollen arm into sight, oozing pus and pulsing red. The pain hit then, and he grit his teeth as it washed over him.

Hands reached down, grabbing his arms, legs, and shoulders, and lifted him. His vision blackened as the agony raced through him.

"Bring him." Antas stood between him and the sun, his blond hair and beard glowing in the light.

Hands supported him, and half-marched, half-carried him forward.

"Antas." Veritt came up to walk beside. Hail Storm fought to focus on his words. "There's more dead than I care to say. I will have a count later. The tents are all torn down and destroyed, but our supplies and gear are in decent shape." Veritt took a breath. "We lost children to those creatures."

Antas stopped dead in his tracks and swore. He stood for a long moment, contemplating the skies. Hail Storm used the precious moments to find his feet and push the trembling from his limbs.

"I'd think the elements had cursed us," Antas said finally. "Except the same death and destruction seems to have fallen on the Heart. Perhaps we are all cursed." Hail Storm caught Antas's glance in his direction. "Still," Antas continued. "No plan survives the enemy."

"Truth," Veritt replied.

Antas dropped his voice. "The other prisoner?"

"Secure," Veritt said. "The tent was torn down around them, and two of the guards killed, but the others kept their post and saw to her."

Antas grunted. "Set a watch on the skies, and have the others scrounge what they may. We will move camp."

Veritt bowed his obedience, then jerked his head toward Hail Storm. "This one cannot ride," he reminded Antas. "The horses reject him."

Antas grunted as they both considered Hail Storm.

"I will be well soon enough," Hail Storm insisted, trying to stand on his own.

"So you have been saying, yet I see no improvement," Antas

said. "I will deal with this," he said to Veritt, who bowed his head again, and headed off, calling instructions.

"Bring him," Antas commanded. Hail Storm found himself moving through the grasses, only now he could see the destruction around him.

They stopped.

Before them was the body of a huge winged animal pierced by a half-dozen lances. Horns on its head, black and curling. The beast still lived, its tail quivering in its death-throes.

"What—" Hail Storm coughed to clear his throat. "What is that?"

"I do not know," Antas said, standing beside him. "I had hoped you would. I do know that whatever they are, they have wreaked havoc on my plans."

"They?" Hail Storm frowned. His wounded arm hung heavy at his side, and throbbed with the beat of his heart. He lifted it, holding it up with his other hand.

"They filled the skies," Antas said. There was pain and wonder in his voice. "I'd gathered my warriors to assault the Council tent and take Essa prisoner." Antas's voice hardened. "We saw a line of black on the horizon, and within moments they were overhead, attacking anything that moved. My proud warriors, dead all around me, and the only safety lay in cowardice. Face down on the ground, still and silent."

The creature before them groaned and rolled, sending warriors scattering. "Get back, you stupid fools," Antas shouted as the tail lashed out in all directions.

All got clear as the beast gave a final moan and died. The tail fell to the ground, limp and lifeless.

"The only good news," Antas said, voice oddly calm, "is that so far as we could see, the Council tent was torn down and their losses are equal with mine."

Hail Storm stayed silent, just looking at the huge beast with its curling horns.

Antas looked around, and Hail Storm followed his gaze. Even with fevered, blurry eyes he could see the ruined tents and the dead warriors still lying where they had fallen.

"So for now, I must rely on allies," Antas almost seemed to be talking to the skies. "Ietha, Loual, and that hot-head Wyrik. They will have to deal with what has happened. The others, the neutral Warlords, will be watching to see how the winds blow. I really don't blame them. The herd follows the strongest mare." He rolled his shoulders. "No. The blame for this rests on Keir and his ilk." He gestured toward the creature.

"How so?" Hail Storm blinked away the sweat from his eyes, swaying slightly. The two warriors grabbed his arms in support.

Antas turned to him, and his eyes burned with hate. "They came from the north. From Xy."

"We will be avenged." Hail Storm straightened, his own hate rising and giving him strength. "I will heal and we will see it done."

"About that." Antas nodded to one of the warriors at Hail Storm's side. "Bring him," he commanded, and once again Hail Storm was 'assisted' toward a fire pit.

"We cannot stay this close to the lake," Antas told him as he walked alongside. "The creatures are gathered there, and the skies alone know what they will do next. We will fall back, farther south." Antas stopped by the fire. "Lay him down." Antas gestured toward the edge.

"What—" Hail Storm struggled against the hands that forced him down, stretching him out in the cleared area and holding him to the ground.

"I have no choice now." Antas reached toward the fire, pulling an axe from its depths, its head glowing dull red. "I've instructed my theas to seek out the winter lodges, and secure the young and life-bearers. I've enough warriors left that we can harry them with smaller attacks, seeking supplies, theas, Essa and Wild Winds and any Elders I can get my hands on." Antas nodded in satisfaction at the weapon in his hand. "This is a setback, nothing more. We will fade into the Plains and build our strength for another season."

"What are you—" Hail Storm struggled again, but the warriors over him were grim-faced and hard. One of them grabbed his injured arm and pulled it straight out from his body. As the pain flared, Hail Storm bit through his lip in an effort not to scream.

"I'd grant you mercy, warrior-priest," Antas said, stepping closer, "if I did not need you. Although your value is doubtful. So I will cure you in my own way."

"No," Hail Storm snarled. "I will not survive—"

"Need finds a way," Antas said.

"Do this, and I will kill you," Hail Storm shrieked, but Antas was unmoved.

"You have to live," Antas said, shrugging. "Then I will fear." He brought the axe down in a swift, powerful blow.

Bone shattered and flesh burned.

Everything stopped, even his breath. It was as if it was happening a distance away, to another. Hail Storm watched as the warrior lifted his severed arm, and tossed it into the fire.

The arm lay there, reddened by the coals, charred at the end. His fingers…its fingers moved. Hail Storm reached with his power, and watched as the singed fingers formed a fist.

But then everything crashed down on him. The sounds of

the warriors, the sizzle of scorched flesh. His lungs demanded air.

Hail Storm gasped, and then screamed until his breath was gone and the pained darkness claimed him.

CHAPTER THIRTY-FOUR

Simus crawled to the edge of the rise, keeping to the taller grasses. This was where he'd first encountered Wild Winds and Snowfall; it would give them a good view of the Heart and the lakeshore nearby. Elois was next to him, keeping her head as low as she could.

Simus just stared at the destruction. The Council tent was flat, covering the stone Heart, a pile of shredded leather and splintered poles. Bodies, too, of warriors that had fallen trying to defend themselves. "Skies above," he swore.

All along the shoreline, as far as one could see, a writhing mass of wyverns flew, flapping their wings and snarling and hissing at one another.

Nothing else moved. Nothing dared.

"They had no warning, I'm sure," Elois choked, but kept on. "The warning horns mingled with the ceremonial ones and the chanting. They didn't have a chance."

"Smart move on your part, knocking down my own tent," Simus said.

"We waited, Tsor and I." Elois's voice hitched. She paused, then continued. "We waited for you. Else we'd have been down there with them."

"Has there been any sign of survivors?" Simus nodded toward the devastation.

"Not so far," Elois said. She sighed. "At one point, something moved within. The beasts attacked the tent and then tore into it like it was a living thing. I don't know if any are still alive underneath. Two rescue attempts failed," she added, nodding toward where a cluster of warriors lay dead.

"Tsor took some of the younger warriors, to stalk the beasts," Elois continued quickly. "Not to attack, but to watch and learn. He told them to stalk as if hunting prey, but to make no attacks."

Simus grunted, still considering the mound that was the collapsed Council tent. It was—it had been—the largest of the tents on the Plains, covering the circular stone with tiered seating for the Elders. It lay in shambles now, but it was possible that under its weight, someone survived. Perhaps…was Joden under that mess?

Simus squashed the thought. Best to deal with what he knew. Better to focus on the problem at hand.

"And those that have gathered there?" Simus asked, deliberately not looking behind him at the warriors gathered out of sight of the Heart.

"What remains," Elois grimaced. "Thirds and Fourths, and the odd Tenth. All lost since their Warlords and Seconds were within the Council tent." Elois snorted. "And them supposed to take over command if the leaders fall."

"Go easy," Simus said. "They've never had to deal with something like this. We've had to face much that is new and different since dealing with Xy."

"But nothing like this," Elois said.

"No," Simus agreed. "Nothing like this." He took one last look. "Let's return."

They crawled back to the group of warriors waiting, kneeling and sitting in the grass. Their hunched shoulders, and anxious scanning of the skies, was telling.

Snowfall and Hanstau sat to one side. Snowfall, with his permission, was trying to contact Wild Winds. She had a small bowl of water in her hands that shimmered with her power. She met Simus's eyes, and shook her head slightly before returning to her efforts. So, then: Wild Winds was either dead or unconscious under the debris.

Simus sat before the group, Elois on his right. "I will call this senel to order," he said, keeping his voice low.

That brought startled heads up to glare at him.

"By what right," one warrior growled.

"Because no one else did," Simus said firmly. "We must make decisions, and quickly."

There was a muttering, but no further protests.

"Tsor, my Second, has taken warriors to watch and learn about the creatures. When they return, we will mount a rescue attempt." He looked around the group of roughly thirty warriors.

"Another?" one voice said. Simus raised an eyebrow in the speaker's direction. "Nona, Third to Osa of the Fox," she said. "We risk more deaths, and there may be no one to aid." She scowled at him. "My Warlord would say save the living."

"Mirro, Third to Loual of the Boar," a male spoke up, his voice flat and angry. "And why would you try, Simus, when those that opposed you are dead?" Mirro's face contorted as he spoke. "You may be the last living Warlord on the Plains, and you and Keir of the Cat would be free to—"

"I would not want to win that way," Simus said simply. "Nor would I serve a WarKing that would take that path to power."

Silence fell over them.

"Those are our best down there," Simus continued. "Our Warlords, Elders, Seconds, and Token-bearers. We know not if they live, but we must try to save them."

That brought a stir within the ranks.

"How?" challenged another. "Those creatures—"

"How is this different from an ehat hunt?" Simus flashed the warrior a tight grin. "We need musk teams to draw the monsters away, and then we send in rescuers to dig out the survivors. I think—"

There was a roar of hissing from the Heart. "Something is happening," Simus said and crouched to go back to the edge of the rise. This time he was followed by a handful of warriors, and his people.

"Ah, no," Elois whispered.

Simus saw that the edge of the tent was moving as someone struggled out. The wyverns had already caught the movement and were growing agitated.

"Don't move, don't move," Elois whispered, but it was a hopeless plea. The warrior emerged from cover, and bolted directly for them, running with everything she had.

Simus watched in sick fascination, helpless and yet unable to look away. Two wyverns rose with single wing beats, and flew toward their prey with wide, spread wings.

The warrior was close, close enough that they could all hear her ragged breathing. The warriors behind Simus shifted, bringing out bows and crossbows, preparing for—

The nearest wyvern plunged down and hooked its claws in the warrior's back, bearing her down to the ground. As the woman struggled, the wyvern hissed, whipped its tail around, and stung her.

Movement around Simus ceased. All knew what that meant. The outcome was inevitable, or so he had been told. Simus looked down at his hands, knotted in tight fists.

The other wyvern came up, and for brief moments they fought over the body, driving each other off. As if the creatures had lost interest, both took to the air and glided back to the lakeshore.

The downed warrior moaned.

"The poison will take her soon. We've seen this before," Elois whispered. "Poor—"

A stir in the grass and Hanstau took off, running down the rise.

"What?" Simus's jaw dropped. The pudgy healer ran like a pregnant gurtle toward the fallen warrior. The wyverns hadn't noticed him yet, but it was only a matter of—

"That city-dweller has lost his wits," Mirro said harshly.

"I need him," Simus growled. "I need his skills. Elois, Tsor, crossbows and lances. We will try—"

A hand touched his arm. "I can save him." Snowfall looked at him with bright eyes. "Permission?"

Simus hesitated, then nodded, and she was running, following the healer to her death.

* * * * *

Snowfall took off running as fast as she could, following the healer, keeping an eye on the wyverns. The creatures were stirring, their snake-like heads starting to turn toward the movement.

She'd have little time.

Ahead of her, Hanstau slid in the grass, down, next to the wounded warrior, hunching over her as if he could protect him.

Snowfall threw herself down on the opposite side of the injured warrior. "Quiet," she whispered, and drew on the power around them.

Hanstau's eyes went wide, staring at her hands but he shook himself, and nodded, going still.

With a deep breath, Snowfall threw a veil up over all three of them.

The wyverns rose on their haunches, craning their long necks, but after what seemed like an eternity, they lowered themselves down and resumed their squabbling.

Snowfall breathed a sigh of relief, only to feel the power flicker. She'd never attempted a veil this large, and if it failed—

"What are you doing?" Hanstau asked, his voice the barest whisper.

"Hiding us," Snowfall explained. "But they can hear, and maybe scent."

"This may have not been my brightest idea." Hanstau's face was dripping sweat. He was looking at the warrior's back even as he tried to watch the wyverns. "But I couldn't let her just die."

Snowfall grabbed his wrist. "We can't stay here," she said, trying to even her breathing. "I may not be able to keep us safe."

Hanstau bit his lip. "Can we move? Can you help carry her? I can't alone, but—"

"We will try," Snowfall said, but then she glared at him. "But if I say for you to run, you will drop her and leave us, and run for your very life. Simus needs you more than—" She frowned at the stubborn expression on the healer's face. "Swear it."

"No need for dramatics," Hanstau said. "Let me get her up, and her arms over our shoulders."

Snowfall didn't have the time to argue. "Move slowly," she

said.

"About all I can do," puffed the healer as he eased the unconscious woman warrior into a seated position, her arm over his shoulder.

Snowfall moved in on the other side, and they got her to her feet.

Hanstau cast one last look back. "So far, so good," he observed.

Snowfall nodded. "Move with me," she cautioned and then put all her focus on maintaining the veil and carrying the warrior, trusting Hanstau to guide them.

Her steps blurred into the weight of her burden, the pain, and the power.

CHAPTER THIRTY-FIVE

Simus's stomach sank into a deep pit as the flame of his heart ran toward certain death.

He'd found her and to lose her now, without knowing her mind, without sharing their bodies, without telling her everything he wanted to share with her for all of their lives—

"Ready lances," he croaked as he watched Hanstau and Snow-fall throw themselves down by the wounded warrior. They'd no chance against two of the beasts.

Snowfall put her hand on Hanstau's shoulder, who was leaning down, reaching for the warrior.

"Run back," Elois whispered. "Get back here now and may-be—"

They disappeared. Suddenly there was nothing but grass and…

Simus sucked in a breath, as the warriors around him gasped.

"Where—" Nona breathed.

"There." Mirro pointed with his chin. "Watch the grass."

Simus focused, and saw the grass was moving. Slowly, surely, toward them.

"A Xyian," Mirro breathed. "A city-dweller. No weapon in hand, and he charges down there."

"There is more to them than you know," Elois spoke up.

Simus said nothing, casting glances between bent blades of grass and the wyverns. Until finally he heard Snowfall's breath, and the shallow panting of a wounded warrior. And the heavier panting of his Xyian healer.

With an audible 'pop' they appeared at the edge, and willing hands pulled them over and down, out of sight of the Heart. Simus had Snowfall in his arms. Relief filled him as her arms enclosed him, and he felt her warm, solid body against his.

She pulled back, and there was a smile in her eyes she'd let only him see. "Just tired, Warlord. I had to carry, and concentrate, and move." She shook her head. "Not as easy as I thought."

"Faela," exclaimed a warrior as the wounded woman was laid down on the grass, Hanstau at her side, digging into his satchel. Willing, careful hands were cutting back the armor, exposing the sting to his view.

"You had to know you were dead," Mirro said, kneeling by the healer. "Why would you—"

"I am a healer," Hanstau said absently, in broken Plains language. "I have my own oaths. Now be silent and let me work."

Elois knelt at the wounded warrior's head, offering a waterskin. The warrior took a swallow, then spat it out. "I am Faela, Token-bearer to Ultie. I bring word—" Her mouth snapped shut against a groan. Hanstau was working on her back.

Simus knelt beside Elois. "Tell us," he commanded.

The warrior blinked against the sweat on her face, and strained to look up. "Many live, some badly hurt, but yet they breathe. If you could—"

"Wild Winds?" Snowfall asked.

Faela grunted against the pain as Hanstau pressed down on the wound. "I do not know," she said through gritted teeth. "Osa,

Ultie—although Ultie is wounded badly in the leg. Other voices, whispering in the darkness. No one dares move." Her breath was gasps now, her words broken. "I…closest to the edge. My choice, to bring word…"

Hanstau swore under his breath and spoke in his own tongue. "Warlord, whatever this poison is, nothing I have counters it. It eats at her from within." He sat back, his lips pressed together in a thin line. He glanced at his bag again, as if considering his options, then shook his head. "Grant her mercy, Warlord."

Simus was surprised, but he knelt by Faela's head. "Faela," he said. "The healer can do no more."

Faela let her head sink down on the grass. "The snows will cool this pain, Warlord," she gasped out. "Let it be done."

"You will be remembered," Simus said.

Faela mumbled something Simus didn't catch, and then made a final effort to lift her head. "I would see the sky," she said.

Willing hands turned her, and Simus stepped back to let those that knew her best conduct the rite.

"The fire warmed you," someone began the chant.

The warriors around her responded in unison. "We thank the elements."

Hanstau moved back, making room, swallowing hard as he angrily shoved jars and bottles back into his satchel.

"Lara fought against the granting of mercy," Simus said softly.

Hanstau paused and took a deep breath. "My Queen is a gentle lady, and a Master Healer, but she lacks my years." The pudgy healer with the soft hands looked up at Simus with hard eyes. "I know when to offer my surrender to Lord Death."

* * * * *

We can kill them," Simus said. "Just like we bring down ehats."

"With all due respect, Warlord, ehat musk does not eat flesh and bone," Nona said.

They'd given Faela mercy and seen to her body as best they could. Now Simus had gathered them once again, out of sight of the Heart. Hanstau sat beside Simus, staring at the satchel in his lap.

"So now we know some live beneath that wreckage," Simus said.

"Without the Warlord, there are no raids. Without raids, there will be no Plains," another offered.

"Without Elders, there is no Council," another said glumly.

"Lances work to kill the creatures," Simus continued, not letting them sink into despair. "Crossbows may, with a good hit. But we need not kill. Just create enough of a fuss to draw them off and let others move in, and pull those that live from the debris. I have an idea—"

A rustling from the grass around them. Simus stopped talking at the sound of a soft bird call. Tsor, and a handful of younger warriors, crawled into view, all grass-stained and sweating.

"Tsor, what word?" Simus said, as the group made room for the newcomers.

Tsor crawled up and sat cross-legged next to him. The young ones sprawled out in the grass before him, sharing a waterskin.

"There's so many, Warlord," Tsor said. "They fill the shoreline as far south as we ranged. But only on the shoreline. They seem drawn to the water's edge." He took a long drink. "They are mock-fighting, and seem to have an area that they defend against all comers. An area that they return to if they are roused. Also, they are piling up their kills."

"Kills?" Simus asked.

"A few have a small heap of dead gurtles close by," Tsor said. "Ouse there has an idea."

Ouse sat up, facing Simus, waiting for permission to speak.

"Give me your truths, warrior," Simus nodded.

Ouse swelled with youthful pride. "Warlord, they remind me of young stags at mating season. Testing themselves against each other."

"Mating?" Simus narrowed his eyes in thought. "Can you sex them? Are there females?"

They all shook their heads. "Not that I've seen," Tsor said. "Not that any of us have seen. No teats, so we think they might be egg layers." He hesitated, and then continued. "I think they may be more like night-flyers than hawks. But that is as good as asking the wind. I've no proof."

"I wouldn't want to bet my life on it," Elois said.

Simus considered for a moment, then shook his head. "If you are right there would be a benefit to delay, but I will not wait on a guess." He looked at the younger warriors. "You five take the healer. Find what is left of his tent and scavenge his gear with him. Watch the skies."

"Aye, Warlord." They scrambled to their knees, ready to go.

"The wounded should be brought to me," Hanstau said firmly. He shifted closer as the others crawled away. "We can set up an area, hidden in the grasses." He gave a sick sort of chortle. "My poor oxen are probably dead."

"What of your powers?" Elois asked Snowfall.

Snowfall shook her head, the twists in her black hair dancing. "It has limits, being unseen. Movement, trying to cover others, all add to the difficulty. Like sparring with five warriors at the same time."

"Maybe if I could use that glow like you do, I could have saved that man." Hanstau pursed his lips.

Snowfall's eyes went wide. "You can see—?"

"Why risk more death in a fatal attempt?" Nona interrupted, spitting her words. "It's useless to—"

"Enough," Simus commanded.

Silence fell, and no one met his gaze.

"Go back to your warriors," Simus said. "Tell them to gather what gear and supplies they can and head out away from the Heart, to regroup. Tell them to warn the theas, protect the herds, and watch the skies at all times." Simus took a breath, awaiting protest.

None came.

"Those that are willing to aid us are welcome," Simus continued. "Return here, with ten of your best warriors, ones willing to take a risk. The winds favor the bold," he concluded.

The wind rustled the grass around them.

"Agreed," Mirro said. "My Warlord may be within and alive. I will return."

"I don't know," Nona said, as the others around her looked uncertain.

"We will proceed," Simus said. "With or without you."

CHAPTER THIRTY-SIX

Simus was alone on the edge of the rise, lying flat, watching and waiting to issue commands.

Almost all of the warriors had returned, bringing others with them, with saddled horses and lances to spare. They were back behind him, hidden by the rises, waiting for his command. They'd organized quickly, once Simus had explained it in terms of an ehat hunt, putting on helmets and strapping shields to their backs for protection against the stings.

Simus drew a breath, taking a moment to appreciate the afternoon sun on his face, the blue of the skies above. One could plan and plan and plan, but it might all come to naught. "Aid us, elements," he whispered in a final prayer.

All was ready.

Simus rose to his knees, the better to see. It was a risk that he might draw the wyverns' attention, but he needed to be seen by his people. The risk was small, given the distraction he was about to unleash.

He raised both fists in the air, and dropped them down.

Behind him, two groups of horses began to run, charging past him and down the slope toward the Heart. As they galloped past, they called out battle cries and sounded horns. Their charge was swift, and they split as they reached the Heart, each taking a side, riding straight for the wyverns.

The wyverns noticed.

The monsters raised their ugly heads with their long, curling horns, focusing on the warriors and horses. Some started to turn, hissing, spreading their wings—

Simus's breath caught, but his warriors never faltered. Both groups charged close to the lake and then as soon as they had the monsters' attention—

—they each turned in the opposite direction, running along the lakeshore, rousing every wyvern that could be seen.

The wyverns launched, but the turn had caught them by surprise, and a few tumbled into one another, hissing and biting each other. But more than enough took to the air, following the riders.

"Move in," Simus bellowed, and resisted the urge to stand in order to see better.

Warriors rose from the grasses around the ruined tent, Snowfall in their midst. It had taken time for them to position themselves, but it had been time well spent under her protection. They darted under the debris as others attached ropes to the edges of the collapsed tent.

Simus watched for the wyverns. But the beasts were all up, pursuing the riders. As they moved along the shoreline, more beasts rose into the air, adding to the congestion.

Simus held his breath as the first of the wyverns closed, but the musk teams darted away from the lake as planned, turning away from the water, still calling, still taunting the creatures. Some had strips of cloth in their hands, letting them flutter out behind them.

The wyverns screeched, and followed. The area was clear.

Simus raised his hand, drew a circle in the air, and then

dropped it.

More warriors charged in on horseback, some with spare horses. They swooped in to grab those climbing out from under the tent debris.

"Come on, come on," Simus urged as the wounded were aided to mount, and some bodies were flung on saddles. Once mounted, the riders wheeled and galloped back, forming a long line of activity that was sure to be noticed. They would keep going, leading the others to where Hanstau had set up his camp. Far enough from the Heart to be safe.

They hoped.

Simus caught a glimpse of Essa mounting, and Haya on the back of another horse. Simus let himself look for Snowfall, but once he saw she was well, his gaze returned to the skies. Tsor had been right. The wyverns had broken off their pursuit of the riders, and were starting to return to their places on the shore. Not much time left.

The last of the riders cleared the area, riding hunched down. Simus waited a breath or two, and then bellowed, "Pull."

Snowfall and her team had also laid the long ropes, and now a team of horses pulled, attempting to shift the debris off the Heart. Simus had proposed this with the vague idea of repairing and preserving the tent, as well as shifting any warriors too tangled to emerge from under. It wasn't the best of plans; shifting the mess might in fact kill those within. Better that than a slow death, was Simus's thought.

The ropes grew taut; the pile began to move. Snowfall and her team began to run, getting out of the way, moving toward the rise where he sat. All of them cast anxious glances above and behind.

The wyverns seemed to care more for reclaiming their territory. Except for one. It flapped its wings, gaining height, focused on the tent.

Simus tensed, waiting…

Snowfall saw it and barked a command, throwing herself down in the grass. The warriors with her dropped, crawled close to her, the shields strapped to their backs glinting in the sun. Simus caught a glimpse of Snowfall's face, the sheen of sweat and strain—

They disappeared.

Circling above, the wyvern seemed more curious than anything else, watching as the debris shifted. The mass caught when it hit the grass, but then continued to slide, the scattered poles rising up like broken bones.

The wyvern snorted, and turned back toward the lake.

The tent debris slid further into the grass, almost clear of the stone of the Heart. Small debris was left behind. Shards of tent poles, kavage pots, a ceremonial drum…and a limp body, covered in tattoos and blood.

Wild Winds.

The wyvern started to circle back.

Simus heard a scream of anguish then, and saw a flickering below him where the warriors lay hidden. The warriors that were with Snowfall appeared, running for his rise.

Snowfall ran for Wild Winds.

Simus's heart jumped, but he didn't waste breath. He picked up the horn at his side, and blew a short blast.

Tsor and his kill team thundered past him toward the Heart.

The running warriors mounted the crest and threw themselves down at Simus's side. "She ordered us back," one gasped.

Simus just sat, forcing himself not to move, a lump in his throat. "Beloved," he whispered, and prayed again to the ever-silent skies. "Elements…please."

The wyvern screeched, and started another circle.

Snowfall ran, beautiful and strong, her long legs eating up the distance, screaming to get the creature's attention. Or maybe Wild Winds's, who had rolled over to hands and knees, struggling to rise.

The wyvern started to dive—

Snowfall stopped dead, and raised her hands. The debris from the tent, including the ceremonial drum, rose in the air and struck the wyvern full on the snout.

The creature hissed. Snowfall now had its full and undivided attention. She stayed where she was, flinging bits of debris.

Undaunted, unhurt, the creature started for Snowfall.

Tsor galloped in, raised up in the saddle, and flung his lance at the creature, burying it in its chest. With a shriek of pain, the creature fell from the sky, perilously close to Snowfall.

The kill team didn't stop. Two warriors brought their horses to Wild Winds's side, and heaved him up behind one of the riders.

Tsor guided his horse toward Snowfall, and pulled her up behind him. They charged back for Simus's rise, riding away before the other wyverns could react.

Simus was mounted and ready when they arrived. He urged his horse alongside Tsor's as they galloped away from the Heart. Snowfall had her head pressed to Tsor's shoulder, her hands around his waist.

"That was stupid," Simus snapped, his anger getting the best of him. "You could have been killed."

"Ride, Warlord," Tsor said, beaming like a madman, flush with success. "Yell at her later."

* * * * *

Dusk was more than welcome.

"We've only allowed small fires," Tsor reported. "Dug down and well shielded. Enough for kavage, and hot water to aid the healer."

Simus nodded, sitting to hear the reports of his warriors. "Scouts?" he asked.

Nona spoke up. "All around us," she said. "With horns to warn of the wyverns' approach. I've four watchers near the Heart as well. They will sound a warning if the creatures take flight."

"Hanstau still tends the wounded," Elois reported. "Those healthy enough have rejoined their warriors." She shrugged. "As to who will live and die, Hanstau said we would know more in the morning."

Simus nodded, knowing full well that some of those included the Elders. But all he could do was wait. "Supplies?" he asked.

Mirro gave him a tired smile. "Our losses were not so bad," he said. "Of more concern will be fresh food, since the gurtle herds have moved even farther off. But for now, we are fine."

"The same is true of the horses," Nona said. "Scattered but alive, and willing to come to our hands."

"The tent debris is being sorted," Elois said. "The skies alone know if it can ever be raised again. But we are saving what we can."

"What of our losses, Warlord?" Tsor asked.

"None of ours," Simus said. "But the dead from the others' camps are far too many."

There was a studied silence then, as they considered his news. Weariness crept into his body, but Simus fought it off. Later. He would sleep later. One piece of good news. Simus had asked, and his people had searched. Joden was not among the dead. Wherever he was, Simus hoped he was safe.

"The other armies have scattered wide, fearing the monsters will return. There are others scavenging the destroyed camps, and keeping watchful eyes on the beasts. It could have been so much worse," Tsor said, bringing Simus's thoughts back.

Elois nodded. "Still, it is not good. So many good warriors, the pride of their Tribes, dead. Especially the death of Kiza of the Cat. Her Second and some of her warriors have approached me, asking if you would accept their swords."

"That is for tomorrow," Simus said, feeling his grief settle in his bones. "If there is nothing further, I think we should seek our tents."

Eyes cast up, looking at the darkening skies before rising to their feet.

"This night might prove your idea," Nona said to Tsor. "That they are not night-flyers."

"I would offer to the skies that they aren't," Tsor muttered.

Elois stood at Simus's side as the others drifted off. "I'll set you a small tent here, for the night."

"Good," Simus said.

"There's a bathing stream along that path." Elois nodded toward it. "Rinse off, and I will have hot kavage for you when you return."

Simus was almost too tired to care, but the dried sweat in his hair was starting to itch. "I will. My thanks, Elois."

He forced his legs to move. Once past the first few steps it got easier. The path had been cut through the bushes that lined the stream, leading to a small bank of stones.

His skin prickled, anticipating the cold water, a welcome relief. He stripped, listening to the noises of his army around him, and then waded into the water. He washed off the sweat and grime, using handfuls of sand. He sat and lay back, letting the cold water wash over him.

Where had these creatures come from? He'd never seen anything like them, nor did he know of any animal with poison such as this, that would eat away at a warrior's flesh. He shuddered, and not from the water.

At least they knew that the wyverns could be killed. Not easily, but what is easy on the Plains, eh? He could almost hear the words in Marcus's dry tones, proclaiming the obvious.

Which led his thoughts to Xy. What if these things had come from there? What did that mean for Lara and Keir and the other warriors left behind. For certain, they had stone walls and stone buildings, but Simus knew full well that one couldn't cower within forever. Would Keir be able to travel to the Plains? Had everything they had strived for been destroyed?

The cold water was taking his breath, and making his teeth chatter. He waded back to the bank and dried off with his tunic.

Gathering up his armor and weapons, he trudged to where his tent should be. Simus sighed. He didn't want to sleep. He wanted to be the one watching the wyverns, or aiding in the healing. But Hanstau had made it clear that he wasn't welcome back at Hanstau's tent until after sunrise. Well after sunrise. And his team had things well under control.

He shouldn't have yelled at her.

Simus stopped, and rolled his shoulders, trying to ease the knots. Wishing he could take back words he'd yelled in his fury. He hadn't seen Snowfall since they'd thundered up to Hanstau's camp, willing hands reaching for a half-conscious Wild Winds. She had gone with him. Simus had stormed off to see to his warriors, dead and alive. His anger had worn off as he'd worked.

He closed his eyes, and admitted to himself that it hadn't been anger. It had been fear. His fear that she'd be hurt, injured, killed, or worse. What if she'd needed mercy at his hand from the deadly sting? Even now the image rose in his mind and made his stomach churn.

He opened his eyes, and continued walking, filled with regret, running over what he might have said. Should have said.

His small, one-man tent was where Elois said it would be.

Snowfall was standing next to it.

His breath caught at the sight.

Her grey eyes were steady, and cool, but she showed her uncertainty when she lifted her chin before she spoke. "I thought we might combine our tents," she said.

"Yes," Simus said, suddenly tongue-tied.

Elois appeared then, with a pitcher of kavage, gurt, and dried meat. "We can see to the tents," she said to Snowfall. "Go and wash."

Snowfall nodded, and stepped past Simus to head down the path. He caught a whiff of her scent as she brushed against him, and watched as the curls of her black hair gleamed in the light.

"A hand, Warlord?" Elois was kneeling beside his tent, a slight smile on her face.

"Of course," Simus said, setting his armor and weapons to one side.

A matter of moments, and the tents were combined. Small enough to sit in, but not so high as to draw attention.

Elois stood, brushing off her knees. "I'll bed down now," she said. "Hanstau is insisting that everyone sleep. Tsor is posting watches for both land and sky." She gave him a side glance. "Try to get some rest, Warlord."

She disappeared just as Snowfall emerged from the bushes, carrying her armor and weapons. Simus watched as she approached, naked, water glistening on her shoulder tattoos.

"Kavage?" he managed to say with a mouth dry with desire.

"No," Snowfall said. "You."

CHAPTER THIRTY-SEVEN

Simus resisted the urge to reach for her. He just held open the tent, and let her slide in first, handing her their sleeping pallets and climbing in behind. They worked together to pile up the gurtle pads, and spread out the bedding. It was a bit awkward physically, and they bumped elbows more than once moving around each other. But having her close, working together—that was comfortable, and easy, and arousing all at the same time.

And when her elbow ended up in his eye for the third time, Simus felt his heart ease, and even sing a bit at the look of amusement in her eyes. Such a small thing. Such a great comfort.

They left the tent flap open, for light and air. Simus might have preferred to sleep under the open skies, but the idea of a tent over his head this night was a good one.

He let Snowfall have the pick of which side, and once she had her weapons arranged to her satisfaction, he set out his armor, sword and dagger within easy reach. Snowfall gathered up the kavage and food bowls, and urged him to take a mug. All in a silence that he felt no need to fill.

She drank as well, studying him over the rim of her mug.

"Gurt?" she asked as they both finished the kavage.

"Later," he said.

She set aside the bowls, and when she turned backed, he reached out and cradled her cheek in his hand, stroking it with his thumb. Her skin was warm and silky against his skin.

She closed her eyes, and tilted her head into his hand.

"I'm sorry," he said softly. "For earlier. For yelling. You are a warrior, entitled to make your own decisions. I was angry because I was frightened for—"

She leaned forward and kissed him.

* * * * *

He tasted of kavage, sword oil, and strength.

Snowfall moved closer, pushing him down, demanding more. Simus obliged, opening his mouth, falling back to let her press him to the blankets and deepen the kiss. She took every advantage, straddling him so that her hips rode his, anticipating what was to come. But for now all that mattered was their lips locked together.

And when she finally needed to breathe, she pressed soft kisses to his face, his nose, his closed eyes as he panted beneath her.

Simus arched his neck as he ran his hands over her back, cradling her buttocks and then moving up again, long sweet strokes across her skin.

Snowfall nuzzled his neck, her teeth biting playfully before her lips sought the skin beneath his ears. She cradled his skull in both hands, using her short nails to scratch at his scalp. She shifted back as she did so, pressing down, feeling his hardness against her stomach.

Simus moaned and arched, then grasped her hips and lifted her up slightly before rolling her to the side. She chortled softly into his neck as he tried to calm his ragged breathing. She'd done this to him, had him quivering under her hands. She took a deep breath of the scent of their bodies together. There was so much more to come, and she ached in anticipation.

She let go, and allowed her tattoos to dance.

Simus caught his breath, watching as the vines swirled and moved, as the flowers bloomed along their lengths. They moved over her shoulders, and down her arms. Snowfall closed her eyes in the pure pleasure of it as Simus stroked her skin and pressed his mouth to the blooms.

"These," he said. "They weren't there before."

"I flower for you," she whispered, and kissed him again, hard and fierce, claiming his mouth.

Simus closed his eyes and kissed her back. "You taste of a sweetness all your own," he murmured against her mouth. He didn't deepen the kiss, letting her control their soft and slow touching of lips and sharing of breath at an awkward angle.

Snowfall stroked her hand down his side, over his hip, and then reached between his legs. Simus caught her hand. "Slow," he whispered. "Slow is good."

Snowfall leaned in, her forehead against his. "It's been some time since I've shared," she admitted to his ear.

"Why so, a warrior as lovely as you." Simus rolled back, pulled her down to stretch out on top of him, skin on skin.

Snowfall shrugged, reaching to run her fingers over his chest. "So much to learn, I think. Then Wild Winds grew ill, and, to be honest, no warrior-priest held much appeal to me."

"I trust I appeal?" Simus asked.

"I wouldn't be here otherwise," she said quietly. She lifted an arm and pulled him into another kiss.

Simus was more than willing, and now his hands were free to explore, stroking her soft skin; Snowfall returned the caress.

It became a long, slow exploration that left them both breathing harder, and their bodies warm and filled with desire. Simus's hands slipped lower, to her core, stroking her folds with the tips of his fingers but not going deeper. A simple, slow touch.

Snowfall shifted to her side, putting one leg over his hip, trying to thrust herself against his hand.

"Slow," Simus reminded her, chuckling against her mouth.

"Simus," she moaned, looking at his with dazed eyes. "Death comes in an instant," she said him.

Simus drew a breath. "Truth," he murmured in her ear, and for a moment they stilled, memory of the day hanging between them.

* * * * *

She'd almost died.

Simus looked at the lovely, strong warrior beside him and his heart almost thumped out of his chest. He could have lost her so easily…

Simus eased her onto her back, moved between her legs, and pierced her heat in one strong thrust.

Snowfall gasped, her hands clutching at his shoulders, her eyes wide.

Simus froze, keeping his weight off of her. "Snowfall?"

"Simus," she said, arching her neck back. "Elements." It was almost a prayer as she shuddered around him, adjusting her legs, spreading them wider. The movement made him gasp, and he sucked in a breath, trying to forestall his own release.

Simus watched as her eyes and face reflected all of her passion and pleasure, there for him to see. "You are so beautiful," he whispered, shifting to cradle her head in his hands, kissing her face and neck.

Snowfall's nails dug into his back. "Move, move," she said, bucking under him. "I want—"

"Whatever you want," Simus said. He moved his mouth along her skin, trailing kisses further down. He took one breast in his hand, pinching her nipple and then sucking it into his mouth.

"Ah, Simus." She pulled his head up and kissed him again. "Please," she mouthed against his lips. "Please."

He moved then, watching her face, feathering kisses all over. Her face, so quiet, so calm and still, now showed every emotion, every feeling as he began his strokes, waiting and watching, wanting to wring out every bit of pleasure he could for her.

—Until the moment she cried out, arching her back, clutching at his shoulders. Then and only then did he allow himself to lose his focus. He followed her in a burst of pleasure, easing off to one side a moment later, limp and languid with delight.

Snowfall murmured something and reached out, flailing a hand about until it met his tunic. She used it to clean them of the worst of it, and then tossed it aside, her eyes only half-open. She cuddled back down against his chest, and Simus pulled her into his arms.

"Sleep," she said and he nodded into her curls and allowed himself to drift off.

* * * * *

The cooler air from the open tent flap woke Simus, his skin prickling as a breeze swept in. He reached out for their bedding and pulled it up and over both of them. Starlight spilled through the opening, giving just enough light to see.

Snowfall had spooned up against him, cradled in his arms. The blankets warmed around them as he breathed in her scent.

Unable to resist, he nuzzled the soft skin behind her ear, her curls tickling his nose.

Snowfall tilted her head to give him better access. Simus pressed kisses along the line of her neck and shoulders.

He held her breasts, tweaking her nipples, and felt her hum of appreciation. His hands drifted down, stroking her stomach. She shivered in his arms, and, with one hand, encouraged him to drift lower, seeking…

Her stomach let out a loud growl.

Simus couldn't help but let out a belly laugh.

Snowfall twisted in his arms, and gave him a sparkling smile that took his breath away. She rose to sit cross-legged, facing him, letting the blanket fall away. The flowers in her tattoo had hidden themselves, but he could see traces of color under the green leaves.

"I love your smile," Simus whispered. He watched in delight as a blush rose on her brown skin.

"Our training," she explained. "A warrior-priest must be enigmatic and mysterious. Your eyes and face shouldn't reflect your thoughts." She reached for the dried meat and gurtle.

"Yet your stomach growls," Simus said, poking at her belly.

Snowfall blocked his hand and looked offended, but he saw through that in a heartbeat.

"Best fill your stomach." Simus danced his eyebrows. "Before I fill your—"

She popped a piece of gurt in his mouth to shut him up.

Simus grinned around the food, but the taste of the cheese reminded his own belly of its emptiness. He sat up and took a strip of the meat.

Snowfall reached for kavage.

"It will be cold," Simus warned. "We could get fresh."

"No," Snowfall said, filling their mugs even as she shook her head. "Let us stay private. Morning, with its demands, will come soon enough."

"Truth," Simus said, taking his mug.

Both their moods changed. Simus contemplated his kavage as he tore into the meat.

"There are matters to consider," Snowfall said. "I would not offend, but I would speak some truths."

"There is no need for tokens between us," Simus said. "I welcome your truths."

"It's still complicated, Simus. Not between us, but with—"

"Say my name again," Simus demanded.

"Simus." Snowfall gave him an exasperated look. "You should name Elois your Token-bearer."

"Not you?" Simus considered her face, open and concerned.

Snowfall shook her head. "Not me. I have thought this through. Yes, I can keep your tent and be your voice, but it's your warriors that concern me. Elois has their trust and respect."

"I trust you," Simus said.

Snowfall leaned forward and fed him another piece of gurt. "But they do not and that is the critical point."

"What of you?" Simus asked.

"I am what I am," Snowfall said. "An advisor, a warrior in your army." She glanced out the tent flap at the night sky. "I will need to check with my superior for my duties in the morning."

"You are wasted collecting dung," Simus said.

"Perhaps." Snowfall was serious. "But those are my duties."

"I would make no secret of what lies between us," Simus said, matching her tone.

"You must do what is best for our people. Give me no special treatment," Snowfall insisted. "I will report back to Destal. I will earn my place." She held out another piece of dried meat.

Simus took it with a reluctant nod. They ate in silence as he thought. "Elois has done well," Simus said. "Both she and Tsor, in dealing with all of this."

"From what I have seen, Tsor is also a solid choice."

"He is," Simus said, nodding. "But Yers would have been better." He paused for a moment. "I wonder—"

"I saw him," Snowfall said. "When I was aiding with Wind Winds. He was on a sleeping pallet. But I cannot say how well he is." She played with a strip of meat between her fingers. "Would you take him back?"

"No," Simus said, pressing his lips together, feeling again the betrayal. "He returns to Xy and to Keir."

Snowfall nodded her understanding.

"Wild Winds?" Simus asked.

Snowfall shrugged. "Hanstau took him under his care. He was not conscious when I left to find you. Essa was there, as were other elders." She frowned again. "Simus, Hanstau sees the power in the land." Her worry was clear. "I do not know how or why a city-dweller can do so, but he sees it. If he can see it, he can use it." She took a deep breath. "He is a danger, and needs training."

"Something to talk to Wild Winds about," Simus said.

Snowfall looked relieved, as if she didn't expect Simus to believe her. "Sometime, I would have you tell me more of Xy. About their stone tents, and their ways. Even maybe teach me chess." She looked pleased when Simus gave her a nod, then let her hand rest on the scar on his thigh. "Simus, how will Keir react to us? To this? His hatred of warrior-priests is known."

Simus smiled at her. "I do not know. But I do know that Keir set out to use the city-dwellers to his benefit, and then lost his heart to one. I would hope he would listen to our truths, Snowfall."

Snowfall nodded. "There are other worries. I do not see how Essa hopes to summon a Council to confirm you as Warlord. Of what strength their choices will have, given their numbers." She offered him more food, but he shook his head. "There is sure to be opposition to your confirmation," she continued, setting aside the bowls and mugs. "Even if it is clear you are the right choice. Even if you have made the right choices for our people. I fear that—"

She continued to talk, offering her insights into the candidates from the days she had spent watching. Simus listened, nodding, but...

This was what Keir had spoken of. What Isdra and Epor had found. What Othur had tried to explain. About the difference between sharing for pleasure and bonding for life.

Here was an equal partner in his life, a strength at his side. Agreeing, disagreeing, resolving those differences. The excitement of challenging one another even as they supported on another. Building a life together. A Bond of purpose, of commitment, to each other, to the Plains, to their world.

Exactly like Lara and Keir.

That was why he loved this woman.

Simus stretched out on the bedding, and put his hands behind his head, a sense of peace, of satisfaction, of fresh strength flooding through him. He let himself grin like a fool.

Snowfall stopped, and gave him a questioning look. "What?"

"You love me," Simus said, smiling at her.

She lifted her chin, and his heart swelled. "I have not said," she said.

"You don't need to," Simus chuckled. "I hear it in your words.

In your fears. In your plans, in your thoughts. You love me."

Snowfall snorted. "That would be the arrogance."

Simus rolled to his side, and placed his hand on her knee. "It's not arrogance," he said slowly as he rubbed her warm skin, and then let his fingers trace closer to her depths. "It's not arrogance, if it's backed by performance..." His hand drifted even closer.

Snowfall moved then, pushing him onto his back and straddling his hips. She leaned down, letting her mouth brush his. "Less talk, my Warlord," she whispered.

Simus couldn't agree more.

* * * * *

They loved again, bringing each other pleasure in all ways before deciding to sleep.

Simus lay on his side, pulled her close, and held her with one arm as he drifted off, breathing softly in her ear.

Snowfall didn't close her eyes. Not just yet.

How was it that Simus could see what she had been blind to? That what lay between them was more than just a sharing of bodies, minds, and goals.

Not that she was going to tell him that. At least, not just yet.

Wild Winds had said to look deeper, and she had. And found surprises, and contradictions, and fascinating possibilities.

When had their goals, their lives, intertwined? Snowfall wasn't sure. It had all happened so fast, and yet it felt as if it had always been between them. In her heart, in the depths of her soul, she knew that between them, love could only continue to grow. Her heart tingled at the thought. Still...she feared his people's response, or even Keir of the Cat's reactions to their relationship. It hurt her that Simus might be hurt by this.

But not enough that she could let him go.

* * * * *

Blaring horns woke Simus in the morning.

There was a moment of confusion as they both reached for weapons at the same time. But the sleep cleared, and Simus waited, letting Snowfall gather her things first and plunge through the tent flap to dress outside.

"The wyverns hunt," Elois's voice came from outside. Snowfall's response was muffled.

Simus buckled the last of his straps, reached for his weapons, and stopped. He had to bite his lip to stifle a shout of joy.

Snowfall had taken his dagger.

CHAPTER THIRTY-EIGHT

Simus was pleased to see that Elois had set up an area with gurtle pads around a small fire pit. Cimor and his scouts were already seated there, eating and waiting to give their report.

Simus settled next to Cimor, putting his sword on the ground next to him. In the distance, he could see the wyverns circling the Heart.

"The monsters roused early." Cimor was stuffing his face.

Simus's stomach growled at the scent of roasted gurtle.

"They're solitary hunters," Cimor spoke around his mouthful. "At least, from what we have seen. They are not launching in swarms." He took a mug of kavage from Elois with a nod of thanks. "And what kills they make, they are carrying back to the lake."

"They eat them and roll in the remains," one of the scouts offered, making a rolling motion with his hand. "The older and more rotted the better."

Simus made a face at that thought, and Cimor nodded. "It explains their smell."

Snowfall hesitated at the edge of the group, but Elois thrust the kavage pitcher into her hands, and gestured for her to serve. Simus relaxed; he didn't want her to leave him just yet.

"You won't want first meats from those kills, Warlord," one

of the other scouts chimed in. "Foul tasting, and the smell," she grimaced. "But their tough skin should make for good leather and bone is bone." She held up a claw, cut from a carcass. "We took claws and those curled horns as well. And their teeth are sharp as any blade."

"When they sleep, there by the lake?" Cimor said. "They curl up in tight balls, covering their heads and bodies with their wings." He demonstrated, curling into a ball, his arms over his head. "You'd think them large rocks if you stumbled over them in the night."

Elois offered Simus a pocket of bread, stuffed with meat. "Best get something in you quickly," she said. "Before you're needed."

Simus started eating. "Do they fly at night?" Simus asked, as he spoke around his food.

"No," Cimor said. "And they are sight hunters, not scent." He took a swig of kavage. "I've set watches on them." Cimor wiped his mouth. "They'll keep eyes on the beasts until you give orders otherwise."

Voices were being raised behind him, an argument from the sound of it. Someone was shouting in Xyian. Hanstau, most likely. Simus ignored it for the moment. "So we are safe to walk about, then?"

"As long as none are in the air about you." Cimor shrugged. "And the horns will warn of their approach. But my truth, Warlord, is I'd almost rather be in Xy and have a nice stone wall between me and them. And the ehats? No one has seen one since the flight, and there are usually one or two—"

The argument grew loud enough to drown him out.

Cimor grinned. "Seems your day has begun, Warlord."

Simus grimaced in agreement.

It was a sight Simus had never expected to see: the wounded of the Plains being tended by a Xyian healer.

Hanstau had gathered the wounded together outside his small tent. The pallets were laid in rows, with wounded warriors sprawled on and under blankets, with bandages covering their wounds. Other warriors were moving about, serving kavage and bread to those that could feed themselves.

Simus paused, as the memories of Lara tending his leg came back. Snowfall came up to stand next to him. She said nothing, but he knew she was looking for Wild Winds.

Hanstau was looming over a wounded warrior, Cadr looking miserable at his side. Hanstau was yelling at—

Loual of the Boar.

"Oh, skies," Snowfall breathed. "He'll kill him."

Simus quickened his step, certain that Loual was going to gut the pudgy healer for insults. Loual was seated on a blanket, cradling his bandaged arm, and looking…confused.

"Take to the ice?" Hanstau was almost purple with rage as he ranted in Xyian. "Idiot! Fool! What is the word?" He looked at Cadr. "What is the word?"

"Stupid," Cadr sighed, looking unhappy. A look of relief came over him when he spotted Simus. "Warlord, please. The healer is—"

"You'll answer to the God of the Sun if you waste your heart's blood on the grass," Hanstau declared, and nudged Cadr to translate. "Waste your life and your skills when your people need you the most. The feeling will return, I tell you. The wrist is splinted, the swelling will go down if you have a care and take the fever's foe."

For the first time, Simus noticed Loual's hand, swollen so

badly the fingers looked discolored.

"But go ahead, shove a blade in your guts. Just don't do it on my blankets. Go off in the grass or better yet, better yet—" Hanstau drew himself up in a picture of righteous fury, waving his hands for emphasis. "Better yet, feed yourself to those monsters for all I care, and wander off to your precious ice."

"Snows," Cadr said weakly. "The word is 'snows'."

Loual of the Boar looked up at Simus. "Does he know?" he asked in the language of the Plains, his voice strained with pain. "That our truths are different? That I oppose you?"

"I doubt it," Simus said. "But it wouldn't matter to him, even if he did."

Hanstau huffed out a breath. "Might as well save my breath, for all that anyone listens to me." He knelt down in front of Loual. "Do this," he demanded in rough Plains language as he held out his hand and made a fist.

Loual tried and winced, but the swollen fingers moved.

"Hah," Hanstau snorted. "See? See?" He huffed as he got to his feet and switched back to Xyian. "Tell him, Cadr. Tell him to give it a few days, to take the fever's foe as he was told—" Hanstau brushed off his tunic and trous. "And if there is no improvement—no improvement, mind, not perfection—" Hanstau waggled his finger at Loual, "—then he can kill himself with no objection from me. Stupid, impatient, thick-headed—" Hanstau muttered until he caught sight of Snowfall. "You, woman. Come with me. Wild Winds is awake and asking for you. Over here."

With that, the healer was gone, dragging a startled Snowfall in his wake.

Cadr duly translated the words to Loual, and scrambled after the healer.

"Any other would be bleeding at my feet for the insult," Loual said. "But he is weaponless, and fat, and oddly angry." Loual looked up at Simus, his brow furrowed. "What is my life to him?"

"The same as mine," Simus said simply. "That is his truth."

"You should have seen him charge toward a wyvern," Mirro said.

"What?" Loual asked, staring up at his Third, looking even more confused.

Mirro knelt beside him, eager to tell the tale. Simus excused himself with a nod, and followed Hanstau to where Wild Winds lay.

* * * * *

Wild Winds stretched out under his blanket, working out the stiffness in his muscles. He drew in a sweet breath, feeling the ache in his ribs as his chest expanded. He let the air out slowly, thanking the elements for the pain. A wet cloth covered his eyes, and he relished the damp, cool darkness.

He had little memory of the attack, other than pain.

Footsteps approached, and he heard the Xyian healer, Hanstau, say something in a voice too soft for him to hear.

A warm presence knelt at his side. "Master," came a soft, calm voice. Wild Winds smiled at the familiar sound.

"Snowfall," he said, taking care not to move his head. "How goes it with you? That feeling, that dread? For me it has faded. For you?"

"Faded as well." Snowfall's voice was soft. "More important, how goes it with you?"

"Alive." Wild Winds drew another deep, satisfying, painful breath. "Bruised and sore, and alive."

"He is well," Hanstau said haltingly. "He—" The man proceeded to rattle off something in Xyian, then paused. Wild Winds could just imagine that Snowfall had lifted her eyebrow at Hanstau.

"His head," Hanstau said.

Someone was peeling back the wet cloth. Wild Winds winced at the light, and then blinked his eyes open.

"Your eyes," said the two Snowfalls of his doubled vision crouched beside him, their lips moving together.

"Head blow." Wild Winds said, and nodded, only to regret it as a wave of nausea washed over him.

"Sickness." She frowned. "Is your sight affected?"

"Yes." Wild Winds smiled at her concern. "But I am not the first to suffer this, nor the last. It will pass."

"With time," Snowfall reminded him.

Cadr came running up, breathing hard, to stand next to Hanstau. He said something in Xyian, clearly scolding the healer.

"Hanstau was yelling at Loual," Snowfall said quietly. "Cadr is explaining the risks."

Hanstau folded his arms over his chest, and looked stubborn. "He wants to get better," Hanstau said. "He will listen."

"You have not answered my question," Wild Winds said. He focused on Snowfall's serene face, which could hide so much. "Are you well? You were not in the Council tent."

"I was with my Warlord," Snowfall said.

Wild Winds squinted, studying her face. Was that a blush on her cheek?

"We were attacked," she continued. "But he killed the beast."

"With your help," Simus said as he walked up and knelt at her side.

Wild Winds squinted at the man. "Simus of the Hawk, I

thank you for my life."

"I am honored to have assisted you, Eldest Elder." Simus bowed his head. "And I am sorry to see that you are injured."

"Pain is better than death."

Snowfall was not fooled. "I have mushrooms," she offered, pulling out a few tiny dried pieces.

Wild Winds held out a shaky hand and took one.

"What is that?" Hanstau demanded, nudging Cadr, pointing at the mushrooms. "He's already had willow-bark tea."

Wild Winds slipped a small piece between his teeth and gums. "You explain, Snowfall," he said, waiting for the dulling effects to begin.

"I will," Snowfall promised as she gave the healer the rest. "But first I must tell you, Master. This healer sees the power in the land."

Wild Winds snapped his eyes open. "What?"

Cadr huffed out a breath and started translating the flurry of questions and answers that followed.

"A Xyian," Wild Winds breathed out in wonder. It had never occurred to him that they might be able to use the magic of the Plains. "You must come with me, when I leave," Wild Winds said. "You must be taught."

"Leave?" Simus asked.

"I must return to Lightning Strike and the young ones," Wild Winds reminded him. "Who must also be trained. He must come with me."

But Hanstau was listening to Cadr, shaking his head. "No. My place is with Lord Simus, by the command of my Queen. I will not leave his side."

Wild Winds closed his eyes, gathering his thoughts. "Our 'healing' powers were mostly illusion. Certain plants, dried mushrooms, were our only tools." He waited for Cadr to translate.

"I have power," Wild Winds continued slowly. "But I have no idea how to use it to heal, even though I know it can heal. Each who has the gift uses it in different ways. In any event, you must be trained."

Hanstau listened, and then stood as if lost in thought. "I wonder," he said slowly. "I wonder if it could be used to counter that poison?"

"And that is how you get in trouble," Wild Winds said. "Wondering and trying without guidance."

"Hanstau," Simus said, speaking in Xyian. Wild Winds looked at Cadr, who quickly translated for him. "I respect your abilities, and you are an asset to my people." Simus pointedly looked out over the wounded. "To all our people." Then Simus drew a breath. "But I also know the Warprize. If Lara thought there was a chance, any chance, that you could bring magical healing to Xy and the Plains, she would want you to seek it out."

Hanstau looked thoughtful. "I will think on your words, Lord Simus. In the meantime, I pledge to you," he shifted his gaze to Wild Winds, "I will not experiment with the glow. With the power."

"Thank you," Wild Winds said.

"I will talk to you later, about these." Hanstau held up the mushrooms before tucking them into his satchel. "But now, I will return to my duties," Hanstau said, and walked off, Cadr right behind him.

"And I must to mine," Snowfall said. "Lest I be seen as neglectful."

"But—" Simus cut off his words. Wild Winds watched as

the blurry pair exchanged a long look.

"Tonight?" Simus asked.

"Tonight," Snowfall whispered back, and now there was no doubt as to the color on her cheek and the glint in her eye.

Well, well. Wild Winds cleared his throat. "So you looked deeper?" he asked.

Simus looked confused, but Snowfall gave him a nod, her smile behind her eyes. "I did," she said, then whispered, "and I found something...amazing."

"Ah." Wild Winds tried very hard to suppress his satisfaction. "My thanks for the mushrooms," he said as Snowfall rose to her feet.

She gave a nod and walked off. Wild Winds couldn't help watching Simus watch her go.

Very well, indeed. Wild Winds relaxed under his blankets, well pleased. At best, he'd hoped that Snowfall and Simus might learn to trust one another. But this attraction showed much promise.

Wild Winds smiled to himself. He was a meddling old man, and well satisfied in the role.

Simus remained at his side. A silence fell between them then, surrounded as they were by the buzz of talk. Wild Winds could hear horns in the distance. "Horns?" he asked.

"To warn of the monsters," Simus explained. "Of the wyverns."

"Describe them," Wild Winds said. "Tell me what happened. All I knew was the collapsing tent and pain."

Simus obliged him, describing the creatures in detail, explaining what he knew of the attack and the rescue.

"There is nothing like that in my memory," Wild Winds said. "Or in the memories passed down to me. Perhaps the Singers know more. Essa lives. He was here, earlier, speaking of our losses.'"

"Did he have numbers? Names?" Simus asked.

"I do not—" Wild Winds sighed. "We spoke, but it is a hazy memory."

"Of course." Simus shook his head. "Forgive me."

"We of the Plains are diminished, not defeated," Wild Winds said. "Seek Essa. He will be the one to decide how we proceed."

"I will," Simus said.

The mushroom was beginning to dull his pain, but did nothing for his eyes. Wild Winds winced again at the light, and fumbled for the wet cloth. Simus took it from his fingers, and settled back over his face.

"My thanks," Wild Winds said, grateful for the relief from the light. "And Simus?'

"Yes?'

"Be good to her," Wild Winds said.

"My oath on it." Simus's voice held a note of joy he'd not heard in a long time. "Never fear. She is the flame of my heart, Wild Winds."

Satisfied, Wild Winds let the mushroom pull him down into sleep.

CHAPTER THIRTY-NINE

Simus finally gave up trying to locate Essa among the wounded and went to ask Hanstau and Cadr for help.

The truths he'd discovered searching for the Singer, however, were dark. He'd walked between the pallets, speaking to a few, observing others, taking a head count and wincing internally at the results. There was no saying this was all; there may be many others that were with their own people, not needing Hanstau's care. But the living were few.

And the dead numbered far too many.

The wounded and the healthy were starting to stir in the camp. The shock of the recent events was wearing off. He could feel their eyes on him and the weight of their questions.

Pity he had no answers.

He found Hanstau at Haya's side, cleaning a wound in her upper arm. "We will not use bloodmoss," he was explaining through Cadr. "The claws of the beasts are filthy and I fear for infection."

Haya glared at Simus. "Finally," she said. "Seo? My camp?"

Simus knelt. "Minor injuries, no deaths," he reported, and watched the tightness clear from her eyes. "Seo was taking the children to a winter lodge for safety."

"Good," Haya grunted. "Smart. But what of the future, Simus

of the Hawk?"

"Wild Winds told me to seek out Essa," Simus said.

Haya gestured outward with her good arm, toward a thick patch of the tallest grasses. "Behind there, off by himself," she said, then sniffed. "Sulking, to my way of thinking."

Hanstau paused in his work, looked at both of them, and spoke in rapidfire Xyian.

Simus nodded, and Cadr translated for the benefit of the others. "He says that as to Essa, he can heal wounds, not hearts. I don't understand."

Haya just huffed a breath. Simus looked at the young warrior, just starting his second season in the army.

"You will," Simus said. "You will."

* * * * *

When Simus found him, Essa was sitting alone, looking out over the Plains, his back to the Heart. Simus approached slowly, crunching the grass beneath his feet and clearing his throat to announce his presence.

Essa looked back over his shoulder. The side of his face was purple and bruised. He looked away pointedly.

Simus stood, waiting.

"Sit," Essa said finally, with a grudging tone, resignation in his shoulders.

"My thanks, Eldest Elder." Simus circled around the man, and sat facing him.

Now Simus could see that Essa's entire face was bruised and swollen, his eyes mere slits. Simus could barely make out Essa's Singer tattoo around his eye. Essa wore the tatters of fine colorful silks, clothing he would have donned for the ceremony.

"Today was to have been a day of celebration." Essa's voice had an odd lisp to it, as he spoke slowly through swollen lips. "Solemn ritual, with singing and drumming, and offerings to the elements. We'd have raised the Council tent, the wisdom and strength of the Plains gathered within. We'd have chosen our best to enter the season of war and secure the needs of the people of the Plains."

Simus nodded, but didn't speak.

"I'd thought there would be debate," Essa continued. "Hours of it, perhaps even days. Bitter words spoken, insights revealed. Then, as it has always been, the chosen Warlords would have been honored and their oaths taken. A full day of celebration afterward, before they and their armies departed." He drew in a deep, clearly pained breath. "Now all that is left is to sing for the dead."

"Wild Winds said that we are diminished, not defeated," Simus said.

"I am not so sure," Essa murmured.

"He also said that there is nothing like these monsters in his memory, or in the memories passed down to him."

Essa stiffened, a flash of pure anger in his eyes.

Simus paused, taken aback. But when Essa said nothing, he cautiously continued. "What of the Singers?" he asked. "Do you—"

"Nothing," Essa spat. "There is nothing in my memory, or in the memories or songs passed down to me, about these creatures."

Simus raised an eyebrow. "I should ask for your token, Eldest Elder."

"No, no," Essa said, deflating. His rage faded as quickly as it had come. "My anger is not aimed at you." Essa raised his eyes to Simus. "And yet what have you unleashed upon us, Simus of the Hawk?"

"Eldest Elder Singer Essa," Simus said carefully. "Is that your truth? That I somehow called down all of this upon us?"

"There are those that will blame you, and Keir," Essa said.

"I will face their truths with my own," Simus said.

"You think that will be enough?" Essa asked wearily.

"Yes," Simus said simply, and then focused on Essa. "You do not support Keir, then."

He didn't make it a question.

"The role of the Singer is to hold to our ways and to pass on the knowledge of the Plains," Essa said. "I don't know what I support, what I think, what to sing, or even if I should sing of this."

"You are the Eldest Elder of the Singers," Simus said. "Your duty is to summon—"

"And if I don't?" Essa lashed out, his words cutting and cruel.

"We will have lost more than we did to the wyverns," Simus said.

Essa sat silent, his head bowed. Simus waited, as the wind rustled the longer grasses, as horns blew in the distance.

"The wind blows," Essa whispered. "The grass bends." He rose to his feet slowly, brushing off his tattered silken trous. Without looking at Simus, he limped off toward Hanstau's tent, moving slowly and carefully.

Simus rose and followed.

The healing area held more people, standing and sitting around the wounded. Heads turned as Essa passed, and those that could struggled to their feet, to stand respectfully in the Eldest Elder's presence.

Essa ignored them. He limped to where Wild Winds lay.

As if he'd sensed his presence, Wild Winds pulled away the cloth from his eyes, and blinked up at Essa. They looked at one another for a long time, and then Wild Winds spoke. "All endings are beginnings, old friend." His words carried over the crowd. "And in turn, all beginnings mark the end of something."

Essa closed his eyes. Simus couldn't help but think that the man was trying to block out the truth for but one moment more. But then Essa opened his eyes, and straightened against his pain. "I summon the Council to meet." He turned, raising his voice, so that the words carried. "I summon it to the nearest winter lodge we can find. Send word to all that we will gather at—" he glanced up at the sky, "—at the nooning."

"Will there be enough room?" Wild Winds asked. "They're not designed for large meetings."

"I fear our numbers won't be an issue," Essa said drily. "Not anymore. But it will be safe. All the living will attend, even if they must be carried."

"I will come," Wind Winds said.

"Let the word be passed," Essa commanded, and the warriors around them moved to obey. "The Council meets at the nooning. Let the candidates present themselves, with their Seconds and Token-bearers." Essa's gaze met Simus's. "There let it be decided and done."

* * * * *

Simus strode back toward his tent, excitement burning through him. Essa's words had lit a fire within the warriors that had surrounded them, and they'd quickly moved into action. Many had run off, to spread the word to their own Warlords. Others had gathered around Essa, pointing to where the nearest winter lodge was located. Simus waited just long enough to learn its location, before heading back to his camp.

Elois stood naked before her tent, her tanned skin glistening in the sun. She'd clearly already heard the word. "Good," she said. "This Council is sure to take all the hours left in the day. There's time to eat more than just the few bites you got this morning, and clean up before we have to appear. Strip."

"Not sure there's time—" Simus started, but Elois cut him off with a scowl.

"There's more than enough time if you don't waste it," she said firmly. "No need to make a sorry showing before the Elders and the Eldest Elders." She raised her voice, looking behind her tent. "Destal, bring your warriors here and get the Warlord's armor." She turned back and glared at Simus. "They will clean and oil our leathers, and do what they can for the chain. Strip," she demanded again, giving him the once over. "And where is your dagger?"

At the mention of Destal, Simus's interest perked. Snowfall was assigned to her. But he still argued. "There are still things I need to do. They may need help carrying the wounded to the lodge."

"I've seen to that," Tsor said as he walked into camp. "Between all the warriors here, we will see it done."

"Strip," Eloise commanded. "Both of you."

Tsor obeyed, his hands going to his belt. Simus followed suit. They each peeled out of the armor, handing off various parts to the young warriors who appeared. They took the gear, and then disappeared behind the tent. Simus heard Destal lecturing one on how to clean chain properly.

"Food next," Elois commanded. Simus and Tsor sat on the gurtle pads she had set out. Simus raised his eyebrows at the meal, which included roasted tubers and boar.

Elois settled on the pad next to him, and a young warrior approached with water and towels for the washing ritual. Simus murmured his thanks to the elements, then dried his hands.

"My thanks for your efforts," Simus said to Elois before helping himself. Tsor nodded enthusiastically around his mouthful.

Elois smiled, clearly pleased with the praise, but then she grew serious. "I am your Token-bearer, am I not?"

Simus paused in mid-bite. "I haven't named either of you formally, have I?"

"No," Elois said. "You have not." Tsor nodded, but didn't stop eating.

"I do so now," Simus said. "Elois of the Horse, you are my choice for Token-bearer. Tsor of the Bear, you are my choice for my Second."

"Our thanks, Warlord." Elois looked off to the side, and gave a nod.

Snowfall came forward with kavage and cups.

Simus grinned up at her as he took the drink from her hands. Snowfall's face was calm and serene, as usual. But her fingers brushed against his as he took the mug.

Tsor swallowed, and spoke. "Word on the wind is that there may not be enough Warlord candidates."

Elois hissed in a breath. Simus stopped mid-bite. "Truth?" he asked.

Tsor shook his head. "No one claims such, but all repeat the words."

Simus exchanged a long look with Snowfall. He chewed slowly, thinking. "This is not good news."

"Isn't it?" Tsor asked. "Won't they have to make you Warlord?"

Simus shook his head. "Even if they do, that means the armies will be thinly spread. I suspect those Warlords named will try to go for richer targets, which means higher risk of the loss of warriors."

"Or choose lower risk ones," Elois said. "That yield less."

Simus sighed. "I do not know."

They finished the rest of the meal in silence.

When the food was gone, Elois stood, brushing crumbs from her thighs. "Tsor, you need to bathe. I will check on the cleaning process."

"Destal knows the ways, she'll not let the young ones slack," Tsor rumbled. "Come and bathe with me." He waggled his eyebrows. "You can make sure I get every spot."

"None of that, now," Elois growled, scowling and sounding so much like Marcus that Simus had to laugh. Tsor joined in, and Elois grinned.

Snowfall looked confused, but shrugged. "I can clean this," she offered, gesturing to the bowls and cups.

"No." Elois shook her head. "Take the Warlord off, and trim his hair for him, less he cut himself and shame us all."

"There's bloodmoss," Simus reminded her, but looked at Snowfall. "But I would not decline the help."

Tsor and Elois both snorted. "Off with you," Elois said, and gestured them off.

Simus reached for Snowfall's hand and pulled her away, out of sight of the young ones and anyone else who might be watching.

* * * * *

As soon as they were out of sight of the others, Snowfall threw down the gurtle pad she'd grabbed. "Kneel," she commanded.

Simus knelt as she drew the dagger at her side. "Is that my dagger?" he asked as she ran her hand over his close-cropped hair.

"It was shockingly dull," Snowfall said, scratching at his scalp gently with her nails. "You don't need much of a trim, really."

Simus hummed, leaning in close, and pressed his face to the bare skin between her trous and her corselet. "You smell so sweet," he said as he rubbed his nose lightly against her.

"Do that again, and you might lose an ear," Snowfall scolded. His touch warmed her, made her tingle, but she didn't move away.

Simus just hummed again under his breath, then frowned. "Have you noticed," he said, lowering his voice. "Have you noticed the despair of some of the warriors?" he asked. "It was only at Essa's summons that they started to move. Started to think."

Snowfall scraped at the hair around his ear. "I did," she said. "Stay still."

"But not so much my people," Simus said. "I wonder if being exposed to Xy, to new ways of thinking, make them better able to cope with the new and different."

"Not to add to your arrogance, my Warlord," Snowfall said, "but I think it is you. Your people reflect your strength, your decisiveness, your courage." She ran her hand over his scalp, brushing loose hairs away.

Simus brought his arms up to wrap around her hips, and looked up into her eyes. "I want nothing more than to peel these trous right off your long legs and—"

"Your unwavering attention to the duties and obligations of a Warlord are unparalleled," Snowfall said drily. But then she smiled at him, letting her admiration shine. "They trust you to see them through. As do I." She took a step back, eyeing him critically, and with satisfaction. "There," she said. "As befits a Warlord."

* * * * *

Done?" Simus asked. At her nod he rose to his feet and put his hands on her hips with a sigh. "I wish you were going to be beside me in that tent," Simus said. "Perhaps if you aided Wild Winds?"

Snowfall shook her head. "My oaths are to you now, and my absence at his side makes that clear. In truth, enough tradition has been broken today." She sheathed the dagger at her belt. "But I would not deny you a kiss for luck, my Simus."

"Your Simus?" he grinned.

That lovely red flared in her cheeks. But she didn't contradict him. Joy flared in his heart, not appropriate for the day, but still there. Between them.

Simus pulled her in, and kissed her, relishing her taste, the softness of her lips, the way her strong body felt against his, her willing response. He pulled her close, wanting—

"Warlord," Elois was calling, and sounded like she was not to be ignored.

Snowfall broke the kiss, and would have stepped back, but Simus held her a second longer. He hesitated, suddenly fearful. 'My Snowfall', he thought to say, but he changed his words.

"Your Simus," he whispered, a promise in her ear.

His reward was her gentle smile in those warm grey eyes, and another kiss. Simus held her close, and tugged at her hips, wanting to draw her down, to lie in the grass and warm sun and—

"None of that, now." Elois stalked up to them like an encroaching storm. "Time's a' wasting. Get back here and put on your armor."

CHAPTER FORTY

The winter lodge wasn't even close to full.

These ancient underground dwellings, used in the worst of the Plains winters, had been dug deep within the earth. No one knew when or how they had been created, and Simus knew of none that had been built in recent times.

The winter lodges were low-ceilinged, and most adult and young warriors walked stooped over within. But the sleeping chambers were warm even when the Plains grew frigid and the snows came. Each lodge had the same pattern. Multiple sleeping chambers off one large gathering place, the floor hard-packed dirt, with rough stone walls covered in faded stylized paintings and support pillars evenly placed.

The air vents had been opened, and all the torches lit. Simus sighed as he walked in, hunched over to avoid hitting his head. As a child, he'd enjoyed the darkness and warmth; as an adult he'd disliked the confinement, especially when crammed with warriors. But then again, he'd welcomed their warmth when the winter winds blew and the snows came.

Essa stood, the top of his head touching the ceiling. The Singer had placed himself at the far end of the gathering place, opposite the main entrance, where all could see him. Essa had his arms crossed over his chest, clearly waiting as the room filled with latecomers. Simus was pleased to see that the man had cleaned up, and was armored, his weapons at his side.

No silken robes for this meeting.

Wild Winds had insisted on walking in, and looked like he regretted it. He seated himself to Essa's left. Haya sat to Essa's right, her familiar scowl firmly in place.

All of the Elders were seated before them, and with them, all of the Warlord candidates, their Seconds and Token-bearers. Simus caught a glimpse of Osa seated not far from him; he could hear Ultie's rumble in the back. Ietha had also survived, as well as Nires, Loual, and Reht, Simus's opposition all seated together.

Tsor was right, there were too few candidates remaining for the traditional four Warlords for each of the four elements. Simus drew a breath, and wondered what Essa would do if—

"I am Essa, Eldest Elder Singer of the Plains," Essa said, his words rolling against the stone walls. "Draw close and heed my words. I summon this Spring Council into session and I call this Council to order."

Clothing rustled as everyone sat, all eyes on Essa.

"The Council of Elders has always been presided over by the four Eldest of the Elders," Essa said. "I am the Eldest Elder of the Singers, and Wild Winds is the Eldest Elder of the Warrior-Priests. Haya of the Snake is here to serve as the Eldest Elder of the Theas. That leaves the Warriors." Essa turned and looked over to the side. "Nires of the Boar. You are an Elder of the Warriors. At the last Council meeting held before the snows, you agreed to serve as the Eldest Elder of the Warriors. Would you again take up the responsibility?"

Nires rose, and stood, hunched to avoid the ceiling. "I would."

"Do any offer objection to this?" Essa asked as Nires moved to sit at Wild Winds's side.

Silence was the only answer.

Simus briefly considered offering to serve, but he'd already tried that once before, when the Warprize had faced the Council. He wouldn't try it now. But in the future…he smiled to himself. Elois gave him a questioning glance, but when he shook his head at her she accepted his decision and looked away.

"That done," Essa continued, "let us speak of the beasts that have attacked us, and driven us from the Heart. I would share what knowledge the Singers have, which is none. Wild Winds? Nires?"

"None," Wild Winds said as Nires also shook his head in the negative.

"Haya? Do the Theas have any knowledge of these creatures?"

"If we had," Haya said drily, "we would have mentioned it before this."

Essa nodded. "Nothing then, from the knowledge of the Plains. I would have us share any truths that have been gathered."

There was a stir, but no one spoke. Simus rose to his knees. "I will share what truths I have." He spoke of Hanstau's tale, and then shared the observations of his scouts. "The beasts seem concentrated around the lake for now," Simus concluded. "It will take time to learn more."

"Interesting," Ietha drawled. "That Xyians have a name for the monsters, but gave no warning."

"Your truth, Ietha?" Essa asked.

Ietha mimicked Simus, and rose to her knees. "What should be clear to all of us. The creatures were sent to destroy us. They came from the north, out of the mountains of Xy, and laid waste at the exact moment the Elders were gathered. At the exact moment that Simus and his people were not within the tent—were, in fact, nowhere to be seen." Ietha glared at Simus. "Keir and his city-dwelling *bragnects*—"

"Silence," Essa said sharply.

Ietha pressed her lips together, breathing hard. She glared at Essa for a long moment, then obeyed and sat back down. Simus sat as well.

"A Council of the Elders is called and presided over by the four Eldest of each branch," Essa recited in what Simus thought of as a 'Singer's voice'. The very tone seemed to calm the room. "A Council names the Warlords, make major decisions on behalf of all the Tribes." Essa paused, scanning the room. "There are decisions we must make, prey we must pull down, at this Council," Essa said. "But as we speak our warriors and armies are at risk. There are also our thea camps, each of which must be warned." He looked out over all of them. "So I will cut short the hunt. We've not enough candidates for all the Warlord positions. All here are worthy. All here have met their Trials." His face grew stern. "I will not waste breath or time. Here is the heart of the matter: Should Simus of the Hawk be named as a Warlord of the Plains?"

Simus's tongue dried in his mouth.

"How is this fair?" Elois hissed, but he placed his hand on her knee. Thankfully, the anger that erupted around them covered her outburst. Anger from both sides, to Simus's shock, from friends and foes and in-betweens.

Tsor said nothing, but shifted slightly to take in more of the room, so that he could watch Simus's back.

"We have always debated," Ultie said loudly. "You'd silence our truths?"

"Our people are at risk," Essa's anger flared, cutting through the noise. "They are exposed, and in need of guidance. Would you leave them in harm's way?"

Haya spoke up. "The supplies for the Tribes must be gathered. We can't delay the raiding season any further."

The muttering subsided.

"If the tent were raised, if our skies were clear, we could exchange truths and argue for hours, days." Essa folded his arms over his chest. "But I will deal with what is, and if in doing so I make the choices necessary for all, so be it. We have time for little else. I would call for a vote. Here. Now. Raise your hands in support of Simus of the Hawk as Warlord of the North."

Simus had to clench his jaw to keep it from dropping.

He wasn't alone. Wild Winds was staring at Essa like he'd never seen him before, but then he raised his hand.

Haya's hand shot up beside him.

Simus glanced around as hands were raised for him. Some anticipated, some a surprise. The hands not raised were not unexpected. Nires of the Boar. Ietha.

But the vote was divided equally. The look of satisfaction on Ietha's face grated.

Simus watched as Essa drew a long breath, and lifted his chin as if still counting, but Simus knew the result. Essa's bold move had not resolved the issue, but there was still hope. Now there would be debate and division. Simus resigned himself to—

Loual's splinted hand slowly rose in the air.

"What?' Ietha exploded. "Why?"

Loual lowered his hand and rose to his knees. "Because of what I have witnessed," he said. "A city-dweller caring for me and my people." He gestured to Mirro. "Because of what I have been told by Mirro, who was my Third, and now serves as my Second.

He tells me of an unarmed city-dweller, a healer, who charged forward to render aid where no warrior would go."

"You favor them," Ietha accused.

"Do I?" Loual raised an eyebrow. "Sending Simus and his people north? To where the monsters came from? To where they and their get will likely return?" He gestured to Simus. "It will be their problem. Let them deal with the havoc they have wrought."

"So it is done," Essa intoned, to be interrupted when Ietha jerked to her feet, hitting her head on the ceiling in her haste.

"No," Ietha growled. "I will not be a party to this, Singer. This is not our way. Already they have destroyed everything they have touched."

"Ietha, listen to reason," Wild Winds said. "It was not they that caused the Sacrifice, it was—"

"To the snows with your reasoning," Ietha snarled. "I go to Antas." She stomped out, keeping her head low, followed by her Second and Token-bearer.

Essa spoke. "Let us waste no more time. We will take the oaths of the Warlords and disburse."

"Let it be done outside," Wild Winds said. "For the skies and all the people to witness."

"Agreed," Essa said.

They emerged, blinking in the sun to find a gathering of warriors awaiting news. Destal was standing there, arms crossed over her chest, her young warriors clustered behind her.

Simus's heart caught in his throat. Snowfall stood with them.

He walked over as the others emerged from the lodge and organized themselves along Essa's wishes. Other warriors, attracted by the sight, started to gather, leading saddled horses.

"Wyverns?" he asked Destal.

"They've settled since the nooning—the horns have not sounded for some time," she said. "But I wouldn't linger."

Simus repeated her words for Essa, then turned back to Destal. Simus lowered his voice. "My thanks," he said.

"It will be instructive for my charges to watch the Council administer the oaths," Destal said. "Nothing more."

Simus grinned at Snowfall.

Snowfall puffed out a breath from behind Destal. "Well?" she demanded, showing cracks in her reserve. "What happened?"

Simus opened his mouth to answer her, but Essa's voice cut him off. "Simus of the Hawk," the Eldest Elder Singer called. "Come and be the first to be sworn as Warlord."

Snowfall's smile was blinding and quick, for his eyes only.

Simus laughed, turned, and strode to where the four Eldest Elders stood, surrounded by the Elders and other Warlord candidates, and all the other warriors gathered to watch.

He stood before them, tall and proud, trying to take it all in.

"Kneel, Simus, and offer your sword."

He pulled his sword, and knelt, offering his blade between his two hands.

Essa spoke loudly, his voice carrying over the crowd. "Simus of the Hawk, Warrior of the Plains. You come before us as a candidate for Warlord. Do you wish to serve the Plains?"

"I do," Simus said.

"Name your Second," Essa said.

"Tsor of the Bear," Simus said. Tsor stepped forward and rested his right hand on Simus's left shoulder.

"Name your Token-bearer," Essa said.

"Elois of the Horse," Simus said. Elois stepped forward and rested her left hand on Simus's right shoulder.

"Have they passed through their Trials?" Essa asked.

"They have," Simus said. "I am witness to this truth."

"Do any deny this truth?" Essa asked the crowd. There was no response.

"Tsor of the Bear. Elois of the Horse. Has Simus of the Hawk passed through his Trials?"

"He has," Tsor said. "I am witness to this truth."

"He has," Elois said. "I am witness to this truth."

"Do any deny this truth?" Essa asked. There was no response.

"Simus of the Hawk, we of the Council entrust you with the lives of the Warriors of the Plains. Will you take responsibility for these lives and hold them dear?"

"I will," Simus vowed. "I will be their Warlord in all things. Their flesh is my flesh, their blood is my blood.

"Simus of the Hawk, the Council of the Elders names you Warlord of the North." Essa drew a deep breath, and placed the tips of his fingers on Simus's blade. "May the very air of this land grant you breath."

Wild Winds moved closer and placed his fingers on the blade. "Simus of the Hawk, the Council of the Elders names you Warlord of the North. May the very earth of this land support your feet."

Haya placed her fingers on his blade. Her voice sounded oddly rough, and Simus glanced up to see tears in her eyes. "Simus of the Hawk, the Council of the Elders names you Warlord of the North. May the very fires of this land warm your skin."

Nires was next, and there was no hesitation in his actions or voice. He placed his fingers on the blade. "Simus of the Hawk, the Council of Elders names you Warlord of the North. May the very waters of this land quench your thirst."

"Rise, Warlord, and serve your people," Essa commanded.

Simus did, sheathing his sword and standing tall. And ever after remembered his pleasure in the moment, for the goal achieved, for the blue skies above, for the horns in the distance, for the cheers of the warriors around him…and the joy in Snowfall's eyes.

CHAPTER FORTY-ONE

Amyu was dismayed to discover a man at the cheese cart instead of Kalisa. She hesitated, letting the crowd swirl around her in the busy marketplace. With the wyverns gone, life had returned to normal in Water's Fall.

She tried to settle her nerves. She'd the permission of the Warprize, and she was an adult in this world. A warrior. She could do this. And if the old one knew anything of airions…

Amyu marched over before she let herself think.

"Excuse me," she said.

The man was finishing a trade of cheese and hard bread. He flashed her a grin as he pocketed the coins. "How may I aid you, m'lady?"

"I am Amyu," she said, repeating the words the Warprize had said she should say. "I am in the service of Queen Xylara. I wish to speak…to hear the words of Kalisa, the cheesemaker."

"I am Anser," the man replied. "Aunt Kalisa could not work the cart today, due to her aches. I cannot leave the trade," he continued. "But my wife will be by soon with my midday meal, and she would gladly take you to her."

"I wish to hear her tales," Amyu said. "Because she is old. As old as any the Queen knows."

Anser barked out a laugh. "Well, don't tell her that, or she'll bite your ear off. Old Auntie is sensitive about her age."

Amyu raised her fingers to her ear.

Anser laughed again. "I forget you Firelanders…those of the Plains…take everything at its word." He sliced some of the yellow cheese, and put it between two crackers. "She would not bite your ear off. She would be offended if you tell her she is old." He offered her the food.

"Ah," said Amyu. "That is good to know." She frowned at the food. "I have no coin."

"You serve the Queen," he said with a smile. "That is payment enough. Take it." He offered the food again, and nodded over to a shaded spot, against a wall. "Tuck yourself up over there. Mya won't be long."

Amyu did so, nibbling on the cheese and crackers, trying very hard to be patient. She wasn't even sure that this Kalisa would hold any answers, but both the Warprize and Iian had said it was worth a try.

She stared glumly at her hands.

The glow was back. Since the night of the pillar of light everything seemed tinged with golden sparkles that looked like the rings of light that had swept through the Castle that night. She'd had odd headaches too, usually when the sparkles were at their brightest.

Master Eln, when she'd finally been able to speak to him, hadn't known what to do other than give her willow-bark tea for the headaches. She wrinkled her nose; she drank it but it wasn't very nice. It did help with the headaches.

But not with the sparkles.

Master Eln had promised to keep her words close, and she'd

decided not to share these truths with anyone else. There were more than enough troubles; she'd not add hers to the mix. It didn't hurt, really. It was just distracting.

Amyu took another bite of cheese and cracker, and distracted herself watching the city-dwellers be about their ways.

Finally, a woman appeared with a basket and jug, and a smile meant only for Anser. He greeted her with a hug, taking her burden and leading her over to Amyu, explaining as they came. Amyu rose to greet them.

"You want to hear Auntie's tales?" Mya said with surprise. She was a plump woman, her hair tied up in a knot. "You'd be more than welcome, but I fear she'll talk your ear off."

Amyu blinked.

"No, no," Anser said, and smiled. "She means—"

"I'll explain," Mya said when she saw the confusion. "You'll be home at close of market?"

"Aye, my love." Anser kissed her, and slipped a packet in his wife's apron pocket. The days' earnings, Amyu suspected, from the rattle of coins.

She followed Mya through the main streets, until they turned into side streets where the buildings towered over them, so close together that they leaned over the street, blocking out the sun. Amyu knew enough to expect it, but she wasn't used to it.

"It's not far," Mya said. "Auntie will be glad of the company, her hands are paining her so."

"Auntie," Amyu said. "I do not know that word. Is she your life-bearer?"

"You mean is she Anser's mother?" Mya shook her head. "No, no, she's family on Anser's side, but I am not sure of exactly how." Mya paused before a flight of stone steps. "She's our blood, though, and took Anser and me as her apprentices, to keep the cheese in the family."

"You keep your animals here?" Amyu asked.

"No, the herds are on the mountain side, outside the City walls. We hid them in the caves when those monsters came." Mya shuddered as she started up the steps. "Thanks be to the Goddess that we only lost two cows, and that my sons took shelter." She paused before a heavy, wooden door, opening it wide. "Auntie, someone to see you."

"And who might that be?" came a strong, clipped voice.

"I am Amyu," Amyu said as she stepped within. "In Queen Xylara's service."

There was a woman seated before the hearth, in a chair that rocked. She was hunched over, her crooked and swollen fingers holding a mug. She looked at Amyu sideways with bright, curious eyes and a welcoming smile. "Well, then, you are welcome, child." Amyu could have sworn that her gaze flickered to her arms.

Amyu stiffened, then relaxed. Her cloak was on. There was no way this woman could know—

"Ah, forgive these old eyes. You are a Firelander, and a warrior. I mean no insult."

Kalisa gestured toward a stool at her side. "Come, sit where I can see you, and tell me why you have come."

"I will leave you," Mya said, jiggling the coins in her apron meaningfully.

"Good, good," Kalisa assured her as Mya vanished to another room. "Now, tell me what you want of an old woman, Amyu of the Plains."

Amyu sank down on the stool and took a deep breath. "I want to fly."

The old woman stared at her, her eyes wide with shock. But then her gaze dropped to her own hands, tight on her mug. Amyu could see the very bones through the thin skin of the crippled fingers.

Kalisa shook her head, muttering under her breath words that Amyu didn't quite catch. Something about 'lifetimes of waiting.' That couldn't be right. But Xyian was so odd. She opened her mouth to ask, but Kalisa turned back, her eyes now piercing and narrow.

"Explain yourself, and quickly."

Amyu explained, her words tumbling out of her mouth as she talked about the wyverns and the airions and the tapestry and the scroll.

And as she babbled, she looked at Kalisa, for she'd never seen one so old, so warped by age. Her crooked, swollen fingers, where she could see every line, every bone. The humped back. The face, almost a skull, with thin skin worn and wrinkled. Kalisa's white hair was braided back, but it was thin and the braid yellowed at the ends.

How long had she lived, to reach such a state? There were no aged on the Plains. One lived as long as one was useful, and then one day the old one was gone.

Kalisa listened, her eyes sharp, nodding at times to show her understanding. Amyu finally ran out of words.

Kalisa eased back in her chair, and rocked back and forth, her mind elsewhere.

There was movement close by, and Amyu looked up to find Mya standing next to her, with a mug. "You must be thirsty," she said, and offered the drink.

Amyu took it. "Thank you," she said politely. It was cool and refreshing. Some kind of herbal tea, she guessed.

Mya smiled, and looked over at Kalisa. "Auntie, you've someone to tell your tales to," she laughed. "Someone interested. My boys never were."

"No, no," Kalisa said. There was a sudden quaver in her voice. "Not today."

"Elder." Amyu set her mug down. "I have permission from the Queen to seek you out. She told me to listen to all you had to say, for as long as it took."

"Oh dear," Mya muttered.

"There are old tales." Kalisa seemed to shrink in on herself, her eyes dimming. The mug in her hand threatened to slip from her fingers. "Tales of the Chaosreaver, and his love," she whispered. "But not today." Her eyes drifted closed.

"I'm so sorry," Mya said, frowning. "This isn't like her, but she does tend to sleep quite a bit." She leaned over and took the mug from Kalisa's gnarled hands. "Hold this." She passed the mug to Amyu and pulled a colorful blanket from a trunk. She gently covered the old lady. "She'll sleep now, probably for hours."

Amyu rose slowly, not really wanting to leave. "Can I come again?" she asked as she handed the mugs to Mya.

"Of course." Mya smiled and lead the way to the door. "But Amyu, you need to know that Auntie is old. I can't promise that she will talk to you."

"I understand," Amyu said.

Mya opened the door. Amyu cast back a quick glance at Kalisa before stepping out into the colder air. She caught her breath, but Mya already had the door closed before she could speak.

Kalisa had been glaring at her. And the old woman's eyes gleamed with hate.

CHAPTER FORTY-TWO

Simus felt a deep sense of satisfaction as he stood witness to the oaths of his fellow Warlords. Elois and Tsor stood with him, slightly back, but he could feel their pride and approval like the sun on his back. Destal held the younger warriors back, as was proper, but that was fine. Simus's delight was that much sweeter knowing that Snowfall was close.

First Ultie, then Osa swore their oaths as Warlord, and then with a nod were gone, taking their Seconds and Token-bearers with them. Simus looked at them carefully. Ultie, in particular, seemed diminished somehow. Not in strength, but perhaps in heart. The loss of his Token-bearer had hit him hard.

Osa, on the other hand, seemed cool and unshaken.

They each gave Simus a nod, mounted, and with a glance to the skies, rode off. Simus didn't blame them. They'd be eager to gather their warriors and set out to start the season. He wished them well, but his was a different path.

Still, it raised questions. Simus turned his head slightly toward Tsor.

Tsor already knew his concern. "We're ready, Warlord," Tsor assured him, keeping his voice low. "Destal has had everything packed and loaded on the horses. We've but to mount and go to where your army waits."

Simus gave him a nod, satisfied.

The four Eldest Elders didn't rush the oaths, but they didn't waste time either. Still, the sun had moved down toward the horizon by the time they finished and the last Warlord departed.

Still, Simus waited.

Now the four Eldest Elders turned to face him. Niles of the Boar folded his arms over his chest and fixed Simus with a glare. "You delay in running off after Keir to do his bidding, like a foal after a tit?"

Elois drew in a sharp breath; Tsor rumbled.

Simus laughed.

Niles studied him through narrow eyes.

"You think to offer me insult," Simus said. "So that I will pull my blade?"

Niles shrugged.

"I take no insult." Simus grew serious. "Keir of the Cat sees what could be for our People, in ways I do not. He is a true leader whose sight is long and clear. But without the aid of strong warriors like me, his vision for the Plains cannot happen." Simus flashed his grin again. "And I'll not risk all I've won by pulling a blade on you."

Niles nodded, as if satisfied somehow. "I do not promise I will not oppose you in the future," he warned.

"Understood," Simus said.

Niles turned to the others. "I've thea camps to find and warn. Haya, have you some idea of where they might be?"

"With those monsters in the sky? As far away as they can be," Haya said. "But you'll want to check the winter lodges."

"My thanks," Niles said. "I can escort you back to your camp, if you wish."

"No," Haya said. "Simus will. I intend to take my charges north with his army."

That raised eyebrows, especially Simus's.

Haya snorted at their surprise. "It's that or cower in the lodges all summer, and I'll have none of that. My children and life-bearers will be safer with Simus, and there will be a new crop of warriors in the Spring to bolster his ranks."

"I'd offer my thanks," Simus started, but Haya shook her head.

"Don't," she said. "I've added to your burdens, Warlord. Just keep them safe. Send warriors with me, and we will meet up with you and your army." She turned to Niles. "Come. We will talk before we go."

They both nodded their heads to Essa and Wild Winds, and strode off together.

"I wished to express my thanks, Eldest Elder Singer," Simus said. "That was well done."

"No, it was not," Essa snapped through swollen lips. "It is not supposed to be this way. There are supposed to be many voices raised in Council, talking, sharing truths, with the four Eldest Elders presiding. Not a single voice. Not a single warrior."

"Yet, you were the lone voice," Wild Winds said. "Just as a WarKing would do."

A chill passed over Simus's skin.

"It's true that a WarKing doesn't have to be a warrior of our people," Essa said. "And in truth, I am not sure I trust any of you to preserve our people or our ways." He paused, then gave Simus a very neutral look. "But I can see no way back. You and Keir have put things into motion better left alone."

"Who's to say?" Simus said, keeping his voice as neutral as

Essa's.

"The Fall Council," Essa said.

Simus narrowed his eyes. This was not a challenge he had foreseen.

"But that is an issue for the Council in the Fall," Essa said. "If we can summon one. If the armies bring back enough to keep our people alive. If the wyverns haven't destroyed the Heart." He shrugged. "We will see what we see when that time comes." Essa turned to Wild Winds, and his voice grew considerably warmer. "It appears we must part, old friend. I must go, for I have work that needs doing."

"Joden?" Simus asked.

"Not that it is any business of yours, Warlord," Essa said, frowning. "But if you must know, I go to administer the Singer Trials to all candidates." He focused on Wild Winds. "Come with me, at least until you are healed."

Wild Winds started to shake his head, then winced. "No," he said. "I must return to Lightning Strike and the young ones. They need my teaching." He faced Simus. "I would take Hanstau, and the warrior that translates for him, with your permission. The healer should get training."

Simus nodded. "If he agrees, and I think he will. For Lara's sake."

"For all our sakes," Wild Winds said.

"You could come with us," Simus suggested.

Wild Winds shook his head. "No. I do not yet trust that Keir wouldn't kill us all. But maybe, in the future. Snowfall knows how to reach me, should the need arise."

Essa's warrior escort came up with their horses. "The elements go with you, Wild Winds." Essa mounted and took up the reins.

"I will see you in the Fall."

"As the elements decree," Wild Winds said.

Essa raised his hand in salute, and urged his horse on.

"I will go with you, to fetch Hanstau." Simus said.

Wild Winds looked behind him, to where Snowfall stood waiting with Simus's warriors.

"You know I will burn you to ash if Keir hurts her," Wild Winds said.

"He won't," Simus said. "Trust me."

* * * * *

Simus felt an even deeper sense of satisfaction once they'd seen Wild Winds off with Hanstau and Cadr. His warriors moved around him, their horses saddled and ready to ride.

"Haya is ready." Tsor pulled himself into his saddle. "There's time to gather her camp and still reach our army before sunset."

"That's well," Simus started to mount his horse, but Destal came up, Snowfall following behind, leading their horses.

"Warlord." Destal's voice was dry. "Let's not play this game any longer. Snowfall is a full adult warrior, with enough experience that she need not be under my command. She should be at your side, advising you and out of my hair."

"I should earn my place," Snowfall said firmly.

"Your dung collecting skills have been proven," Destal snorted. "The best place for you is at our Warlord's side."

"If that is your judgment, Destal," Simus said. "Snowfall will take duties under Elois."

Elois snorted. "I can't wait to see Keir's face when he hears this tale."

Tsor laughed. "I can't wait to see Marcus's."

"Mount up," Simus ordered, and pulled himself up into the saddle. His horse danced a bit, stamping its hooves, eager to be off.

"Have Cimor and his scouts been pulled away from the Heart?" Simus asked.

"Not until I warble," Tsor said. "I wanted eyes on those monsters at all times."

"Then let's be about it," Simus said.

Tsor lifted his head and warbled a cry that was echoed around them by the scouts.

"Lead the way," Simus said.

Tsor started off, and the others followed, with Simus at the center.

Snowfall moved her horse up beside Simus, looking cool and collected and content. She favored him with a glance from under her dark lashes.

His heart swelled with the joy of the moment. To have her at his side, to be Warlord, to have survived to reach this time, this moment...

Only one thing remained for perfection.

"Elois," Simus bellowed. "Let it be known that I would trade with any in my army for the finest gold wire, beads, and small gems. The finest, mind."

"As you say, Warlord," Elois said. "But you'd find those things easier in Xy."

"No, no," Simus said. "For I would weave a bonding in the ear of Snowfall of the Plains long before we reach Xy."

The looks of shock and horror around him made his happiness complete. But none more than that of Snowfall, stunned, her mouth hanging open.

Simus smiled.

"You," Snowfall sputtered, her usual calm countenance alive with outrage and anger.

"You arrogant, stupid, insufferable—"

"One usually asks one's bonded first," Elois noted. "Usually under the bells."

"There is no 'usual' with Simus," Tsor pointed out.

"You and I shall be bonded," Simus said to Snowfall. "You are the flame of my heart, Snowfall."

"Your wits never existed," Snowfall yelled. "Much less having been taken by the winds. Warrior-priests do not bond. Warlords do not bond while—"

"Yes, they do," Simus said, smiling at her. "We will bond, Snowfall of the Plains, and you will be my star, my flame, my night wind, and my morning sun. You and I—" Simus moved his horse in closer, and swept Snowfall from her saddle.

She didn't resist. Instead, she wrapped her arms around his neck, letting him settle her in his arms. "You arrogant, foolish—"

"Say 'yes,'" Simus said.

Snowfall huffed. "As if I'd agree to bind myself to—"

Simus laughed. "Yes, you will, my heart's delight."

"And why would I do that?" Snowfall leaned back to look him in the eye.

"No one else makes your heart pound as I do," Simus said simply. "No one else makes your mouth go dry with desire. No one else makes you laugh as I do." He paused, and then grew serious. "As you do for me. Bond with me, Snowfall of the Plains."

She looked away, and Simus's heart sank. He'd acted without thinking, but it was his truth and—

The tattoos on her shoulders started to move, and flowers appeared. Red, blue, yellow, all the colors of the Plains in springtime.

He lifted his eyes to find Snowfall giving him a warm look with grey eyes that sparkled.

"What do you say?" Simus asked, daring to hope.

"We will bond, Simus of the Hawk, Warlord of the Plains." Snowfall pressed her forehead to his. "And you will be my star, my flame, my night wind, and my morning sun."

Simus blinked away tears, and kissed her, softly at first, then—

"None of that now." Elois rode closer and rolled her eyes. "You will fall off the horse, and then where will we be?'

Simus roared out his laughter. "Truth," he said. He helped Snowfall regain her saddle, then looked around at his warriors, all grinning at him.

"There's work to be done," he called out. "To Xy!"

EPILOGUE

Hanstau just knew that his buttocks would be sore for days if he ever got off this godsforsaken horse.

It wasn't that he didn't know how to ride; he'd been taught the basics, and ridden in his younger years when he'd served as healer to the army. But that had been many years ago, before his marriage, before obtaining his Mastery. The Lords and Ladies of Xy rode horses. Craftsmen like him walked, or took pony carts.

He smiled despite his misery. How horrified his wife would have been to see him riding on the Plains, following a Firelander warrior-priestess, surrounded by Firelander warriors.

But she'd have been proud and pleased as well at the bargain he'd struck. Their children were now well placed, in good apprenticeships, holding promise for their futures. A practical woman, Fleure had been. For all that their marriage had been an arranged one, they'd done well together.

It still hurt to think of her death, of the lump in her breast, and her wasting away. He'd been helpless, and Master Healer Eln as well, though they'd tried every remedy they had. All to no avail.

Hanstau looked ahead, where Wild Winds rode, keeping them at a swift pace. If there was any chance that he might be able to learn to heal magically...the very idea took his breath. It was worth it, this discomfort, if there was any hope…. Besides, Wild Winds had to be hurting as well, what with that wound to his head.

The horse under Hanstau's legs huffed out a breath, apparently as tired of Hanstau as Hanstau was tired of it. Oh, for his oxen cart, or the pony carts he rode in Xy, or just to be able to get off and walk for a while. Was there really this need to rush?

Cadr rode next to him, and gave him a grin. "Straighten your legs," he called, showing by example. All fine and well for him, Hanstau groaned. But there was only so long that he could hold that pose, and they'd been riding for what felt like hours.

He was just promising himself at least three cups of willowbark tea as soon as they camped, when a buzzing noise went past his head.

"What?" was all Hanstau had time for. Cadr reached over, grabbed his arm, and yanked him from his saddle.

Hanstau clung to Cadr's arm, hanging for a long moment before Cadr dropped him to the ground. Harder to fall off then he'd thought; he lost his breath and his wits as he hit the ground.

The horses continued on, but Hanstau followed his instructions to stay down, and hidden.

He hunched in the grasses for long moments, breathing hard, listening to the sudden sounds of combat. There were shouts, and horses neighing, and the clang of sword on sword. It took a moment for him to realize they were being attacked.

He raised his head slowly.

Warriors had surrounded Wild Winds and his people, and the fighting was intense. Hanstau jerked back down, but he caught a glimpse of a downed warrior near him, groaning.

Hanstau started crawling.

The warrior was dead by the time he got to her, but there was another close by. Cursing at the waste, Hanstau crawled over.

A thigh wound, a bad one, cut right through the leather. Hanstau got to his knees and spread the edges open further. A clean wound. He took out a small bit of bloodmoss and got to work. The warrior never roused, but he was breathing evenly.

The fighting continued, joined with flashes of fire, and the smell of burning flesh. Hanstau refused to be distracted, concentrating on his patient until the wound was sealed. He dropped the bloodmoss, now pale green. It would grow and sprout for the future, with any luck.

But there was another warrior, moaning, well within reach. Hanstau crawled over, and flipped the warrior over.

It was Cadr, white and pale, his limp, bloody hands sliding away from his neck.

Hanstau reacted without thinking. He clapped bloodmoss over the cut, regardless of its state. It was the boy's only chance. He slapped a bandage over that, which quickly soaked with blood. "Aid him, God of the Sun," Hanstau prayed, knowing the wound was beyond anything he could close. He'd done what he could. Hanstau looked at the lad's pale face with deep regret, then moved on.

The noise around him had subsided, but there was another warrior down nearby. Hanstau crawled again, focused on saving what wounded he could.

But when he turned her, the chest wound was too frightful to close. And the life had already faded from her open eyes.

"Have mercy on her, Goddess of the Moon and Stars," Hanstau whispered, and reached to close her eyes.

Except a large, gloved hand reached down and grabbed his wrist, wrenching it away and up.

The hand forced Hanstau up onto to his knees. A warrior towered above him, a bloody sword in his other hand. Hanstau blinked into the sun at the large, solid man looked down at him, his blond hair and beard glowing in the light.

"Antas," a voice called, and only then did Hanstau realize that the sounds of fighting had stopped.

"Here," the blond called out.

"Wild Winds is dead." Another warrior approached. "We couldn't take him alive."

"No matter," the blond above him said, his eyes never leaving Hanstau's. "I've found something better."

Hanstau jerked his wrist, trying to free himself, but the warrior…Antas…just laughed. His white teeth gleamed against his tanned skin, as he leaned down and spoke.

Hanstau's blood went cold. He knew that word.

"Warprize."

ACKNOWLEDGMENTS

No one writes a book without major support from friends and family. I can't name all of you, but know that I am grateful for your love and support.

But there are some special people who must be thanked:

As always, my writer's group: Helen Kourous, Spencer Luster, and Marc Tassin.

To Mary Gustafson, for her help with my lovely and yet disgusting wyverns.

To Carolyn Wielinski, my dance advisor, who said 'let me show you' and twirled me around the salon like I was a princess.

To Dylan Birtolo, my knight in shining armor. Literally. A member of the Seattle Knights, Dylan was willing to answer questions about prolonged periods of combat with different opponents.

To Elizabeth Candler, Beth Cogley, Stephanie Loree, Denise Lynn, Patricia Merritt and Molly Reed, all victims of various versions of the book, and willing to give comments to a needy writer.

To Maurice Broaddus, Gay Mercer, and Jewel Strahan, who patiently answered any question I asked.

To my editor, Anna Genoese and my copy editor, Katherine Crighton for all their efforts to make me a better writer.

Finally, to Kathie McMillan. Really sorry about that night at gaming when I rolled that critical greater cleave into your paladin's body. They were using you as a shield and I honestly thought you were already dead.

ABOUT THE AUTHOR

Elizabeth Vaughan is the *USA Today* Bestselling author of *Warprize*, the first volume of The Chronicles of the Warlands. She's always loved fantasy and science fiction, and has been a fantasy role-player since 1981. By day, Beth's secret identity is that of a lawyer, practicing in the area of bankruptcy, a role she has maintained since 1985. More information can be found at her website, WriteandRepeat.com.

Beth is owned by incredibly spoiled cats, and lives in the Northwest Territory, on the outskirts of the Black Swamp, along Mad Anthony's Trail on the banks of the Maumee River.